Into the Battle

THIS LAND, THIS TIME

Dobrica Ćosić

Into the Battle

translated by
Muriel Heppell

A Harvest/HBJ Book
Harcourt Brace Jovanovich, Publishers
San Diego New York London

Library of Congress Cataloging in Publication Data

Ćosić, Dobrica, 1921–
Into the battle.

(This land, this time / Dobrica Ćosić; 1) (Harvest/
HBJ book)
Translation of: Vreme smrti, v. 1.
1. World War, 1914–1918—Fiction. I. Title.
II. Series: Ćosić, Dobrica, 1921– . Vreme smrti.
English; 1.
PG1418.C63V7213 1983 vol. 1 891.8′235s 83-10703
ISBN 0-15-644991-9 (pbk.) [891.8′235]

This paperback volume is a translation
of *Vreme smrti,* Volume I, which previously appeared
in a condensed form
as the Prologue to the hardcover version
of *A Time of Death* (Harcourt Brace Jovanovich, 1978).

Printed in the United States of America

First edition

A B C D E F G H I J

Into the Battle

Prologue

VIENNA
THURSDAY, JUNE 28, 1914

FROM *Neue Freie Presse* (SPECIAL EDITION):

NEWS CAME TODAY FROM SARAJEVO WHICH HAS SHAKEN THE ENTIRE MONARCHY TO ITS FOUNDATIONS. THE IMPERIAL HOUSE ANNOUNCED A TERRIBLE TRAGEDY.

THE HEIR TO THE THRONE, ARCHDUKE FRANZ FERDINAND, AND HIS WIFE, ARCHDUCHESS VON HOHENBERG, TODAY WERE THE VICTIMS OF AN ASSASSINATION PLOT IN SARAJEVO.

ACCORDING TO THE REPORT FROM SARAJEVO, THIS HORRIBLE CRIME HAPPENED IN THE FOLLOWING WAY:

WHEN HIS IMPERIAL AND ROYAL HIGHNESS THE ILLUSTRIOUS ARCHDUKE FRANZ FERDINAND AND HIS WIFE, ARCHDUCHESS VON HOHENBERG, SET OUT THIS MORNING TO ATTEND A RECEPTION IN THE TOWN HALL, A BOMB WAS HURLED AT HIS CAR, WHICH HIS IMPERIAL AND ROYAL HIGHNESS DEFLECTED WITH HIS SHOULDER. THE BOMB EXPLODED AFTER THE ARCHDUCAL CAR HAD PASSED. COUNT FOS-BALDEK AND COLONEL MERITSI, THE ADJUTANT OF THE PROVINCIAL GOVERNOR, WHO WERE IN THE NEXT CAR, WERE SLIGHTLY WOUNDED.

THE WOULD-BE ASSASSIN, A COMPOSITOR FROM TREBINJE NAMED ČABRINOVIĆ, WAS IMMEDIATELY ARRESTED.

AFTER A FORMAL RECEPTION IN THE TOWN HALL, HIS IMPERIAL AND ROYAL HIGHNESS THE ILLUSTRIOUS ARCHDUKE CONTINUED THE TOUR WITH HIS WIFE.

A HIGH-SCHOOL STUDENT FROM GRAHOVO NAMED PRINCIP FIRED SEVERAL SHOTS AT THE ARCHDUCAL CAR WITH A BROWNING REVOLVER. HIS

IMPERIAL AND ROYAL HIGHNESS THE ILLUSTRIOUS ARCHDUKE WAS WOUNDED IN THE FACE, AND HER HIGHNESS THE ARCHDUCHESS VON HOHENBERG IN THE LOWER PART OF HER BODY. HIS IMPERIAL AND ROYAL HIGHNESS AND THE ARCHDUCHESS WERE TAKEN TO THE PALACE, WHERE THEY DIED FROM THEIR INJURIES

THE ASSASSIN WAS ALSO CAUGHT

THE EMPEROR WAS IMMEDIATELY INFORMED OF THIS TERRIBLE EVENT.

NIKOLA PAŠIĆ, PRIME MINISTER OF THE ROYAL GOVERNMENT OF SERBIA, TO ALL EMBASSIES OF THE KINGDOM OF SERBIA:

BELGRADE

JULY 19, 1914

THE PRESS OF AUSTRIA-HUNGARY, IMMEDIATELY AFTER THE ASSASSINATION AT SARAJEVO, BEGAN TO PLACE THE BLAME FOR THE HORRIBLE CRIME ON SERBIA, CONSIDERING THAT THIS ACTION WAS THE OUTCOME OF THE GREATER SERBIAN PRINCIPLE. . . .

BOTH THE COURT AND THE GOVERNMENT OF SERBIA, ON RECEIVING NEWS OF THE ASSASSINATION, EXPRESSED NOT ONLY THEIR SYMPATHY, BUT ALSO THEIR CONDEMNATION AND LOATHING OF SUCH A CRIME.

IN SPITE OF THIS, THE PRESS OF THE NEIGHBORING MONARCHY CONTINUES TO HOLD SERBIA RESPONSIBLE FOR WHAT HAPPENED AT SARAJEVO. FROM THE VERY BEGINNING THE SERBIAN GOVERNMENT HAS EXPRESSED ITS READINESS TO COMMIT FOR TRIAL ANY OF ITS CITIZENS WHO CAN BE PROVED TO HAVE PARTICIPATED IN THE ASSASSINATION AT SARAJEVO. . . . FINALLY, THE SERBIAN GOVERNMENT AFFIRMED THAT IT WAS READY TO CARRY OUT, AS IT HAS DONE UP TILL NOW, ALL THE NEIGHBORLY OBLIGATIONS WHICH ITS POSITION AS A EUROPEAN STATE WOULD REQUIRE. . . .

MEANWHILE, THE CAMPAIGN AGAINST SERBIA IN THE AUSTRO-HUNGARIAN PRESS CONTINUES UNABATED, AND PUBLIC OPINION AGAINST SERBIA IS BEING STIRRED UP BOTH IN AUSTRIA-HUNGARY AND IN THE REST OF EUROPE. . . .

THE SERBIAN GOVERNMENT CONSIDERS IT VITALLY IMPORTANT TO THE INTERESTS OF SERBIA THAT PEACE AND TRANQUILLITY IN THE BALKANS SHOULD BE ESTABLISHED AS SECURELY AND FOR AS LONG AS POSSIBLE. BECAUSE OF THIS, THE GOVERNMENT IS NOW AFRAID THAT THE INFLAMED STATE OF PUBLIC OPINION IN AUSTRIA-HUNGARY MIGHT CAUSE THE GOVERNMENT OF AUSTRIA-HUNGARY TO TAKE SOME STEP THAT WOULD HUMILIATE THE NATIONAL DIGNITY OF SERBIA, AND TO PRESS DEMANDS THAT WOULD BE UNACCEPTABLE. . . .

HOWEVER, WE COULD NEVER ACCEPT DEMANDS CONTRARY TO THE

DIGNITY OF SERBIA, DEMANDS NO STATE COULD ACCEPT THAT VALUES AND GUARDS ITS INDEPENDENCE.

BARON GIESL VON GIESLINGEN, AUSTRO-HUNGARIAN AMBASSADOR IN BELGRADE, TO LAZA PAČU, DEPUTY PRIME MINISTER AND MINISTER FOR FOREIGN AFFAIRS:

BELGRADE
JULY 23, 1914

I HAVE THE HONOR TO SUBMIT TO YOUR EXCELLENCY THE ENCLOSED NOTE WHICH I HAVE RECEIVED FROM MY GOVERNMENT, ADDRESSED TO THE KINGDOM OF SERBIA. . . .

IT IS CLEAR FROM THE EVIDENCE AND FROM THE CONFESSION OF THE PERPETRATOR OF THE ASSASSINATION OF JUNE 28 THAT THE CRIME COMMITTED IN SARAJEVO WAS PLANNED IN BELGRADE; THAT THE WEAPONS AND EXPLOSIVES SUPPLIED TO THE MURDERERS WERE PROVIDED BY SERBIAN OFFICERS AND OFFICIALS, MEMBERS OF THE NATIONAL DEFENSE; AND FINALLY THAT THE TRANSPORTATION OF THE CRIMINALS TO BOSNIA WAS PREPARED AND CARRIED OUT BY CHIEFS OF THE SERBIAN FRONTIER SERVICE. THE RESULTS OF THE INQUIRY MAKE IT IMPOSSIBLE FOR THE IMPERIAL AND ROYAL GOVERNMENT TO CONTINUE THE ROLE OF A CALM AND PATIENT OBSERVER WHICH IT HAS MAINTAINED FOR MANY YEARS TOWARD DISTURBANCES OF WHICH BELGRADE IS THE CENTER, AND WHICH HAVE SPREAD FROM THERE TO THE TERRITORY OF THE MONARCHY; ON THE CONTRARY, THESE RESULTS IMPOSE ON US THE DUTY OF PUTTING AN END TO THESE PLOTS, WHICH ARE A CONSTANT THREAT TO THE PEACE OF THE MONARCHY. . . .

TO ACHIEVE THIS PURPOSE, THE IMPERIAL AND ROYAL GOVERNMENT IS COMPELLED TO SEEK FROM THE SERBIAN GOVERNMENT THE FOLLOWING OFFICIAL PRONOUNCEMENT:

"THE ROYAL GOVERNMENT OF SERBIA CONDEMNS ALL PROPAGANDA DIRECTED AGAINST AUSTRIA-HUNGARY, THAT IS, ALL EFFORTS WHICH HAVE AS THEIR ULTIMATE AIM THE SEPARATION FROM THE AUSTRO-HUNGARIAN MONARCHY OF TERRITORIES THAT FORM PART OF THE MONARCHY, AND EXPRESSES SINCERE REGRET FOR THE DISASTROUS CONSEQUENCES OF THIS CRIMINAL ACT. THE ROYAL GOVERNMENT REGRETS THAT SERBIAN OFFICERS AND OFFICIALS HAVE TAKEN PART IN THE ABOVE-MENTIONED PROPAGANDA AND THEREBY COMPROMISED THE GOOD NEIGHBORLY RELATIONS TO WHICH THE ROYAL GOVERNMENT IS SOLEMNLY COMMITTED BY THE PRONOUNCEMENT OF MARCH 31, 1909.

"THE ROYAL GOVERNMENT OF SERBIA CONDEMNS AND REPUDIATES ANY IDEA OR ATTEMPT TO INTERVENE IN THE FATE OF THE INHABITANTS OF

ANY PART OF THE AUSTRO-HUNGARIAN MONARCHY; IT CONSIDERS IT TO BE ITS DUTY TO ISSUE A SERIOUS WARNING TO THE OFFICERS, OFFICIALS, AND ENTIRE POPULATION OF SERBIA THAT IN THE FUTURE IT WILL DEAL VERY SEVERELY WITH INDIVIDUALS WHO COMMIT THE OFFENSE OF DEVOTING THEMSELVES TO SUCH ACTIVITIES, WHICH THE SERBIAN GOVERNMENT WILL PREVENT AND PUNISH BY EVERY MEANS IN ITS POWER."

THIS STATEMENT MUST BE SIMULTANEOUSLY COMMUNICATED TO THE ROYAL ARMY IN THE ORDERS OF THE DAY ISSUED BY HIS MAJESTY THE KING, AND PUBLISHED IN THE NEXT NUMBER OF THE SERVICE LIST. . . .

IN ADDITION, THE ROYAL GOVERNMENT BINDS ITSELF . . .

THE REPLY OF THE SERBIAN GOVERNMENT TO THE AUSTRO-HUNGARIAN NOTE:

BELGRADE
JULY 23, 1914

THE ROYAL SERBIAN GOVERNMENT HAS RECEIVED THE COMMUNICATION FROM THE IMPERIAL AND ROYAL GOVERNMENT OF THE TENTH OF THIS MONTH AND IS CONVINCED THAT THIS REPLY WILL REMOVE THE MISUNDERSTANDING THAT THREATENS TO DISTURB THE GOOD NEIGHBORLY RELATIONS BETWEEN THE AUSTRO-HUNGARIAN MONARCHY AND THE KINGDOM OF SERBIA. . . .

SERBIA HAS SO MANY TIMES GIVEN EVIDENCE OF HER PEACE-LOVING AND MODERATE POLICIES DURING THE BALKAN CRISIS THAT SHE HAS SEVERAL TIMES PRESERVED THE PEACE OF EUROPE BY SACRIFICING HER OWN DEMANDS IN THE INTERESTS OF THAT PEACE.

THE GOVERNMENT OF THE KINGDOM OF SERBIA CANNOT ACCEPT RESPONSIBILITY FOR PHENOMENA OF A PRIVATE CHARACTER, SUCH AS LETTERS TO THE PRESS AND THE PEACEFUL ACTIVITY OF PATRIOTIC SOCIETIES, WHICH ARE USUAL IN ALMOST ALL COUNTRIES AND WHICH AS A RULE ELUDE OFFICIAL CONTROL, AS IS WELL KNOWN. . . .

THE ROYAL GOVERNMENT WAS THEREFORE PAINFULLY SURPRISED BY THE ASSERTION THAT INDIVIDUALS FROM THE KINGDOM OF SERBIA HAD PARTICIPATED IN THE PREPARATION FOR THE ASSASSINATION CARRIED OUT IN SARAJEVO. . . . HOWEVER, IN RESPONSE TO THE DEMAND OF THE IMPERIAL AND ROYAL GOVERNMENT, THE ROYAL GOVERNMENT OF SERBIA IS READY TO TAKE THE APPROPRIATE STEPS AND BRING TO TRIAL ANY OF ITS CITIZENS, IRRESPECTIVE OF RANK AND POSITION, WHO CAN BE PROVED TO HAVE TAKEN PART IN THE CRIME COMMITTED IN SARAJEVO.

IN THE EVENT THAT THE IMPERIAL AND ROYAL GOVERNMENT IS NOT SATISFIED WITH THIS REPLY, THE ROYAL SERBIAN GOVERNMENT, CON-

SIDERING THAT THE GENERAL INTEREST WOULD NOT BE SERVED BY AN OVERHASTY DECISION ON THIS QUESTION, IS PREPARED, AS IT ALWAYS HAS BEEN, TO ACCEPT A PEACEFUL SETTLEMENT BY SUBMITTING THIS QUESTION TO THE DECISION OF THE INTERNATIONAL COURT AT THE HAGUE, OR TO THAT OF THE GREAT POWERS. . . .

COUNT LEOPOLD BERCHTOLD, AUSTRO-HUNGARIAN MINISTER FOR FOREIGN AFFAIRS, TO NIKOLA PAŠIĆ, PRIME MINISTER OF THE ROYAL GOVERNMENT AND MINISTER FOR FOREIGN AFFAIRS:

VIENNA
JULY 28, 1914

SINCE THE ROYAL GOVERNMENT OF SERBIA HAS NOT GIVEN A SATISFACTORY ANSWER TO THE NOTE DELIVERED BY THE AUSTRO-HUNGARIAN AMBASSADOR IN BELGRADE ON JULY 23, 1914, THE IMPERIAL AND ROYAL GOVERNMENT HAS BEEN OBLIGED TO TAKE MEASURES TO PROTECT ITS RIGHTS AND INTERESTS, AND FOR THIS PURPOSE TO HAVE RECOURSE TO FORCE OF ARMS. AUSTRIA-HUNGARY THEREFORE CONSIDERS HERSELF FROM NOW ON TO BE AT WAR WITH SERBIA.

THE KING OF MONTENEGRO TO THE REGENT OF SERBIA, PRINCE ALEXANDER:

CETINJE
JULY 28, 1914

. . . IT IS THE FATE OF THE SERBIAN NATION TO SACRIFICE ITSELF ONCE MORE FOR THE DEFENSE OF ALL THOSE WHO BEAR THE NAME OF SERBS. . . .

THE PRIDE OF THE SERBIAN PEOPLE DOES NOT PERMIT THEM TO YIELD ANY FURTHER! SACRIFICES MADE FOR TRUTH AND FOR INDEPENDENCE ARE INDEED SWEET. IN GOD'S NAME AND WITH THE HELP OF OUR POWERFUL PROTECTOR RUSSIA AND THE SYMPATHY OF THE CIVILIZED WORLD, THE SERBIAN NATION WILL EMERGE VICTORIOUS FROM THIS GREAT MISFORTUNE. MY MONTENEGRINS ARE ALREADY ON THE FRONTIER, PREPARED TO GIVE THEIR LIVES IN THE DEFENSE OF OUR INDEPENDENCE.

REPORT OF THE AUSTRO-HUNGARIAN AMBASSADOR AT THE VATICAN, COUNT MORITZ PALFI, TO HIS GOVERNMENT ON HIS AUDIENCE WITH THE STATE SECRETARY, CARDINAL MERI DE VALA, AND POPE PIUS X, WHOM HE INFORMED ABOUT THE WAR AGAINST SERBIA:

JULY 28, 1914

. . . DURING THE LAST FEW YEARS HIS HOLINESS HAS ON SEVERAL OCCASIONS EXPRESSED HIS REGRET THAT AUSTRIA-HUNGARY HAS NE-

GLECTED TO CHASTISE ITS DANUBIAN NEIGHBOR. THE POPE AND THE CURIA SEE IN SERBIA A CORROSIVE EVIL WHICH HAS GRADUALLY PENETRATED THE VERY MARROW OF THE MONARCHY AND WHICH WILL IN TIME DISMEMBER IT. NOTWITHSTANDING ALL THE CURIA'S EXPERIMENTS IN RECENT DECADES, AUSTRIA-HUNGARY REMAINS THE BEST CATHOLIC STATE AND THE BULWARK OF THE CHRISTIAN CHURCH IN OUR TIME. THE COLLAPSE OF AUSTRIA-HUNGARY WOULD MEAN THE LOSS TO THE CHURCH OF ITS MOST SOLID SUPPORT IN THE STRUGGLE AGAINST ORTHODOXY; IN THIS COLLAPSE THE CHURCH WOULD LOSE ITS STRONGEST DEFENDER. . . .

HENCE, JUST AS AUSTRIA-HUNGARY MUST, IN ORDER TO ENSURE HER CONTINUED EXISTENCE, DESTROY THIS EVIL IN HER ORGANISM, BY FORCE IF NECESSARY, SO THE CATHOLIC CHURCH MUST DO ALL IT CAN TO SERVE THIS PURPOSE. . . .

WILLIAM II OF GERMANY TO NICHOLAS II OF RUSSIA:

JULY 28, 1914
10:45 P.M.

IT WAS WITH THE GREATEST ANXIETY THAT I LEARNED OF THE IMPRESSION PRODUCED IN YOUR EMPIRE BY THE AUSTRO-HUNGARIAN MEASURES AGAINST SERBIA. THE THOUGHTLESS AGITATION THAT HAS BEEN GOING ON IN SERBIA FOR YEARS HAS RESULTED IN A TERRIBLE CRIME, OF WHICH FRANZ FERDINAND WAS THE VICTIM. YOU WILL UNDOUBTEDLY AGREE WITH ME THAT IT IS IN THE INTERESTS OF BOTH OF US, ALONG WITH ALL OTHER RULERS, TO SEE THAT ALL PERSONS MORALLY RESPONSIBLE FOR THIS FOUL CRIME RECEIVE THE PUNISHMENT THEY DESERVE.

ON THE OTHER HAND, I UNDERSTAND VERY WELL HOW DIFFICULT IT IS FOR YOU AND YOUR GOVERNMENT TO GO AGAINST PUBLIC OPINION IN YOUR COUNTRY. BEARING IN MIND THE CORDIAL FRIENDSHIP WHICH HAS BOUND US CLOSELY FOR A CONSIDERABLE TIME, I WILL DO MY UTMOST TO PERSUADE AUSTRIA-HUNGARY TO COME TO A FRANK AND PEACEFUL UNDERSTANDING WITH RUSSIA. I EARNESTLY HOPE THAT YOU WILL SUPPORT MY EFFORTS TO REMOVE ANY DIFFICULTIES WHICH MIGHT STILL ARISE.

YOUR SINCERE AND DEVOTED FRIEND AND COUSIN,
WILLIAM

NICHOLAS II TO WILLIAM II:

PETERHOF PALACE
JULY 29, 1 P.M.

I AM GLAD TO HEAR THAT YOU HAVE RETURNED TO GERMANY AT THIS CRITICAL TIME. I BEG YOU MOST EARNESTLY TO HELP ME. A SHAMEFUL

DECLARATION OF WAR HAS BEEN MADE AGAINST A SMALL NATION. THIS HAS AROUSED DEEP DISGUST IN RUSSIA, WHICH I SHARE. I FORESEE THAT BEFORE LONG I SHALL NOT BE ABLE TO RESIST THE PRESSURE NOW BEING PUT ON ME, AND WILL BE OBLIGED TO TAKE MEASURES THAT WILL LEAD TO WAR.

IN ORDER TO PREVENT THE MISFORTUNE OF A EUROPEAN WAR, I BEG YOU, IN THE NAME OF OUR OLD FRIENDSHIP, TO DO ALL IN YOUR POWER TO PREVENT YOUR ALLIES FROM GOING TOO FAR.

NICHOLAS

WILLIAM II TO NICHOLAS II:

JULY 29, 1914
6:30 P.M.

I HAVE RECEIVED YOUR TELEGRAM, AND I MYSELF WISH TO PRESERVE PEACE. HOWEVER, I CANNOT CONSIDER THE AUSTRO-HUNGARIAN WAR A SHAMEFUL ONE, AS YOU DESCRIBE IT IN YOUR FIRST TELEGRAM, SINCE AUSTRIA-HUNGARY KNOWS FROM EXPERIENCE THAT SERBIA'S PROMISES ARE WORTHLESS WHILE THEY EXIST ONLY ON PAPER. IN MY OPINION THE AUSTRO-HUNGARIAN ACTION SHOULD BE REGARDED AS AN ATTEMPT TO SECURE A GUARANTEE THAT THE SERBIAN PROMISES WILL BE KEPT. I THEREFORE THINK IT IS POSSIBLE FOR RUSSIA TO REMAIN AN OBSERVER AND THUS NOT DRAG EUROPE INTO ONE OF THE MOST TERRIBLE WARS THE WORLD WILL EVER HAVE SEEN. . . .

MILITARY MEASURES ON RUSSIA'S PART COULD BE SEEN BY AUSTRIA-HUNGARY AS CONSTITUTING A THREAT AND COULD PROVOKE THE VERY MISFORTUNE WE WISH TO PREVENT, THUS RENDERING IMPOSSIBLE THE MISSION OF MEDIATOR WHICH I HAVE GLADLY ACCEPTED, FOLLOWING YOUR APPEAL FOR MY FRIENDSHIP AND ASSISTANCE.

WILLIAM

WILLIAM II TO NICHOLAS II:

JULY 30,1914
1 P.M.

. . . AUSTRIA-HUNGARY HAS MOBILIZED ONLY AGAINST SERBIA, AND THEN ONLY WITH PART OF HER ARMY. IF RUSSIA MOBILIZES AGAINST AUSTRIA-HUNGARY, WHICH IS NOW CERTAIN AFTER THE ANNOUNCEMENT MADE BY YOU AND YOUR GOVERNMENT, THE MISSION WHICH YOU ENTRUSTED TO ME AS A FRIEND, AND WHICH I ACCEPTED GLADLY, WILL BECOME DIFFICULT, IF NOT IMPOSSIBLE. THE WEIGHT OF THE DECISION NOW RESTS ON YOUR SHOULDERS. YOU BEAR THE RESPONSIBILITY FOR WAR OR PEACE.

WILLIAM

NICHOLAS II TO WILLIAM II:

PETERHOF
JULY 30, 1914
1:20 P.M.

THANK YOU VERY MUCH FOR YOUR PROMPT REPLY. TODAY'S MILITARY PREPARATIONS WERE DECIDED ON FIVE DAYS AGO AS A PRECAUTIONARY MEASURE IN RESPONSE TO THE AUSTRIAN MILITARY PREPARATIONS. YOU MUST EXERT STRONG PRESSURE ON AUSTRIA TO COME TO AN UNDERSTANDING WITH US.

NICHOLAS

NICHOLAS II TO WILLIAM II:

PETERHOF
JULY 30, EVENING

MANY THANKS FOR YOUR INTERVENTION, WHICH GIVES ME HOPE THAT THERE MIGHT YET BE A PEACEFUL OUTCOME. INDEED IT IS IMPOSSIBLE FOR US TO STOP THE MILITARY PREPARATIONS PROVOKED BY THE AUSTRIAN MOBILIZATION. WE ARE FAR FROM DESIRING WAR, AND AS LONG AS NEGOTIATIONS WITH AUSTRIA ABOUT SERBIA CONTINUE, MY TROOPS WILL CERTAINLY NOT ADOPT A HOSTILE ATTITUDE; I GIVE YOU MY WORD OF HONOR. I HAVE FAITH IN GOD'S MERCY, AND HOPE FOR THE SUCCESS OF YOUR INTERVENTION IN VIENNA FOR THE GOOD OF OUR COUNTRY AND THE PEACE OF EUROPE. FROM THE BOTTOM OF MY HEART, I REMAIN

YOUR DEVOTED
NICHOLAS

WILLIAM II TO NICHOLAS II:

JULY 30, MIDNIGHT

ACTING ON YOUR APPEAL TO MY FRIENDSHIP AND YOUR REQUEST FOR MY HELP, I HAVE UNDERTAKEN TO INTERVENE BETWEEN YOUR GOVERNMENT AND THAT OF AUSTRIA-HUNGARY. MEANWHILE, THE MOBILIZATION OF YOUR ARMY AGAINST MY ALLY AUSTRIA-HUNGARY WAS CARRIED OUT, RENDERING MY MISSION PRACTICALLY FUTILE. EVEN SO I CONTINUED MY WORK OF INTERVENTION. HOWEVER, I HAVE NOW RECEIVED RELIABLE INFORMATION CONCERNING MILITARY PREPARATIONS ON MY EASTERN FRONTIER. MY RESPONSIBILITY FOR THE SECURITY OF MY EMPIRE COMPELS ME TO TAKE APPROPRIATE DEFENSIVE MEASURES.

I HAVE DONE THE UTMOST IN MY EFFORTS TO PRESERVE WORLD PEACE. I SHALL NOT BE RESPONSIBLE FOR THE MISFORTUNE THAT NOW THREATENS THE ENTIRE CIVILIZED WORLD. AT THE PRESENT MOMENT YOU ARE

STILL CAPABLE OF PREVENTING THIS MISFORTUNE. . . . MY FRIENDSHIP TOWARD YOU AND YOUR COUNTRY, WHICH MY GRANDFATHER CHARGED ME TO CONTINUE, HAS BEEN A SACRED TRUST, AND I HAVE REMAINED LOYAL TO RUSSIA IN HER MOST DIFFICULT TIMES, PARTICULARLY DURING HER RECENT WAR.*

TODAY ONLY YOU CAN SAVE THE PEACE IN EUROPE, IF RUSSIA DECIDES TO STOP PREPARATIONS FOR A WAR AGAINST GERMANY AND AUSTRIA-HUNGARY.

WILLIAM

PRINCE HENRY OF PRUSSIA TO GEORGE V OF ENGLAND:

JULY 30, 1914

. . . WILLIAM IS IN CONSTANT TELEGRAPHIC COMMUNICATION WITH NICHOLAS, WHO HAS TODAY CONFIRMED THE NEWS THAT HE HAS GIVEN ORDERS FOR MILITARY PREPARATIONS AMOUNTING TO MOBILIZATION. WE HAVE ALSO BEEN INFORMED THAT FRANCE IS MAKING MILITARY PREPARATIONS, WHILE WE HAVE TAKEN NO MEASURES OF ANY KIND, BUT AT ANY MOMENT WE WILL BE COMPELLED TO DO SO IF OUR NEIGHBORS CONTINUE WITH THEIRS. THAT WOULD MEAN A EUROPEAN WAR. IF YOU TRULY WISH TO PREVENT THIS TERRIBLE CALAMITY, MAY I SUGGEST THAT YOU USE YOUR INFLUENCE WITH FRANCE AND RUSSIA TO PERSUADE THEM TO REMAIN NEUTRAL. THIS WOULD BE EXTREMELY USEFUL. I SHOULD LIKE TO ADD THAT NOW MORE THAN EVER IT IS NECESSARY FOR ENGLAND AND GERMANY TO ACT TOGETHER, IN ORDER TO PREVENT A CATASTROPHE THAT IS OTHERWISE INEVITABLE. . . . THE MILITARY PREPARATIONS OF BOTH WILLIAM'S NEIGHBORS HAVE AT LAST FORCED HIM TO FOLLOW THEIR EXAMPLE, IN THE INTERESTS OF THE SECURITY OF HIS EMPIRE. I HAVE INFORMED WILLIAM ABOUT THIS TELEGRAM, AND I HOPE YOU WILL ACCEPT MY COMMUNICATION IN THE SAME FRIENDLY SPIRIT IN WHICH IT IS SENT.

HENRY

GEORGE V TO PRINCE HENRY OF PRUSSIA:

JULY 30, 1914

I WAS DELIGHTED TO HEAR OF WILLIAM'S EFFORTS TO REACH AN UNDERSTANDING WITH NICHOLAS FOR THE PURPOSE OF PRESERVING PEACE. IT IS MY EARNEST DESIRE TO PREVENT A CALAMITY SUCH AS A EUROPEAN

*The Russo-Japanese War of 1905. [Translator.]

WAR, WHICH WOULD DO IRREPARABLE HARM. MY GOVERNMENT WILL DO ALL IT CAN TO PERSUADE FRANCE AND RUSSIA TO POSTPONE FURTHER MILITARY PREPARATIONS, PROVIDED THAT AUSTRIA WOULD BE SATISFIED WITH THE SEIZURE OF BELGRADE AND THE SURROUNDING AREA AS THE PLEDGE FOR THE SATISFACTORY FULFILLMENT OF HER DEMANDS; MEANWHILE, OTHER COUNTRIES WOULD HAVE TO CEASE THEIR PREPARATIONS FOR WAR. I AM SURE THAT WILLIAM WILL USE HIS CONSIDERABLE INFLUENCE TO PERSUADE AUSTRIA TO ACCEPT THIS PROPOSAL. IN THIS WAY HE WOULD DEMONSTRATE THAT ENGLAND AND GERMANY ARE WORKING TOGETHER TO PREVENT AN INTERNATIONAL CATASTROPHE. PLEASE ASSURE WILLIAM THAT I AM DOING EVERYTHING IN MY POWER TO PRESERVE THE PEACE OF EUROPE, AND WILL CONTINUE TO DO SO.

GEORGE

WILLIAM II TO GEORGE V:

JULY 31, 1914

MANY THANKS FOR YOUR FRIENDLY COMMUNICATION. YOUR PROPOSALS AGREE WITH MY UNDERSTANDING OF THE SITUATION AND ALSO WITH THE COMMUNICATION THAT I RECEIVED LAST NIGHT FROM VIENNA AND THAT I LATER DELIVERED TO LONDON. I HAVE JUST BEEN INFORMED BY MY CHANCELLOR THAT LAST NIGHT NICHOLAS ORDERED A TOTAL MOBILIZATION OF HIS ARMY AND NAVY. . . . I AM LEAVING FOR BERLIN TO TAKE THE NECESSARY MEASURES FOR THE SECURITY OF MY EASTERN FRONTIERS, WHERE LARGE CONCENTRATIONS OF RUSSIAN TROOPS HAVE ALREADY ASSEMBLED.

WILLIAM

THE GERMAN CHANCELLOR TO THE GERMAN AMBASSADOR IN ST. PETERSBURG:

AUGUST 1, 1914
12:52 P.M.

IF THE RUSSIAN GOVERNMENT HAS NOT GIVEN A SATISFACTORY ANSWER TO OUR DEMAND BY FIVE P.M., YOUR EXCELLENCY IS TO HAND OVER THE FOLLOWING DECLARATION:

"FROM THE BEGINNING OF THE CRISIS, THE IMPERIAL GOVERNMENT HAS TRIED TO SECURE A PEACEFUL SETTLEMENT. IN RESPONSE TO THE DESIRE EXPRESSED BY HIS HIGHNESS THE CZAR OF RUSSIA, HIS HIGHNESS THE EMPEROR OF GERMANY, IN AGREEMENT WITH ENGLAND, WAS READY TO ACCEPT THE ROLE OF MEDIATOR BETWEEN THE CABINETS OF VIENNA AND ST. PETERSBURG, WHEN RUSSIA BEGAN THE MOBILIZATION OF HER ENTIRE MILITARY AND NAVAL FORCES, WITHOUT WAITING FOR THE OUTCOME OF THIS INTERVENTION.

"AS A RESULT OF THESE THREATENING MEASURES, WHICH WERE NOT PROVOKED BY ANY MILITARY PREPARATIONS ON THE PART OF GERMANY, THE GERMAN EMPIRE FINDS ITSELF CONFRONTED BY AN IMMEDIATE AND SERIOUS DANGER. IF THE IMPERIAL GOVERNMENT TOOK NO MEASURES AGAINST THIS DANGER, IT WOULD COMPROMISE THE SECURITY AND INDEED THE VERY EXISTENCE OF GERMANY. HENCE THE GERMAN GOVERNMENT WAS OBLIGED TO ADDRESS TO HIS HIGHNESS THE EMPEROR OF ALL THE RUSSIAS A REQUEST TO STOP THE MILITARY MEASURES UNDER WAY. SINCE RUSSIA REFUSED TO COMPLY WITH THIS REQUEST, AND BY DOING SO SHOWED THAT HER ACTION WAS DIRECTED AGAINST GERMANY, I MAKE THE FOLLOWING COMMUNICATION TO YOUR EXCELLENCY ON THE ORDERS OF MY GOVERNMENT:

" 'HIS HIGHNESS THE EMPEROR, MY EXALTED SOVEREIGN, IN THE NAME OF HIS EMPIRE DECLARES AND REGARDS HIMSELF IN A STATE OF WAR WITH RUSSIA.' "

WILLIAM II TO GEORGE V:

AUGUST 1, 1914

I HAVE JUST RECEIVED A COMMUNICATION FROM YOUR GOVERNMENT IN WHICH IT OFFERS FRANCE NEUTRALITY UNDER THE GUARANTEE OF GREAT BRITAIN. TO THIS OFFER WAS ATTACHED THE QUESTION OF WHETHER GERMANY WOULD DESIST FROM HER ATTACK ON FRANCE UNDER SUCH CONDITIONS. FOR TECHNICAL REASONS MY MOBILIZATION, WHICH I HAVE ORDERED TODAY ON TWO FRONTS, EASTERN AND WESTERN, MUST CONTINUE. COUNTERINSTRUCTIONS CAN NO LONGER BE ISSUED, SINCE YOUR TELEGRAM UNFORTUNATELY ARRIVED TOO LATE. BUT IF FRANCE OFFERS TO REMAIN NEUTRAL AND THE NEUTRALITY IS GUARANTEED BY THE ENGLISH ARMY AND NAVY, I WILL OF COURSE STOP THE ATTACK ON FRANCE AND USE MY TROOPS ELSEWHERE.

WILLIAM

August 3, 1914: Germany declared war on France.
August 4, 1914: Great Britain declared war on Germany.
And so World War I began.

It began with an attack on Serbia. The Austro-Hungarian Empire sent a punitive expedition (*Strafexpedition*) against the Kingdom of Serbia, to destroy it and open up to Germanic conquest the way to the Bosporus and the East. The first bullets of World War I were fired at Serbian soldiers; the first man killed in the war died on the right bank of the Drina River; the first artillery shell was hurled against Belgrade, and the first house was destroyed there—and then more houses than anybody could remember. August 1914 witnessed the first cases of women and civilians being hanged by the victors; the first murders of old men and children, raping of women, and looting; the first destruction of Orthodox churches and poisoning of village wells. All this was on Serbian territory occupied by the armies of the Austro-Hungarian monarchy.

At dusk the drum sounded in Prerovo, around the district office, but it did not penetrate far into the lanes, as if the drummer did not wish the village to hear it. Even so, the old men and women gathered in front of the stone steps of the district office more quickly than ever before; for about ten days not a single letter had arrived from the front, no telegram from the Command announcing anyone killed, wounded, or missing.

Aćim Katić was the last to arrive and he did so only with great effort. The silent crowd of women, old men, and boys, who now stood huddled together at the door of the district office, stopped him at its fringes. He leaned against the scorched trunk of an elm and supported himself with his cane; for the last two weeks there had been no news from his grandson Adam.

The gathering dusk extinguished the whiteness of the walls and the women's kerchiefs; faces were indistinguishable in color from the roof tiles and the bark of the elm. Waves of breathing and sighing from the crowd mingled with the occasional barking of dogs. A stream of yellowish light issued from the district office. The drummer opened the window. The village mayor called out from the office in a clipped, ominous voice:

"The Command has announced that since the last bulletin the following soldiers from Prerovo have been killed. . . ."

Aćim Katić held out until the mayor finished reading the names of those who had been killed, and of the conscripts who had to report to the Command in Palanka by seven o'clock the next morning. But immediately after the lamp was extinguished and the wailing villagers set off through the lanes, Aćim slid down the trunk of the tree and sat on the ground. He remained there until the crowd had disappeared into the dusk. Then he got up and walked through the village, going wherever the winding lanes led him. He could not go home. "Be quiet, you poor creatures," he whispered to himself, "or you'll scare the children. Till daybreak at least. Let the children and the animals sleep. Keep quiet so that the conscripts can get off to sleep—this is the last night they'll sleep in a bed or a dry place. It's not good for them to take the sound of wailing to the battlefield. Life must go on. We haven't seen the worst yet."

He walked past several carts filled with corn which had been left in front of the gates; he silently passed the houses where there had been no deaths, and paused in front of the open door of a house belonging to a man who had been conscripted: the open door revealed a big fire on the hearth; in the darkness a suckling pig was struggling for breath under the knife. "Good luck to you, Ljuba," Aćim said. "Go to bed and have a good sleep. And remember: if you want to live, death can't touch you."

They invited him in, but he continued on his way past the courtyards of the enlisted men; he gripped the fence of a house where a man had been killed.

"You women stop wringing your hands! You haven't gathered in the corn. Your vineyard is rotting away. You haven't sown any seed. The snow will come, and you haven't cut any wood. You've got children and grandchildren. Or if you haven't got children, you've got animals. And plants. Life must go on."

He reached the school: through the open window he saw lights burning and smelled wax. He walked up to the window, grabbed one of the shutters, and looked inside.

Kosta Dumović, the schoolmaster, was walking slowly through the classroom, silent and bareheaded: on the desks at which the boys from Prerovo who had perished in battle used to sit, candles burned, which he, their teacher, had lit for the repose of their souls. He wrote the names of his students who were killed on the board with a piece of chalk; he had begun the list in the summer, and this evening he had added some eighteen names, almost filling the board. He paused between the desks and surveyed the candles: those that had fallen and were burning feebly he relit and put back in their places; he nipped the restless flames with his nails and made sure that those that were burning low did not set the desks on fire; when a flame began to flicker in its last drop of wax, he blew it out. He kept returning to his desk to jot something down in the logbook. Then once more he would stand between the blackboard and the abacus, lost in thought, watching his candles burning.

"How are we going to get through the night, Kosta?"

"In silence, Aćim."

"Come out. Let's talk."

"Tomorrow, Aćim."

"Did you know another twenty young men are leaving Prerovo for the Command tomorrow?"

The schoolmaster continued striding between the deserted desks in the candlelight.

Aćim turned toward the village: moans and wails were fused into one long, mournful note. He walked toward the schoolmaster's house to have a talk with Kosta's daughter. In his own heart he had long ago adopted her as his grandchild; that was how much he loved her.

He knocked on her window with his cane: "Prerovo is crushed, Natalia my child."

"She left for Šljivovo at dusk, to read letters for the women. The letters that arrived today from the front," announced Natalia's mother from the darkness.

"An evil night, that's what it is. And no one to talk to," Aćim said to himself, and set off toward his own house.

The moon seemed to be disintegrating in a mass of clouds. The fences blocked his path; the posts lunged at him. The eyes of dogs and women stalked him. Someone stopped him in the darkness: "I've been looking for you, Aćim. Can you give me ten dinars for Svetozar? He has to go to the Command in the morning. I'll give you some grapes."

"Here's thirty dinars. You don't owe me anything, Gvozden."

They reached for each other's hands: Gvozden's trembling fingers could hardly gather up the coins from Aćim's palm. They parted without a word. Aćim continued on his way until he heard the sound of a flute: that was Tola Dačić playing. He hurried toward Tola's house and banged on the gate with his cane.

"Prerovo is wailing and lamenting, your son was killed forty days ago, and here you are playing music!"

"Music for the three who are still alive. I'm playing because, of my four sons, only Živko's gone, thank God. Things could be a lot worse."

"Lots of houses have been left empty, the life crushed out of them, you idiot!"

"I'm singing for life that hasn't been crushed, Aćim. Let those wail who must. One man wails and another sings. That's the way of the world. A man wails if he must and sings if he dares. There's always some evil worse than the one that's upon us."

Djordje was sitting on his doorstep, smoking. Aćim stopped: what should he say to his son now? He had nothing to say, nothing to ask. Djordje does not dare listen to the reading of the telegrams from the Command. When the names of those killed are read out, or when a letter arrives from Adam, he gets drunk on strong brandy.

"Where've you been all this time?" grumbled Djordje, catching hold of his trouser leg.

"No mention of our boy."

"Did you hear right?"

"Yes, I did. None of the cavalry were killed. About eighteen of the infantry. Eighteen, my boy!"

Aćim heard an ax fall on the cobbles.

"What are you doing with that ax, Djordje?"

"I want to cut some barrels and pour off the wine."

Aćim sat on the doorstep of the winery and lit a cigarette. Djordje's face was indistinguishable from the bricks, his breathing inaudible because of the wailing from the village. Tola played on.

Djordje was sobbing. With a shudder Aćim got up and hurried to his old house He paused on the porch and listened to Djordje's crying; it occurred to him that he had just called Djordje "my boy." He had not called him that since Adam's birth.

"My boy," he whispered, in order to hear the words that now he addressed only to his grandson Adam. But Djordje was the one who would make the arrangements for his funeral. Who else? Vukašin might not come home to Prerovo, even then.

He went into his room and lit the lamp to read his grandson's letters. He had received only three—Djordje had grabbed one and wouldn't show it to him. He would read them in turn. This was the first from the battlefield. He read in a whisper:

Dear Grandfather and Father,

I hope you are well. Dragan is behaving beautifully. You wouldn't believe it, but he's the quietest horse in the regiment. He's as serious about his King and country as a regular soldier.

Yesterday at dawn we charged when the first shot was fired. The rifles were firing away one after another like machine guns. Grandpa, I was scared to death. I thought a bullet was sure to get Dragan—you know what a great big horse he is.

"Well, so long as one doesn't get you, my boy!"

Dragan made himself small and thin, like a dog about to spring, and did everything right. The minute he heard a shell or a piece of shrapnel, he lay down.

All sorts of things happened. One meadow was black with soldiers lying dead, theirs and ours, but the two of us never got a scratch. Only I'm having a lot of trouble getting oats.

"The officials and contractors are eating them all. Where would the soldiers and horses get them?"

So please send me some more money. Then I'll have it in case oats get even more expensive. Don't worry about me. I hope you are all well.

Adam
Cavalry Squadron, Morava Division,
Second Draft, First Army

This evening there were more deaths from the first draft of the Morava Division. The fighting was in the mountains, beyond Valjevo. But when they came down into the plain, there would be cavalry charges.

He read Adam's second letter aloud:

Last night Dragan was wounded near the village of Lipolist. The shrapnel just grazed the skin of his left shoulder, thank God.

"Thank God. You poor, miserable idiot!"

I felt it when the shrapnel hit him. My heart nearly stopped beating. When the charging and stampeding was over, I got down to loosen his girth, and my hand fell wet and sticky. I struck a match and saw the blood. Dragan turned his head to the left and didn't make a sound. I cleaned the wound with brandy and he trembled like a leaf, poor thing.

"Why don't you tell me when your horse has pissed. And to find out how you are I'll look at the stars."

I rubbed some special ointment on his wound and it stopped bleeding. Luckily the battle at Cer, the one in which we drove the Fritzies out of Serbia, was over. We are now resting near the Drina, and Dragan's wound is healing. Just think, Grandpa, and you too, Father, what would have happened to Dragan if he had galloped a few inches to the left! Give my greetings to everyody who asks after me. If Natalia doesn't ask, I don't care.

"So you've got yourself tied in a knot. You can't have every woman you fancy. It's better for you to learn it from Natalia than for some whore to set your brain on fire."

Aćim pushed the letter away into the shadow. *It's as if the horse were my grandson,* he thought, *and Adam his groom.* He blew out the lamp. Darkness enveloped him, shot through with the sounds of lamentation from the village. He took off his boots, lay down on the bed in his clothes, and put his hands over his ears. *That poor, motherless boy, that idiot, the one creature left to live on after me, will lose his head because of his horse.*

Aćim's fingers grew still in his beard; once more he was remembering how Adam had gone off to war.

The church bells were tolling, the drum beating, the women wailing; at dusk poor folks and hired men from Prerovo and the surrounding area filled his courtyard, coming in from the apple orchard and over the fences, as if the gate were too narrow for the last debts they were going to incur: they asked for ten dinars for the war, for themselves, for a son, or for a brother. For the first time, Djordje refused no one and did not reproach anybody for an unpaid debt; he gave with a kindly hand everything that was asked of him. "Give them what they want! Help them!" Aćim called out. He looked toward the apple orchard, waiting for Adam, who had sneaked out from behind the hayloft as soon as the summons to mobilization sounded. Aćim wanted to have a good look at Adam, to give him some advice, and to tell him his wishes for his own funeral.

He remembered the times over the years he had waited for his grandson to come through the apple orchard: Tola's creaking fence, the rustling of the apple trees, Adam's furtive steps on his way back from some woman; he would always come to the porch where his grandfather was sitting and have a long drink of water from the pitcher, and then greet his grandfather and sit down on the step. Neither of them would speak: Aćim would breathe in his grandson, hunting for the smell and sweat of the woman. Trembling, he would struggle painfully not to ask Adam who he had been with that night and what she was like. Adam would give a loud, relaxed yawn, and Aćim would say: "The best thing for you is a glass of cold milk. Then sleep until I wake you." After Adam had gone, he would smoke, filling the dark room with women, Adam's and his own from times gone by, always on the earth, among the plants, fragrant and silent.

A solitary firefly appeared in the apple orchard and flew around a tree. Adam still hadn't returned: even on this last night before going off to war nothing was more important to him than a woman.

Adam too would betray him. Those who love women love only themselves. The gate creaked; waves of sound filled the courtyard. Perhaps he would not live to see so many people gathered together again. The war was taking away voters and political supporters. This was his last assembly. Aćim got up from his chair, gripping a porch post, and surveyed the crowd in the dark courtyard.

"Where are you going, brothers? The war is here at home. Our boys shouldn't be killing the German emperors; they should be hanging the thieves in our government! Pašić has lost the election, so he's pushing Serbia into war! And what are we going to fight with? All right, we had to fight the Turks. And the Bulgarians deserved what they got. But how are we going to fight Austria and Germany—two empires? The people are naked and barefoot; we're worn out by war and poor harvests. Not even our great-great-grandchildren will be able to pay off our debts. The crops are poor; our animals all have worms; the rains are ruining the soil. What have we sown? What have we reaped? Our granaries are empty, our sheepfolds deserted, the people are hungry and dying of disease—and Pašić is driving us into war! What good is a state without justice for the people? Can there be a worse war than the war we are fighting for this miserable existence?"

On the other side of the fence Tola Dačić began playing his flute, overwhelming the wailing with a folk song and striking Aćim speechless. The peasants too fell silent. They were never silent when he spoke; they had never greeted his words with silence. Did they think differently now? Was he no longer for them what he had once been? He fumbled for his cane, walked inside, and lay down on the bed.

Djordje shouted to Tola: "If you're just drunk, go and sleep it off; if you've gone crazy, we'll tie you up."

The playing did not stop.

Aćim was trembling: what if he died while the war was still on? While the men were on the battlefield? All his supporters would go away and be killed. Only cripples, children, and a few old men would remain in the villages. Surely Aćim Katić would not be escorted to the cemetery by women? Women and silence. All his hopes rested on his funeral. For fifteen years he had not entered a single election. His son Vukašin had betrayed him, and Pašić had cooked his goose at the executive committee of the Radical Party and buried him in Prerovo. All he had to look forward to was his funeral, when all of Serbia would learn who had the backing of the Morava folk. If there was no other way, let the people vote for Aćim Katić with candles!

Those votes could not be bought with brandy. Pašić and his district clerks couldn't tamper with the election lists that would stretch out behind his coffin. The people would dance the *horo,* twisting and turning in the Prerovo cemetery, and sing peasant songs from the time of the rebellion in Prerovo and the Timok country. This would hurt Vukašin, that traitor who was no true son.

The crowd had dispersed from the courtyard; the soldiers had gone away to get ready for their departure. Tola began another song on his flute but did not finish it.

Aćim dragged himself out of his room and once more sat on the porch. The solitary firefly was still anxiously circling the red apples.

Did Adam really have to spend this last night with a woman? Those who like to enjoy themselves love only themselves. Did Adam know this? *One of these days you'll need your home and family, you restless creature. When troubles and evil times beset you, when you are left alone, my boy, you'll need a big tree to shelter you and a grandfather to comfort your soul. Plant your roots deep, so a strong sun doesn't kill you, scoundrels and bullies don't uproot you, the winds from the Morava don't blow you away. But tonight everything that matters to you is underneath you. Now you need nothing but yourself. You love yourself. You're not afraid of anything. There's nothing you can't do. The war hasn't got to you yet.*

The firefly was climbing up an apple, up its steep green slope.

Enjoy yourself, my boy! Grow up, young man! Grow up and don't let life break you. And may none of your women forget you; may their breasts be full of glowing embers when they meet me! I want each one to blush when she sees me; I want to know every woman you have had; every one of them must ask me about you, ask in a whisper when you'll be home on leave. They must stop when they pass our house, creep past our ash trees, our fields and meadows. I want them to think of you all night long, to go barefoot into the haylofts and keep vigil where you used to meet them. Let them wait for you like aspens; let them shiver as they stare at our fence.

"What's that boy doing all night? It's nearly midnight. When is he going to get his sleep?" cried Djordje from the doorstep of the winery.

"Never mind," Aćim said in reply, but inside he felt afraid: Adam might fall asleep without hearing his final instructions about the kind of funeral he, Aćim Katić, the old Radical champion of Pomoravlje, wanted to have. The man who had driven cabinet ministers from the rostrum of the Assembly with his cane when they maligned peasants and enacted laws against them, who had thrashed district chiefs and tax collectors like oxen when they violated law and justice. Even

King Milan shuddered when he heard Aćim's name mentioned. That was until his son Vukašin betrayed him. That fine gentleman, a doctor of law from Paris, on whom he had set his hopes. An unnatural son. Pašić had strangled Aćim with his son's hands and buried him alive. But he could do nothing against his own son. He did not want to do anything. He did not want to trample on his son's head, break his arms, or halt his footsteps.

"Where is he?" cried Djordje, throwing away his cigarette and walking across the apple orchard toward the fence. *Why does Adam have to be with those women tonight? He'll catch a disease; death goes for those who shove themselves between women's legs. Why must he trample the flowers around somebody's house, mess up someone's hay, and frighten some poor man's chickens? Why tonight, why?* Djordje sat down by the fence which Adam's legs jumped every night and seized hold of the fence post which Adam's hands gripped every night. *Those who wear themselves out with women have a short life,* he thought. *They are blinded by a midnight star which only they can see. Its spark falls into their hearts and burns them up. Then tuberculosis starts. Some star! Some spark! Those who break people's fences to get to women are killed by an ax. They are attacked by dogs, knives, bullets. Death rushes at those who run after women. They perish by night.*

Djordje strained his ears, listening to the dogs, trying to determine by their barking where in the village Adam might be. The sky was bright: the green apples and leaves glistened in the moonlight. Adam would not be back until sunrise.

Djordje got up, gripped the fence post with both hands, and dropped his head onto the binding rope; actually, it would be better if Adam didn't make it to the Command. In fact, he must not go there! He can't hold back Austria and protect Serbia! What was one trooper to Serbia? He, Djordje, would buy him out with a bagful of ducats; he would bribe generals, kneel before Putnik and Pašić and tell them he had never been involved in politics or listened to Aćim. There was nothing he wouldn't do to save his son. He would dig a passage under the Morava River so that a whole division would not be able to find him. And the war wouldn't last long; how could Serbia fight against two empires? He had hoped there would be no war, and he never went to the Command to see to things, to have Adam placed on the staff or in a hospital; he could be a telephone operator—after all, he could read and write. Vukašin could arrange this easily. If only Adam had a good horse, but he was rushing off to war with Dragan. How Adam had screamed and yelled when Djordje had implored him that evening: "Let's get Flower ready for you, my boy. She's a mare, always quiet and obedient. What will you do with Dragan when the cannon fire?" "Flower? You can keep her! Dragan is my horse and I'm taking him." A horse was a target a blind man could not miss. Especially Dragan—a beautiful, big horse, and so well groomed. The Fritzies would think it was a general on such a fine horse and would aim right at him, the swine. It was Aćim's fault that Adam had done his military service in the cavalry; the old man had gone crazy because he no longer had political power, and he insisted that his grandson should be a cavalryman so he could brag about him. Three days was all he needed to fix things in the Command! Just three days, and he would go to Belgrade, to Vukašin; but this evening the tolling bells and the drum had ordered the men to the Command by daybreak.

The rope snapped, and Djordje jerked his head from the fence post. He stared at Tola's plum orchard. It was Tola, moving quickly in the moonlight, carrying a lamb in his arms. A stolen lamb.

"Whose sheepfold did that come from, Tola?" he called out, hoping to exchange a few words about Adam with him—the boy had no mother, and Djordje could not talk about him with Aćim.

"Not from yours, Djordje. There're four soldiers in my house, and they must take four shoulders of roast meat with them. I can't give them a suckling pig each."

"Have you seen Adam?"

"Now how could I see him? Everybody knows where he is now."

"Do you need anything else? Don't steal tonight, Tola! Take what you need. Don't worry about money. I'll give your four boys a ducat each for the war."

"Please don't. My sons didn't have any ducats in peacetime, and they don't need any now. Give them ten dinars each, if you must. And bring a bottle of brandy for each of them. And a bottle of that wine that you serve to important guests." The lamb began to bleat; Tola pressed on its throat and hurried home.

Djordje lit a cigarette and leaned against an apple tree. *If only his mother, Simka, were alive,* he thought. *If she were alive, Adam would not be chasing women so much. A man without a mother has no shame. Anyone who has had no mother to love can't love his father either. Well, never mind, my boy. Just go on living. Hate me as much as you like, but stay alive!*

Suddenly he felt numb. He dragged himself to the winery, poured off some wine, drank a whole jug, then tottered to the stables and sat down on the trough next to Adam's horse, Dragan; he leaned his face against the horse's shoulder, then against his chest, rubbed his neck and stroked his head, wept and implored him: "Take care of him for me, Dragan. When the shooting starts, lie down. Run for cover. Don't charge. And don't run like a race horse; this is war. Run fast only when you are being chased. Look after Adam for me. He won't go off to war without you. I'll have you shod with ducats."

The horse was silent, sniffing at Djordje and breathing down his neck: Djordje wept and caressed him. Suddenly Tola's flute sounded. Djordje jumped up and went out: the cobbles gleamed in the moonlight. A big fire was burning next to Tola's barn, over which the stolen lamb was being roasted. Tola's sons were asleep, as they should be. All the enlisted men were asleep now. Except for Adam.

Again Djordje went into the winery, and drank another jugful of wine, then sat down on the doorstep: he listened to Aćim coughing on the porch, and to the sound of Tola's flute beside the fire, over which Andja was turning the lamb on a spit. He hated Aćim because he was waiting for Adam; Aćim would take Adam away from him. He hated Tola because there he was playing his flute, and at dawn his four sons would go away to their death.

He crossed into Tola's yard and stood between him and Andja.

"Do you have to play your flute tonight?" he asked, making a threatening gesture.

"I want to cheer up my boys. I don't want them to go off to war sad and worried. I'm playing to taunt fate. And because I feel like it."

"How dare you do such a thing?"

"Well, when a man's giving the state four soldiers, when three of my boys will be firing rifles for Serbia and Aleksa will be doing his bit with his cannon, I can play my flute."

"I don't understand you," Djordje whispered, and went back to the doorstep of his winery.

Tola went on playing his flute. He played all the songs he knew his sons liked. He put aside the flute only to chide his wife when she was sniveling and not turning the spit evenly, to poke the fire, or to take an occasional swig of brandy from his flask.

Tola had done everything in his power for both the state and his sons. Then the war came. What could a man do? What did it matter that a man didn't want the war when the emperors wanted it? The world just wasn't to their fancy. Some people want more than they have, others won't give up what they have. So now the devil has seized God by the beard and God has got the devil by his horns.

He shoved the flute into his pocket and threw some more wood onto the fire: four soldiers from his house, four sons; no one else from the whole district of Prerovo was giving away so many to the state. Once these hard times were over, someone would acknowledge it, reward him for it. If the state didn't, maybe the King would, and if he shut his eyes, God would. Tola Dačić would not be the same after the war. War turned everything upside down. It was not for him to say who would come back alive and who wouldn't. So many children died of sickness, but he had lost only two. There were four left, and all boys to boot. He who has life has hope. If it's your fate to die, you can die of eating a plum. If Serbia collapsed, it would not be the fault of Tola Dačić and his sons. If, God willing, Serbia was victorious, the sons of Tola Dačić would be victorious. Four soldiers: three rifles and one cannon. And what was his employer, Aćim, yelling for now? *You masters are feeling the pinch,* he thought. *Your hired men and servants have gone away. Your fields and vineyards will become wasteland; there's no one to mow your meadows. The war's come to you Katići too. Now we're all the same, no one better than anyone else. Not a bad thing, Aćim, that the war makes us equal, that the same pains hurt us, that we have the same hopes and fears.*

"There's a war on, Aćim!" he shouted out loud, and went on playing his flute.

Aćim swore and banged the wall with his cane, then fell silent and dropped the cane between his legs. Adam was crossing the apple orchard, carrying a watermelon in his arms; he went hesitantly up to Djordje, who was sitting on the doorstep of the winery and smoking; he knew his father had had too much to drink. Aćim announced his presence with a cough, but Adam did not hear: he was cutting up the watermelon for Djordje.

He's stolen a melon; we have none on our property. He knows that Djordje likes melons. Even tonight he's remembering his father, but he's forgotten me. A lot he cares about his grandfather! His father has plenty of time to despise and to forgive. His grandfather dare not even be angry. He has only a little time left; he must love. Yes, that's what I must do. Adam is both roots and leaves for me.

Trembling slightly, Aćim watched Adam slicing the melon on the cobbles by the light of the moon. Then he called out:

"Adam, I've been waiting for you!"

Djordje said something to Adam, who went up to the porch and leaned toward Aćim. The roosters were beginning to crow when Adam said crossly:

"I'm tired, Grandpa. I want to go to sleep."

"Do you know where you're going and what's waiting for you?"

"I'll think about that when I have to."

"Do you have any idea why you're going off to war?"

"I'll let you know when I do, Grandpa. Now I want to go to sleep."

"All right, Adam. Out there on the battlefield see that you sleep whenever you can. See to it that you have a faithful friend, a full bag, and dry socks. Never eat by yourself. If your commanding officer is a sensible man, pay more heed to him than you have to me or to your father; if he's a silly fool, keep quiet and keep out of his sight. Always stay with other people. When there's a charge, don't be the first or the last. Keep in the middle when you flee too. And now go and get some sleep. Your father will get you up on time."

Adam walked slowly away to the new house. "Sleep well, my boy," whispered Aćim, and put out the bitterest cigarette he had ever smoked. On the way to his room Aćim stopped and pressed his forehead against the door of Vukašin's room: since Vukašin's departure on Christmas morning twenty-two years ago, nobody but Aćim had crossed the threshold of his room. Aćim kept the key attached to his watch chain. He entered the room every autumn, to throw away the rotting and withered apples and quinces from the cupboard and the grapes from the window and to replace them with the reddest apples, the biggest quinces, and the finest grapes from the old vineyard. He observed that day in silence, sighing furtively; that day he did not go to the inn or read the newspapers. He would also go into Vukašin's room when all his thoughts and memories fused into the old, familiar suffering over Vukašin; he could never free himself from the pain of his son's betrayal. He would look at the old photograph: Vukašin, a student at Belgrade University, wearing peasant clothes, and he, Aćim Katić, Vice-President of the Serbian National Assembly. He would gaze in silence at the tall, handsome, serious young man who had been for everybody, including his teachers, Aćim's son, who was studying in order to bring wisdom and justice to Serbia; in the Radical Party, he had stood side by side with his father, a peasant fist raised against the petty tradesmen who fleeced the people. Then Aćim had sent him to Paris so that he might be more learned than those frock-coated gentlemen. But Vukašin had become a different person. The son had betrayed the father. Pašić had strangled Aćim with Vukašin's hands.

Once during those twenty-two years he had spent a whole day in

Vukašin's room: one morning, Kosta Dumović, the schoolmaster, came to the house; pale and breathless, as if announcing Vukašin's death, he stammered: "The Independents have formed a government, and Vukašin's been made a cabinet minister!" His hands shaking, Aćim got dressed, then went into Vukašin's room and sat there till nightfall, looking at the photograph of the two of them. He was glad that Vukašin had become a minister. Yes, he was happy, he had never been so happy and sad at the same time; several times he said to himself: "I'm in the Opposition, you know." When the government in which Vukašin was a minister fell and every time he was excluded from a new cabinet, Aćim remarked casually to Djordje, "Those scoundrels have again thrown him overboard." And then he would once more relapse into silence about Vukašin, as if Vukašin were a runaway slave, concealed in the empty room whose door was now burning his palms and forehead.

He took the key fastened to a silver chain on his waistcoat, unlocked the door of Vukašin's room, went inside, and stood before the photograph of the two of them, taken in the days when he believed there was no happier father in Serbia, when his word was law to the Morava people. He and Vukašin loomed dark on the wall. He was about to strike a match and take a close look at Vukašin but his hand trembled. He flung himself onto Vukašin's bed, into the creaking, rustling shadows. *Vukašin too is a father. He won't be asleep tonight either; his son is going off to war. My grandson Ivan, whom I haven't seen. I haven't seen my granddaughter Milena either.* What force had dug such a chasm in his own hearth? Why were they, people of the same blood, warring with one another?

His thoughts were gloomy. Vukašin's bed felt uncomfortable. He went to his own room and lay down. It was dawn, the dawn of war. Tola was playing his flute.

If Adam did not come back from the war, bats and barn owls would settle in his chimneys; thieves and rain would demolish his houses. Tola's sons would burn down the fences and steal everything that could be stolen. The vineyards would become wasteland; the fields and meadows would be covered with thorns. The poor would cut down the apple trees.

"O God, where are You? Take care of Adam for me! Thou knowest how I have grafted him onto my own blood, Thou knowest how deeply he is implanted in my soul. Save him for me, O Lord, and do not let the entire Serbian race perish."

The sun shone on the lower branches of the ash trees when Adam mounted his horse in front of the stables and rode up to Djordje, who was standing in the middle of the empty courtyard. Adam jumped down from his horse and kissed his father's hand, then straightened himself up, tall and large-eyed like his mother. Djordje looked at him with tearful eyes.

"When did you grow up to be so tall and handsome? Why did you reach the age for military service and war so soon?" muttered Djordje.

"I could have been born a cripple, you know. Then you'd look at me as if I were going off to war every day."

"That would be different."

"If I weren't going off now, I'd hate the sun."

"Why did you have to grow up, my boy?"

"What can the Fritzies do to me? Don't worry, Father."

Just as Adam embraced his father and kissed him on both cheeks, Aćim banged his cane. Adam had already said good-bye to him in his room and to his grandmother, Milunka, and his stepmother, Zorka, in the kitchen. This was what his father had ordered. The father was seeing his son off to war; this final act belonged to the two of them alone. For the first time in his life Adam embraced his father and kissed him on both cheeks. Djordje was unable to move; he felt himself slipping down onto the cobblestones, their curved gleaming surfaces coming upon him like water, rising up to his throat; his voice was barely audible.

"Promise me, Adam."

"What do you want me to promise?"

"Please, my boy!"

"I'll do anything."

"Not to run after women while the war's on."

Adam smiled and rode off. The cobbles resounded with the singing of Tola's sons. The ash trees enveloped Adam, hiding him from sight as he trotted down the lane.

On the doorstep of the winery the rosy slices of watermelon lay scattered. Djordje picked them up, carried them into the winery, placed them on a barrel, and burst into tears.

The rains were so heavy that not even the underside of a bird's wing could stay dry. What would happen to the men? They couldn't, dared not, light fires. *It will pour tomorrow night too,* thought Djordje.

He was leaning against the house under the metal eaves, listening to the rain and the cries of lamentation from the village. Where should he go first: to Vukašin in Niš or with Tola to the battlefield near Valjevo? He had not seen Vukašin in over fifteen years, but he must go to him for Adam's sake. Did that unnatural brother have a heart? Had he forgotten that they both nursed at the same breast? He had paid for Vukašin's education in Paris and given him three hundred ducats that last Christmas, but that was between him and God. First he must find Adam. He must go to Valjevo and look for the second draft of the Morava Division. He would hide him somewhere, anywhere, until the war was over. And then? Well, he would approach some people with tears and others with ducats. Who cared whether it was Franz Josef or the German Emperor so long as Adam was alive. Even if he had to be a slave. Djordje stood against the wall, listening: at this early hour Prerovo was a graveyard. Foul smells drifted over from the stables and sheep pens. Aćim knocked on the floor with his cane. A cane in his hand invariably meant fear or some evil thought in his head.

A group of women called to Djordje from the lane, and he walked over to the fence. Their sons had been drafted; at dawn they would leave for the Command. The women begged for help.

"What do you need? Just ask."

"A few dinars!"

"Will a hundred each do?"

"That's too much! How can we pay it back?"

"The boys can—when they return from the war."

He was glad to give them the money. He thought of Adam, who loved to give to the poor and would give them anything they asked for. God must know that

It began to rain as he trudged into Tola's courtyard. He thought of Adam, who would be in the rain and the cold all night, hungry and unable to sleep. Well, so be it. He knocked on the window, and Tola came to the door.

"Are you dressed?"

"I had a dream that the barrel of Aleksa's cannon burst. Burst like a pumpkin. So I got dressed and I've been waiting around, listening to the rain. Hard to take this rain, even for a dead man."

"They're all dying, you know, Tola. The Fritzies are destroying Serbia."

"Yes, they're dying. But not all."

"What do we do if one of these days they all get killed?"

"Well, I suppose there is Someone in this universe who sets a limit to evil."

"If there is, I don't dare put all my trust in Him. Let's go to Valjevo and find Adam and Aleksa."

"Let's. And we'll take some food and dry clothes for them."

"We'll leave at dawn. Get ready, and meet me at my house. Take whatever you need."

Tola stood in the doorway with his hands pressed against the post. As Djordje walked away he whispered: "No, Djordje, I'm not taking anything from you. I'm not taking the boys anything that isn't mine. No, sir! It has to come from my hands. Now what do I have?" He walked toward the plum tree where his hens roosted for the night. One scrawny rooster for three hungry soldiers? Yes, one scrawny rooster, and yet eight people from his household had worked the soil of Prerovo, and four soldiers were sent to the war; four Dačići gone to take on the German Empire. If only he had known ahead of time, he would have caught a few turkeys last night. A good night to catch turkeys. He could have grabbed a sackful. Let's see now. Who has chickens roosting on low perches? And who feeds them well?

Cautiously jumping over fences, he went through the Prerovo plum orchards. He would take nothing from those who had lost someone in the war or from those who were leaving for the Command at dawn. But those who were fast asleep and would live through the war like moles—they were the people whose roosters he would take for his heroes. He crouched under a quince tree: that coward had fought neither the Turks nor the Bulgarians, and he wasn't going to fight the Germans either. Tola seized his hens by the neck and felt their tails and combs, searching for a rooster. The hens cackled loudly, took fright, and flew away. The roosters flew into the mulberry trees. His hands still empty, Tola jumped over the fence and hurried to a hen roost on a mulberry tree. That thief was serving time as a convict; he was safe, the bastard. The hens flew off to the top of the mulberry tree. They were thieves too. They were all thieves. He ran down the road looking for low hen roosts, no rooster in sight.

Tola returned home without a rooster. In desperation he seized one of his neighbor's chickens, which gave a squawk. He squeezed its head and jumped over the fence. He yelled to his wife and daughters-in-law to make a fire and heat some water; how dare they sleep while the Serbian soldiers were out in the rain all night, hungry and barefoot. Under his own plum tree, he grabbed some hens and felt them; they were scrawny. He managed to catch one; the others dispersed into the darkness of the courtyard. He asked his daughter-in-law to catch one more, the biggest. He killed the chickens on the woodpile, and the women carried them into the kitchen. Aleksa would get the rooster, he decided. Aleksa was in the artillery, the only person from Prerovo in the artillery; he was the best gunner in the Morava Division and deserved the Karageorge Star. Blagoje and Miloje wouldn't mind when he told them there was only one rooster. They'd get the same kind of bread and a bottle of Djordje's strong brandy. And the quinces and bacon—the same for all of them. Djordje would give each a ducat; he would give whatever they asked for. He had been giving to everybody since the war started, but bullets ran after ducats and money. If they have to die, let them die as poor men. Soldiers with empty pockets. Let the Fritzies see that we're an honest nation. Let the heavens know that the Dačići were hired men and that they stayed that way in the war, fighting for the state and freedom. But why did Zivko stay out there at Cer? His son without a grave, in the soil for which he gave his life. A man without a grave hasn't been born; a man has not existed if he leaves no mark behind him. Why did he tread this earth if he doesn't have a cross to honor him? The best digger in Prerovo has gone naked into the ground. A great big man like him without a grave. Gone. Never was.

"Andja, where are you?" he called to his wife. "Make some cheese pies. I don't want my boys to be ashamed in front of the soldiers and the corporal when they open their bags."

"I don't have anything to make them with."

"Take what you need from those who have it. If our folks haven't earned the right to a cheese pie after fifty years as hired men, then we've no reason to fight a war."

He got up from the woodpile and stood under the eaves: boiling pitch was pouring from the skies; he must be with his sons now that the world was falling apart. If they were alive, he would give them food fit for a feast and bring them a change of clothing; if they had to die, he would give them a proper burial, a place marked with a cross, so that their existence would not be wiped out. Now where in Djordje's courtyard had he lately seen a nice piece of wood, already planed? You could cut three crosses of the right size out of that piece of white wood. There would be room for the surname and Christian name. And my name in the middle. Date of birth, Prerovo, Morava Division. And the year when Serbia perished. He would have to find wood for the coffins at the front. He would tear apart somebody's house if he had to, but he would make a coffin for his soldier son; while I'm alive no son of mine will go naked into the earth, and he won't lie in the mud with the dogs and wild beasts. He would take the tools with him. The Fritzies were looting, and people were running away, taking with them whatever they could. Yes, he would need tools—an ax, an adz, a plane, and a saw. And nails. All he had was an ax. His master, Djordje, had everything. And where would he find some blue paint? Where would he find it? Unpainted wood gets covered with lichen, and turns black. Looks ugly and old. A little more of this damned rain, and unpainted wood will rot before the man underneath it. He would have to find blue paint in Palanka. Never mind the war. He just wasn't going to the battlefield without blue paint. Candles, and incense. And a censer. He would have forgotten the censer. It might rain and the candles would go out. But first he must find that piece of planed ashwood.

From Aćim's room Djordje saw Tola wandering around the barn; Aćim was telling him his dream about Adam. "I am going to Valjevo, to help Adam," Djordje said. "I'll find a way of getting him out. The army and the state are up to no good."

Aćim looked hard at him, a dark figure etched against the window in the early dawn light. "Dare we do that, Djordje?" he said with a slight tremor in his voice. "In times of great misfortune, a man mustn't try to get himself out of trouble on his own."

"We each have only one head, and we have to keep it out of trouble."

"No harm will come to Adam!" Aćim said after a pause. "Not all our boys will get killed. There are limits, even in war. Even in the greatest evil there is some justice."

"What if he does get killed?"

"Go and see him if you have to. But let him stay where there are men and rifles. Anything else would be far worse for him."

Djordje pulled down his hat and went out into the rain.

"Do you have any blue paint, Djordje?" cried Tola from some distance away; he was carrying a plank of white wood, a saw, and a few other tools.

Djordje did not understand: he stared at the wood, deafened by the sound of wailing from across the way, beyond the ash trees.

"Why blue?" he asked.

Tola lifted his head toward the cloudy, grim early-morning sky: "I don't know why coffins and funeral crosses are painted blue. But they must be blue."

Djordje hurried to the stables and ordered the servants to get the horses and cart ready for a long journey.

Fully dressed, Aćim sat at the window, looking at the courtyard, the main gate, and the road beyond the ash trees. The horses were being harnessed. They had all left at daybreak, he recalled: Vukašin, Adam, and now Djordje. He gazed at the early-morning light and thought of those departures. Departures with no return. What was left to him after so many years of life? What evil had he done to deserve what was now in store for him?

From a distance came the rattle of a cart and the thud of horses' hoofs on the cobblestones. The small bell sounded from the Prerovo church, soon joined by the large one, announcing the death of a man.

The bells unbolted the gates of his memory and transported him into the hazy world of recollection. His eyes fell absently on the previous day's newspaper.

Bulletin from the High Command of the Serbian army. As a result of the great numerical superiority with which the Austro-Hungarian enemy has penetrated into our country, our troops are gradually retreating in order to battle under the most favorable circumstances. . . . The Bulgarians are demanding Macedonia. . . . Will Bulgaria attack Serbia? . . . Turkey's entry into the war is expected. . . . The Russians are advancing. . . . How long will the war last?

Aćim pushed the paper away and finished drinking his coffee. Every morning after breakfast he would go to the inn to tell the peasants what was in the newspaper, curse Pašić and the government, predict the fall of Austria-Hungary, and firmly declare that mighty Russia would be victorious. Every morning it was the same routine. Now, he picked up his cane and paused by the door. The church bells were ringing.

Natalia Dumović walked in through the gate. Aćim was not pleased to see her, nor did she smile at him ass was her custom when she came up to kiss his hand.

Natalia stopped under the eaves to wipe her daamp face with the edge of the dark-blue scarf tied around her head. In herr bosom was Bogdan's letter. Strength and warmth. And joy, which she wanted to express to Aćim, even though the bells were announcing death. She looked at him timidly.

He's aged since yesterday, she thought; *he won't last long.* She had never seen him so unhappy. He had never said a word to her about Vukašin and his grandchildren in Belgrade. It was a known fact in Prerovo that if anyone wanted to offend Aćim and make him angry, all he had to do was mention Vukašin. But surely he must now be glad to have news of his grandson.

The bells boomed; Aćim's forked white beard was quivering. Every day he would ask her whether she had heard from Bogdan. Then he would comfort her and scold the male sex. He liked to talk about Bogdan, who was a student and a socialist.

"I've received a letter from Bogdan, Grandpa!" she said. Aćim was looking beyond her as if he couldn't hear her. Stepping toward him, she raised her voice: "Bogdan says he's in the same platoon with Ivan Katić." Aćim nodded and continued to gaze at the ash trees. "He says he is a good man. And Bogdan is severe in his judgment of people." Aćim banged his cane on the step. Could it be that he was not pleased?

"Read me the letter."

Natalia was surprised. How could she share such a personal letter?

"Read it to me, Natalia."

"Well, Grandpa, here it is. 'Ivan Katić is in my platoon. He's the son of Vukašin Katić. He studied at the Sorbonne. Where else?' "

"Don't skip anything, Natalia." Aćim moved closer to her; frightened, she quickly put the letter back in her blouse.

"Natalia, read it all to me, from the beginning."

"Bogdan loves Ivan. He says Ivan is a wonderful young man and a marvelous friend."

"Read it!"

" 'He's far from being a chip off the old block; and he confirms the old rule.' "

"Ah, my unhappy boy!" the old man said with a sigh.

"I thought I was giving you news that would please you," Natalia said disconsolately.

"Read on. And don't be sorry for me."

" 'Young Ivan does not think the same way as his father.' "

So Vukašin too has lost his son, Aćim thought, then added sharply: "Go on, Natalia."

" 'He despises the reformers and the middle-class Progressives. He has a wise head on his shoulders and a feeling for justice and goodness. The conditions in his home and his strange passion for books are to blame for the fact that he hasn't become a socialist sooner. Inexperienced as he is, young Katić finds it hard to judge his own father and his class. There is something tragic about him, something that arouses sadness and pity.' Well, there it is, Grandpa."

"Read that last sentence again."

"It doesn't necessarily apply to your grandson, you know. Bogdan is reflecting."

" 'They'—Bogdan is thinking of the bourgeoisie—'condemn themselves to destruction through their children. In their homes, under their wing, among their spoiled and well-fed children real opponents grow up. They make them uneasy and unhappy even when they are at their most powerful. The seed which will destroy the oppressors sprouts right at their hearts.' "

"What makes Bogdan think that Vukašin is an oppressor? A bullet's sprouting right there in Bogdan's head."

" 'I attach great significance to rebellious and discontented individuals from bourgeois homes. They may not always be the seed of the future, but they constitute open wounds on every coat and uniform. It is from such children that the bourgeoisie and the tyrants will experience their first defeats.'

"So Vukašin has lost his son too!" Aćim said, and disappeared into his room.

Natalia did not know what to do. She had intended to read him only the first sentence and give him pleasure. It was not enough to share the letter with her mother or to read it to herself countless times through the night.

The bells fell silent: the gurgling in the gutter merged with their dying echoes. Natalia moved away from the wall. The main gate banged shut behind her. Once again the small bell began to peal, this time mourning the death of a field hand of Prerovo.

A woman stepped over the threshold of her house and grabbed hold of the doorpost, swaying and moaning, while a small boy sat down on a pile of pumpkins and poked one of them with a stick. His father was an awkward, swarthy man who laughed easily: several times Natalia had seen him beating his oxen until blood gushed from their nostrils. Where had the bullet got him?

She stopped at a sheaf of cornstalks stacked against a mulberry tree, took Bogdan's letter out, and read:

At night when I am on sentry duty, I look at the stars. I am stunned by the feeling that if I did not have you, I would doubt my own existence. Will we be able to love each other even in a time of bondage? In the Student Battalion every doubt is like treason these days.

An old man was unfolding a mourning flag by a gate. So Radoš was dead too. Natalia and Radoš had gone to school together; he used to bring her birds' eggs. He was the best singer in Prerovo. His grandfather glanced at the house filled with the sound of wailing, then walked over to the hayloft and buried his head in a haystack.

Natalia hurried along the lane. *The voice of the bronze bell sounded the same for everybody,* she thought; *the sexton tolled every death with the same force, with equal length; the telegrams announcing a death were the same. And yet they had not been the same men. They had been good, bad, stupid, amusing, miserable, brave.*

Behind a bend in the lane someone sang and then fell silent. Natalia stopped: she saw two conscripts carrying bags, accompanied by their mothers and grandfathers. She recognized them. What could she say to them? Should she wish them a happy journey? Zdravko, a silent young man, began to sing; his mother begged him to stop.

"I want to sing today! I may die tomorrow," he cried. "Good morning, Natalia! Good-bye, Natalia!"

"Have a good journey, Zdravko," she murmured.

"Some journey! Promise me though that you'll write letters to me for my mother and grandfather. They can't write."

"I will, Zdravko."

"And promise that you'll read mine aloud, to all the neighbors. Will you do that?" asked the other young man, who had pulled his cap down over his eyes to hide his tears

"Yes, I will. Be sure to write often."

Once more Zdravko began to sing; his mother wept and pulled at his bag.

Natalia hurried on so as not to see and hear them. She paused in front of a small house without a fence, the most poverty-stricken house in Prerovo. A disheveled woman was walking slowly and silently around the house; she would stop for a moment, beat her chest with her fists, then continue circling the house; clinging to her skirt, a barefoot, half-naked little girl rolled in the mud.

Duka, Djordje Katić's swineherd, lived here. He hadn't written a single letter from the front. And Natalia had written three. In the last one she herself had scolded: "You should be ashamed. You are the only man from Prerovo who hasn't written home. Write at once, or I'll tell your commanding officer what kind of husband and father you are." Without him they would starve.

"Natalia, come have a drink for the repose of Borivoje's soul. You went to school together," called Borivoje's father from over the fence.

She wiped her eyes and went into the house. On the table lay Borivoje's new suit, a body whose head was a chain of lighted candles; his mother and widow moaned quietly.

The crumpled, empty suit would never hold the body of the swarthy, hot-tempered fellow, a good dancer who used to pick fights, break up the kolo dances, and rush at his rivals with a knife.

"Will Serbia be defeated, Natalia?" whispered Borivoje's father, staring at his son's peasant shoes.

"Not with Russia fighting on our side."

"Well, what can we do? God gave him to us, and God took him away. Some sickness could have carried him off while he was still sucking at the breast. But we lived to see him a grown man and a soldier. Both the meadows and the state have profited from him. He brought us both joy and worry," Borivoje's father whispered above the empty suit on the table.

Leaving the house, Natalia walked on between the fences, slipping in the mud, pursued by lamentation and the tolling of church bells, meeting conscripts heading for the Command; fearfully she wished them a good journey. She stopped beneath an ash tree and took out Bogdan's letter.

Our army is retreating. Perhaps we're on the brink of defeat. But we students feel like victors. Can you understand that this isn't just some kind of craziness? It's horrifying to shoot at people, but I'm convinced that I'm fighting for freedom and justice for the poor and oppressed. They are my homeland. And for you, Natalia. Believe me, that's how I feel: you are my other reason for fighting.

"I understand and I don't, my dear, handsome, crazy boy," she said to herself. "Oh, why did I leave the train at Lapovo? What frightened me so much? Those overpowering words of yours, falling like stones. I felt stunned with desire; everything turned black. That's all I could think about when I was crossing the Morava—no, before that, as soon as I read your letter."

Be sure to get here on Wednesday afternoon, because on Thursday we leave for Skoplje. I'm going off to war. So come one night earlier; come, if you trust me; come without fail the night before we leave. There's a war on, Natalia.

I fell out of the train; somebody pushed me, Natalia thought; *I never wanted to do it for a minute.* But suddenly she had felt frightened; she had a vision of him hovering over her, showering her with words, dazzling her with his eyes. Then she had jumped out of the train and fled behind the station, into the corn and pumpkin stalks: far away the train whistled on its way to Ralja. She wanted to cry, but the tears wouldn't come. She dragged herself to a tree and leaned against it. Why was she so afraid of him?

When the crickets became silent, just before dawn, she came out of the cornfield and went to the station to catch the morning train for Belgrade. She arrived at Ralja before midday. Pushing her way through the rows of young student volunteers, she caught sight of Bogdan lying on his back, his hands behind his head; he didn't move, just waited for her to come to him, then raised himself slightly. For the first time he didn't smile at her, and gave her a limp handshake, very different from his usual firm grasp. He never mentioned her belated arrival or his imminent departure. He talked about how he had parted from Dimitrije Tucović, the leader of the Serbian socialists; she looked straight ahead, feeling sad and ashamed. Why had she been afraid of him? Why couldn't she trust him? He was so different from all the others who used to come to the Students' Club; different until now; now he was just an ordinary student volunteer, defeated by masculine vanity, who at a shout from an officer hoisted his bag and went to the platform where the train was waiting, walking with a light step, as though he were going on a trip. She could no longer restrain herself.

"Forgive me, Bogdan!"

"What's there to forgive?"

"My fear. The thing that makes us different from you men."

"You mean what gives men the right to consider themselves superior?"

"No, it's what deprives you men of that right, Bogdan. Don't look at me like that. I'm not ashamed to be crying."

She would have left him standing in front of the train and fled into the cornfield if he had not immediately said, in a quiet, stammering voice: "Can you understand what it means to go off to war? If I come back, I won't be the same person. I'm not afraid of death, Natalia, but I am afraid of the war. Horribly afraid."

It was this trembling, whispering Bogdan that she loved, not the one who spoke momentous words, who threatened her. "Natalia, Natalia . . ." he whispered her name slowly, beseechingly. In the train the students were singing and embracing each other. Natalia trembled under the touch of his broad, soft hands on her shoulders; she swayed as her forehead touched his chin; she saw the nearby wood growing denser in his eyes, and the corn bursting into flame: that was where their bed would have been if she had arrived last night. She pulled his head down onto her breast, which pounded with words she couldn't understand. A numbing pain gripped her whole being with the desire to remain in his arms. All she could see was laughter, wagons full of laughter moving slowly past her, gradually receding on their way to war.

Nikola Pašić, Prime Minister of Serbia, stood behind his desk, listening absently to Jovan Jovanović, his assistant for foreign affairs.

"Another note from the British embassy, Prime Minister. The English consul in Skoplje has complained to the Foreign Office that we've levied a heavy tax on some Turkish merchants who are friends of theirs."

"Tell the district chief to exempt those Turks from the tax."

"And the English vice-consul in Bitolj is angry because we're levying taxes on two villages where they shoot partridges. Sir Edward Grey has no hunting dogs, so he uses peasants instead."

"Exempt those peasants too. Keep the consular gentlemen happy so that the British embassy doesn't send us these notes."

When Jovanović had gone out, Pašić leaned over his desk, piled high with the morning's disagreeable telegrams from the Allied capitals and recent reports from the battlefield: *The situation could not be more critical, Prime Minister.* "It will certainly get worse, Colonel," Pašić murmured, and the thought struck him that a man who didn't think in time of misfortune that things could be even worse didn't belong in his cabinet. As he stood bent over his desk, he reflected on his speech for the next day's secret session of the National Assembly: what should he take care *not* to say? He considered Serbia's position, one part of her territory conquered by her enemies, another part being taken away by her friends, and the army barely able to hold out at the front. The Allies wanted to give Macedonia to Bulgaria and failed to send munitions and military equipment; meanwhile, the Opposition was blaming him for the country's troubles! And the mob believed them. In this situation, how could he say as little as possible, when everyone was expecting him to tell everything, even the worst? Today any fool could prove that Serbia's position was hopeless. And yet it was his duty to give reasons for hope without providing much evidence. Curiously enough, people have little faith in a policy buttressed by proofs. But there was the Opposition, determined to crush him. If only he could silence Vukašin Katić in the Assembly tomorrow. He was the one member of the Opposition who spoke sensibly, and the people believed him. There would be no political agreement without Aćim's son, who persistently opposed any suggestion of a political coalition. How could he win him over, his old and dangerous opponent. If the truth be known, the Austro-Hungarian attack on Serbia had saved him from being defeated by Vukašin in the summer elections.

"The chief of the High Command is on the telephone, Prime Minister," said his secretary, adding, "My office is full of foreign journalists demanding an interview."

"Tell them I'll see them the day after tomorrow."

When his secretary had left, Pašić sat down, slowly lifted the receiver, and waited for Vojvoda Putnik to speak.

"I've thought long and hard, Prime Minister, before deciding to inform you that our army is on the brink of catastrophe."

"I take it that our army is still in the trenches, Vojvoda, and resisting the Austrians and Hungarians."

"It's no longer resisting them. Our front has cracked at Mačva and Jagodnja. The Austrians have broken through and are pushing relentlessly toward Valjevo."

"Do what you can to stop them."

"We have rifle ammunition for about ten days, but only ten shells for every cannon. Without substantial help from the Allies we can barely hold out for two weeks."

"I'll press the Allies again for munitions. But we dare not hope to receive fresh troops from them."

"The Commander in Chief has authorized me to summon you and the cabinet to Valjevo immediately to discuss the situation. Hello, Niš! Can you hear me, Prime Minister?"

"Tomorrow there's a meeting of the National Assembly. The High Command must decide for itself what should be done at the fronts, as it has done up till now."

"Prime Minister, I repeat that the situation on all fronts is extremely critical. I must ask you to come at once."

"If the situation is as you describe it, we should refrain from making hasty decisions."

"I believe that we must now make a crucial decision."

"And I believe that we made that crucial decision when we rejected the Austro-Hungarian ultimatum. Everything else must conform to that decision. It must be the basis of all our actions. I am firmly convinced of this, Vojvoda. No, I'm not evading any responsibility; certainly not. Please convey this to the Regent. I'll think things over and call you tomorrow evening."

Pašić replaced the receiver, for the first time cutting short a conversation with Vojvoda Putnik. This soldier, always so calm and sensible, who never acted hastily, talked as though Austrian shells were already falling around the High Command. His voice had trembled. If Putnik said the army was on the brink of catastrophe, it was. But that meant the end of Serbia. What should he do in the face of this calamity?

Pašić got up and leaned on the table as though he were leaning on the railing above a precipice. *Now wait a minute, Nikola, take your time and go back to the beginning. Where did you make a mistake? Could you have done anything different? Was there any way of avoiding the war, before it was declared on Serbia in that open telegram from Count Berchtold?*

From the time that he received the ultimatum from the Austro-Hungarian government on July 23, he had never for a moment thought that the murder of Franz Ferdinand was Vienna's main reason for going to war against Serbia. Actually, Austria-Hungary had seen Serbia's victory over Turkey as a declaration of war on herself. And it was. Turkey had protected the Hapsburg monarchy from the South Slavs, but the Turkish presence in the Balkans had also postponed Austria's attack on Serbia and the Germans' *Drang nach Osten*. He could not believe that the shots fired by that boy Gavrilo Princip had given Vienna a cause for starting a European war. By her victories over Turkey in 1912 and Bulgaria in 1913, Serbia had brought herself into direct military confrontation with the Danubian monarchy. And by refusing his guarantees of good neighborly relations, Vienna had made it perfectly clear in 1913 that there could be no peace between Serbia and Austria-Hungary while they possessed common frontiers. *There could only have been a truce between us*, Pašić thought. But a truce was vitally necessary for Serbia. Colonel Apis had thought that the truce would be prolonged by the assassination of Franz Ferdinand. Neither he, Nikola Pašić, nor the Serbian government was responsible for the fatal mistake of that band of conspirators. No great historical event has ever been set in motion by the dictates of reason, nor have its participants been guided by moral principles. A man can plan a small action well; he can even act honorably in a small matter. In great affairs this is difficult. Vienna had found an excuse and had pressed its advantage by attacking Serbia when she was at her weakest, after two exhausting wars.

Every word of the Austro-Hungarian ultimatum was, for Pašić, clear proof that she had decided to destroy Serbia. After reading the ultimatum, he had for a long time hovered in a kind of limbo; then he had felt a strange buzzing inside his head: this was the declaration of a war in which either the Kingdom of Serbia or the Hapsburg monarchy would cease to exist. Us or them. War was unavoidable. But he knew very well that Serbia must accept such a war in a conciliatory spirit. In replying as he did to the ultimatum, he was replying not to Vienna and Budapest but to London, Paris, and St. Petersburg: they must be convinced that Serbia had absolutely no desire for war, that she was ready to satisfy the Austro-Hungarian demands up to the point beyond which her independence would be destroyed and her national honor annihilated. He also had to ensure that Europe and the entire world would regard Serbia as the victim of German conquest, the first victim of Germany's advance to the Dardanelles and the East. But he was certain that Russia would defend Serbia, and he firmly believed that both England and France would find it in their interest to take Serbia under their protection and acknowledge her as an ally. With Allied support Serbia could win the war, in spite of the disparity between her and Austria-Hungary.

Pašić's belief in Serbia's victory had been reinforced by the conduct of the Austrian Ambassador, Baren Giesl, to whom he had personally taken the Serbian government's reply to the ultimatum of July 23. The Baron had received him in hunting costume, wearing a hat decorated with feathers. In the tradition of the Austrian and Hungarian aristocracy, always contemptuous toward the Serbs, the Baron had run his pencil vigorously over the Serbian reply, comparing it with the demands of the ultimatum, searching for the least sign of insubordination. After a few sentences he had found it; he had raised his head, smiled cynically, and pushed aside the Serbian papers with the words *jawohl! jawohl!* Observing the facial expression and gestures of this imperial huntsman as he read the Serbian reply, Pašić had felt the knot of fear loosen in his throat; he felt an easing of the strain caused by the tremendous uncertainty and his own personal responsibility for the sacrifices that would have to be made; he felt confident that the correct reply had been given: war was unavoidable and could be won. An opponent who despises you to such an extent is not invincible, no matter how strong. When Baron Giesl did not offer his hand at parting, but just briskly clicked the heels of his hunting boots, Nikola Pašić stood looking at him calmly until the imperial diplomat nodded slightly; then he gave a sudden start and thought: *Yes, you have to be persistent with them, very persistent, that's all!* Aloud he said: "Your Excellency, please convey to your government my sincere wishes for peace and good neighborly relations. Please make them understand our respect and admiration for the great Austrian nation and the brave Hungarian people." As he slowly said these words he felt that he was declaring war on the Hapsburg monarchy. A war that would end in victory.

Now, after three months of successful fighting, after winning a great victory at Cer and driving the imperial Balkan army across the Drina and the Sava, now that the Entente powers had accepted Serbia as their ally, was it really necessary to make yet another crucial decision? What other decision would lead to victory?

Pašić walked up and down his office, recollecting every word spoken by Putnik, remembering his trembling voice. If the army was really on the brink of catastrophe, then surely the wisest course was to take the government to Valjevo that very evening and calm down the High Command. But why should the Opposition be freed from the heaviest responsibility and the most serious anxiety? Why shouldn't they come with the government and share in his mistakes the following day, if the situation was as bad as Putnik said it was?

His secretary came to tell him that the foreign journalists were still waiting.

Pašić pondered a moment: what should he *not* say to them? Then he set off behind his secretary. From the open doorway of the journalists' room he bowed politely and said in French: "I am at your disposal, gentlemen."

"What can you tell us about the situation in Serbia today, Prime Minister?" asked the French journalist Henri Barbi.

"In wartime people should talk about the war as little as possible, monsieur."

"But what will become of Serbia if the Austro-Hungarian advance continues?"

"Things will be extremely difficult for us, gentlemen."

"It seems to us, Prime Minister, that the situation is critical."

"No, gentlemen, it is not. We are resolved to be victorious."

The journalists looked at him in amazement. Nikola Pašić bowed slightly and returned to his office.

At dusk Vukašin Katić hurried through the streets of Niš toward the bridge over the Nišava River. After spending the day in the wartime office he shared with seven other deputies, who perpetually railed at Pašić and assailed the Allies for not helping Serbia, and after dining in the house into which several families from Belgrade had been squeezed, Vukašin couldn't bear to stay in the room crammed with possessions and suitcases, where all he could do was lie in silence if Olga wasn't there. He couldn't bear the cafés, where at least ten military strategists and national prophets sat at every table and where he'd have to wait for hours for a glass of wine. Neither could he wander through the streets, crowded with frightened women, agitated young girls, refugees, wounded soldiers, and young boys enjoying their boundless freedom. He longed for the quiet of the fields, a world that silently endured everything, the only living world that possessed something of perfection.

As soon as he crossed the Nišava, the gloomy expression left his face: he was alone and free. He turned around: the great expanse of sky over Niš, to which the mountains lent a troubled depth, had contracted and descended over the hills surrounding the town. A flat and ashen sky. A north wind scattered the fallen leaves, plucked the last ones from the tops of the poplars, and sent a tremor through the dark, scorched fields. The smell of dying vegetation filled him with foreboding and anxiety for his own and himself. Could he compose his speech for the next day's secret session of the National Assembly in this fast fading light?

With long, slow strides Vukašin walked along the damp paths between the harvested fields, breathing in deeply and hungrily the smell of decaying crops and vestiges of summer. Stopping under a large aspen, whose golden leaves had been shaken by frost the night before, he dropped his cane and knelt, grabbed handfuls of leaves, gazed at them, smelled them. A shuddering breath of old age emanated from them. He had never before felt anything so clearly: something pressed on his heart, a dark, pungent residue of time through which his blood and thoughts flowed, making everything seem smaller and less important, making him doubt his highest aims. He scraped some leaf spots with his nail and the leaf fell apart. This last remnant of summer and sunshine, this concentrated essence of light, this fragment of time now dead and gone would soon, after the first rains, decay. This sweetish smell was the odor of a dead body—the most beautiful body in this ugly, monstrous world. He opened his hand and let the leaves drop, heard them rustle as they fell. What did the last throb of the human heart sound like? He would rather hear that than the sound of the first heartbeat.

Vukašin picked up his cane and walked on, stepping carefully over the leaves, listening to the crunch of dry stalks. He couldn't help feeling that everything he saw was coming to an end. Yet freedom had meaning and purpose only for a man who had hope, who didn't see the dregs of death in the falling leaves. How could he convince himself that no price was too high for freedom? That the country that would emerge from the war would be sufficiently good and just to compensate for the great sacrifices Serbia must make? He must weigh carefully every word he would say in the Assembly tomorrow. Everything he said must be clear, firm, consistent.

A nation that identifies freedom with its own existence chooses suffering.

Suffering or uncertainty? Both, really. Just in front of him a hare rose from a clump of withered flowers, stared at him, then moving slowly, as though playing, it jumped off into the unharvested corn.

Then he would say:

Today we must have the courage to speak the truth.

After these opening sentences he would say a few words about a nation having been robbed of time by its conquerors. History has not given us time to make historic decisions or to take the wrong path. He would say these words firmly, looking hard at Pašić, an optimist who bided his time, so that everyone would notice. He would ignore interruptions. He wasn't speaking to the voters and the press; he was speaking to a refugee Assembly, to soldiers on the battlefield at a time when Serbia perhaps stood on the brink of catastrophe.

Vukašin walked through a patch of watermelons, entangling his feet in their dry stalks; a small flock of partridges suddenly rose up, curved around in a short, low flight, and fell into some peppers. Lowering his voice to a whisper, he would allude to Pašić:

There are politicians who on the pretext of patriotism hold secret meetings and make secret decisions. Only tyrants make decisions in secret about the fate of nations. Only tyrants and conspirators deliberate in secret about matters of state. People for whom politics means serving the homeland perform that service publicly.

That was uncalled for. What were the right words, timely yet enduring, words that would mean something to everybody, that would be heard on the battlefield? Certainly it would be better not to attack Pašić immediately, but to begin with a review of the general situation. But what gives hope? What faith impels men to kill and be killed? Was this the faith that inspired his children, Ivan and Milena? With such faith people were ready to die. Was that the only thing people could feel today, the only thing they could think about?

He went on his way, stumbled over a head of cabbage, and walked out of the cabbage field; he stopped and leaned against a willow. He must find some way of expressing the truth simply, in a manner worthy of the moment: My friends, we are alone. Serbia is alone in this European slaughter. She is alone, even though she is fighting alongside her allies.

This wouldn't make a good beginning either. A hopeless tone wouldn't do; war couldn't be fought without hope. But could hope be separated from illusion, from blindness and stupidity? Pašić's authority rested on gullibility, a prime national trait. Tomorrow the government would again face accusations of dishonesty and sabotage in provisioning the army. Flour adulterated with sand, sandals made of cardboard, thieving in the warehouses, rampant influence-peddling. An army of draft dodgers was wreaking havoc behind the lines.

No, he wouldn't talk about that. A whole nation was being killed off; tomorrow it would be Ivan's and Milena's turn. His words must be the parting words to a son, words he hadn't dared say to Ivan before he enlisted as a volunteer.

Vukašin gripped his cane and hurried along the bank of the Nišava away from Niš, into the twilight seeping through the willows, the underbrush, and the borders of the fields.

"What long steps you take, Mr. Katić!"

Vukašin turned around. A policeman was running toward him.

"What do you want?"

"I've got orders from Mr. Pašić to bring you to him right away."

"Why are you running? Who told you where I was? I'm not Pašić's clerk." Vukašin walked on rapidly. So Pašić wanted to see him? Why? For twelve years they had spoken to each other only across the podium of the Assembly. What did he want now?

"Please stop, Mr. Katić. I have to take you to his office. Things look very bad. Some very serious telegrams have come."

Vukašin quickened his steps. "Don't accompany me. Go on ahead. I know where I have to go."

Did Pašić really want to see him, after all that had happened? After his speeches during the summer elections, when he had opposed Pašić in his own constituency, determined to defeat him where he was strongest? After his article "The End of Nikola Pašić and the Old Political Era"; after his attack on Pašić's foreign policy in the Assembly a few days ago?

Vukašin stood still. Above Niš the blue evening smoke twisted among the trees and chimneys. When the lights went on, he would go into the town. No need for people to see him going into Pašić's office following a policeman. War made people more stupid and brazen. He sat down on a fallen willow trunk and lit a cigarette, the chill murmuring of the river behind him.

The first time he had talked with Pašić alone it had also been dusk, the sultry August dusk of Belgrade. Milena had just begun to walk. He had felt uneasy as he pushed his way slowly through the milling crowd, past the tables and chairs on Terazije Square, saturated with the unpleasant smell of charcoal, shish kebab, and chopped onion. With a feeling of awe he had entered Pašić's house and then the room where Pašić was waiting for him in the darkness. Pašić with his long, gray beard. Pašić had greeted him in a whisper and offered him a slice of pear. He did not ask him to sit down.

"May I sit down, Mr. Pašić?" Vukašin asked, confused and somewhat offended because he had been standing before Pašić for a few minutes.

"Sit down, my boy. Make yourself at home," Pašić said, in such a warm and fatherly way that Vukašin felt ashamed of his wounded pride.

It was not until he had finished eating his piece of pear that Pašić said: "I've asked you to come here to tell you that we've decided to elect you a member of the executive committee at the party's general meeting, and then we'll nominate you a deputy. After that your own wisdom and sense will see you through. After all, you're Aćim's son. Well, that's what I wanted to tell you. Choose your path accordingly." He said the words quietly and distinctly, with frequent pauses.

Pašić's wife appeared with a lamp, but Pašić waved it away. "We don't need a lamp," he said. In the darkness they heard dogs barking; lightning flashed across the sky. Vukašin was glad Pašić had refused the lamp. At that moment, in the darkness, he had realized quite clearly that all the plans he had made in Paris and all his efforts after returning to Belgrade had come to nothing. *In our milieu,* he thought, *failure makes a man a fool, disgraces him, humiliates him.*

Ideas are met with contempt and curses. Knowledge is mocked; truth is hated and despised. He even touched Pašić's hand out of gratitude for this unexpected graciousness, something that had not been asked for but freely offered, help through which he would indeed "go further and higher." Pašić was his savior; this he believed, had to believe. Even before the painful breach with his father—after his rupture with the socialists and the friends of his early youth—and especially after his father-in-law's humiliating refusal to give him money to build a plow factory, Vukašin had doubted whether he could make a clean break with the past. His new ideas would not enable him to do something for Serbia; he was prepared to abandon the political struggle and take a university post. And now unexpectedly, here was Pašić, a powerful man in his party, asking him to share in the leadership of the biggest political party! Easily, with few words and without laying down conditions, Pašić was offering the possibility of success to a man who had always been an outspoken opponent, to the son of his bitterest enemy in the party. At that time he certainly hadn't reflected on Pašić's motives.

Vukašin could not remember whether he had said a single word after Pašić's generous promise. He did remember clearly that they had sat in the stifling darkness and eaten the pear that Pašić had cut into slices. He had eaten Pašić's pear, and already saw and heard himself making speeches at the general meeting of the Radical Party, at large gatherings, and in the National Assembly. He saw himself a deputy, a minister, a president under whom Serbia would be reborn, the man who would transform her into a European nation. And he wasn't the only one who thought that. The youthful ambitions of his entire generation had been imbued with a crazy notion of historical greatness. Peasants had become tribunes; students were now prophets. People were entering history's stage from sheepfolds and plum orchards. French and Russian writers had inflamed their hearts with great ideas and a new faith.

When a cool gust of wind suddenly swept into the room, Pašić stood for a few moments at the window gazing toward the west, his beard lit up by a flash of lightning and twisted by the wind. In that scene just before the storm he had looked great and powerful, the Pašić who had been the friend and disciple of Bakunin. Vukašin looked at Pašić, the follower of Svetozar Marković,* forgetting that

*A prominent socialist writer and publicist in late nineteenth-century Serbia. [Translator.]

Pašić had later renounced his convictions. Afterward he remembered his father, Aćim, who that summer had held meetings up and down the Morava valley denouncing "that traitor Pašić, the leader of petty shopkeepers," and had tried to have him expelled from the leadership of the Radical Party. No, Vukašin hadn't thought about that for long, or he would have had to draw certain conclusions—or at least to doubt the sincerity of Pašić's good intentions toward himself. Later, much later, came pain, shame, and remorse. Perhaps he had not said good-bye when he went out into the street emptied by the approaching storm.

The most important decision after his return from Paris had been made that evening in Pašić's room—not in his father's house in Prerovo that Christmas Eve when they had clashed head-on. The turning point in his life had come when he ate Pašić's sweet, sticky pear smelling of honey. That was the sharp break, and not the general meeting of the Radical Party, when he made a speech against old men and reactionaries, after which Aćim had walked out, a scene reported in all the newspapers. For just a few moments he had been torn two ways, while his father dwelt on Serbia's poverty and lawlessness; but his feelings changed the moment his father banged his cane on the podium, threatening the "pen-pushers and skinflints," to the noisy approval of the peasants, who shared his opinions. It was the expression on their faces and their yelling and shouting, as much as Aćim's words, that had goaded him into speaking against his father. Of course the provocation had been submerged beneath his passionate determination not to yield an inch to anyone and his urge to prove his strength despite the consequences. He did not feel guilty because he and his father were opponents. His father had long ago, even by his love, made him an opponent of beards and low ceilings. The old story of sacrifice and betrayal, of conflict between old and new, of father killing son and son killing father in the struggle for power and authority was being played out in a Serbian setting. But with this difference: while the original tragicomedies had been enacted in city squares and royal palaces, this Serbian drama was played out in the Paris Café. Its producer was neither Fate nor any other invisible power controlling people's destinies; its producer sat at a table in the café by the kitchen listening calmly, his eyes focused on his long beard. Each actor knew his part well and everything happened as foreseen. Vukašin was gripped by the feeling that perhaps he was simply the victim of that inexorable force which draws all human desires and powers into a tangled knot of eternal futility.

And the greater the sacrifice, the greater the futility. Vukašin shuddered at the thought.

Even today he didn't know if he had spoken immediately after Aćim. Or didn't he want to know? No matter. He couldn't renounce his ideas; he couldn't have spoken a single word differently. His only alternative would have been to take his hat and cane, leave the meeting, walk out of public life for good, and abandon his great aims. He really had believed in his goals. But why hadn't he stopped talking when Aćim got up and pulled his fur hat over his forehead? He could at least have done that. He hadn't stopped talking even when Aćim banged his chair with his cane. Amid the loud laughter, Aćim stumbled and almost fell on his way out. Just in front of the door, Aćim turned around and looked at him. . . . Vukašin went on talking, without the slightest tremor in his voice, people said. No, that couldn't be true. "Then Aćim spat toward the podium," they said. At him or at Pašić?

Suddenly Vukašin felt space contracting around him as the hills drew nearer. Above Niš smoke from the chimneys blended with the sky, darkening it. Since the outbreak of the war, ever since Ivan had enlisted and Milena had volunteered to work as a nurse, Vukašin thought more and more about his father and Prerovo. He was tormented by what he had abandoned. He got up to follow the policeman, his fear and anxiety mounting as he drew closer to Niš.

As he walked through the town the gathering dusk did not save him from verbal attacks from a crowd: "Is it true that we're abandoning Valjevo and Belgrade, Mr. Katić? No more state secrets, we're finished. When is the government moving to Skoplje? You've fixed things for Serbia, all right: what are our children dying for? When is Niš going to be evacuated? What happens when we capitulate? Where are our allies? What's the matter with Russia?"

Vukašin wasn't convinced by his own answers. He could hear curses too, but was not offended. He pulled his hat down lower over his face.

He entered the dimly lit corridor and stopped at the door of Pašić's office. "I've been betrayed by that pup of Aćim's whom I fed with my own hand," Pašić had often muttered into his beard. Without mentioning Vukašin's name, he had said in his pre-election speech: "It wasn't hard for a man who first betrayed his father to betray his party. A man who betrays his father and friends won't find it too painful to betray Serbia." Vukašin was neither offended nor goaded into retaliation.

The policeman opened the door: he saw the broad beard glimmering behind the table. Crossing the threshold, without waiting for the door to close, Vukašin said stiffly: "You asked me to come see you, Prime Minister?"

Pašić looked straight through him and remained silent.

"You sent a policeman to escort me here," Vukašin added brusquely.

"Sit down and have a smoke, Vukašin. I'll be ready in a minute. I just have to finish a telegram." Pašić spoke as though they'd had lunch together, as though he were addressing his nephew and not his bitterest opponent, the man who that summer, just a week before Austria-Hungary's attack on Serbia, had declared political war on him with his article "The End of Nikola Pašić and the Old Political Era," which all his opponents and the majority of his supporters knew by heart, and about which Pašić had said to a group of journalists, as though dropping a casual remark: "I don't read foreign newspapers, gentlemen. One need refute only the Opposition's petty lies. The people will defend us against the big ones." Something remote but unforgotten made Vukašin reject Pašić's friendly overtures. He knew very well how Pašić could conceal his true feelings and real intentions, mention only half of the most important matters, or simply allude to them in passing. He stood and watched Pašić as he slowly and clumsily wrote, his pen squeaking.

"How is Aćim?" Pašić asked in a quiet, kindly tone without raising his head; his pen squeaked more as he strained his ears to catch the reply.

Vukašin stepped toward the desk, shifted his hat from his left hand to his right, and smiled.

"When you write to him, give him my warm greetings. I must finish this telegram to Russia. I'm appealing to the Czar's government not to enter into preliminary negotiations with Italy at the expense of Dalmatia and Croatia, which are resolved to be united with Serbia."

The last time Vukašin had been alone with Pašić he had also asked after Aćim and sent him his greetings; his pen had squeaked loudly in the same way twelve years ago. Vukašin had entered the office of the Radical Party without knocking, not his usual behavior.

It was a winter morning, and the office seemed smaller because of the drifting snow and ice that covered the narrow window. Pašić always sat behind his desk, lying in wait. Protected by his beard, that shield which prevented people from seeing his intent gray eyes, Pašić would say nothing but follow every word, pouncing on it like a hunter as it was torn from the speaker's mouth. Suddenly he and Pašić were standing face to face. They could clearly hear each other's breathing; they were unbearably close: the closeness that precedes an embrace or a wrestling match. Vukašin remembered distinctly that sense of superiority which made him sway on his feet; out of sheer fury he kicked the woodbox. The loud noise settled him and strengthened his resistance to this old man, this second old man, this second beard that had planted itself squarely in his heaven, lowering it to an office ceiling and a tax collector's box, darkening his days and entangling his footsteps. Now he would grab this second beard with both hands and pluck it out of his life, just as he had done with Aćim's black forked beard in Prerovo that Christmas Eve. Pašić had looked at him benignly and sat down again at his desk, stroking his beard with his fingertips.

"Take your coat off and sit down, my boy, or you'll feel cold later." This had spurred Vukašin to say immediately: "I've come to tell you frankly, Mr. Pašić, that I can no longer be your supporter. I feel obliged to tell you because of the pear I ate in your office four years ago."

"Do you feel constrained, working with me?" Pašić asked in the same quiet, fatherly way.

"I do, and depressed."

"It's the times we live in, Vukašin; there's nothing we can do about it."

"In our almost blind political life, people see no further into the future than the door of an office or a cabinet minister's chair. We must live for something else; we must conduct our lives differently."

"In politics today it's either the door of a government office or the door of a prison. The same with a minister's chair. Very close to it, sometimes a bit to the left, sometimes a bit to the right, stands the gallows or the stake and white towel. I'm thinking of the fate of those who have lofty aims." Pašić wasn't threatening; he was talking slowly and evenly.

"Maybe so. But at my age one also sees a third door, a lofty gate a long way off but high up. I don't want to whisper ideas that I believe could pull this nation out of its Balkan poverty."

"That's how it should be. A man should be seeking a new path as long as he lives. That's something I like about you, Vukašin."

"It can hardly please you, Mr. Pašić."

"You've only got to make one small mistake. It may be small, but it lasts forever."

"Maybe. But it's those very mistakes—small but lasting forever—that sometimes bring us the greatest joy. And give meaning to life. Anyway, without those mistakes in youth there's no wisdom in old age." Vukašin gave a broad, confident smile.

"Isn't the price a bit high to pay for wisdom you don't even acknowledge now?"

"That depends on the individual. Only people who gain experience by making mistakes know this."

Pašić passed the tips of his fingers over his lips, as if wanting to wipe away the slight twitch caused by the distasteful recollection of his own youthful mistakes. "Let me tell you something about ideas, Vukašin. They're worth something only as long as they're whispered. The more quietly you utter them, the farther away they're heard. Once you begin to shout them, no one believes you. Nor should they be disseminated through the newspapers. Because newspapers are used for all sorts of things, and once they get soaking wet from the rain, they're no good for anything."

"There are different kinds of ideas, Mr. Pašić. And it's true that some are good only for whispering. Some should be shouted and sung. That's where we differ. I don't believe in whispering about the fate of our people. Those who do aren't helping the people."

"What is it that you want to shout, Vukašin?"

"I'll tell you about that later. I'm leaving the party, along with a group of people who think as I do. We're going to found a new party, a party of genuine young Radicals."

"Why do you need a new party? When someone in your house bothers you, it's much better to push him into a corner than to rush outside and build a new house."

"Apropos of houses, Mr. Pašić, I must tell you that by your ambition and servility at the King's court you've deeply eroded the foundations of our house, or, rather, your house, a house you built honorably and courageously. That was your great mistake. The one that begins in youth."

"Just what is it that you brave and honorable individuals intend to do?"

Although there was no trace of irony in Pašić's voice, Vukašin said:

"Your irony is out of place. We too have decided to make our great mistake. We will announce our political program and fight against you in the elections."

"If that's what you've decided to do, Vukašin, good luck to you. You're young, so you have time both to plunder and to kill," said Pašić in his usual voice. Yet the expression in his eyes, hidden beneath his forehead, darkened.

"As regards youth and time, Mr. Pašić, quite the opposite is true. We haven't got an hour to waste. We can't go along with your ideas, an old man's ideas, for another day. Serbia can't afford to stop or to stray from her path. This is the twentieth century. Electricity and the combustion engine have been invented. Science has mastered the world. Europe forged ahead long ago. What kind of future faces us? What are we doing?"

Pašić shrugged. Vukašin had noticed at their first meeting that if he talked about ideas and principles, Pašić would shrug and raise his eyebrows, pretending to be ignorant and confused.

"What are we doing?" Vukašin repeated, raising his voice. "We're squabbling over dynasties and strangling each other for political power. We've tied our fate to political power. It's only when political power is in the hands of others that we see anything wrong with it. That's how low we've sunk, morally. Political power is our curse."

"And what do you young gentlemen propose to do later on?"

"Afterward we'll follow in your footsteps. We'll fight each other for financial privileges and official positions. So ends our knowledge. Serbia is becoming a country of incompetent officials but competent swindlers. Meanwhile, in Europe people are thinking and building for the future."

"So I hear. They say all sorts of things about Europe. And I see they're doing all sorts of things there. Those who live long enough will see. As for happiness and the future, Vukašin, that's anybody's guess. The more foolish someone's notions, the greater a prophet he's considered. The more crazy a man's suffering, the greater saint he is. The calendar is full of saints and prophets. How is Aćim these days?"

But Vukašin did not allow Pašić to ask after Aćim's health as though they were the best of friends, as though he hadn't driven Aćim out of the executive committee of the Radical Party, as though he hadn't stirred up son against father. Vukašin kept himself under control; actually, those words about saints and prophets pleased him; he even managed to smile. "I shall have neither reason nor occasion to convey your greetings to him."

But Pašić was deaf to irony, insults, or even curses. He heard only what was useful. When Vukašin said to him, as he put on his hat: "You can be sure that my personal feelings will never influence my political program," his voice betrayed him. What if it did? That didn't bother him. Nor did Pašić's words, spoken after a silence which only appeared to be reflective.

"You must decide that for yourself, my boy. You'll have time to think about things properly. Now I shall tell you something I didn't know when I was your age."

"Whatever it was that you didn't know at my age would mean something to me only if you still thought now as you did when you were young."

Pašić's fingers remained buried in his beard, as though forgotten. He began his story about Bakunin and the old man. "I was a student in Zurich, and we were sitting with Bakunin, as we did every night, and he was thundering away about revolution and turning the world upside down. We were hanging on every word. Afterward I couldn't fall asleep till daybreak."

"I've heard that story. I have to be going."

"Wait a few moments. You really ought to hear this. A small old man came and stood behind us and listened. Bakunin suspected that he was a spy and drove him away from the table several times. Poor Mikhail! He suspected anybody who didn't say anything or stood behind his back of being a spy."

Again Vukašin interrupted Pašić. He'd had enough of his stories. Until that moment he'd been slightly afraid of the mighty beard, the calm, quiet, mysterious, and withdrawn opponent who was most dangerous when everybody was convinced that he was completely powerless, whose blows could not be foreseen, whose hand could unexpectedly stretch out to caress and then tighten into a clenched fist. Until the story about Bakunin and the old man he had been keeping his resistance under control. He felt a surge of self-confidence; he became even more certain about the rightness of his ideas. The beard on the table darkened and disappeared into the distance; the desk shrank and sank in front of him; he moved toward the end of the lengthening, dirty room with its broken, rotting floorboards.

"We went on listening to Bakunin's fulminations. The old man came up and said: 'See here, gentlemen, I've been listening to you for more than fifty nights.' 'You've actually counted fifty, you spy?' cried Bakunin, but the old man went on: 'If you're a real revolutionary, just let me say a few words.' Bakunin had got up to drive the old man away again, but stopped; the rest of us pricked up our ears.

'I like all the things you want to do for the people and mankind. I admire your wisdom and nobility. The only thing I don't like is your revolution.' 'There's a wise man for you!' cried Bakunin. 'He likes the aims of revolution, but not the revolution. What drivel!' "

"I think I know what the wise old man said to that half-crazy Bakunin, Mr. Pašić. However, your analogy is inappropriate. I'm not a rebel, and you're not a wise man."

But Pašić refused to interrupt his story. " 'I must tell you the truth, gentlemen,' said the old man. 'You are wise and noble young men, so you ought to know it. I don't like revolution, but not because it overturns palaces, kills a lot of people, and causes bloodshed. People have died since the world began. Blood and sweat are always flowing through the world. Think of all the senseless wars! The magnificent temples destroyed in the name of other gods! Why should we feel sorry about the palaces of the nobles? Half the people born on this earth have been slaughtered in the name of some prejudice. Not to mention the men, women, and children who have been killed for Christ and Muhammed.' 'Listen to him, brothers!' cried Bakunin in a frenzy. 'This poor creature here is our true enemy. Listen to him!' The old man wasn't frightened; in fact, he raised his voice. 'I don't like revolution, gentlemen, because it also overturns the things that Time has created and set in place; Time outlasts us and our works. What would happen to the world if some force began to move around the rivers and mountains and put them down wherever it fancied?' "

At the point in the story when Bakunin clapped Pašić on the shoulder, Vukašin interrupted him and said, smiling: "Admit you are proud that the hand of the prophet of anarchy clapped you on the shoulder?"

"I admit it, Vukašin. And it hasn't made things difficult for me in any way."

"I believe you. With such shoulders it's easier to bend the knee before princes."

Pašić did not blink. Calmly, without any change in his voice, he finished his story.

"Thank you for the political fable; I'll pass it on," said Vukašin. "But there are some concepts of wisdom that I cannot believe in, even after hearing about Bakunin and that wise old man of yours. I'm not prepared to compromise."

"I'm very much afraid of people who don't want to compromise, Vukašin. I dislike conducting political business with fanatics and hotheads. People who are not prepared to compromise should make oxcarts or barrels or tools. They might even compose verse. But I don't want them near me."

Pašić repeated the last words twice in a perfectly calm voice, looking at Vukašin without blinking, his hands crossed under his beard. Vukašin felt uneasy, but he quickly regained the sense of superiority with which he had entered the office.

Pašić handed the telegram to his secretary and replaced his pen in the inkwell, then folded his arms and stared right through Vukašin. A clock in the corner of the office struck the hour, and the Nišava rippled noisily under the window. When the last echo of the clock's metallic clang had died away, Pašić began to speak.

"The High Command has announced that our army has suddenly begun to retreat. Putnik tells me that without help from the Allies we can't hold the front even for two weeks." He fell silent and gazed at Vukašin, stroking his beard gently, almost fearfully.

Their eyes met: for the first time Vukašin detected signs of agitation and anxiety in Pašić. Holding his hat and cane, his coat fastened as if he had just dropped in, Vukašin felt the impropriety of standing in front of Pašić. But sitting down in the chair would give the meeting a tone he didn't want.

"I suppose you'll explain your position fully at tomorrow's meeting of the Assembly. I shall demand that the session be public and that the people be told what confronts them."

"The people know what is facing them better than we do. And they don't need to know that we don't know what's in store."

"When you say 'we,' Prime Minister, I take it you are referring only to the government. Because many people in this country have known for a long time what's in store for Serbia as a result of your policies."

"I know they do, Vukašin. But right now I don't know. That's the worst of it. Now I am ignorant, whereas the people and you members of the Opposition know everything. You're pressing me hard and trampling me, as if we are about to have an election." Pašić shook his beard, tugging at its roots, his voice and eyes increasingly anxious.

"It's possible to be unjust even toward those who rule," said Vukašin, and fell silent. He did not want private deals with Pašić. He must not commit himself in any way. Their heartbeats mingled in the silence of the gathering dusk; an oxcart clattered on the wooden bridge across the Nišava.

"I must tell you, Vukašin, that the Allies are holding a knife at our throat," Pašić said hoarsely. "We must either give half of Macedonia to the Bulgarians immediately or we can no longer count on getting munitions. They won't even hear of sending troops to the Balkan battlefield. Meanwhile, our front has cracked; I told you what Putnik said about that."

The secretary brought in a lamp and set it on the table beside the telephone. A gleam of light spread over the beard.

"Why don't you put the overhead light on? What do you need a lamp for?"

"I don't like light above my head."

The beard gleamed in the lamplight. Vukašin sensed it was a good moment to reiterate his views.

"I think you know me well enough to realize that I'm not one to exult in our misery. It's shameful to be a prophet of evil and misfortune. But surely it's obvious that our victory over Bulgaria last year has already turned into defeat."

"But what should we have done in the face of Bulgaria's trickery?"

"We should have made sure that Bulgaria was no longer our enemy. It was your duty to avoid war with Bulgaria. Our war with Turkey should have been Serbia's last war."

"As long as Serbia exists, the Bulgarians, Austrians, and Hungarians will be her mortal enemies. And the Albanians too, unless we deal with them properly. Vukašin, could we possibly give Bulgaria half of Macedonia after the way the Bulgarians let us down in the war with the Turks? Why, we even liberated Adrianople for them. And yet they want everything as far as Ohrid. What government would dare concede so much?"

"A government that had more thought for the future."

"A government that would not have cared that the Serbian people shed their blood at Kumanovo, Bitolj, and Ovče Polje. A government of blind men and fools."

"But a government that would have been vindicated by history only a year later. I mean today, Mr. Pašić. There were opportunities for avoiding war with Bulgaria."

"You know what, Vukašin? If the people harbor some illusion, it's not wise men or prophets who will deliver them from it, but time and misfortune."

"One expects those who claim to lead the people not to follow misfortune or walk on the heels of time, but to avoid misfortune and overtake time."

"I don't know whether it's a good thing to run after our grandchildren and descendants."

"We must run after our grandchildren if we are ruling their fathers and grandfathers. Nothing is forgiven those who rule a nation, Prime Minister."

"As for history, Vukašin, I don't have much faith in historic destiny. No one who trusts me as a politician expects me to worry about the future. The people have elected me to work for the present. And to tell the truth, I don't believe in the respect and honor of our descendants. It's their affair whom they choose to honor, and why. It's no concern of mine."

"I admit that one can win elections with such views. A war, no. Forgive me for talking like this—but our national interest is best served by working for tomorrow. At least that's how it's been so far," Vukašin said emphatically but calmly.

Pašić gazed silently before him and, without raising his eyes, said quietly: "Tell me, Vukašin, what shall we do now, in this war against a much stronger adversary? Now that both our enemies and our allies are against us?"

"The most important thing is for Serbia to square her accounts with her Balkan neighbors as soon as possible. And to turn her back on the East."

"Turn our back on the East now?"

"Yes. If we don't do this resolutely in the present war, we as a nation have no hope of a peaceful future. The Bulgarians and Albanians will spill our blood. Our geopolitical position gives the Great Powers the right to judge us as long as we exist. We will remain under the heel of either the Russians or the Germans. I see no third possibility."

"What makes you think that, Vukašin?"

"This is not the time for profound discussions, Prime Minister."

"I think it is, Vukašin."

"Let me just say this: we were driven out of the southern part of the Balkan Peninsula when we were defeated at the Battle of Maritsa.* Dušan's empire was the Byzantine Empire. We can't found national goals or political programs on this historical debris. We must not go on moldering with our old illusions."

"There's nothing easier, Vukašin, than calling the faith of a nation

*The battle fought near the Maritsa River in 1371, when the Serbs were decisively defeated by the Turks. [Translator.]

an illusion. And nothing more dangerous. Especially in wartime. Today."

"I've always thought that the hardest thing in politics is to oppose what you call the faith of a nation. But a nation's illusions must be opposed for its own good. Of course, you and I have always differed on this point."

"I don't want us to disagree now. Tell me what's on your mind."

"I will. We don't have the strength, and I doubt if we ever will, to assimilate either politically or culturally the total area that our people have occupied in the course of their wanderings through southeastern Europe during the last few centuries."

"But I maintain that we must always guard our roots and our hearth. We must, my boy, because otherwise the winds will tear off our skin and the wild beasts that surround us will devour us."

"There is something I want to tell you, and not merely as your political opponent: we must not shed blood in vain, and we must not lose time. We must not go on living in the Middle Ages. That's not even practical. Poets have the right to get carried away by national joys or sorrows; you and I don't." Vukašin was surprised that he had said so much; it was his fault that the conversation was taking a direction he did not want.

"And why should we Serbs and no one else renounce our homeland and our past?"

"For the sake of a more tranquil future, Prime Minister. Because we need to consolidate our strength as a nation and stand with our neighbors. That is our first task as a nation. We should not forget that in our final migrations we Serbs moved northward and westward. I am convinced that our national path lies in that direction, and that it is there that our national aims will be fulfilled."

"The Russian government insists that we hand over Macedonia as far as Ohrid to Bulgaria. And Ohrid as well. That's the message we've received from St. Petersburg." He clutched the end of his beard and fell silent.

Vukašin waited for him to explain himself. Was Pašić looking for an ally in capitulation, or a supporter for some new political scheme? He had never before seen Pašić so worried, so strongly moved, or so articulate. His lips were trembling.

"That's what we've lived to hear from our mother Russia, my boy. From our dear brother Czar Nicholas. Unless he doesn't know about this," Pašić whispered tremulously.

Pašić didn't try to hide the pain Russia was causing him. That thread in his life had twisted and turned—from Mikhail Bakunin to Nicholas Romanov. He had abandoned the first, and the second was deserting him. Would he stay loyal to Russia? Here was a man with a single dogma: would he cling to it if he lost his ally? Could it be that Pašić was no longer an optimist? Or was he just pretending to be wrought up? Optimism was his political philosophy; he was a man who played a waiting game and believed that time was on his side. Now he was being pushed to the wall. No, his one talent was patience, which the nation interpreted as wisdom. "Was that the source of his strength now? What role does he have in mind for me?" Vukašin asked himself. He would keep quiet and wait for Pašić to speak his mind.

Pašić gave a start, and his voice became firmer.

"Why are you standing, Vukašin? Sit down, for goodness sake."

Sitting down in the nearest chair, Vukašin said slowly and softly: "There's no point, Prime Minister, in my repeating my opinion about our tragic love affair with Russia, that great mistake of ours, in which we obstinately persist." He stopped as he met Pašić's wide-eyed, startled glance.

"Never mind about that, Vukašin. Tell me what you think."

Pašić stroked the palms of his hands slowly, gently, gazing intently at nothing in particular. Here again was the Radical acrobat who, when supposedly thrown on his head, always landed on his feet, that terrifyingly ambitious politician who conspired against members of his own party, who always fought with the door open for retreat, who hid his aims and policies and had a scapegoat for every failure. Vukašin lit a cigarette and continued.

"Is it not true, Prime Minister, that since 1804 all our national aims have clashed with Russia's in the Balkans? In fact, this has molded our national character. For the Great Powers, there are no people worse than the Serbs. We're disobedient and stiff-necked, and we want freedom at any price. The Bulgarians are very different from us, as you well know. And Russia will always be on their side."

"But we are Slavs, and that, Vukašin, will decide our fate on the European scales and in European wars as long as we exist. Russia is our only protector. We know what lies in store for a small nation in this den of wolves."

"I'm not convinced of that, Prime Minister. Russia's attitude toward Serbia has always been consistent, unfortunately."

Pašić spoke casually, continuing to scrutinize Vukašin. "What would have happened to Serbia if Russia hadn't entered the war this summer as soon as the Austrians attacked us? If Russia hadn't sent us any military aid? She understands us better than anybody. If Russia hadn't helped us and defended us, Serbia would have fallen headlong over the precipice."

Their eyes met and they leaned toward each other with the full weight of the differences between them, the many years of enmity, and the force of their entrenched opinions.

Pašić said, with a note of warning in his voice: "Well, what's to be done now? The roof is falling over our heads, and our foundations are sinking."

"We must act more with Europe and for Europe," said Vukašin softly.

"And if Europe doesn't want us?" whispered Pašić, looking at him askance. "After all, she abandoned us to the children of Muhammed more than five centuries ago, and left us crushed under their heel."

The striking of the clock muted the rumble of carriages and the clatter of horses' hoofs. Vukašin took a long draw on his cigarette. The roaring surge of the Nišava echoed his rising fear of the inevitable disaster that lurked even in the voice of the river, fear of the great evil that was making nonsense of his rational ideas. Today everything followed another kind of logic, diametrically opposed to his. Why did he want to be right about historical events whose course he couldn't influence? For vanity's sake? It was simply ridiculous ambition. Was there any virtue in being consistent about freedom and the fate of the nation? Vukašin began to speak again.

"But this war *is* uniting us with Europe. After several centuries, we are entering Europe with our whole being and with enormous sacrifices. We are becoming part of Europe and sharing her fate. Now we too are helping to draw the map of Europe. And we must become a European state in every respect, or this war has no historical significance for us."

"Today, Vukašin, both the English and the French ambassadors have informed me of the opinion of their governments." He fell silent and did not look at Vukašin. "As for the Bulgarian annexation of Macedonia, they share the view of the Russian government. Not a scrap of difference. They say we must cede Macedonia at once."

"Is that a friendly suggestion or an official decision?"

"The hardest decision to accept is the decision of a friend, Vukašin." Pašić grasped his beard with both hands and kept his eyes riveted on the floor, his voice taut and even. "They insist that Serbia will only make her situation worse and lose out in the West if she delays in ceding Macedonia to Bulgaria. That's how things stand, my boy."

Did Pašić's voice tremble as he spoke the last sentence? Was there no way out? Tomorrow my consistency may make me a traitor and reality show me up as a fool, thought Vukašin. He listened to the clock and waited for Pašić to tell him what he had decided. Certainly Pašić hadn't sent for him just to tell him this.

The telephone rang. Pašić rose slowly, like an old man; Vukašin also got up, and walked toward the window. On the bank of the Nišava crowds had gathered under the bare chestnut trees and dim streetlights, waiting for the latest news, ready to pounce on ministers, secretaries, messengers, and telephone operators as they scurried out of the government headquarters in the evening. The people in front of the building fell silent, huddled together, and looked up toward him. Vukašin drew back abruptly and sank into the black chair.

Pašić slowly replaced the receiver, sighing as he sat down at his desk: "According to what Putnik has just told me, Serbia is giving her last gasp, Vukašin."

The unexpected and unfamiliar tone of voice in which the words were spoken sent a shudder through Vukašin. He would have liked to disbelieve the suddenly broken voice coming from that broad, illuminated beard, to disbelieve those arms folded like a bishop's: powerful white hands, calm and beautifully shaped, which he had described as "filthy and stinking" from political corruption and party politics. But now he could not refuse to believe Pašić.

"What kind of people are we?" Vukašin muttered in confusion. "Caught between Asia and Europe, on the frontiers of religions and empires, we have perished foolishly, mourned by no one, perished more for others than for ourselves . . . and we haven't gained a single faithful friend. Wretched and accursed nation! We're the only country in Europe that doesn't have a single true friend. Not one!" He had not meant to say all this; the words seemed inappropriate. He felt relieved when Pašić at last began to speak.

"I suppose that's all quite true. But God will once again take care of us. For some reason, and for some purpose."

"God takes care of everybody, but for His own reasons, and solely on His own terms. We don't want those terms. We want freedom, we want democracy, we want to form a large united state, we want . . . God doesn't take care of such people!"

"Then what are we going to do tomorrow, Vukašin?"

He met Pašić's stern, merciless glance. That night he would think up his real answer to that simple and terrible question. For the sake of saying something, he answered: "Perhaps a small nation can survive in these times only if it's more quick-witted than the great nations. But not by trickery and cunning, to which the weak and foolish resort. What we need now is creative wisdom. The kind of wisdom that makes a nation great in peacetime."

"But what shall we do in wartime? When we're caught in a vise, when the vojvodas don't want to command the army? What about our national goals, Vukašin? We have inherited them, just as we have inherited the land that feeds us, the land that will receive our bodies when we die."

"We must adapt our national goals, and ourselves, to circumstances, Prime Minister."

"But first we must defeat Austria-Hungary."

"Of course. What we don't agree about is the price to be paid for winning the war. And the way to win it."

"What makes you think so, Vukašin?"

"The time has come when a small nation can no longer lose a war. It can only lose the peace." He would say no more about it. Pašić's expression meant that he was lying in wait. He always divulged facts and asked questions according to a definite plan.

"Tell me, Vukašin, what do you think we ought to do tomorrow? The soldiers are dying, the High Command is wailing, the people behind the lines are cursing. And you people in the Opposition are thinking, thinking. . . . Only agreement can save us now."

"Let's not talk about these things behind closed doors, Prime Minister. I'm not the kind of man who makes decisions about the aims and interests of the state in secret. I will explain my views in the Assembly tomorrow."

Horses' hoofs resounded on the cobblestones, breaking the silence.

"But I thought," began Pašić, speaking in a tight voice, "that when the cart was overloaded and going uphill, it was best to follow the old familiar road."

"If we're quite sure there isn't a better one."

"I don't see a better one. The people choose their road, not through their wisdom, but through their suffering."

Vukašin picked up his hat and cane from the small table and prepared to get up. "It's increasingly hard to believe that the people have ever chosen their own historic path. We know very well who chooses these paths, and how. Of course, democracy has legalized hypocrisy and made it legitimate." He got up and fastened his coat. "We've had a very pleasant conversation. You have never talked to me in this way, or talked so much." Changing his voice and expression he added: "It's quite clear that in your policies what is left unsaid is much more important than what is said."

"It all depends on the circumstances, Vukašin."

"Now tell me what you wanted to say to me before the meeting of the National Assembly tomorrow. Time and our present situation don't permit us to play guessing games and lie in ambush."

Pašić stood up and took a step toward him. "I asked you to come here, Vukašin, to tell you that I no longer regard you as the Opposition. We are one and the same now, my boy; all Serbia may need your mind and hand more than mine. The time has come when she needs everybody's mind and all our hands. Please stop by tomorrow, as early as possible."

"Thank you for this confidence in me, Prime Minister," Vukašin said quickly as he started to leave.

"Are your children well, Vukašin?"

Pašić came up to him and shook his hand affectionately. Vukašin trembled: for twelve years he had been sure that as long as he lived he would not touch Nikola Pašić's hand. As he moved silently toward the door he heard Pašić saying behind him:

"Please come early."

Vukašin paused on the steps of the peacetime Regional Headquarters. Were they really in such a hopeless position that Nikola Pašić wanted his approval and co-operation? Wasn't he a man whose hatred for his opponents had never prevented him from working with them when it was to his advantage, just as his love for his friends and supporters had never prevented him from abandoning them when he no longer needed them?

Vukašin walked quickly down the steps into the street; a dark, silent, expectant crowd waited for him on the bank of the Nišava.

Vukašin turned into the first street, an unpaved, unlit lane. Where could he go? At home the hallway was packed with refugees clamoring for the latest news; and when he had pushed his way through this morass of fear and patriotism, there would be Olga's strained silence, which she would break just before midnight, whispering: "Say something. Anything!" And he would mutter, "I have no words to help you fall asleep, Olga." Then he would lose himself in his forebodings. If only this lane would stretch before him till daybreak, if only this darkness would last until he left for the meeting of the Assembly, if only he didn't have to face the crowds under the yellow streetlights, people who were swallowing the latest news and taking pleasure in poisoning themselves with despair.

Vukašin turned back, walking more slowly. *What is Pašić up to? He says he no longer regards me as the Opposition. But what else am I, when he represents what I've been trying to destroy for the last twelve years? Does he want us to share defeat on equal terms? What a magnanimous expression of patriotism! I won't drop in early. We'll talk to each other publicly tomorrow in the Assembly. A conversation for the official record and for history. But what if being true to my ideas makes me a traitor in this war? What if my sincerity makes me a fool in this hopeless situation? If Austria-Hungary destroys us, will those of us who thought differently be distinguishable from the others? Death, not war, will unite us. How tragic and futile it all is! But only in wartime do we work for history, win honor through suffering and death. Only by dying for the homeland and by suffering in war do we redeem our life; only by death can we make it honorable. A detestable fate!* He leaned against a fence; the strong scent of chrysanthemums rose in the darkness.

Vukašin heard someone call his name, and then short, rapid footsteps: it was she! He recognized her purposeful footsteps and the shawl she always wore when she waited for him at night. How had she got here? Was she still alive after the bombardment of the houses around the Vasić warehouse? Could it be that an Austrian shell hadn't put an end to that love affair of his student days which he couldn't wrench out of his life? The affair had stirred him deeply in his youth, and then after his marriage had tormented him like a hidden crime. He couldn't do without her for long; suddenly, in a single instant, he would again fall headlong. Surely this wasn't going to continue in wartime?

He felt as if he were standing naked in front of a knife. His knees buckled; he paused to wait for her, leaning on his cane: he could hear her sighing. She stopped a few paces away. Did she still have that same expression, and the eyes of an unhappy child?

"It's I, Vukašin. Radmila."

Once more he felt that painful trembling, that overpowering feeling: Radmila was not merely a lover, an irrational longing; nor was she a corrupting vice. She was something different. And when he finally came to believe that the war had saved him from himself, had put an end to a part of his life that he couldn't regret deeply in his present fears for Ivan and Milena and in the general calamity, here she was, standing in front of him in the darkness, silently waiting.

It was wartime; his children were at the front. Who could tell what would happen to them all? Radmila didn't have to start up again something that had died forever.

"I have no one in the world but you, Vukašin. I know you don't like to hear this."

"We're getting old; that madness of our youth is over. I've done wrong, and to you too."

"No, you haven't done me any wrong. Don't say such horrible things. It's just that you and I are something different."

"We were. But it's all finished."

"You're all I've got. And it must stay that way, even after a hundred wars."

"It can't stay that way. There's nothing left, Radmila."

"It must, Vukašin."

She came close to him; he clearly heard her broken breathing.

"Do you have something to live on? Can I do anything to help you?"

"I live in that small yellow house near the hospital. Where the Russian doctors are. Nobody knows you. I'll be waiting for you."

"I have no strength now even to humiliate you, Radmila."

"Yes, you have. I've told you where I am. I'll be waiting for you."

"Never! It's over for good!" he cried, and hurried toward the lights of the main street.

Someone stopped him in the darkness fragrant with chrysanthemums.

"Wait, sir. For a hundred dinars you can buy a prisoner of war."

"What do you want? What kind of prisoner?"

"Don't shout. For a hundred dinars I'll bring you a Fritzie. Tonight the price is a hundred dinars. After the fall of Valjevo and Belgrade, you won't get one for three hundred."

"Why would I want an Austrian prisoner? Who are you?"

"You can get a Croat or a Bosnian for fifty. I'd give you a Czech for seven. But I won't take anything less than a hundred for a genuine Fritzie. If you want an officer, we'll have to bargain."

"Why should we bargain? What do I want an Austrian prisoner for?"

"That's a stupid question! You'll hide him in your attic or woodshed and feed him until their troops get here. They'll be here in ten days. After that you'll have no worries until the war's over."

"Get going, you scoundrel!"

"When you've simmered down, you can find me at Zona's Lane." And he disappeared into the bushes and chrysanthemums.

In the darkness of their room in Niš, surrounded by suitcases and boxes, Olga stood by the open window, waiting for Vukašin: she was anxious to catch sight of him, to touch his hands and face and whisper: "Do you know that Ivan is going to the front? What shall we do? Surely no politics, no principles are more important than the lives of our children? Yes, I know the law—the same treatment for everybody. And then there're your principles. I thought I could sacrifice my son for the homeland. Before the war I really believed that I could."

Leaves from the walnut tree fell onto the cobblestones; the pungent fragrance of chrysanthemums permeated her forebodings.

Tonight she would not wait for Vukašin in bed with a scarf over her eyes, persuading herself that the light bothered her, that she could fall asleep more quickly and sleep longer with the dark-blue scarf over her eyes, a scarf with black Oriental flowers and a curious smell that no amount of airing could remove which her mother had brought back from her last visit to Budapest. For a long time she had deceived both herself and him with this scarf, so they wouldn't feel awkward because they had less and less to say to each other when he came home late at night, frowning gloomily, and when he left punctually at nine in the morning, his brow even more deeply furrowed.

Today he had not wanted to postpone his afternoon walk for half an hour to wait for letters from Ivan and Milena. Had he ever been different? She had loved him just as he was, honorable, stubborn, completely absorbed in his work, hard on himself and everyone else. It was precisely these qualities that she had respected and loved. That was how she wanted him. She had never revealed her disappointment to a living soul, nor to him. He must know that. So that tonight she had the right to say to him: "There is a limit to what I can stand, Vukašin."

Olga kept her eyes fixed on the gate between the yellow dahlias tossing in the fitful wind, their color vibrant under the electric bulb. Not hearing footsteps in the street, she turned and gazed at the letters lying open on the bed pillow.

She had read them countless times before it grew dark; she didn't dare turn on the light; under the electric bulb the disorder of this room among strangers and the poverty of their life of exile became unbearable. She read them, laying bare every word, peering at every letter, hearing the voices that had never spoken them, seeing their faces, their eyes, their lips. She saw Ivan hunched over his school homework, bent so low that his pencil hit his glasses, and gripping the edge of the table with his left hand. She did not want to think of him in the barracks. When she did occasionally, she imagined a wretched little room with forty dirty men sleeping in it—she would never forget the stench of male feet in the hospital full of wounded, after the victory at Kumanovo, when she had visited Milena, who was working there as a nurse. As for Ivan's letter from Skoplje, addressed to her, with only a greeting to his father at the end, she imagined it being written in his room at home, on his tidy, elegant writing table, under his favorite portrait of her, painted in Budapest just before her marriage.

No matter that a shell had fallen on their house, destroying the roof and showering bricks and mortar on their things, on Ivan's books and writing table. She could not imagine anything of hers, anything dear to her, apart from her house and the things in it. Yet Vukašin had seemed almost indifferent when he told her about the destruction of their house on his return from Belgrade after the bombardment. She didn't want to hear about it or to see the wrecked and plundered house. Out of pride she didn't tell anyone that the wealth she had inherited had been destroyed—the furniture that had belonged to her mother, the things in which she felt the soul and hands of those she loved. She was especially proud, not because the things were expensive, but because they were unlike any others in Belgrade houses. If anyone asked her about the bombed house, she would admit that a shell had hit the summer kitchen and slightly damaged the roof of the house; then she would insist that her house was exactly as she had left it that evening at dusk when she reluctantly agreed to go to Niš. She had refused to take anything except her dresses and the family photograph album. "One doesn't move houses and graves. That's for the army to defend. If Serbia collapses, let my house fall too," she had said before a crowd of frightened neighbors. Vukašin had not contradicted her; he had even smiled. It was Ivan who had said: "Quite right, Mother. There's no point in our being survived by grandmother's armchairs and plates."

Milena also wrote hunched over the paper, breathing at the words with the pencil touching her lips; ever since she had begun to copy words from her reading book, she had thrust her head into her exercise book as she had seen her brother do. Her letter smelled of iodine—the same choking odor that had filled the doctor's office the last time she had visited Milena. Doctors were milling around her, smoking, drinking brandy, and exchanging coarse jokes with the nurses, who wore their bloodstained white coats somewhat boastfully. This was the shortest of Milena's letters.

Perhaps that boorish lieutenant of Milena's had written her another jealous letter. What strange creatures men were! To feel jealous in the trenches, facing bayonets and bullets, jealous because a girl worked in a military first-aid station, worked with men without arms and legs, men with gangrenous wounds. To her dying day she would remember her parting from Milena beside the hospital gates. They had said good-bye, and Olga was climbing into a carriage when Milena called out to her:

"Mother, why are men suspicious of us, even when we love them?"

Then Olga had realized that it was not only the hard work and the terrible scenes in the hospital that had cast the shadow over Milena's face that had surprised her as soon as she caught sight of her daughter on the platform of the Valjevo railroad station. During those two months in the hospital Milena had aged ten years.

"What kind of a man could be jealous of you today, Milena?"

"He suffers terribly, Mother. He says if I don't leave the hospital, he will get himself killed. But how can I do that now?"

Olga suppressed her tears and her anger toward this stupid Othello with his medals for bravery and his fame as a guerrilla. She remained silent while considering her answer.

"Men, my dear, trust only women they don't love. Vladimir loves you."

"Then why isn't Father jealous?"

"Your father is different."

Your father is different. But we two are alike. Milena had surrendered the minute she set eyes on him. A wounded man too. Milena, who distrusted every man she met for the first time. To fall in love at first sight with a wounded guerrilla! A few sloping, hastily written sentences, mostly about Vladimir, nothing about herself. That ill-omened Vladimir, as Vukašin described him. As soon as Vukašin had learned of his existence he had feared him.

In Ivan's letter there was not a word of tenderness—even a trace of bitterness when he asked for his glasses, as if he were reproaching her, blaming her because she had given birth to a near-sighted son.

"We will certainly be going to the front any day now. I can hardly wait." The words kept running through her head; she could see them like a chain of fire on the garden wall and on the dark bedspread. Ivan had carefully crossed out a few words; he must have felt sorry for her and so obliterated the hardest words.

How could Ivan shoot at people and stab them with a bayonet? Even if they were Austrians, how could he do it? She could never remember him fighting with other children; he never even wrestled. How many times Milena used to hit him! Tears would well up in his eyes, and he would go to his room. He had never hurt anybody, and now he would have to attack a man with a bayonet. How would he escape when those villains went for him with their bayonets? They would get him in the first battle, as soon as he reached the front! From the balcony he couldn't even recognize his friends at the gate; what would he do in the forest at night? Or in a fog? Soon the autumn rains would bring fog. His glasses wouldn't help, and he was asking for three pairs. Who in the world went off to war with three pairs of glasses?

It was as if the boy were running away from home to spite his father. Vukašin had never played with him as a father should. With Ivan he was always stern and serious, obeying some sort of principles, following ideas about modern education and upbringing. Freedom of personality and self-discipline. Freedom, but without love. Ideas, but no trace of tenderness. That was how it had been since Ivan was in the cradle. Even before Ivan was born, Vukašin had felt some shadow from Prerovo hovering over his unborn son. It was something that she had never understood and had not wanted to.

Olga remembered that bright Sunday afternoon when they were eating cherries in the garden, and she had asked him:

"Will you be very sorry if I don't give you a son?"

"I would rather you gave me a daughter."

"I don't believe you. You, a peasant's son and a Serb, would rather have a daughter?"

"I'm afraid you might have another Vukašin."

"You don't want him to be like you?"

"No. I don't want him to be like me."

"Why? Surely, if it's a boy, he shouldn't be different from you."

"Give me a daughter and I'll love you more than ever."

Why bring up all this now? How dare she doubt Vukašin's love for his son tonight? Did she doubt it?

But that had been her first thought at Ivan's birth, when she heard a shot being fired from the balcony as she regained consciousness and realized that it was her father celebrating the arrival of his grandson. She had at once asked to see Vukašin: she wanted to see for herself how happy he was. It was already daylight and the lamps had been extinguished; he was standing at her feet, holding on to the bed, very sleepy and wrapped in thought. She looked at him from under lowered eyelids: could it be that he wasn't happy? He smiled at her: a long, warm, loving smile as he gazed at her from somewhere far away. His whole face was transfigured by that unforgettable smile. It was that smile, never seen before, which sent her off to sleep. In her sleep she began to cry, probably from happiness, and the midwife woke her up, wiped her damp face, and said comfortingly: "Don't be afraid any more. Your son's a fine bouncing boy." She wasn't afraid; she had forgotten the conversation with Vukašin when they had eaten the cherries on that bright Sunday afternoon in the garden. So why should she have remembered the conversation when she came upon Vukašin standing over the cradle, looking dejected and thoughtful?

"Why are you looking at him so sadly, Vukašin?"

"He's got my forehead. I've been thinking about all the thoughts and ideas he can have under that forehead. If one can inherit a predilection for particular smells and colors, as people say, then other tendencies can be inherited as well."

"Are you really worried because your son takes after you?"

"He will be ruthless. And miserable."

When Milena was born, Vukašin was truly upset that he couldn't bathe the child because he had "coarse Prerovo hands." And when she cried out during the night, he would take her in his arms, babble to her, and sing funny little songs. To justify his tenderness toward Milena he would say:

"Girls have a bad time. If they're not loved and coddled in their father's house, they can live their entire lives without knowing what tenderness is. If their fathers don't show them tenderness, then . . ."

"Then what? A girl's father isn't the whole world," she had said rebelliously.

"A father should give his daughter love enough for all men. If some other man should love her as well as her father, she can consider herself fortunate."

Why was he so illogical in showing Milena tenderness, playing with her, and giving her presents? Why was he indulgent toward all her moods and actions? He would smile as he listened to her telling him how at a party she had refused to dance the polka, the quadrille, or the waltz—or indeed anything but the Serbian kolo. He did not say a word when she refused for patriotic reasons to learn to play the piano. "After the annexation of Bosnia and Hercegovina it's a disgrace for a Serbian girl to play the piano!" she had said. "Isn't that right, Daddy?" He had burst out laughing and tweaked her pigtail. He had not even reproached her when, after the declaration of war on Turkey, she had left high school to work as a nurse in Vranje. It was only after Vukašin found out that she had fallen in love with Vladimir, a lieutenant from Macedonia, that he was sometimes irritated with her, but more from sadness than anger.

Toward Ivan he was a different man: with Ivan it was always methods of upbringing and principles, paternal strictness and masculine, peasant indifference even when Ivan was ill. He talked with Ivan about ideas and history, and Ivan's birthday presents and rewards for success at school were old French books. The only time they spent an evening alone together was just before Ivan's departure for Paris. Maybe he wrote Ivan a few letters. When Ivan came back from Paris, two days before mobilization, he was not pleased to see him and showed his displeasure by his silence, as he usually did. Apart from Vukašin's questions about what the French thought of the assassination at Sarajevo and what the students of Slavic nationality living in Austria-Hungary were saying about the war, Olga did not hear father and son talk about anything. Then came that fateful evening when Ivan announced after dinner that the next day he was going to enlist as a volunteer: his father had stared at him dumbfounded. Vukašin's cigarette had burned down to his lips, and the flame began to sputter in his mustache; he hastily threw the stub into his unfinished glass of red wine; it was unbearable to look at them. She had wanted to cry out, but their fellow refugees were playing cards in the hall; she could hear them discussing their game. Vukašin muttered:

"You're going to enlist as a volunteer, with *your* eyesight, wearing glasses with a diopter of minus seven?"

"That's not my fault, Father. A man goes to war with whatever he has."

"Have you thought it over?"

"I've thought it over thoroughly and considered the matter from all sides." Ivan smiled ironically as he said these words, so frequently used by Vukašin himself. Then he frowned as though angry with himself and added crossly:

"That's why I came back from Paris. Do you want me to look like a slacker in the eyes of my contemporaries?"

"Listen to me, Ivan. I'm glad you're a brave and honorable young man. I've brought you up to act according to your convictions. If your convictions tell you that you should go off to war half-blind, then go. Yes, Ivan my boy, go."

Vukašin spoke in a strange voice, as though the words issued from some dark inner whirlpool, of which Olga had never caught a glimpse, although she had long suspected that it existed. She got up from her chair for a closer look at his face and eyes; he no longer looked like himself. The words "Yes, Ivan my boy, go" were spoken with malice, vindictiveness, hatred, with an expression on his face that she had never seen before. She did not know this man who drained his glass of wine and spat the cigarette stub onto his plate. His voice, his facial expression and behavior frightened her so much that she couldn't even cry out "But this is crazy! It's suicide!" Ivan was confused by his father's words and frightened, so frightened that he sat down again meekly at the small table beside the window, guilt and regret plain on his face. Olga was waiting for him to burst into tears and beg his father's forgiveness. Ivan's lips trembled and he looked straight before him. Olga drove her nails into her thighs so as not to cry, so as not to say anything in front of the father and son—who, after twenty years, had become father and son, compelled at last to drop their hateful masculine playacting about principles and ideas, their disgusting roles of "modern father" and "modern son," that cruel competition in vanity. Finally she began to cry. The two of them, both of them, looked at her scornfully, with masculine contempt. Yet how could she not cry? How could she endure all this in silence while father and son communicated with each other only by their audible breathing? Ivan would not have been able to restrain himself, he would have felt compelled to speak, to admit that his intention was crazy and suicidal, had not Vukašin, with his customary gloom and severity, Vukašin, that man of principle, got up from the table and said in his usual dry voice: "Now the two of you had better discuss what clothes to take to the war." He picked up his hat and cane and buttoned his coat. Not even on that night would he go out of the room, into the darkness of Niš, with his coat unbuttoned.

The room rocked and swayed around Olga; she felt as if she were being swung backward and forward, as if something were tearing her apart. She didn't say a word to Ivan. Her damned pride. She didn't know how long her sobbing lasted. Out of compassion Ivan didn't look at her when he muttered agitatedly: "Mother, you know I've never put our national heroes on a pedestal, the way you and Milena have. I beg you not to let me remember this evening by your weeping." He had dried her tears with the words "I beg you, Mother" and the tone of his voice.

Ivan's whole life flashed before her: from his first cry, when the midwife brought him for his first feeding, to the moment he said good-bye to her on the step of the railroad car, standing among the crowd of singing student volunteers whom the train was taking away to Skoplje. Ivan was the only one who was not singing. Vukašin did not embrace him as they parted. They talked about the future, when trains would run through all the villages of Serbia. They talked seriously, carried away by their subject. Did other fathers and sons part this way in wartime? She didn't want to weep in front of all those people; she merely smiled and waved her hand as if she were his lover, not his mother. As if her son were going on vacation.

Olga heard a clock strike. Eleven o'clock, and still Vukašin hadn't come. She wanted to escape from this sheep pen, this warehouse of refugees where all people did was rail at Pašić, play cards and checkers, snore, tell fortunes, and prepare to flee to Skoplje and Salonika. It was because of the clock, an exact replica of the one in her dining room, that she stayed in this house. When she first heard it strike she imagined herself back in her own home. She refused to move in with a friend of Vukašin's who offered them two rooms and peace and comfort; she stayed to listen to the clock. Her own clock, which her mother had bought from an old Czech countess in Carlsbad, and which had been blown to bits by the shell.

The card players in the hall went off to bed squabbling. A shower of walnut leaves fell onto the cobblestones and flower beds. She gazed at the gate between the windblown yellow dahlias blazing under the streetlight. She would wait for her husband, touch him and say: "Ivan can hardly see; he'll be killed the first time he's in the dark. Arrange things so that he stays at headquarters. Ivan doesn't have to be with General Mišić. Just as long as he isn't in the trenches or the woods; they'll get him with the first bayonet. That's not favoritism. That's justice, Vukašin. What do I care about your party and your principles! It's a crime to let him be killed so stupidly. You must save him. No one should have to die so needlessly and unjustly, so cruelly. No, Vukašin, that is not favoritism!"

Olga pressed her forehead against the iron window bar until it hurt; though she could scarcely stand on her feet, she could not tear herself away. She stared at the gate, her heart pounding.

The gate opened without a sound. Vukašin walked slowly, stealthily over the walnut leaves on the cobbled path between the dahlias and chrysanthemums waving in the wind under the streetlight. Olga tore herself away from the window and sat down on the bed. She put her hand under the pillow to pull out the dark-blue silk scarf for her eyes, but withdrew her hand empty. She would not wait for him with the scarf over her eyes.

Vukašin came in quietly, so as not to wake her. He hung up his hat and coat and began to take off his boots.

Hasn't he noticed me? Or doesn't it matter to him that I haven't put the scarf over my eyes tonight?

"Turn the light on, Vukašin," she whispered.

"Are you there?" he said, also in a whisper.

"Where else would I be at midnight?"

"I thought you were at the benefit concert for the wounded."

"I haven't stirred from the house since lunchtime. We've received letters from the children. Turn on the light and read them."

"You tell me what's in them."

"I can't."

Olga handed him the letters and looked hard into his face. He's lost all hope! He really feels miserable. It's not just because of Serbia; it's not just the situation on the battlefront. He's been gloomy and silent for a long time. It wasn't just filthy party politics. Was she to blame for the change in him: for those wrinkles, that gray hair, his smoking at night, and those stifled sighs when he was alone in a room?

Vukašin had never been a man to whom either laughter or curses came easily. He had always been serious, reserved, and dignified. When Olga had first heard his voice in the "men's salon" at the Krsmanović house, she had instantly concluded that this Vukašin Katić, whom the girls adored and the young men disliked, was thoroughly refined and dignified. She stood in the doorway of the men's salon and watched him carefully: he was not drawing attention to himself by any outward show of passionate feeling; he didn't shout or wave his arms—that pleased her immediately. He wasn't talking enthusiastically about the people. Here was a university graduate who didn't worship the people and village life! He wore his European clothes easily and naturally, as though he had strayed into the Belgrade party from an old château. All those Bazarovs, reformers, and revolutionaries were quite odious. Vukašin wasn't in the least like Bazarov. She was fascinated by his appearance, his seriousness, and his dignity.

Yet something had snapped within her when she had quarreled with her father over the plow factory, for which he wouldn't give Vukašin money; she had been somewhat too forceful in taking her husband's side against her father. How this had dumbfounded old Todor Tošić, a man cruel toward the entire world but infinitely tender toward his only daughter.

"Are you going against your father, my girl? Are you my pet? Are you against me?" His voice had gradually risen from a whisper to a howl. So that her words would carry more conviction, she had remained silent a few moments before saying: "I will always be on Vukašin's side, Father." But even while her father was threatening not to give Vukašin a mite and banging his pipe on the table, she was asking herself: "Where did he get the idea to build a plow factory?" Everybody had expected Vukašin Katić to be appointed Serbian Ambassador to Paris or Foreign Minister, or, at worst, a university professor. She never told Vukašin what she thought, nor did she ever oppose anything he did or said. Not from fear or submissiveness; she genuinely delighted in following him in everything. Even in his periods of adversity. His political failures made her more passionately attached to everything he did; she always found something worthy of admiration, something to be proud of.

It was the year they had broken with her father over the plow factory that Vukašin had begun to slip into those long silences and to write newspaper articles attacking both the government and the Opposition, venomous articles which repelled many of their friends. "Who is this Vukašin Katić for whom nobody is honorable or wise? What does he want, anyway?" they said. But she was pleased just because he was different from everybody else; she saw his isolation as a kind of latter-day chivalry, and in politics too, which otherwise she considered a degrading passion. She loved him just because the street and the cafés didn't; she never felt insulted when the politicians he had attacked in the press didn't speak to her; she would smile contemptuously at the lies about the two of them that circulated in Belgrade. She was proud of Vukašin because he had publicly dissociated himself from those Karageorgević gypsies, Apis and his band of conspirators, and the peasant Radicals who ran Belgrade after 1903. The daughter of a prominent Liberal and friend of the

Obrenović dynasty, a woman whose mother had been among the first ladies at court, Olga was grateful to her husband for giving her reason to hate publicly the scoundrels who had made their names stink throughout Belgrade by shedding royal blood.* If she had sometimes felt dissatisfied with Vukašin and less than delighted with his place in society, it was while Vukašin was serving as a minister in a government of Independents, while he was in power.

She looked at Vukašin's long, dry clenched hands. When had those fingers stopped caressing her? What if she was, after all, to blame for those long solitary walks of his? If only that were true! If she was to blame for at least one of his sleepless nights! It was something else, something terrible, that had furrowed his long handsome face. He wasn't in this state because of the situation at the battlefront and the future of Serbia, because of his damned ideas and principles. Still not a word about Ivan and Milena. He said only as much as he was forced to say.

"What has happened to you, Vukašin?" she whispered behind him, wanting to caress him. He was reading the letters, his head bent over them, his whole body sagging dejectedly.

The one thing about his figure that she had not found attractive was the challenging way in which he puffed out his chest. Even in the days when he had not been gloomy, when he could smile cheerfully and joke, she had not liked to walk beside him, looking at the steep slope of his shoulders, at his threatening, arrogant erectness. She had justified herself by saying "I only like to wait for you," a rationalization that appealed to her femininity. In actuality, that erectness, those strong shoulders, always slightly pushed back, conveyed not only the beauty and defiance of strength, but also a typically masculine arrogance and brutality.

"What does Ivan want with three pairs of glasses? Three pairs . . . We sent him glasses ten days ago," Vukašin whispered to himself. "He's always making me feel guilty about his glasses, revenging himself on me. What wrong have I done to that child?"

Trembling, she got up, walked around the bed, and sat down on a suitcase; any moment she might press her face against his knees. She looked up at him.

"Please tell me what happened."

---

*A reference to the assassination of King Alexander Obrenović and his wife, Draginja, in 1903. [Translator.]

"Pašić asked me to come and see him. He sent a policeman to find me in the fields outside Niš. I was alone with him for two hours."

"What did he say?"

"He said that our situation was extremely critical. Serbia is on the verge of collapse, Olga. Unless a miracle happens."

"Has nothing happened to you, Vukašin?"

"No. Why do you ask?" He met her glance for the first time since he had come in. "What else could happen to me, Olga?" He moved farther away, but then she changed her position to remain close to him.

"Mr. Pašić didn't tell you that they've decided to sacrifice the students too?"

"What do you mean, sacrifice the students? Who told you that?" He bent toward her; their faces were in shadow but they could clearly see each other's deepening furrows and tightening lips. "Where did you hear that the students are going to the front?" he repeated, speaking more loudly, a distinct tremor in his voice.

"All Niš knows, Vukašin. All the mothers with sons in the Student Battalion have been baking cakes since noon and preparing clothing. Their fathers have been making the rounds of various Commands."

"I don't understand. What for?"

She bent her head and was silent for a moment.

"To try to get letters from senior officers and the War Minister."

Keeping his eyes lowered, he wiped his forehead with his palm.

"Olga, those rumors are spread by the relatives of telephone operators and orderlies."

"Pardon me for informing you, a politician and a deputy, about the intentions of Putnik and Prince Alexander Karageorgević."

Her restrained sarcasm made him feel rather ashamed and hurt him all the more. "The government has no thought of this. Pašić would have told me."

"Then why does Ivan ask us to send him three pairs of glasses? You've read what he says: 'We will certainly be going to the front any day now. I can hardly wait.' " Olga no longer wanted to lean her face against his knees.

Vukašin lit a cigarette. Clearly she thought it was his fault that Ivan had enlisted as a volunteer. "My dear Olga, you used to repeat to the children three times a day: I expect you to love your homeland and its poetry. Your homeland and its poetry!" he whispered scornfully.

"Should I have brought up the children to follow more lofty ideals?"

"Olga, there's no sense in our arguing tonight about things we haven't discussed these past twenty years while sharing the same bed and eating at the same table."

She looked as if he had slapped her face. He bent toward her. "Where will we be at dawn if we go on like this, Olga?"

"Do sit down, Vukašin. And keep your hands still. Your hands used to be as calm and still as those of an icon."

The pain in her voice cut him deeply. He felt sorry for her. How had they come to talk in these tones, which foreshadowed the marital recriminations they had so far managed to avoid? She clutched her face with her hands and whispered:

"Something horrible is about to happen. What if my shadow on the wall said something terrible to you, if it began to breathe and to look at you differently from the way I do."

"Everything is coming apart now. Everything."

She removed her hands from her face and looked hard at him: even now he was thinking of everything. And Ivan was simply part of "everything."

He saw scorn in the corners of her dry, frightening, aging eyes and around her suddenly compressed lips. Seldom had he seen her scorn turned against him. She who was tireless in her efforts to charm everyone by her fine feelings and lofty thoughts.

"Tell me what you intend to do about Ivan," she asked unexpectedly, in a listless voice.

"What do you mean, what do I intend to do? What can I do?" he said aloud.

"You can stop him from committing suicide," she said, whispering even more listlessly and looking up at him from the suitcase with a hint of menace.

He jerked as if from an unexpected blow. "How can I stop him?"

"Everybody in the country knows the answer to that."

"I can't ask for special favors for my son, who has volunteered for the army," he said aloud, gripping his knees with his hands.

"You can't do it for your only son? You can't do it for Ivan? Is there actually something you can't give up to save him? Is there something more important to you than Ivan?" she whispered, dumbfounded.

"I can't ask for a letter from the War Minister; I can't ask for special favors for my son. Ten days ago in the Assembly I attacked the government because of the corruption and favoritism at headquarters during mobilization, because of the hordes of merchants and shirkers at headquarters and behind the lines. Last week I published the article 'Vitium cordis: Crime of the Heart.' I can't myself do what I attack in others. I simply can't do it."

"General Mišić is your friend. He knows what Ivan's eyesight is like. He knows that you're not asking for a favor."

"I can't ask for such a service from my friend, from Putnik's assistant," he whispered.

"Then Ivan will be killed as soon as he gets to the front," she said aloud and with such pain in her voice that he was speechless. "Because of your principles! Is it possible, Vukašin? How can you do it?"

She cried out to him, kneeling between the bed and the suitcase. He had not noticed that she had moved closer to him and was kneeling, imploring him with her eyes. "Is this what you are really like, Vukašin?" she repeated to herself. "A man of principles, a man who would sacrifice his son for an idea? Egotist!"

"What are you saying, Olga?" he asked, frightened by her eyes and the rapid twitching of her lips. "Would you like me to go to the front with Ivan? I've thought about that. I could ask General Mišić to arrange for me to be in Ivan's platoon. I can ask that kind of favor. But no other," he said, raising his voice.

"Even today you're thinking of your principles and your ambition. My God, what is to become of us?" She sighed and sat down on the suitcase. Then she leaned back and lowered her head into her hands. "Turn the light out," she said.

It made him feel easier to do something so that he could not see how much she despised him. He turned the light out and stood leaning against the door.

"Can it be that my husband is simply a man of principles? A man who believes that his ideas justify the pain he inflicts? A man who has the right to sacrifice his children?"

"What are you saying, Olga?"

"I was talking to myself."

On the terrace a cat meowed and scratched at the door; her kittens had been taken away. The clock began to strike the hour. Olga was silent as she listened to the voice of her home and her mother. This clock was her beautiful, devoted companion from a world that was going to pieces.

Vukašin heard the cocks crow and realized that it was midnight.

"I can't save him. I can't," he said, looking imploringly and despairingly into her eyes.

Frightened by these words, by their crushing finality, she staggered up from the suitcase and lay down on the bed beside the letters, her face sunk deep into the pillow.

The cat meowed piteously, jumping up and scratching at the door.

Vukašin felt for a chair, sat down beside the window, and lit a cigarette.

She turned over, raised herself, and stared at him; then she spoke, angrily and loudly. "Love can do everything. There's nothing it dares not do, Vukašin."

"There's only one kind of love that dares do everything, Olga."

"Only one?"

"The love of flesh and blood, Olga. There's nothing that that love dares not do."

"And a father's love?"

"It has different laws. Its own laws." Vukašin stood up, and she remained below him, a long, long way below.

"What is this law of yours, this father's law?" she whispered at his knees.

"A law that says I can't do everything. Dare not do everything," he muttered.

Tears blinded her eyes and she began to tremble. Hot, burning words caught at her throat. She gripped the bed convulsively. From a great distance she heard Vukašin's heavy, broken sighs.

"Have pity on me, Vukašin. If you possibly can," she whispered later. "If it matters to you whether I respect you," she said aloud.

Vukašin took off his coat and lay down on the bed, completely exhausted. "Don't you believe me when I say that I can't ask special favors for Ivan?" he asked. "That I can't act dishonorably to save him?"

Olga slowly got up from the bed, pulled the thick curtain over the window, and lay down again fully dressed, taking care not to touch him. She placed her scarf over her eyes.

When did he make his mistake? That once-in-a-lifetime mistake? The mistake a father can't prevent his son from making? Was it when he threw his peasant's clothes into the Seine, breaking his first pledge to his father? Or when he began to believe that being right was more important than success? When he preferred the role of moral gadfly to making a successful career? When he began to believe that to speak the truth was nobler than to avenge the defeat of Kossovo by dying a hero's death? To speak the truth and denounce wrong was not merely a matter of moral principle; it was a consuming intellectual passion, a man's true victory in life. But hadn't it in fact happened quite differently? And much earlier. Everything had been decided right from the beginning.

It had begun that night before he went away to school, when he had fallen asleep to the sound of his mother's wailing; her complaint that "that heartless, cruel Aćim was sending her child into the wide world." At which Aćim had shouted: "You've got Djordje and that's enough. I'm not going to let this one stay an ignorant country bumpkin. I want him to train his mind; I want all those thieving office pen-pushers to bend their necks before him. I want the road and the Morava to make way for him!" What did his father mean? What offices? he asked himself as he covered his head with a coarse blanket so as not to hear them; he wept and prayed to St. George, the family's patron saint, that his father might be struck dead before daybreak, that the Morava might overflow and flood all Prerovo and Palanka. With these thoughts he fell asleep. He was awakened by the sound of swishing blows, his mother's moans, and his father's grunts as he tightened his muscles and delivered those blows. He got up, opened the door of the kitchen a crack, and looked in: his mother stood naked and bent double beside the fireplace while Aćim beat her with a short rope. He threw himself on his father, who grabbed him by the neck and flung him back into his room, where he screamed: "You can kill me, but I won't go to school! I won't! I won't!" He couldn't fall asleep again for crying, tormented by the sight of his mother naked by the fireplace, pushed forward against the fire, the only place to which she could flee. At dawn Mika the schoolmaster pulled him out of bed. His father was already sitting in the cart with the horses harnessed; his mother, still weeping, was loading sacks of flour, beans, and potatoes. His father ordered him to climb into the cart, but he dashed off to the hayloft. Mika caught him, and he remembered nothing more until they were rafting across the Morava. He was lying in the cart between Mika's feet, the schoolmaster's soles pressing against his loins; the idea flashed across his mind that he was crossing the Morava forever. When he began to cry, Mika squeezed him mercilessly with the soles of his feet, trampling him. Like a trussed lamb he was being sacrificed to his father's will to lord it over people.

But the real break in his life came when he left for Paris. He hadn't wanted to take anything from Belgrade except his socialist ideas, his pledge to his father, and his peasant clothes; he loved his father, his homeland, and a few friends, no small thing for a young man setting out for a foreign country. That was what he had believed until he arrived in Paris, until all the fixed points of his former life began whirling around him, until all his momentous decisions became twisted and tangled and he was tormented by his own insignificance.

Ivan had presumably been tormented by something different. He had replied to his father's questions, after his return from Paris, with an ironical smile and silence.

In Paris, Vukašin was soon forced to admit that he lacked the strength for a life of solitude, the precondition for serious study and reflection. His days dragged out in despair. He could not bear to be a nonentity, to pass through that immense, overpowering forest of people unheard and unnoticed, like a mouse or a weasel; he had to crash his way noisily through that forest like a stag or a wild boar. These images had crystallized in his mind some ten years later, when he was forced to look at himself because of another failure.

Women, not one woman, like Radmila, but many women, had offered him the easiest kind of success, the most gratifying sense of importance. During the first two years of his studies in Paris his reputation as a seducer was firmly established, thanks to certain qualities that women described as "un Slave, farouche mais formidable." He loved not beautiful women, but simply women; he didn't pursue only the exceptional ones, he fought for them all: he wanted not love but pleasure. Variety was more important to him than fidelity; the uncertainty of something experienced for the first time delighted him more than the familiar and reliable; wantonness was more exciting to him than modesty. Wantonness was a gift, a woman's greatest gift.

Now, as he approached his fiftieth year, he was forced to pass judgment on himself: there had been no virtue in his passion for women, no trace of spirituality. His passion had been simply a vice, a flaw, which weariness and disgust had finally obliterated. But even in those days he had thought of "uprooting the past and everything connected with it." He was internally preparing for a complete break with the Prerovo world of long beards and low ceilings. He was firmly resolved to think for himself and go his own way. It was not books but fear that had changed him; he was afraid of blundering and ashamed of his poverty, the poverty of Serbia. Seen through the eyes of Europe, everything of value in himself and in his homeland had been threatened and humiliated. He would be eternally grateful to his father for not sending him to Paris to live the life of a poor student. He had never sat hungry over his books; never looked at the world chilled to the bone. He had never suffered from privation, the most common of all humiliations.

In those days Vukašin had doubted that one could believe the truth as seen by a poor man. A poor and weak man is more unjust toward people than a rich and powerful one; his life's goal is easy, and the road leading to it is short.

He had never doubted his own will power. And he gradually convinced himself that he must do the one thing that those who thought they could do everything could not do. Certain general conclusions followed: women corrupted a man, made him superficial and oblivious of time, made him blind to dangers, yielding and defenseless in the face of evil and cunning. He became confused and anxious, isolated himself, and was proud of his new love of solitude.

The role he had assigned himself in Serbia demanded that he convince people of his altruism, a real feat in a nation in which the majority of people have reason to believe that no one would do them a good turn without having some ax of his own to grind. He would have to renounce all forms of pleasure and everything that did not enhance his reputation, that did not compel even his opponents to respect him. A man who intended to acquire the power to reorganize a state along rational lines must first lead a rational life himself.

In working out his theoretical conceptions before returning to Belgrade, Vukašin had thought about the reformers who came back to Serbia dressed in European frock coats and bearing diplomas from European universities, men who sooner or later became "good Serbs" and "fat cats." To avert this fate, Vukašin was prepared to suffer the defeats that lay in store for "hotheads," as the graybeards contemptuously and spitefully described the innovators. He did not want to resemble the run-of-the-mill university graduate, either in his life style or in his opinions. He wanted to be different, to be himself, a man who had changed his entire personality. People revenged themselves on him with mockery and scorn. His convictions gave him the strength to refuse to fulfill the high expectations of his family, his milieu, and his generation; to this day he believed that this was his most painful test of character. And, throughout, Olga had been a tender and steady source of support.

Could he be losing Olga? With whom he had fallen in love as soon as he caught sight of her, leaning lightly in the doorway of the Krsmanović salon, her green eyes seeming to see everything in him at a glance. None of the other young women wore a dress with such a daring low neckline, cut in an unusual delicate floral shape. He had started, and his speech had become broken and confused. "That's the one!" he had said to himself. Afterward he had secretly watched her hands, provocatively tender, sexually exciting in their slim white nakedness, and had repeated to himself: "Yes, this is it!" He did everything possible to look at her and listen to her every day. No other woman had aroused such feelings in him. The houses seemed taller and the winding streets straighter when he went to meet her. He was sorry to fall asleep afterward. She was always different, always saying and doing something new. He loved her freedom, her imagination, her sagacity. No young girl in Belgrade had more beautiful eyes or greater pride. Later there was no wife like her. When had this ceased to excite or please him? Perhaps it was precisely this quality of being different that first lost its charm and meaning. At the beginning their personality differences had made their love more convincing, their passion purer, and their marriage unusual and more interesting. What had changed this? Time had destroyed that quality which set her apart from other women. Or perhaps time had made her uniqueness more difficult to live with. And how did she feel about him? He had been unfaithful to her with Radmila and had broken with her father. He had devoted himself to politics, which she disliked. They had disagreed about the children's upbringing. He had had no patience with her artistic friends. In what other ways had he made her unhappy? By being himself? Yes, that was it, that was the real reason. But he could not have lived his life differently. After the breach with his father, there had been the rupture with his father-in-law.

It had happened when Ivan was ill with measles. After seeing the doctor off, the three of them had remained in the dining room. The winter gale was blowing, the worst in living memory. Todor Tošić tried to persuade him to join the Liberal Party, but he had said firmly:

"I don't want to bury my life in either your party or Aćim's. I don't want a political career and a position of power. In Serbia, anyone who is literate can succeed in politics."

"Then why did you bother to study, spending Aćim's ducats all over Paris, if you didn't want to join a party and feed at the public trough? If you didn't want to ride a horse fed by others? A horse fed by the whole of Serbia. You don't want to go through a door that opens by itself, is that it?"

"I don't want to and don't intend to. I want to use my knowledge in the service of this poverty-stricken country. I want to serve the cause of progress."

"I know many respectable men, good husbands and fathers, who have gone to brothels before their marriage. And they'll visit a brothel whenever they go to Budapest. But they don't open brothels in Belgrade and Kragujevac."

"You may be sure I'm not one of that respectable type."

"So you've definitely decided not to go into politics? You don't want a position of power?"

"Serbia needs factories and professors, not parties and politicians."

"Factories are all we need to ruin this nation completely; it's rotting away already. Europe has factories, Doctor Katić, because she doesn't have our corn, plums, and pigs."

He banged his pipe in his palm; in the next room Ivan began to cry.

"You brought into this house a sackful of rags and a cane. The cane reminds me of Aćim. Is that why you carry a cane?"

"That's one reason why I carry a cane."

"Keep your cane. But just remember this, Vukašin. Since you're a family man, I wouldn't advise you to write in the newspapers the things you've told me tonight about factories and brothels and those other places of ill repute in Europe. Even though papers can stand anything. You won't get a mite from me for your plow factory. My money will go to my grandchildren. The only ducat you'll ever get from me will be a Christmas present. If you're lucky."

Then Olga had come up, put her hands on his shoulders, and said: "I'm on your side, Vukašin." On all such occasions she knew how to put her hands on his shoulders.

After the breach with his father-in-law, Vukašin abandoned his attempt to come to terms with people and circumstances in Serbia; he rejected the principle of modus vivendi and the power and value of guile. Perhaps that had been his fateful step. He had renounced the first gift needed for life, for survival, for coming out on top. He had become a civil servant and parted company with Pašić and the old Radicals; he had not wanted to be tied to Pašić's apron strings after repudiating politics as a skill learned from Machiavelli. Afterward he had left the Ministry of Foreign Affairs to lead a new party of independent Radicals and to become the editor of an Opposition newspaper, the *Echo.* He had alienated himself so thoroughly from his "own kind" that he could not have gone back to them without making things even harder for himself. At a high price he had gained a measure of respect and trust from the people and the reputation of an honorable and obstinate individualist.

Was that all? Certainly he was more respected than loved; that was what he wanted. But what had he accomplished?

What part had he played in leading Serbia into a new age? Where had it got him, his stubborn adherence to his principles, his strict consistency, which people found distasteful, his weighty ideas, which the nation could neither understand nor accept? He was the most popular opponent of Pašić and the "old men." The eternal polemicist. "The moral sword of Serbia," as some professors and students called him. That sword had neither handle nor sheath; it was a bare blade in his hand. What else had he achieved? How long would his success last?

From the time he went away to school, his father had kept drumming into his head: "In Serbia an educated man can become a village policeman; a man of property can die beside a fence; and a man of sense can end up among fools. If you want to do better than that, take care, my boy, that this thieving and malicious world doesn't find out what you want."

When had he made his mistake?

The twittering of the sparrows told Vukašin that it was daybreak. Angry and frightened, the flocking birds were pecking at the gray light filtering into the room at the sides of the heavy curtain Olga had drawn across the window to prolong the night. This was his last chance to find release in sleep, at least for a few minutes. With such a throbbing head, how could he make an important decision today? Should he decide for posterity? Appear as a traitor for the sake of posterity? A traitor in the name of the future? What future? He needed sleep, oblivion, so that darkness might spill over his brain and extinguish that intolerable burning. The sparrows were pecking at his brain. He put his fingers in his ears to shut out the birds; the buzzing hurt too. He couldn't fall asleep. Every subject touched on that night, everything spoken and unspoken, not only tormented him but was somehow defiled forever. Nothing was so filthy and disgusting as certain spoken words. Not even his fear for Milena and Ivan, or the dull pain caused by the war.

Alarmed by his own deep sigh, Vukašin opened his eyes. He was at the bottom of a soft, hot hole, hemmed in and pressed down by the gray light of early dawn and by the relics of Olga's elegant house and their former life.

The gray shapes of suitcases and trunks merged into one another amid the bestial shrieking of the sparrows in the eaves and in the walnut tree. Those objects around him wouldn't burn if he set fire to them; they wouldn't burn because of his words. The heap of whispered words now scattered over the bed and over their possessions. If he had spoken aloud, if he had been able to cry out, the pain would have been different.

Olga had not spoken. She lay there motionless, reproach seeping from her; the room was filled with her disappointment. If she had removed the scarf from her face and looked at him, he would have groaned aloud. He listened to her deep breathing, so unlike her usual breathing. His present feelings for her were indefinable, alien.

Someone opened the hall door; slippers clattered over the cobbled path: the old men were going out to urinate. Housewives and servants called to each other. In neighboring courtyards well ropes creaked and buckets banged. Smokers coughed.

Vukašin closed his eyes to snatch a moment's sleep, so that at least a wisp of darkness might pass through his brain. Somewhere a bugle sounded reveille, the first morning bugle call he had ever heard in Niš. He often heard taps played in the barracks on returning from his walk; then his thoughts would turn to Ivan. The sharp, distant screech of the bugle bored into his veins: Ivan would be getting up now. Still half asleep, he would get dressed, straighten the bed, and hurry out to wash. . . . In the one letter Ivan had written to him—all the others were addressed to his mother with only a greeting to him—he had complained about having to get up early. That was the only thing Ivan had complained about, but just in one sentence, quite casually. Everything else was fine and interesting, he said. No doubt it *was* very interesting in the Skoplje barracks for Ivan. A fellow who went to bed late, read until dawn, and during the holidays slept until noon. Now he was getting up at daybreak. What if they really were sent to the front?

He felt stiff and tense, but managed to doze off for a moment. Even a man at the point of death falls asleep at dawn. The bugle kept calling to Ivan to get up. Maybe it was summoning them for breakfast. Would they have tea, or some kind of gruel? "Don't send me any food, Mother. Not even cakes. I'm really enjoying this awful food and I've gained two kilos." Ivan, who was such a fussy eater that he wouldn't take a bite of anything without smelling it first. As soon as the meeting of the Assembly was over, he would take the train to Skoplje. He would take Ivan his glasses and give him the letter he had meant to give him before his departure for Paris. In that letter he had told Ivan what he wanted for him and expected of him on his return from Paris. But when they parted, Vukašin had been afraid to burden Ivan with his love and ambition. He was afraid of revealing his own wounds. He was afraid of the Vukašin in Ivan, of sharing Aćim's fate. Now he would hand over the letter "to be read one night in Paris." Let Ivan read it in the barracks. Vukašin would tell him what he could not say to Olga, or even to General Mišić. He would explain why he had not played and joked with him, why he had not spent more time with him. He would show Ivan how much he loved him. Did Ivan really not know it? Dare Ivan doubt it because he had been aloof and severe? He had been that way out of fear. Fear of love.

The very roots of his hair were burning. At daybreak even a man at death's door falls asleep. The bugler was stuck fast under the crown of his head. A cricket chirped by the wall.

In the dining room the stoves were being lit, and he could hear people wishing each other good morning, asking each other about their dreams, and ordering *slatko** and cold water. Another day of suffering for the homeland. They must surely have been overheard last night, even though they had talked in whispers. They must get out of this place as soon as possible. He got up quickly.

Vukašin stood in the narrow space between the bed and the suitcases, holding his breath: if only she doesn't draw the scarf from her face.

"Does Vukašin Katić live here?" he heard someone say in the hall.

Who could be asking for him so early? He dressed hastily. As long as she doesn't take the scarf from her face. The neighbors knocked at the door and called to him.

"I'm coming: right away!"

Now fully dressed, he picked up his hat and cane; he heard Olga whisper something but he didn't turn around.

"I didn't want to humiliate you," she said. "I was just trying to save Ivan. With your help. There's no one else I can turn to."

"I know."

---

*A sweet preserve made from different fruits, often served with a glass of cold water and a cup of Turkish coffee. [Translator.]

"I want more than that."
"But if I haven't got anything more, Olga?"
He dared not look at her. The noise in the hall drowned out her whispers. He opened the door abruptly and stepped into the large hall: the refugees, still wearing pajamas and bathrobes, were gathered around the policeman who had taken him to Pašić the previous night.
"What do you want, Sergeant?"
"Mr. Pašić wants you to come to his office at once. As soon as you possibly can."
"I'll come at the beginning of his normal office hours. Don't start explaining things to me. I know what is urgent and what I have to do."
As soon as the iron gate had clanged behind him, Vukašin stood still in the street and took a deep breath of fresh air to dispel the nausea of the previous night. The houses and trees were swaying and floating against the gray softness of the clouded sky. Why did Pašić want him so early in the morning? The collapse of the front, Macedonia, pressure from the Allies? Whatever had happened, things couldn't be worse than they were now, than they had been for a long time. He would go to Skoplje, to Ivan. He would leave at once. He would explain to Ivan the reasons for his apparent indifference to him, why he had kept his tenderness in check, why he had imposed the harsh regimen that people called paternal education. Should he leave for Skoplje before the meeting? In any case he would go today. *I'm not sacrificing you, my boy. I won't sacrifice you for anything in the world.*
Vukašin heard the rhythmic rise and fall of marching feet, murmuring voices, dull thuds. A column of Austro-Hungarian prisoners was coming past, accompanied by women and civilians who were giving them things and taking money. The Serbs, men and women, were selling them food—selling their defeated enemies too. People were selling everything, and killing everybody. The densely packed column trudged wearily past him, stopping from time to time. He could not walk alongside them; he must wait for them to pass, that living remnant of Serbia's victory at Cer that summer. The poverty of these captives had extinguished the hatred engendered by war and evoked the pity of the Serbs. They had become the first slaves of a people who had been enslaved for centuries, who did not see them as enemies but as unfortunate strangers. The Serbs pitied them, these soldiers of a great empire who had become the prisoners of

the small Serbian army, these wretched cowards, Vukašin thought, who have so easily persuaded us that we are the great heroes of this war. These poor wretches have given us the right to indulge in delusions of grandeur, that disastrous Serbian trait. Who wasn't grateful to these defeated foes for their very existence, grateful because every day thousands of them passed through the streets of Niš, enhancing its importance and confirming its position as the wartime capital of Serbia? Were the prisoners actually smiling at him? Yes, they had turned their unshaven faces toward him and were smiling faintly. He rubbed his eyes: why were they smiling? None of them knew him. Perhaps it was because they had seen a Serbian "gentleman," and were glad to see the Serbs making such progress!

Vukašin tottered forward on the pavement; behind him he heard a burst of laughter from the Austrians and wondered what was happening to him. He pulled himself together and hurried on with his usual long stride down the undulating street squeezed by the roofs of the houses.

Vukašin thought he was safe when he opened the door of an empty barbershop. The stench of dirty soapsuds assailed him. The barber bowed to him; he could not turn back, and anyway, where could he go unshaved? He hung up his hat and flung himself into the barber's chair. He saw himself reflected in the mirror: his head was riddled with dry, rusty holes. One eye was missing, a hole under his nostrils obliterated all but the ends of his mustache, his forehead was hollowed out, his silver-gray hair was flecked with rust, no ear on one side, and right under his throat a large patch of rust and flyspecks instead of his tie.

"I want a shave and facial massage, please."

"Don't worry, Mr. Katić. Everything will be just as it was before the war. Absolutely clean."

Vukašin shifted so that both his eyes were visible in his punctured head; then shook it, annihilating his nose and plowing soft furrows under his eyes.

"Keep your head still, Mr. Katić."

"Your hands are shaking."

This old man, nothing but skin and bones, would be the death of him. Let the man chatter away; he would keep quiet. The meeting of the Assembly was due to begin at ten o'clock. Today he had to stake everything he had won during the last twelve years on this Serbian roulette, which was now turned by winds blowing from St. Petersburg, Paris, and London, and which Pašić stopped or pushed forward at will. He must stake his so-called moral and political authority, his reputation as an Opposition leader, the fame he had won as the enemy of Pašić, the freedom to speak according to his conscience. If he came out in favor of fulfilling the demands of the Allies and handing over Macedonia to Bulgaria, the nation would regard him as a traitor. So would his children; certainly Milena would. His children would bear the burden of his shame all their lives. He could no longer be a real opponent of Pašić. Politically he would be finished. If he opposed the pressure from the Allies and defended that miserable Macedonia, he would be risking the very existence of the Serbian state, risking everything that had been created during the last hundred years. He would be deciding in favor of uncertainty and enormous sacrifice. Uncertainty! It would mean suicide for Serbia. By refusing to agree to the Bulgarian annexation of Macedonia, he would be accepting Pašić's alternative. What did General Mišić think? Should he sit through today's meeting in silence? If he did not speak up when the fate of the country was being decided, he would lose the right to concern himself with its fate; he would have to keep silent forever. That would be the end of his hopes and dreams, of the great role to which he had dedicated his life, bringing upon himself hatred and enemies. He would lose all peace and joy. And his children. Olga's words last night had already shaken him to the core of his being.

"You're shivering, Mr. Katić; you're feeling cold. I must start heating tomorrow. Wood is very expensive; the peasants are making the gentry pay a high price for the war."

"I'm not cold. It's you that's shivering." Vukašin gripped the arms of the chair to stop his shuddering. He must write to Milena immediately. Presumably they would evacuate the hospital from Valjevo in good time. Since life is governed by eternal laws and since everyone knows the consequences, why do people always make fatal mistakes? Why don't we take a different road to the grave? Is there another road?

"Backo dropped by a short while ago and told me about the telegrams that came last night. Our great allies have sure made things hot for us. Serves us right, too, seeing as how we're dying like cattle for the bourgeoisie and the imperialists."

"Are you a socialist?"

"I've been a Red ever since I can remember, Mr. Katić. And I'll die one. I used to listen to Svetozar Marković in Kragujevac, and I shaved him for nothing several times, as a favor to a comrade. I hate

Pašić and his thieving Radicals more than the Turks. I don't care if we're ruled by Bulgarians or Fritzies or Turks as long as they get Pašić off Serbia's back. Tell me—since you Independents are different from Pašić's crowd, or so you say—why does my only son have to get killed by the Fritzies? Whose country is he giving his life for? For the King and the bourgeoisie? For your freedom to persecute and oppress us?"

Vukašin flinched. "Calm down! You'll be the death of me!"

"I'm really glad you're my first customer today. People think you're honest and willing to do things. I don't know; you weren't a minister for very long; you didn't have much time to put your hand in the till."

"Stop, you're skinning me!"

"When is that scoundrel Pašić going to run to Skoplje? Backo told me that you and Pašić were shut up together for two and a half hours last night."

"The government isn't going to move to Skoplje. And with your son at the front, my friend, there's no sense in spreading false news and panic. The most important thing today is to stay calm and have faith in yourself."

"The most important thing today, my dear Mr. Katić, is that the heads of peasants and workers are cheaper than those of sheep. And that café owners, merchants, and the gentry have got themselves safe berths behind the lines and at headquarters. What homeland are the peasants and workers dying for?"

"Excuse me, but my son is a volunteer. And my daughter is a nurse in Valjevo."

"That's all to your credit. You've still got red blood in your veins. I've heard what you said in the Assembly. I've got a newspaper that tells about how you rescued Vasa Pelagić from a lunatic asylum. I've also kept a picture of you and Vasa Pelagić, when you were our friend. Would you like me to show it to you?"

"No, thanks. I'm in a hurry."

The barber went on reviling and cursing Pašić, the Allies, and the capitalists.

Vukašin didn't listen. What a day! He had passed several barbershops and he had to pick a socialist. A man who reminded him of the past, insulted him, spewed out his petty working-class hatred in the name of a great idea. A fatal idea for a small nation, the spiritual obsession of the poverty-stricken Balkans, Serbia's tragicomedy. Yes, he had seriously believed in all that; he had been a socialist too.

Could it be that only Ivan and Milena were now saving him from the scorn of this angry barber? Ivan and Milena bore witness to his honor as a citizen and to his patriotism. What pass had he come to? Now his face had no chin and only one eye. Why had Pašić again asked to see him so early? Maybe Pašić was really preparing to capitulate. Was he looking for support before beginning peace negotiations? With Pašić it was never all or nothing; he never put all his eggs in one basket. He'd rather be sure of a little power than unsure of full power. Probably that consummate politician wanted neither to capitulate nor to go on with the war. Pašić didn't worry about principles or consistency. If he beat around the bush today, they would demand his resignation; they would attack him as a timid and incompetent war leader.

"Don't bother with the facial massage. I'll wash my face myself. At least you've got some water, even if there is a war on. Rinse my face with cold water."

"I've heard that in Budapest and Vienna the barbershops don't stink, Mr. Katić."

Vukašin didn't respond and paid the man double. "I don't take tips in wartime," the barber snapped.

Vukašin went out into the street without saying good-bye. He felt sick and wretched. Walking slowly, he headed for the Prime Minister's office. It was quarter to eight. He must have a cup of coffee and pull himself together. He went into the nearest inn. It was full of people. He could drink his coffee in peace. He pushed his way to the bar through the noisy crowd; he didn't even mind being pressed against the wall. The whole place reeked of brandy, cigarettes, and people. He ordered two cups of strong coffee; while waiting he overheard a flurry of voices:

"A double brandy, Ćira. What you've heard is very bad, Backo. It's a good thing for you that you don't know it. And for the dead too. I didn't sleep a wink last night, Backo. They're still retreating. I ran away from the wailing women before daylight. The Second Army was fleeing all night. Don't wash those dishes now. Hey, you folks in the corner, don't bang those dominoes on the table so early in the morning! Has Belgrade been abandoned? Yes, gentlemen, I'm sorry to say. People are at each other's throats. Pašić has been sitting alone in his office since dawn. He isn't receiving anybody. Neither Protić nor Paču dares show his face in the room. Only Joca goes in, with the telegrams. Ninety-two percent of a man's body weight, gentlemen, consists of water. It's just stinking vapor. The world is rotten to the core. There's been no worse injustice since Cain killed Abel. Serbia is settling accounts for all the Balkan countries. Tell me what Pašić says. He doesn't say anything; just tears at his beard. We are done for. Another round, Ćira. Now, Backo, we're all Serbs, so tell us what the Czar's minister Sazonov said in his telegram. Pašić could deal easily enough with Sazonov, who would know what to whisper to the Czar. But last night there were new telegrams from the British minister, Grey, and from the Frenchman, Delcassé. They're not giving us munitions, but they're selling Macedonia. That's the English and the French for you, gentlemen. Judas Iscariots, both of them. Now, boys, we must control ourselves and not curse the Allies. Niš is full of spies. All that about spies is rubbish, Doctor. We're too small a country to have spies. Don't get so upset, folks! We endured five centuries under the Turks, and we'll put up with today's emperors and all their Greys and Sazonovs. But it's not good that Pašić is keeping quiet. You're right about that. See here, folks, isn't there a single house in this damned town without any mice? What can you do now, Inspector? The mice rushed in when the Fritzies took Mačva. What's that about the Fritzies? Don't worry, Stepa and Putnik will stop Potiorek. So now Serbia's fate hangs on mice. There's a mouse right in the heart of this poor country. The Russian ambassador, Strandmann, couldn't sleep again last night for the mice, never shut his eyes. Do you mean to say that the ambassador of an empire like Russia is scared of a mouse in Niš? Russia is full of bears, and now this Strandmann is afraid of a Serbian mouse. Watch your manners and don't shout; the man's got sensitive nerves and hasn't had enough sleep, so you can just imagine what kind of telegrams he's writing to the Czar from Niš. We'd better catch those mice, boys. You know, folks, those mice will gnaw the threads that Serbia's hanging on to. Pašić, you mean, not Serbia. Ćira, pour out a glass all round for the soul of my son Slobodan. When did you get the news, Judge? Last night. A shell got him. God have mercy on his soul. They'll destroy us all. The Serbian artillery's been inactive for three days."

"The Serbian cannon haven't any shells! They're silent!" cried Slobodan's father.

Vukašin stared at him and trembled. Slobodan's father was more bitter than grief-stricken. He didn't want compassion. He wanted people to grasp the importance of the Serbian artillery.

"This war is a war of artillery!" shouted Slobodan's father.

Vukašin couldn't drink his second cup of coffee. He paid his bill and moved toward the door. Could he now ask for special favors for his son? It was all loathsome.

"What do you say about what's going on, Mr. Katić?"

Backo had grabbed the lapels of his coat. Never had Vukašin seen such a deeply lined face as this one under the large black hat. The noise around him died down.

"I'll be speaking today in the Assembly. You'll hear then. Excuse me, I'm in a hurry. Yes, the situation is serious. We haven't any ammunition for our artillery. But I'm not a pessimist, definitely not."

Vukašin walked slowly, staring at the dead, fallen leaves. He had no right to feel sad, still less right to feel miserable. Because he had to deceive people and show that he wasn't a pessimist. He had to today, out loud. In front of that father who was holding a funeral service for his son in the inn. Pitiable hypocrisy. He would stay a whole week with Ivan, spend some time with him every evening. After Ivan's return from Paris they had talked about the front casually over lunch. He would tell Ivan all he ought to know and give him that parting letter. It was too late. Love could not make up for lost time. Yes, it could. That feeling had its own time, but it came only once.

Vukašin was halted by a sudden silence.

A crowd of Serbian wounded was coming up from the railroad station. The people stood silently in rows by the road, as though a funeral procession were approaching. Vukašin stood back against the wall. It was not right to stride along while those men with bandaged hands and arms, unshaven and exhausted, carrying canes and on crutches, wearing ragged uniforms, dragged themselves wearily on, looking askance at the silent civilians. Not one of the hundreds of wounded men was wearing glasses, Vukašin noted, and hurried across the bridge toward the Prime Minister's office.

In the anteroom of Pašić's office there were a dozen ministers and party leaders, looking glum. Vukašin lingered at the door and greeted them in hushed tones, as if someone had died. He leaned on his cane and looked straight ahead: for two months his political duties had kept him from visiting his son at the school for junior officers. He sighed loudly but attracted no one's attention.

Pašić peered out and quietly called to him. Vukašin quickly entered the large office and felt a little better when the attendant shut the door behind him.

Pašić bent forward and said thoughtfully: "I've been thinking about what you said last night. If we capitulate, then we're back to where we were before the First Uprising. Or do we fight to the last man?" He raised his eyes toward Vukašin. "Is there a third possibility?"

Vukašin remained silent for a while, then said with dry lips: "I don't know if I can give you good advice at this time, Prime Minister." He felt better for having spoken spontaneously and sincerely.

"Can we take anything off the people's backs? Can we do anything to make things easier for them? Their spines will crack."

"You know my opinion, and the Opposition's views on your policies. Who knows if we are entirely just and objective? Perhaps the time has come for other truths." Was Pašić smiling at him? He could see yellow sparks in his eyes.

"Opposition has never bothered me, Nikola Pašić. I've suffered the greatest inconvenience and harm from my supporters and those who think as I do."

"I suppose you want to tell me something about today's meeting of the Assembly," interrupted Vukašin, changing his tone.

"The meeting of the National Assembly has been postponed. Vojvoda Putnik has asked that tomorrow the government be in Valjevo, at the headquarters of the High Command. The army is on the verge of collapse. We must decide together what to do. I will not make a decision about the fate of Serbia without the Opposition. Besides, it's high time we formed a coalition government, Vukašin. We must come to an agreement and form a united front, if it's not too late."

3

A long time ago the powerful Austro-Hungarian Empire resolved to crush the small nation of Serbia, a freedom-loving democratic country. Serbia, being free, attracted Austro-Hungarian citizens of Serbian origin and presented an obstacle to the much desired route to Salonikă. It was essential to prepare the people of the Dual Monarchy for the task of destroying their inconvenient neighbor. With this aim in view the Austro-Hungarian press, faithfully followed by that of Germany, began a campaign of systematic calumny against the Serbs. According to what one reads in their newspapers, there are no greater barbarians, no more repulsive people than the Serbs. They are thieves and regicides, infested with lice, possessed by a lust for blood. They cut off the noses and ears of their captives, castrate them, and gouge out their eyes.

The Austro-Hungarian soldiers who found themselves among the people whom they had always heard spoken of as barbarians were frightened, and it was probably fear that caused them to commit the first atrocities, so as to avoid being mutilated themselves. But once a man has seen blood, he changes into an animal. The troops became possessed by a collective sadism.

Thus the responsibility for these cruel actions rests not with the simple soldiers, victims of the bestial instinct that lies dormant in man, but with their superiors. What I have just described, along with eyewitness accounts of atrocities committed by Austro-Hungarian soldiers, reveals carefully thought out preparations for slaughter on the part of their leaders.

An extraordinary document which I have faithfully translated from German begins as follows:

"K. and K. 9. Corps Command

"Instructions for conduct toward the population of Serbia

"The war has brought us to a country whose inhabitants are inspired by a fanatical hatred for us, a land in which murder is legally permitted and regarded as a heroic deed by the upper classes, as was demonstrated by the disastrous event at Sarajevo.

"It would be a mistake to show any humanity or kindness toward such a population; moreover, it would be harmful, since the kind of consideration that is sometimes shown in war would put our troops in serious danger.

"I accordingly order that throughout our military operations, all the inhabitants be treated with the greatest severity, toughness, and mistrust."

This was written by an Austrian general, the representative of a government which, as we know, wished to send an enormous number of people to their death on the basis of false documents composed in its embassy in Belgrade.

The instructions continue:

"First of all I will not allow any persons in the enemy country who are carrying arms but not wearing uniforms, whether encountered singly or in groups, to be taken prisoner. They are to be summarily executed."

The Austro-Hungarian General Staff was well aware that the Serbian soldiers of the third draft and at least half of those of the second draft never received uniforms. Hence the instructions were a clear summons to slaughter these soldiers, and one which the army followed to the letter.

Subsequently we find the following statement regarding hostages:

"During our march through populated areas, hostages should be taken, if possible, while the column is passing through, and if a single shot is fired at the army, they should be summarily executed.

"The ringing of church bells is forbidden, and if necessary the bells are to be removed; every bell tower must be surrounded by a patrol of soldiers.

"Religious services may be held only in open areas in front of churches.

"A squad prepared to shoot will stand near the church while a service is being held.

"Any inhabitant found outside a village, particularly in the woods, should be regarded as a member of a band which has concealed weapons; we have no time to search for the weapons, but the men should be executed if they appear suspicious."

Here is an undisguised invitation to murder. Any person found outside a town or village is a guerrilla fighter who should be killed!

I can only describe this extract as a summons to slaughter the civilian population.

(R. A. Reiss: *Comment les Austro-Hongrois ont fait la guerre en Serbie.* Observations directes d'un neutre, Paris, Armand Colin, 1915)

His telephone conversations with Pašić left Vojvoda Putnik deeply troubled about his assessment of the defeats suffered during the last few days. Even before his first conversation with Pašić, fearing that he might be exaggerating the defeat, he had tried out his conclusions on his assistant, General Živojin Mišić, whose opinion he valued highly.

"If you were in command of the Serbian army, Mišić, how would you assess its present position?"

"I agree that our position is very unfavorable."

"That's all?"

"Yes. As long as we keep fighting, our position can always change for the better," Mišić replied.

"Do you really believe that, Mišić, when our army has been reduced to half-strength after only three months of fighting? Our troops don't have ammunition—you tell me that every morning. They are naked and barefoot, and winter will soon be upon us. Meanwhile, the enemy is doubling his strength and steadily advancing on the fronts held by the First and Second armies. So you are an optimist?"

"Yes, I am, Vojvoda. The side that can endure defeats longest will win the war. No enemy can match our capacity for endurance."

So ended the conversation. There was no point in arguing with Mišić, who had such a limited and simplistic view of the present state of the Serbian army. Mišić's optimism even strengthened his own convictions and prompted him to speak his mind without mincing words. But Pašić's persistent cold-blooded refusal to accept his estimate of the Serbian army's plight confused and alarmed him. Although Pašić had agreed to come to the High Command the next day with the government, his callous attitude toward the frightful losses in the army implied a sense of superiority that transcended his official position—the superiority of good health, which he, Putnik, lacked. But Pašić's sense of superiority also derived from the strength to stand firm in the face of adversity, and it was precisely this strength that he needed more than the other members of the High Command. Perhaps he no longer possessed that strength, despite the fact that he had so far refused to make changes in the High Command that would indicate a state of emergency; in fact, such changes had been demanded by Prince Alexander in his capacity as commander in chief and were supported by General Mišić. Just as he insisted on maintaining the "normal state of affairs" in the High Command, Putnik also clung to his own daily habits. He called to his orderly to carry his chair to the window, so that while waiting for night to fall he could look at the bare lime trees in the rain and watch the last leaves falling. If the earth were not swathed in clouds, he would have driven that evening to a small hill overlooking Valjevo and gazed at the constellations, in whose presence he experienced a deep tranquillity and became most fully conscious of eternity and the infinite—thoughts never far from his mind.

Wrapped up in his overcoat, Vojvoda Putnik moved toward the window of the main hall of the district court, but in the middle of the huge empty room containing his table and a single chair, he was stopped by General Mišić.

"Vojvoda Stepa is on the telephone, sir. He insists on talking to you."

"Tell him we'll talk here tomorrow. I suppose he's received the telegram about tomorrow's meeting."

"Yes, he has. But he says he won't come to Valjevo tomorrow."

Vojvoda Putnik walked slowly up to his desk and lifted the receiver. "Well, Stepa, what do you have to tell me?"

"I've just this minute got back from the positions of the Morava Division. The Austrian heavy artillery has leveled the trenches and blown our artillery earthworks to smithereens. Yet my gunners can't fire back because I've ordered them to keep their last three shells."

"Go on, Stepa. I'm listening."

"Putnik, you should have seen how a single salvo wiped out entire platoons. This is butchery! Sheer butchery of the Serbian army!"

Vojvoda Putnik put his hand over the receiver and whispered to Mišić: "He's weeping!" Speaking into the telephone, he said: "Just a minute, Stepa. This is my fifth war too. And I know what an artillery barrage is!"

"No, you don't, Putnik! This isn't a war between two armies. This is the slaughter of the Serbian army! The slaughter of helpless men!"

"I told you last night, Stepa, that for the third time I have made urgent appeals to both Pašić and the Allied ambassadors, asking them to deliver as soon as possible the munitions we've already paid for."

"That's no help at all to me. I no longer want to command an army that doesn't have any artillery. I've called to let you know that I am resigning my command of the Second Army. Please convey this to the Commander in Chief."

"That's all very well for you, Stepa." To calm himself, Putnik sat down. "And to whom can I submit *my* resignation, as head of the High Command, in a country that has no munitions factories, a country being attacked by a European empire with fifty armaments factories? To whom can I show my anger and despair because I am suffering defeats in this unequal war, and because I am being undeservedly battered by Herzendorff and Oscar Potiorek? In the name of my honor and the pity I feel for the army, to whom, Stepa Stepanović, can I submit my resignation?"

"To the King and Pašić! To the politicians! Let those gentlemen come to the trenches!"

"Why don't your subordinate commanders submit their resignations to you? Why don't they, since they have more right to do that than you and I?"

General Mišić left the courtroom.

"They sure have, Putnik! Because someone is to blame for the fact that we have entered the war in this helpless state, with nothing but our bare hands. And you know very well who it is."

"Listen, Stepa . . . you and I are both old soldiers. In our first year in the Artillery School in Kragujevac we learned what a soldier's duty is. Let's not now assume rights that don't belong to us. Because the Austrian sergeants will make us grooms for their horses!"

"They won't do that, Vojvoda! I can always die standing on my feet!"

"Now you should *think* standing on your feet! Our duty is to think, not to die. But we'll talk about this when we're alone together. Please come and see me at once." He put down the receiver and remained seated behind his empty desk. He didn't answer Stepa's second call.

The Regent, Prince Alexander, came and without a word, as if he were alone in the room, stood with his hands behind his back staring at the military maps on the wall. The Regent's habit of gazing at the maps and demanding to discuss the state of the fronts filled Putnik with a rage he could barely control. That was how lieutenants imagined great commanders poring over maps; well, let him get on with it. As long as he didn't propose a flank attack today. As commander in chief, the Regent was perpetually suggesting flank attacks. And as long as he didn't again berate his Montenegrin cousins for not fighting on their front. He wouldn't say anything to the Regent about Stepa. Let that sentimental vojvoda hand in his resignation to the Prince in person tomorrow.

General Mišić put some papers down on the desk. Putnik did not hear from whom the report came. Nor did he care. He already knew far more facts than he needed to make a wise decision. He watched Mišić walk slowly out of the room with a certain gloomy self-confidence. Mišić was always self-confident and always gloomy. He never ventured to give an opinion unless asked, and he was always optimistic. He regularly repeated his requests for ammunition for the artillery and machine guns; occasionally he would speak his mind about the Allies. But he never showed any of that characteristic initiative that had prompted Putnik to appoint him his assistant. Mišić was obviously taking his revenge for being forced to retire the previous year. Well, let him get it out of his system.

"The Drina Division must withdraw from elevations 420 and 426 this very evening," said Prince Alexander, without so much as casting a glance at him as he went out.

Putnik felt like retorting: "Don't bother me now with divisions and elevations!"

Placed as he was, between Stepa and Mišić, in fact, above Stepa and Mišić but under Pašić and Prince Alexander, how could he think straight or act judiciously? When there were no real grounds for hope? And yet without hope wasn't it impossible to wage war and command an army? For Pašić, all the major decisions had been taken when he resolved to go to war. He expected from him, Putnik, only victory. Pašić was an optimist too. Ah, these optimists, this optimism, that philosophy so dear to fishermen. One of them was his assistant, the other was the Prime Minister! If the war ended in defeat, he, not Pašić, would bear the blame. Pašić would be praised for his boldness and sense of honor in going to war with two European empires in defense of freedom and independence. Pašić's hardest duty was to be steadfast, to persevere—something any fool or heartless man could do. He, Radomir Putnik, would savor the grandeur of defeat. Grandeur indeed! Dying on one's feet, as Stepa said, and the Serbs perishing to the last man, incited by militant patriots behind the lines. Or should defeat involve as few sacrifices as possible, so that you live to fight another day? But that meant acting rationally, not dying like a hero, as the militants thought. Greatness in defeat meant to think heroically, to think sensibly, to think clearly and independently without regard to superiors or subordinates.

Putnik rang for his orderly and moved slowly to the chair at the window. He was always fascinated by the transition from light to darkness. He disliked being in an enclosed space when dusk fell; during those moments he could not work; he wanted to be alone.

Before the incomprehensible universe, his own doubts became more certain; the unknowable darkness and clusters of stars sharpened his perception of everything within and around him, making perfectly clear the most important thing of all: that we are but dust, here for a moment, then gone. His orderly draped a blanket around him and went off to light the stove. Putnik called him back to open the window; he wanted to feel the wide space, the earth, the autumn.

"It's very damp outside, Vojvoda."

He glanced at Sergeant Zarubac and the man hastily opened a casement. Eagerly he breathed in the freshness of the autumn dusk and the smell of the damp trees, restraining his cough. His orderly brought him a lighted cigarette, but he waved him away. Even the fire in the stove behind his back disturbed him as he tried to concentrate his thoughts on the utmost limits of the Serbian army's endurance, on which he must base his argument at the next day's meeting of the government and the High Command. He stared at the wet black lime trees, from which the wind was tearing the last leaves. He recalled the times he used to press his ear against the thick trunk of the walnut tree in his vineyard so as to hear the sap flowing to its roots. If you could hear the sap flowing in the forest, descending in autumn and rising in spring, what music that would be, what poetry! But man cannot hear it, no more than he can see the most beautiful things, know the most vital truths, or do his best. Man is an imperfect creature who will not accept the fact of his own imperfection, who is always hankering after more than he needs. That makes him suffer, and rightly so. Just as it was right that he, Putnik, should be tormented by the fate of his army. In the darkness of northern and western Serbia he saw the long line of the Serbian front cracked and broken.

Where did such enormous crows come from, and why is there such a mass of them flying toward Valjevo, Vukašin wondered as he hurried to the meeting of the High Command. He would have to oppose sending the students to the battlefield. Whatever the military reasons, the sacrifice of her entire intelligentsia was contrary to the vital interests of Serbia. He would tell them that, whatever they thought or said about him the next day. He would say: The nation has already lost the war. Today only one generation may lose its freedom—that's water under the bridge. But if any nation loses its intelligentsia, then it loses the war, no matter what the result on the battlefield. *The officers will tear me to bits,* he thought.

He could scarcely push his way along the pavement through the townspeople and refugees from Mačva, who stood silently beside the roadway, staring at the long column of oxcarts full of wounded coming to Valjevo from the front. The creaking and grinding of the carts reverberated in the early twilight, filling the street with anger and despair.

Yes, and I'll tell them this: Today a nation left without intellect and knowledge has no reason to rejoice at peace. What kind of future can justify such a sacrifice? This war might prove more significant for Serbia in terms of what she loses than what she gains. *Is it reasonable to say that now, this evening? That's what's so terrible: to be right today might well make one a traitor tomorrow.*

He stood in front of the entrance to the district court, which housed the High Command of the Serbian army. The officer on duty greeted him from the steps, but he walked past him, feeling a little awkward at being the last to arrive at this discussion that, as Pašić had asserted on the train, "would decide the fate of Serbia." Officers were hurrying along the corridor; the tramping of military boots was distasteful to him, as were the sheepskin hats, the epaulets, and the clanking of sabers.

The officer opened the door, and he entered the dark courtroom, where total silence reigned around a table covered with military maps, where army commanders sat on one side, and ministers and Opposition leaders on the other. At this table—a battlefield where victories were easily won and defeats cheaply bought—there were only two empty chairs: one at the head, obviously for the heir to the throne, Prince Alexander, the official Commander in Chief of the Serbian army; and another at the foot, for him. He greeted the company with a slight bow, removed his hat and coat, and took his seat, placing his cane between his knees. Only Pašić and General Mišić returned his greeting, and they did so loudly and with pleasure. He could hear the asthmatic coughing of Vojvoda Putnik, chief of the High Command and the real commander of the Serbian army. Opposite Putnik sat the Prime Minister, rhythmically tapping the floor with his cane and staring at a war map of Serbia. The generals and all the officers were gray-haired, and all of them, except General Mišić, looked angry and offended; at this court their look and bearing implied accusation, in the name of some remote and superhuman power. The politicians glowered, their anxiety apparent in their posture, as though waiting for a verdict.

Whose fate, Vukašin wondered, was being decided there that evening, over the war map of Serbia? That of Serbia or the political and military careers of those sitting around the table? The people here around the map or the men on the battlefield? The rain-soaked wounded, the peasants, the refugees? And what if the verdict had already been pronounced? If so, what was he here for—as a witness? Or perhaps a culprit, whom a process of historical inevitability would pronounce guilty of the defeat in the name of the homeland, that there might be implanted in his descendants, through jeers and curses, the fear of the slightest disobedience to any demand: for the cause of freedom, all must sacrifice themselves! But whatever he said and did, whatever decisions were taken at this meeting in the district court, over this military map of Serbia, above those crisscrossing and overlapping lines—a veritable chaos of lines, designated by names and numbers—it was not here that the outcome of the war would be decided for Serbia. By no means! Here, there was no November rain falling, no groans of the wounded. He felt like smashing the ceremonial officialdom with something closer to the reality outside this courtroom, something like the bloodstained jacket full of shrapnel holes that a medic had brought out of the casualty station, holding it by the collar as he told Vukašin that his daughter, Milena, was in the operating room and that he dared not call her. Vukašin coughed and scraped his chair; he looked at the silent civilians—ministers and members of the Opposition—and wanted to say to them: "Look at that rain!" He wanted to say a few ordinary human words, but all those present suddenly rose to their feet, saluted, and clicked their heels: Prince Alexander, the heir to the throne, entered the room and returned the salute.

On taking his seat, the Prince started awkwardly when he saw Vukašin opposite him, for Vukašin had frequently criticized the monarchy; the Prince gave him an angry and hostile stare. Vukašin returned his look firmly and calmly, looking him straight in the eye. The Prince's hands fidgeted; apart from Pašić, they all noticed this, and waited for a flood of impatient words.

"Shall we begin, Your Highness?" said Pašić, looking at his knees and still tapping the floor with his cane, though more gently.

Prince Alexander looked nervously toward the windows; he was bothered by the clamorous cawing of the jackdaws outside.

No one could ever remember seeing him calm, or not provoked to anger by something or somebody in his presence. To this overly serious heir apparent, there was a sense of pressure everywhere; this ambitious prince, who in fact already ruled, had grasped the eternal law of power with remarkable ease and speed. But whatever his position, and whatever sort of man he was, he was the King under whose flag Vukašin's son, Ivan, would go out to face bullets and buckshot; he was one half of the national pledge and military oath, "For King and Country," in whose name thousands were perishing every day. This thin, desiccated young man took his position too seriously, alongside these bearded ministers and gray-haired generals. He said something in a quiet voice. Pašić stopped tapping with his stick.

"Gentlemen, not since the Battle of Kossovo in 1389 have the Serbs had a more fateful meeting than the one we are holding this evening in Valjevo. Every uprising and every war we have fought since 1804 is being decided once again. The King, my father, has empowered me to ask of you a conscientiousness in the service of the homeland equal to the courage shown by our soldiers on the battlefield. I will now ask Vojvoda Putnik to explain our military position."

Everybody except General Mišić looked at Vojvoda Putnik, who began to speak softly, almost in a whisper, with his fists on the military map of Serbia.

"It is my duty, gentlemen, to convey to you the extremely critical facts about our condition. The state of our army, and the situation on the battlefronts—"

He paused to control a wheezing in his chest, making an effort not to cough, his face turning crimson above his short white beard. Ravens croaked from the branch of the lime tree outside the window. He continued in a whisper.

"Our divisions are reduced by half. From forty to sixty percent of the officer cadres have perished. Our ammunition is exhausted. The infantry has enough for two weeks at the most, and the artillery has about ten shells for every cannon. Our soldiers, gentlemen, are barefoot and naked."

All the heads around the table bent forward in his direction; necks craned over the military map. Vojvoda Putnik raised his voice slightly, looking over the heads of the ministers.

"Any day now it will start snowing. In all respects, our enemies are incomparably stronger and better prepared for war. We cannot halt their attacks; we are unable to defend Valjevo—or Belgrade. The Albanians are simply waiting for us to weaken; then they will strike from the rear. The Turks are penetrating our frontier. The help offered by our Allies is, as you are aware, spasmodic and inadequate.

Every day our High Command presses the government for more help—well-deserved help—from the Allies. We have received nothing. Our troops are exhausted and have turned their backs on the enemy."

Everyone present held his breath, trying to catch the asthmatic, almost inaudible words of Vojvoda Putnik.

"Before the ink is dry on my instructions, the troops have abandoned the positions that I order them to defend at all costs." He stopped and straightened himself; moving his head slightly, he cast his eyes around the table, then moved his fists to the edge of the map, to the frontier of Serbia. "Gentlemen, the Serbian army has done its utmost." He spoke the last sentence in a firm, clear voice.

"What are you trying to say, Vojvoda?"

"In my opinion, Your Highness, our military effort is about to collapse. The fate of Serbia now rests with the diplomats—if it is not too late. In any case, it is no longer within my competence."

Over the military map of Serbia there was dead silence; outside, the jackdaws croaked, and the oxcarts carrying the wounded continued on their grinding way. The faces of the officers were frozen, and amazement darkened those of the ministers in the failing light. Was it possible that Vojvoda Putnik—the man who had planned the strategy that had brought victories over Turks and Bulgarians—could now really believe that the Serbian army was facing inevitable defeat? Could he believe this—the man whose knowledge, seriousness, and determination had implanted in the Serbian army and nation a belief that it could win in an unequal struggle with the Austro-Hungarian Empire. Vukašin gave a start, then looked hard at Vojvoda Putnik, who was now shaken by his thick, asthmatic cough: the exhausted, sick old man was supporting himself against the table.

Vukašin then looked at the rest of the company: some of the ministers and Opposition leaders were taking out cigarettes; their glances met those of the generals, whose confusion blunted their vengeful anger against the politicians and the government. No one ventured by the slightest movement to break the deathly hush around the conference table, on which the homeland lay spread out in the shape of a military map. Pašić was staring at it, noiselessly tapping his fingers on the edge of the table, as if playing some simple childish ditty.

Only Pašić paid no attention to a new and significant development; with wide, overemphatic movements, General Mišić had struck a match and lit his cigarette. This relaxation of tension caused some of those present to sigh audibly and look hard in the direction of

Vojvoda Putnik. Mišić's lighting of a cigarette seemed to Vukašin like a gesture of exultation: perhaps Mišić's hour had struck. He had been persecuted and twice pensioned off; after his victories over the Turks and Bulgarians, he had been thrown off the General Staff like a village constable—he, a man whose conviction was always matched by his courage and dignity. He was calmly smoking and gazing out the window. It was clear from his look that he did not believe in the collapse of Serbia.

But who will listen to my opinion? thought Vukašin. He dropped his cane on the floor. The sound startled him. Once more he was aware of the contempt and irritation of the officers. Perhaps he would have made some apology, but at that moment Prince Alexander rose and, turning his back to the table, stood tensely for what seemed a long time, as if he might explode or do something terrible; however, all he did was to open the window, as if unfastening a tight button, and the conference room echoed with the cawing of birds. He turned back to the table and looked uncertainly at his officers and ministers. They moved their chairs, and all eyes turned to the battlefields marked on the map, to the thick, broken lines and twisted arrows converging on the center of Serbia.

Three carts carrying wounded passed the courthouse. Vojvoda Stepa Stepanović, commander of the Second Army, spoke: "A lot of birds retreating from the front, driven off by the Austrian fire."

"Birds are always restless before it snows," said General Petar Bojović, commander of the First Army.

"They're taking a bath in the slops from the officers' mess," said General Pavle Jurišić-Šturm, commander of the Third Army.

Vukašin was waiting for General Živković, in charge of the defense of Belgrade, and for General Aračić, commander of the Užice Brigade, to add their explanation of the flocking of so many birds; then they would know the opinions of all the top commanders of the Serbian army about the advance guard of the Austro-Hungarian army, operating in the Balkans under the command of Field Marshal Oscar Potiorek.

"Colonel Pavlović, please tell the guard to shoot at that black mass crawling on the prison roof!" ordered Prince Alexander.

"Please don't frighten the people, Your Highness. What will they think when they hear shooting now? Shooting at jackdaws!" said Pašić.

"They'll be thinking a lot worse things when they see us covered with ravens. You might as well hoist a mourning flag, Prime Minister," said the Commander in Chief, turning his back on the High Command and the members of the government.

"The people aren't frightened of anything because it's black, Your Highness. They've got used to black and all it stands for. But there's no need to remind them that things are black for us too."

Colonel Živko Pavlović, head of the Operations Section of the High Command, hesitated at the door, then whispered, "I'll do something about it," and left the room.

Vojvoda Putnik coughed painfully. Carts carrying the wounded to the hospital creaked and shook along the road. Was Serbia to fall one more century behind Europe and to remain forever at her lowest point, confined to the East? Vukašin looked questioningly at Mišić. What if he thought the same as Putnik? They had surely talked things over. Vojvoda Putnik's adjutant brought him a cup of tea; he took a little bottle of medicine from the upper pocket of his jacket and poured a few drops into the tea. Everybody watched him, waiting for something else to happen or for the meeting to be adjourned until the next day.

Nikola Pašić could feel the embarrassed and angry looks thrown at him by the generals, ministers, and Opposition leaders. Once again he must decide, as on July 24, when an answer had to be given to the Austro-Hungarian ultimatum. He could feel his beard quivering; his cane, resting between his knees, was shaking slightly in his hands. For a few moments at least he must remove himself from the range of those glances and calm the mental turmoil provoked by Putnik's words. He got up and walked slowly over to the window; the prison courtyard was filled with the screeching of the jackdaws enshrouding the bare lime trees and the roof of the prison.

If Putnik firmly believed that further resistance was hopeless and that it was necessary to capitulate, how long would it be before the soldiers in the trenches were also convinced of this, with their empty bags and cartridge belts, their tattered peasant shoes, without overcoats, and continually spattered with bullets? When the most intelligent soldier in Serbia, the steadiest head in the High Command, considered that catastrophe was imminent, dare he, a politician, refuse to accept this? Dare the government believe something different? The fate of Serbia was in the hands of the diplomats! That meant in his hands. What should he do? Was there anything at all he could do to change the course of events and halt the process of collapse? All those people sitting in silence behind him were waiting for him to speak first, to take some definite line, although he had brought them here so that he would not have to make a decision alone. What line should he take? If he agreed to capitulation now, then why had he not accepted the ultimatum from Vienna on July 24? Why had over a hundred thousand soldiers perished and the people been reduced to utter exhaustion? If he refused to accept Putnik's suggestion and went on with the war, convinced that it was hopeless and would not last long, what was the point of exposing the army and the people to destruction? *A war for honor and glory, for heroic defeat, is not my sort of war,* he thought. *The only war for me is a war to save Serbia, but salvation can be found only in victory.* As soon as Austria-Hungary's punitive expedition began to kill, indiscriminately, men and women, old and young, those who resisted and those who surrendered, there was no doubt that Vienna and Budapest had decided to implement their old slogan: *Serbia delenda est!* And how could you seek peace from an enemy with such a war aim? How could you ask for mercy and conduct diplomatic negotiations? They would not concede this right. All they wanted was capitulation, in which Serbia would renounce her very existence and disappear completely. How could he conduct diplomatic negotiations after three months of fighting when Vienna had refused to have any dealings with him even before the war? It's we or they. How can Putnik not see this? Or perhaps he thinks the war has already been decided for us. *He hasn't convinced me, though.* A sick man has a jaundiced view of everything. If we must be annihilated, then the only thing left for us is a fight to the finish. This must be clear to the generals. While we can scratch those who attack us with our fingernails, we will not surrender. This sort of patriotism had always made him shudder. But victory was possible in such a war. Never mind how improbable it seemed now. But he would not be able to convince anyone of this gambler's hope this evening. The Allies were his last hope; they wouldn't dare permit the collapse of Serbia. It was not in their interests to have Serbia destroyed. For the sake of the Balkans and the Dardanelles, they must defend her, since they were thereby defending themselves. But which of the generals, who among all these people, would believe this when he informed them of the Allies' firm demand that Macedonia should be given to Bulgaria? He could not possibly dispel Putnik's lack of confidence in the possibility of further resistance by faith in the Allies alone.

Pašić dropped his cane, and the sound roused him. Vukašin Katić came up to him and whispered:

"I was surprised by Putnik's reaction. It's extremely dangerous. The effect on the army will be disastrous."

"We ought to patch up our differences. Agreement could save us, Vukašin."

"The only kind of agreement that can save us is one that settles our differences of this evening."

"It would be better if you were to keep your opinions to yourself until the war's over."

"Perhaps our fate is indeed being decided this evening. But please let's not accept that too easily."

"Listen, Vukašin. If we don't accept our fate like sensible men, fate itself will decide against us. The officers will tear you to bits like mad dogs. And you know all too well what Alexander would like to do with you."

"I do, indeed, but you must know that I can't support you against my own convictions."

"Are your convictions more important than the survival of the country? I've talked to you like a son and told you what you should know."

In the courtyard soldiers were shouting and throwing stones at the prison roof and the branches of the lime trees; the flight of the jackdaws cut across the windowpanes.

As she stared at the huge shrapnel wound, the gaping hole in the man's back, Milena Katić was thinking about Lieutenant Vladimir Tadić: Let him lose an arm, both arms, even his legs, as long as his head was unharmed so that she could look at him, look at his face and his eyes. As long as she could look at him and listen to his breathing.

Doctor Sergeev's shadow fell across the wound. The wounded man gritted his teeth and gave a barely audible groan under the skillful probing of Sergeev's tweezers; he was removing pieces of shrapnel from the wound, muttering "Good, very good" in Russian. The wounded man was sweating. Milena stroked the nape of his neck.

The best thing was a light wound. In the leg, through the thigh. No, not the thigh, the bullet might pierce a vein and he could bleed to death before he got to a hospital; or the leg would be badly bandaged and perhaps turn gangrenous. The arm was near the heart, so not the left arm. What if he was simply concussed and brought to the hospital? No. There might be brain concussion, burst blood vessels. Please, God, no concussion. Suppose a bullet passed through his shoulder, but without touching his lungs or a blood vessel? He was a hero; he'd already been wounded twice; he could bear one more wound so that she could bandage it, look after him, and watch him while he slept; so that they could be together for at least a month, even if it was in the hospital.

"Don't stroke me like that, nurse!" snapped the wounded man.

She jerked her fingers away from his hair and felt a flush rising to her cheeks. Then she once more stared at the wound, which was bleeding copiously under the doctor's tweezers.

"A letter for Milena Katić!" cried the hospital clerk from outside the door.

She threw the dish containing instruments onto the table, jumped over two wounded men lying on the floor, went out into the corridor and grabbed the letter: was it from Vladimir or from Ivan? From Ivan, she whispered, disappointed; leaning against the wall she read:

Dear Milena,

In your letter, which arrived only this morning, you raked me over the coals, just like a sergeant on parade, for my "lack of patriotic spirit" and my "faintheartedness," for the "foreign and bookish ideas which have poisoned my soul." But I must tell you once more that I am not at all happy that you have become "a real Serbian girl," a "fascinating Kossovo maiden." *

She stopped reading, frightened and hurt by Ivan's words. She stared at the page as the orderlies carried past her a wounded man screaming for help. Did her brother really think that? She read on.

Worn out by the most stupid drilling we have had since I came to this "school," and disappointed by your letter, this evening I again thought about what Father calls "the people" and about your Serbia; I can no longer understand either what this Serbia is or how anyone can love the people. The Serbia of my school days has been trampled underfoot during our drill and torn to shreds by sergeants and lieutenants. In the barracks, in front of the cauldron, and in our dormitory (that realm of snores) I feel revolted by the mob, the mass, those sheer numbers that are called "the people." The people en masse are horrible when they are literate and educated; but what will the real people be like, the illiterate peasants? I dare not think what is waiting for me when I find myself cheek by jowl with them at the front.

Milena wiped away her tears with the edge of her nurse's veil. She must send this letter to her father.

But don't be afraid, my dear sister. Your brother is not a coward or a deserter. That is precisely why I came back from Paris and why I am here now. I do not lack resolution to "die for the homeland." I will die, not because

*A reference to the legendary Serbian girl who succored the Serbian soldiers at the Battle of Kossovo in 1389. [Translator.]

of "King and Country," but for purely personal reasons, which are not of a heroic nature; they lie beyond history and national ideals.

What was he saying? What was happening to him? Why had he enlisted as a volunteer when he was such a feeble creature?

I repeat, Milena: there's no aim in the world worth being herded into barracks for; no ideal for which one should spend a single day drilling under the sergeant's orders; no flag that deserves to be saluted. Just listen to this! "Chests forward, stomachs in, hands straight at your sides, heads up, eyes straight ahead, keep absolutely still and don't move a muscle even if there's a bullet on your nose." Don't you find that ridiculous and shameful?

No, she didn't. He was the one who was bringing shame on himself, and disgrace to their father!

For me there is no freedom that justifies the hierarchy of the military, that gives the commander and the officers the right to curse us and box our ears. All on account of a missing button, or laughing while standing in line, or not extinguishing the lamp the minute the bell rings for "lights out." What sort of sacred traditions are these, in the name of which the sergeants make us drill all day long and march through underbrush until we're "torn to ribbons"? First they humiliate you by these "rules of military service," which degrade a man totally, then they ask you to "die like a hero for the homeland." Don't you find all this business of the state, the army, and the homeland loathsome?

She'd never heard any Serb talk like that! Not even the socialists! Either he was a great weakling and coward, or else they had addled his brain there in Paris. It would break their mother's heart.

I have ceased to believe in any freedom and democracy that contains such a senseless instrument of human degradation as the army. And it's only invalids who are not liable for military service. It's only moral nonentities who can avoid the army today. I don't want to be a moral nonentity among my contemporaries; I want to go through this total degradation with people like my friend Bogdan Dragović, with whom I share a pallet and who is my partner in the line—that's why I am a volunteer and why I am fighting in this war. Please try to understand and don't write me any more letters containing the words "national" and "patriotic."

Your loving brother,
Ivan

Milena gazed in surprise at the last word, "Ivan," written in large, calligraphic letters, quite unlike Ivan's usual handwriting. It was as though someone else had signed the letter. That is how cowards think, she concluded unhappily, putting the letter in her bosom and hurrying into the bandaging room.

Once more she was gazing at a wound: a man's shattered hip. It could be Vladimir's or Ivan's.

The orderlies brought three badly wounded men into the bandaging room and put them down on the floor. The banging of the stretchers and the groaning of the men made her hands tremble. Doctor Sergeev frowned as the tweezers and scissors clinked in the instrument dish, and removed the shell splinters from the wounds more roughly and quickly.

"Is there anyone here from the Drina Division?" she asked, raising her voice above the groans of the wounded and the quarreling of the orderlies; no one answered. Dr. Sergeev banged his tweezers on the edge of the instrument dish.

"Give me some gauze, Milena!"

"Please answer me: what's your division?"

"The gauze, Milena!"

She gave him the gauze, then repeated her question.

"I'm from the Fifth Regiment of the Drina Division," said one of the wounded men from his stretcher; he was lying across the threshold with only his head in the bandaging room.

"Which battalion?"

"Third."

"Is anyone here from the First Battalion? Do you know Lieutenant Vladimir Tadić, the commanding officer of the Third Platoon of the First Battalion?"

"No, I don't; there's a lot of them out there. And they're still bringing them in."

Milena put down the dish of surgical instruments, wiped her bloodstained hands on her apron, and went up to the stretchers on which the newly arrived wounded were lying. She bent down quickly and stared at an unshaven, ravaged face. In the fading light she could see the man's strong spasmodic shaking.

"Do you know Lieutenant Vladimir Tadić?" she asked timidly. "He's my cousin."

"I don't know him. The officers are getting killed now too. Everybody is getting killed."

"But aren't you from the First Battalion of the Fifth Regiment?"

"I don't know him. And I don't care."

She leaned over a third man: she could see his damp face, the dried blood on his lips. She put her hand on his forehead.

"Are you from the Fifth Regiment of the Drina Division?" she asked; under her hand she felt the convulsive movements of his weeping. "Don't be afraid. Everything will be all right. Do you know Lieutenant Vladimir Tadić? He's in the First Battalion of the Fifth Regiment."

"A lot of them got killed this morning," he whispered.

She straightened up and went into the corridor. *What did I do this morning? I went to bed at daybreak and fell asleep at once. I was asleep, and he was charging, with shells falling all around him.* She went outside and stood on the steps: the lamps were being lit in the gathering darkness, orderlies were shouting, and men and oxen were moaning. Men groaned as they were being loaded onto stretchers. If anything has happened to him, I'll cut off my hair, put on a uniform, and leave for the front tonight. Trembling, she ran down the steps. In her letters she had not dared to tell Vladimir of her resolve to join him at the front. Other protestations of love were not enough. She would write and tell him tonight. If he had not already been brought here. His last letter was so lighthearted and funny, the only one free from jealous suspicions. Heroes feel cheerful before their death; she had heard this from several wounded men.

She went from cart to cart. "Is anyone here from the First Battalion of the Fifth Regiment of the Drina Division? Don't swear at me, soldier; I'm looking for my cousin. Please answer me, and I'll bandage your wounds. Where are the wounded from the First Battalion of the Fifth Regiment, drivers?"

"Hey, lady! You're pretty, real pretty, but you're not wearing pants and you don't have an officer's stripes, so don't yell at us."

"Yes, I do!"

"What stripes do you have?"

"I'm eighteen years old and I'm a volunteer nurse. Where is your daughter? And what's your sister doing?"

Jumping over the shafts, she walked around the oxen, stepping over puddles and excrement, and looked into another cart. "Do any of you boys know Lieutenant Tadić?" she asked imploringly.

The wounded men were raging and cursing because they were not being taken into the hospital. "He's my commanding officer," said one of the men.

"When did you last see him?" she asked, leaning over the whisper coming from the straw in the cart.

"This morning. When we were ordered not to abandon our position. But more than half our battalion was killed between noon yesterday and daybreak today. I got hit about breakfast time."

"What was he doing the last time you saw him?"

"When I last saw him he was swearing at the sergeant and running toward our machine gun."

"And you didn't see him again? Or hear anything about him?"

"No. The Fritzies rushed out of the wood, and the stubble field suddenly turned green. Then the howitzer mowed us all down one by one. That's when they chopped off my legs."

Milena walked up to the hospital building and pressed her forehead against the wall.

"Tell Colonel Pavlović to come here! That's enough banging!" ordered the Commander in Chief sternly, standing at the window beside Pašić.

"Soon it will be dark and the birds will settle down, Your Highness—we can wait a bit," said Pašić, returning to his place at the conference table.

"We don't have time to wait!"

"There's always time for everything, Your Highness."

"Put the lights on!" ordered the Commander in Chief, shutting the window.

Before the Prince could reach his place at the head of the table, Vukašin took his seat at the foot, but with his eyes fixed on the floor. Was he about to make an irrevocable mistake? No, he was not! He could feel questioning and worried eyes upon him. He would disappoint some people who respected him, and his prewar supporters too. People did not want wise counsels at a time of suffering; they wanted a united front and identical opinions. He lit a cigarette. Light poured down from the ceiling. After a few long puffs, he felt slightly dizzy. But he could hear them talking quite plainly.

"So. Vojvoda, you suggest we capitulate?" said the Commander in Chief at last.

A deathly silence crept over the conference table, over Serbia, between the uniforms and the frock coats; Vukašin could feel its cold, sharp edge on his face. In the light, everything is remembered; but people have their shadows, their doubles, and the conference was full of people and shadows. He had a vague desire to seize General Mišić by the hand, look him straight in the eye, and ask him: Do you realize what's waiting for us if we vote for ending our defense and the war effort? Mišić was gazing thoughtfully at his crossed fingers. Pašić was scratching the edge of the map with his nail. The eyes of all the others were on the pale, swollen face of Vojvoda Putnik, meeting over his gray, aging head. Putnik leaned more firmly against the table and coughed with unconcealed exasperation.

"You have heard the facts. I have drawn my conclusion from them. That is my duty and my right before the homeland."

"Are you suggesting we ask Austria-Hungary for peace? That we abandon our centuries-old struggle for freedom and unity?" Prince Alexander gave him a challenging look, turning around in his chair and leaning on its edge.

Vojvoda Putnik turned toward him and raised his eyes. "I suggest, Your Highness, that we save what can still be saved. If that is possible. That is the function of every national army."

"You are proposing capitulation. Speak plainly, Vojvoda!"

Vojvoda Putnik rose from his seat, glanced at the map of Serbia, and at all those present. Then he turned toward the Commander in Chief and spoke in a deep, choking voice, full of pain and despair.

"I am proposing peace, Your Highness. Peace—for our wretched, bleeding people!"

"It's a disgrace! It's a betrayal! You would defile your country!"

"Peace is no disgrace and does not defile a people struggling against a much more powerful enemy. For this people, one third of our army has died heroically. Peace is a disgrace only for a defeated conqueror. Peace—" Vojvoda Putnik was seized by a choking cough and sank back exhausted.

Nikola Pašić passed him his cup of tea and said in a quiet, anxious voice:

"You had better stop talking now, Putnik. Let others talk, and you listen. Just nod your head when you agree."

Vukašin felt a tremor of sympathy and admiration for the wisdom, conscientiousness, and courage of this aging soldier, who had the rare honor of the supreme military command in a small country whose army had been victorious in two wars. Only a man whose love for his country had no limits could show such moral courage today; and only an innate bravery could be combined with such prudence when all the rest had lost their heads. *Not for anything in the world must I abandon my convictions,* he thought. *A man who does not betray himself does not betray anybody.* He clung to his chair to keep his hands still.

"Vojvoda Stepanović, what do you have to say on this matter?"

"The situation could not be worse, Your Highness," replied Stepanović, the victor of the Battle of Cer, speaking in a clear tenor voice, with a stern expression on his stiff, official face. The scraping of chairs and restless movements of hands and eyes that followed his announcement indicated the surprise it had provoked. Even Mišić made no attempt to conceal a frown. Vojvoda Stepanović continued in clear, clipped tones.

"After fifty days of ceaseless fighting and bloodshed, our army has suffered a moral collapse. Only by superhuman efforts can we keep our troops from cracking up completely."

Nikola Pašić began tapping with his cane again, staring at his knees.

"I have brought up the last reserves of manpower and munitions," continued Stepanović. "For three days my army has had no ammunition for its artillery. What more can I say?" he cried in a quavering voice and dropped his eyes.

Vukašin stared at this officer who had won the first decisive battle for Serbia and the Allies and justified hopes of a final victory. Vojvoda Stepanović toyed with the pencil in his hand; around the conference table nobody spoke.

General Petar Bojović, commander of the First Army, looked at all the ministers and politicians in turn, then said in an angry voice, as though slapping their faces:

"We can't carry the wounded from the battlefield. The army is naked and barefoot; only one man in ten has boots and an overcoat. The delivery of food supplies is irregular. We already have looting and mass desertions. The soldiers are demoralized by the corruption and graft behind the lines. If there is no immediate change, disaster is inevitable. If the Allies don't send reinforcements at once—"

"And what do you suggest, General Bojović?"

"I think, Your Highness, that Mr. Pašić and his government should immediately tender their resignations. They are not capable of directing a country at war."

"You're right!" shouted the generals and officers. "The offices and cafés are full of draft dodgers. It is the government's duty to supply war matériel to the army. And what is our government doing? Quarreling in Niš and getting ready to flee to Salonika with their wives and sisters-in-law. It is not the Austrians who have demoralized our army, but you, the party politicians. 'Who are we dying for?' the peasants ask. 'And will you civilian gentlemen tell us why we have to have blood on *our* pants?' "

So they shouted without even asking permission to speak, hurling threats at the ministers and party leaders; all their bitterness against Pašić's Radical supporters—and politicians and civilians in general—

exploded over the conference table, which now itself became a battlefield. Prince Alexander listened to the quarreling with concentrated attention and almost exultant curiosity, but said nothing.

"It's you and your Radicals, Mr. Pašić, who are to blame for the fact that three thousand Macedonian enlisted men have fled to Bulgaria. Because you sent thieves and swindlers and political agitators to be district chiefs and officials in Macedonia. You sprang your supporters out of jail and sent them to the liberated areas to represent the government of Serbia. And they looted Turkish houses, blackmailed prominent citizens, stole taxes, and sold entire forests. Deputies to the Assembly bought estates for trifling sums. It's the fault of you Radicals that the Bulgarian guerrillas are destroying our railroad."

Yes, that's all quite true, thought Vukašin. Hadn't he once written about these abuses in the *Echo* and spoken about them in the Assembly? But hearing it now from the officers, he felt ashamed. Why was Prince Alexander smiling in that curious way? And why was Pašić keeping quiet? He was tapping the floor with his cane and looking straight ahead, as he had done at Niś while they were waiting for the train. Colonel Apis, enormous and indifferent, moved suddenly in his chair and stared at the military map with a lighted cigarette hanging from his lower lip. Perhaps this attack on the government by the officers was Colonel Apis's doing—a flare-up of the bitter feud of the last ten years between his band of conspirators and the politicians to gain complete control of Serbia? Well, if Serbia under Pašić and the Radicals had no future, under Apis and his military junta it would have only a past. Should he open fire on them immediately? But the ministers were hitting back.

"You officers also brought carpets and other things from Macedonia. The colonels and generals did their share of looting; do you want me to give their names?"

"You ministers had better keep quiet! Just before mobilization you found safe jobs on the railroad for your party supporters. You appointed rich peasants as signalmen, stokers, and engineers! Who's to blame for that bad train crash last week? And the time has come, gentlemen, to put this question to you: Why is it that since the beginning of the war the Serbian army—the army that defeated Turkey and Bulgaria—had had a higher sickness rate and more deaths than any army in Europe? It's only in the Spanish colonies and the Philippines that people die as they do in Serbian barracks. And while this is going on you're squabbling over ministerial portfolios and advancing your careers. And getting the state deeper and deeper into debt."

"If the Serbian peasants had such a poor opinion of their government as you military gentlemen, they would have already surrendered to the Austrians," Pašić broke in, speaking in a tired, distant voice.

Silence descended upon the meeting. The jackdaws and crows had stopped cawing, the movement of the carts carrying the wounded was only a distant rumble. There was no sound but the labored breathing of Vojvoda Putnik. Vukašin looked at Pašić's white beard nodding over the map of Serbia and listened to his measured, even words.

"Fortunately for Serbia, her people do not think their government is the worst in the world. If the government were really as bad as you gentlemen say it is, what are the people showing us then by dying on the battlefield? They show that they are indestructible! And that they love their freedom so dearly—even our very imperfect freedom—that they are ready to defend it by any sacrifice. Because this freedom of ours, made up of many different things, is still freedom. It is my belief, gentlemen, that this evening it is our duty to take into account the opinion of the people."

Mišić laughed aloud; in the general amazement he prolonged his laughter and made it sound even more scathing.

"What is so funny, General?"

"There's always a time and a place when truth will out! That's what I'm thinking, Your Highness."

"And what do you think of our military situation?"

"In the presence of my Commander in Chief, I give my opinion only when asked."

"Well, I'm asking you now."

"We haven't yet lost the war. And if we do things right, we won't lose it."

Everybody waited for Mišić to say something more. But he just stared at the Commander in Chief, who reflected for some time before finally answering: "What do you suggest?"

"First of all, that in both the High Command and all branches of the staff, three words be strictly forbidden under the severest penalties: 'defeat,' 'catastrophe,' and 'capitulation.' "

"That's some wisdom," cut in Vojvoda Stepanović, without looking at Mišić.

"No wisdom at all. It's what I believe—a belief by no means shared by all the people around this table. In my opinion, it is vital that they should share my convictions."

There was a scraping of chairs and a rustling of the war map of Serbia. Putnik restrained his cough, staring wide-eyed at his assistant.

Vukašin gave Mišić a questioning look. The situation could not be as straightforward as Mišić made out, nor could the solution of an obviously difficult situation be achieved by such simple means, which Mišić reduced essentially to an attitude of optimism—optimism regarded as a duty and an obligation. Still, he felt a certain pride that he and Mišić were friends.

"Is that all you have to say, General?"

"No, Your Highness. It's the beginning."

"Then tell us how you think we can get out of this situation!" The Commander in Chief banged the map with his fist, then almost jumped up from his chair, as though frightened by this action. "What are we to *do*, Mišić?"

"Instead of the extreme and extraordinary measures to raise the morale of the troops proposed by Vojvoda Stepanović and General Bojović, I suggest simply the conscientious application of ordinary military measures—measures familiar to all competent brigade commanders and responsible officers." Mišić fell silent and began to roll a cigarette.

All eyes were fixed on his fingers holding the paper into which he was slowly and carefully packing silky yellow strands of tobacco from a leather pouch. Vukašin wanted to catch his eye, and at least by this means to convey to him the dissatisfaction, even disappointment, that he felt at his very modest and perhaps pointless proposals in a situation that required exceptional attitudes and decisions, and that gave him, Mišić, the opportunity to convince everybody present that he was the man who should immediately be given the supreme command.

The Commander in Chief rose nervously from the table, walked quickly toward the other end of the room, and stood by the window, now darkened by the evening sky. The murmuring sound under the eaves filled the conference room. It was sharply interrupted by the quick steps of Prince Alexander walking back to the table.

"Do you really think, General Mišić, that what you propose is enough at a time like this, when absolutely everything is against us except, perhaps, God?" he asked in an unexpectedly appealing voice.

"Everything has always been against us, Your Highness. Nobody has helped us to survive during the last few centuries. We have survived only thanks to our own patience and our will to survive. Nothing else has helped us. Now our confidence in ourselves seems to be wavering. The lack of all the other things we don't have will not decide our fate."

"Wars are fought, Mišić, with soldiers, weapons, and munitions. With food and clothing. With supplies! With capable commanding officers," said Vojvoda Putnik, obviously angry.

Pašić stopped tapping with his cane.

"Quite right, Vojvoda. When you think about our situation, you naturally have in mind, first and foremost, the war and the facts relating to the war. But I am trying to consider the fate of the people. You are concerned about the soldiers, while I am looking at the people. To you, munitions are all-important, whereas for me it is the will to survive."

Vojvoda Putnik spoke with a great effort, from the depths of his chest. "To whom are you addressing these words, Mišić?"

"To all of us, if I may say so."

He was cut short by a buzz of dissatisfaction and reproaches and the entry of Putnik's adjutant, bringing telegrams from the front. Everybody except Pašić and Apis watched Putnik anxiously while he read them. Vukašin began to have doubts as to whether Mišić would support him when he protested against sending the students to the front. Maybe Mišić was the very man who was pressing for this most strongly in the High Command. Would he have to come to grips with him now?

Vojvoda Putnik sipped a few drops of tea, still holding the telegrams. Then, with a look at the Commander in Chief, he spoke slowly and without a trace of agitation.

"Tonight we will have to abandon all those positions we have somehow managed to defend until today. The High Command must leave Valjevo tomorrow evening."

In front of Vukašin's eyes, Serbia seemed to sag on the military map: trees moaning in the forests, rain drenching the unharvested cornfields and vineyards, muddy streams rushing forward, swollen rivers meandering through the small country, unaware of where they were going.

In the hospital courtyard, Djordje Katić and Tola Dačić were going from cart to cart looking for their sons. Tola went in front and asked the questions, and Djordje followed him with a lantern.

"What's your division, soldier?" asked Tola, grasping the upright post of a cart and leaning toward a wounded man covered with wet hay.

"Morava."

"Morava first draft?"

"No, second. Do you have a drop of brandy? I haven't seen a piece of bread for two days."

"I'll give you some brandy." He couldn't give him any bread; it wouldn't do to bring his sons half-eaten bread. He handed the wounded man his flask.

"Are there heavy losses among the cavalry?" asked Djordje, clutching one of the drivers by his sleeve.

"I'll say! I saw with my own eyes a stream full of dead horses."

Djordje lowered his lamp: its light flowed over the bloody puddle in which he was standing; his knees buckled and he moved back with a jerk. He stared at the bloody puddle in front of him and saw the stream full of dead horses.

"What about the troopers?" he whispered. The driver did not hear him.

Tola bent over the wounded man and poured some brandy between his lips; a wet, emaciated ox stepped toward Tola, splashing through the bloody puddle, and began to lick and sniff at his bulging bag, to which some blue laths and a small ax were tied. The pouring rain obscured his vision, drenching the oxen and carts with blood; about noon a wounded trooper had said to Djordje: "After we fled across the bridge, I never saw Adam again."

Tola moved on and called to him to shine the lantern on the wounded men lying in the carts, covered with straw, rarely with a tent flap or overcoat. Djordje walked cautiously, afraid of stepping in a bloody puddle or patch of mud. He hardly heard Tola's questions.

"Do you know the Dačići from Prerovo? They're my sons. Three of them still alive, if the good Lord hasn't deceived me. And d'you know Adam Katić, my boy? What's your regiment, soldier? How come you don't know the gunner Aleksa Dačić? He should be sewing on his corporal's stripe by now. Nearly got the Karageorge Star at Šabac. Mike and Blaža—they're in the infantry, Seventh Regiment, Third Battalion. How come you don't know your comrades in arms? Adam Katić is a trooper in the cavalry squadron of the Morava Division, second draft, the best-looking trooper in the whole division, a real fine young man; you must know him if you're a trooper. D'you know when he was last seen alive? Was there heavy fighting when you came past that mill? Take a swig of brandy. Go on, have another. D'you know who was wounded in that field?"

Djordje banged his head against a cart.

"They all got out of the field, d'you hear, Djordje? What are you doing hiding under your cart, driver? Those two men inside are both dead. Do you know their names? What d'you mean that's none of my business? If a man walks this earth with a name, pays taxes, registers for military service, and dies for his country, the poor guy should go underground with his own name. So what, if he rots away; at least he'll rot under his own name. Don't you shirk. There're men dying back there, waiting for you, so harness your oxen and get going. Have an apple, soldier. D'you know anyone by the name of Dačić, or Adam Katić? What are you getting so mad about? Four rifles fired their bullets for Serbia from my family; three still left. And I'm looking for them; that's the least I can do! If I don't manage to find them, I hope somebody will give them a change of clothes and a bite to eat; I don't want them to be buried naked and without a cross. Why, soldier, my sons in the infantry are in that battalion! Was everybody killed? How could *everybody* get killed, for God's sake? You say Blaža got hit in the leg? You mean Blaža Dačić? What d'you mean, you don't know his surname, damn you? Who told you they're going to cut off both his legs? You hear that, Djordje? They're going to cut off his legs; the doctors will cut them off with a saw."

"Now it's your turn, Prime Minister," said Prince Alexander, sitting on the edge of his chair, his hands under the table.

Vojvoda Putnik sipped his tea and leaned toward Pašić. The ministers frowned. Nikola Pašić twisted his beard as though in surprise, raised his eyebrows, and stared at the map. Dare he inform them of the Allies' demands? That would shatter the last miserable illusion about those Allies. What kind of courage and wisdom could save a people being annihilated by its enemies and sacrificed by its allies and friends? No cunning or worldly wisdom could save such a people.

"The Allies have demanded that we immediately cede Macedonia to the Bulgarians—as far as the frontier proposed in 1912," said Pašić, directing his glance toward Vojvoda Putnik.

"What's that?" said Mišić, evidently disturbed, or perhaps dissatisfied, by Pašić's tone.

Pašić did not look toward him; he kept his eyes on Vojvoda Putnik, whose face was contorted by a fit of coughing. For a few moments there was total silence, while they waited for Pašić to say something even more shattering.

Vojvoda Stepanović could no longer restrain himself. "Never!" he shouted angrily, then added, "Not at any price!"

The other senior officers, equally indignant, supported him. "Never—not while there is a single Serbian soldier left! It's a disgrace! While we die for the Allies, they hand the Bulgarians Serbian territory on a platter!"

"That, gentlemen, is the price the Bulgarians demand for entering the war on the side of the Triple Entente—that is, our Allies," said Pašić, implying both by his tone and by his words that he was trying to make a case for the demands of the Allies.

Vukašin noticed that Prince Alexander too was confused, and did not know what to do with his hands. Pašić said nothing, but continued to look straight at Vojvoda Putnik.

"Let them give the Bulgarians Thrace!" said Ljuba Davidović, the leader of the Independent Party, indignantly. "Or let them have the Dardanelles as the price of their entry into the war, but *not* Serbian territory. Turkey has declared war on Bulgaria—why don't the Allies compensate her at Turkey's expense?" He turned to Vukašin, his political ally, with a significant look—a look of warning, enjoining silence, which Vukašin understood.

The leaders of the other Opposition parties, Ribarac and Marinković, hastened to explain themselves. "We are a sovereign state, gentlemen! It's in defense of our sovereignty that we are fighting Austria-Hungary! Surely we don't have to sacrifice our sovereignty for the Allies—to pay for their having the Dardanelles by sacrificing Macedonia? To defend their colonial interests in the East by giving up Serbian territory? Not at any price!"

"The Russians and the English insist, and the French share their opinion, that if we don't allow the Bulgarians to occupy Macedonia immediately, they will openly support Germany and Austria-Hungary. And if the Bulgarians don't join the war on the side of the Allies, neither will the Rumanians or the Greeks." Pašić continued to speak in the same firm, calm voice, looking at each of the commanding officers in turn.

"The Bulgarians will never fight on the Allied side!" broke in Vojvoda Putnik.

Pašić appeared to attach no importance to this remark.

"If the Rumanians and Greeks had entered the war against the

Triple Alliance," he continued, "Austria-Hungary would soon have capitulated in the face of the big Russian offensive in the Carpathians." He stopped speaking in order to observe the officers better, and nodded affirmatively to Vukašin, who did not understand this gesture. "And we would have been saved. That's what they tell us in St. Petersburg and London. The collapse of Turkey and the fate of the entire Balkan Peninsula, so our Allies assert, depend entirely on our surrendering territory to Bulgaria. Let us give up Macedonia first, and the rest will follow."

Pašić had begun speaking ironically, but ended in a trembling voice, almost a whisper. Over the conference table, with Serbia spread out upon it, amid the glances and audible breathing, there suddenly developed a sense of agreement between the officers and the politicians, the High Command and the government. Prince Alexander's face had the expression of a hurt, cheated schoolboy. At last Vukašin understood Pašić's tactics that evening: the mention of Macedonia would reduce Putnik to silence and put an end to his extremely dangerous despair. The military leader who had liberated Macedonia, and won fame and recognition from this victory, could not sacrifice that territory now without jeopardy to the very core of his being; his sober appreciation of facts would have to yield to an irrational, but higher and more personal, inconsistency. Putnik would have to opt for suffering, or his actions would cease to have any meaning for either the army or the people. He must go on fighting, even to defeat.

Carts carrying wounded still passed along the street, and the rumbling of their wheels on the cobblestones dampened the conversations among the ministers and Opposition leaders.

The revelation of Allied pressure on the Serbian government—Vukašin continued to sort out his impressions—rendered any further attack on that government's policy by the High Command and the officers impossible and meaningless. The dissatisfaction of the officers with the government, and with Pašić at its head, was transformed into anger directed against the Allies and the Bulgarians. What would be the next step? No vital problem had been solved; the crisis was getting worse; military collapse was inevitable, with increasingly serious consequences. That masterly politician had won, that evening, a political victory that was in fact meaningless: agreement between the government and the High Command that the demands of the Allies could not be accepted. But what then? What would Serbia gain from her traditional decision in favor of pie in the sky?

She would cease to exist as a state, and sink once more to the lowest point of historical significance.

"And what compensation would we receive, Prime Minister, in return for the territory between Skoplje and Struga?" asked Ribarac, the leader of the Liberal Party.

"A guarantee for Bosnia and Hercegovina, and some territory on the Adriatic coast."

"How much?"

"Well, something. Because Italy doesn't want us united with Croatia and Slovenia. Italy is demanding the whole of Dalmatia and Istria as a price for entering the war on the Allied side. So that's all we would get for our great sacrifice."

"And they're still annoyed because we won't give the Bulgarians *our* territory!" cried Prince Alexander.

"Macedonia to the Bulgarians, and Dalmatia to the Italians! Our lands are the price to be paid for their military co-operation with the Allies. *Our* Allies!" Prince Alexander continued to speak in an agitated tone, saying that not since the Battle of Kossovo had Serbia faced greater trials.

I should have made my position clear immediately, thought Vukašin, shuddering. Now that all the others had made up their minds, he would appear not only a traitor, but also a fool. He would be alone against them all. No, he couldn't do it. But he must speak. He must see it through to the end.

"Your Highness, may I say something?"

"Please do," replied Prince Alexander, giving him a withering look.

That look helped him to pull himself together, and gave him courage.

"It is obvious, gentlemen, that our survival as a nation and all our future progress are now at stake, because of both the situation at the front and the attitude of our Allies. But we must also consider our own reaction and behavior." His voice seemed to fail him; he could see that they were all against him. "We must take as our starting point the fact that the Serbian question has become a European question. Until today we have never solved any of our national problems according to our own will, and by our own efforts. We have fought, but the Great Powers of Europe have decided the outcome of our struggles according to their interests. They have assigned us sometimes victories, sometimes defeats."

"We have no time for your theories, Mr. Katić."

"But we have no time for misconceptions either, Your Highness. We have no time at all to take the wrong road now."

"Then tell us which road will save us, Mr. Katić!" said Prince Alexander in a challenging tone.

By now Vukašin was calm and sure of himself; he no longer felt those waves of fear. Strength seemed to pour into him from his opponents. Convinced that he was right, he also felt an unusual sense of joy—the delirious, excited satisfaction of defending the truth and sacrificing himself for a great cause. He continued in a quiet, intense voice.

"I can't tell you that, Your Highness. But let me finish what I was trying to say. I want to turn your attention to the following facts. Our entire future as a nation is conditioned by this European war. At no time in history have there been such favorable circumstances for a final decision on the Serbian question—that is, for uniting the Serbian people. But such a union might be achieved with the full support of the Allies, though not without it. Any divergence between our national program and that of the Allies will be catastrophic for us as a nation."

"From one point of view, you're quite right, Vukašin," broke in Pašić, who continued drumming his fingers on the edge of the map.

"What do you suggest, Mr. Katić?"

"I propose, Your Highness, that we accept the Allied demands," he said decisively. All the faces around the table had the same expression—astonishment succeeded by gloom. He raised his voice. "But we must make firm conditions."

"What conditions and recompense can there be for territory that has been ours for centuries?"

"We must insist that, after the defeat of Austria-Hungary, the Allies will guarantee that all the South Slav peoples shall be united; that their entire ethnic area shall be included in our new state."

"What use are such guarantees to us? Why should we fight for the union of all the South Slav tribes? You are advocating the betrayal of our nation, Mr. Katić!"

All the generals and most of the ministers supported the Prince with shouts of anger. Pašić stared at the war map. General Mišić looked gloomily at his fists crossed over the map. He too thinks I'm a traitor, concluded Vukašin, but that didn't bother him. On the contrary; he looked at them all in turn, sure of himself and convinced that he was right.

"I consider it vital to the interests of Serbia that part of Macedonia be sacrificed to Bulgaria."

"It's not just a part. It's more than half of Macedonia, which we, and not the Bulgarians, liberated from the Turks."

"I don't dispute that, Vojvoda Putnik. But let me finish what I have to say. It's you who sought this conference, not me. But now that we are here, we must be on an equal footing or I'll leave the meeting." The murmuring stopped suddenly. "Here are the facts I want to put before you. By accepting the demands of the Allies, we put them under an obligation to send us immediate help. And if Bulgaria enters the war against Austria-Hungary—which the Allies assure us she will, followed by Rumania and Greece—then, gentlemen, the war will end sooner. The sacrifice of Serbian lives, which has so far been enormous, will be smaller. In short, Serbia will be saved—yes, gentlemen, saved!"

"No, Serbia will not be saved! And if there is smaller loss of life, there will also be fewer victories. And the centuries-old aspirations of the Serbian people will be betrayed."

"I repeat, Your Highness, the war will be over sooner. We will get out of the present crisis—which might more aptly be called a catastrophe. Is anything more urgent today than that?" He wanted to catch Mišić's eye, but Mišić continued to stare at his fists on the war map. "Anyway, if we don't come to an agreement with the Bulgarians over Macedonia, they will settle the question themselves to their own advantage, by war—together with the Germans, of course."

"In the name of what future are you suggesting that we renounce the fruits of victory from two wars? Sacrifice your own patrimony, but not Macedonia!"

"That is a small sacrifice compared with those we will make if we fight alone in the Balkans against Austria-Hungary and Germany. I would like to stress once more, Your Highess, that the sacrifice of half of Macedonia is the greatest contribution we can make to the future peace of the Balkans. The Bulgarians will be deprived of any historical or political justification for hostility toward Serbia. And we will be saved from our present plight."

"Vukašin, the Bulgarians would not join the war on the side of the Allies even if we gave them Niš as well as Macedonia. In any war the Bulgarians will always be against Serbia. That's part of the geopolitical situation in the Balkans," said Pašić, avoiding his eye.

Once again Tola Dačić was pushed down the steps of the hospital. The doctors had no time to look at lists of newly arrived wounded, whom nobody had been registering since noon, anyway. Some nurses promised to give him information in the morning. But how could he wait until then—and Blaža without his legs? If he at least knew where they had been cut off. If it was only one leg, and under the knee, then he would still look like a man. He would not be able to mow or spray the vineyards, but he would be able to dig.

"Go ahead, Djordje. Ask that nurse."

"I'm afraid to, Tola."

"You heard two of them say that Adam crossed that bridge. Just a minute, miss."

Milena stopped in front of the hospital steps and lifted her lantern. She saw a burly peasant with a big mustache carrying some blue laths on his back, and behind him an oldish man, hidden by his beard, who was looking at her with a scared expression.

"What can I do for you?"

"I've given four rifles for the defense of Serbia. So I don't deserve to be kicked out of the way like a dog in a butcher's shop. This man here is Vukašin Katić's brother; he's looking for his only son. I've got three still alive."

"Which Vukašin Katić?"

"Him that's putting salt on Pašić's tail. But that's their business. You're an educated girl, you must know him. Now don't get mad, miss."

Milena felt embarrassed and also ashamed for some reason. Something really awful must have happened, since her father had not once mentioned his family after breaking with them. He had never talked to her about his childhood or his native village. When she had asked him whether she had a grandfather, he had replied irritably:

"You have. When you've finished at the university, you can go to the village and meet him."

"Why don't you take me now?"

"I'll explain why when you're a university student."

Something terrible must have happened between them. Should she tell them that Vukašin Katić was her father?

"Don't you think Vukašin Katić's brother should be told whether Blaža Dačić's legs were cut off—Blagoje Dačić from the Seventh Regiment of the Morava Division, second draft. Even if you're one of the fine folk, you can surely understand that all a man without legs can do is husk corn and shell beans—if he has any."

"What's your name?"

"I'm Tola Dačić from Prerovo. Servant and neighbor to Djordje here, who is Vukašin Katić's brother. We were real pals when we were kids, Vukašin and me; later, well, you know what happened.

And it's my son Blaža that's got hit in both legs. Be a good girl and see if he's been brought in. If they haven't cut them off yet, for God's sake don't let them take both."

Milena moved nearer to Djordje, her lantern upraised. He didn't look like her father; he seemed miserable.

"And what's your name?" she asked him, lowering the lantern so he could not see her face.

"He's told you my name. Please do what we asked, if you can. And don't ask me a lot of questions," said Djordje angrily, moving away from the lantern.

"I'm Vukašin Katić's daughter," she murmured, and put the lantern behind her.

Djordje gripped Tola's sleeve, astonished; he wasn't sure it was a good thing that this girl was his niece. He stared hard at her: she looked like her father.

"And what is your son's name? My cousin."

"Adam."

"The first man. A wonderful name," she murmured excitedly. So she had a cousin as well as a brother; perhaps she would be bandaging him too. "Excuse me—I didn't tell you that my name is Milena," she said, more embarrassed than ever. What terrible thing had they done to her father that he hadn't forgiven them after twenty years? Or had he hurt them in some way? Her father couldn't do anything bad. Did Ivan know the secret? She would write to him tonight and tell him that they had a cousin, and that she had met her uncle. "I'm afraid I didn't hear you. What did you say?"

"I said first go and see about Blagoje Dačić, Seventh Regiment, Morava Division, second draft. Then come and talk to your uncle."

"All right. Wait here for me." She lifted the lantern to see her uncle's face.

Djordje bowed his head. Where was her brother? Vukašin must have fixed things: sent his daughter off to be a nurse and got his son a safe berth as a clerk in the High Command. So the wolves had eaten their fill and no sheep missing, and he was still a great man among the Serbs. But Adam could die for the sake of his uncle's ministerial portfolio, for the power of the bourgeoisie. Damn their stupid hides!

"Why is that niece of yours walking so slowly?"

"She's a fine lady. Takes after her mother."

"To me she's the image of her father."

"Stop babbling, Tola. I didn't tell her to look for Adam too. Even if he did get across that bridge, there was more fighting and a lot of people got killed. And when a man's riding such a great big horse, you can see him miles away."

"But the Fritzies will shoot at the horse, not the rider. A foot soldier is by himself; he's the only target, Djordje. It's always the infantry that gets it worst. If it's only one leg, he can manage. But if it's both, what in heaven's name will I do with him?"

They fell silent: an orderly came out of the hospital carrying a pail full of bloody limbs; keeping in the shadows, he walked along the wall and disappeared around the corner. Djordje shut his eyes.

"Surely they're not throwing those legs that've been cut off to the dogs? Why don't those damned orderlies give them a decent burial? A man has only two legs, and they take a long time to grow. They're half of a man. We use our legs to save ourselves. We dance on them. A man without legs is nothing but a log, damn them!"

"Shut up! I'll leave you here. I can't stand it any more." Djordje averted his head so as not to see a dead man being dragged out of the hospital by two orderlies; one held his head and the other his feet as they hauled him down the steps and along the wall into a corner.

Tola was about to follow them and see where they threw the body, but just then Milena appeared on the steps with a worried look. She came slowly down, scrutinizing Djordje, who was staring at the puddle in front of him, stooping under his bundle: he wasn't like her father; he was a small man. And he was unhappy. *How can I comfort him?* she thought.

"What news?" asked Tola, coming forward to meet her.

"A wounded man was brought in this evening with a piece of paper inside his jacket. It had the name 'Blaža' written on it, nothing else."

"Blaža? Nothing else?"

"No. Neither his regiment nor his division."

"And?"

"Both of his legs have been amputated. But he will certainly live Doctor Sergeev, the Russian doctor, operated on him. He hasn't regained consciousness yet, so I couldn't ask him any questions."

"Those must have been his legs that bastard brought out a while back!" Tola grabbed Djordje by his shoulders and shook him. "He threw them to the dogs!"

"Now listen, Tola! Your Blaža isn't the only Blaža in the Serbian army! Just be patient; in an hour or so he'll regain consciousness and I'll ask him who he is. Sometimes the drivers change the names on wounded men."

"Thanks, miss. I'll see for myself if those are Blaža's legs," he said, walking after the men who were carrying the dead soldier. They sure were big shanks, from a big, burly man. *So help me God, they could be Blagoje's legs,* he thought.

"Come under the eaves out of the rain, Uncle."

"Will you go right now and check all those lists? Look for Adam, cavalry squadron, First Army," he muttered, not budging.

"I will. Don't worry. Did you know that my father arrived in Valjevo today? They told me he was looking for me." He wasn't pleased by her news. "My father would be very pleased to see you. Several times he was ready to go to Prerovo, to see you and Grandfather. His duties prevented him. Three wars in three years, you know. And then, he's in the Opposition, and you can imagine what his life has been like with Pašić ruling the country."

Djordje shrank under his bag and hung his head under his sheepskin hat. He looked uneasy, as though he was ashamed. *He* must have been to blame for that family quarrel. But he was unhappy. Her father ought to forgive him; he must, now that there was a war on.

"My father told me a lot about your childhood together," she said.

"Your father's lying," interrupted Djordje, raising his head. He looked hard at her: she was just like her father. "And if you want to do something for me, go and look at those lists."

She gazed at him, dumbfounded.

Tola came back, silently took the lantern from Djordje, and ran off into the darkness behind the hospital. At the corner he collided with the orderly. The pail was empty.

"Stop! Where did you empty that pail?"

"What business is that of yours?"

Tola shook him by the shoulders, raising the lantern to see his eyes. "Are a man's legs trash? Cut off, they're still a man's legs."

"Let me go or I'll throw you into the pit." The orderly tried to wrench himself away.

"Aćim Katić's bull couldn't free himself from my grip!"

"All right, what do you want?"

"You tell me whose legs you threw away and where you threw them." He would crush the man's shoulders to powder if he didn't tell him.

"How should I know whose legs the doctors are sawing off, for God's sake? I wipe away the blood and clean up the mess."

"What d'you mean, *mess*?" Tola shook him again. "You filthy little draft dodger, you call a soldier's arms and legs 'mess'? A soldier fighting for Serbia!"

"I'm telling you in plain language all I do is clean up the operating room. Now let me go."

"Don't you be such a bastard. I've given the state four sons. Did those legs come from Blagoje Dačić, Seventh Regiment, Morava Division?"

"I don't know, I tell you."

"Did they come from a big man?"

"I didn't look closely. All I noticed was that the sole of one foot was broken clean off."

Tola let the man go.

"Tell me, my boy, when he was yelling, while those torturers were cutting off his legs, who did the poor fellow mention?"

"They all cry out for their mothers."

"How about a drink? I've got some good brandy." Tola held out his flask.

"I can't now, I have to go."

"All right, but first tell me where those legs were cut off."

"Above the knee."

"Poor devil! Where did you throw them?"

"Into the trash pit. Behind the acacia tree. You'll see piles of limbs and trash there."

"It's not trash, you idiot! Nothing that comes from a man and a soldier is trash."

Tola headed for the pit. He walked slowly past the hospital windows, listening to the groans mingled with shouts and curses. He would recognize Aleksa's ankle at once; he had ankles like an ox. And he could spot Mika's shin in a pile of shins from the scar left by an ox. But Blagoje had only his crooked toe. If the foot was broken off, how would he recognize Blaža's legs? He was stopped short by the stench of rotting flesh and lime. He shone his lantern over the pit: several legs and two arms were sticking out of the lime.

"Your idea amounts to treason, Mr. Katić! If the soldiers could hear you, they'd tear you to pieces!" interrupted General Bojović.

"And who will be the traitor, General, if we do not accept the Allied demands and they refuse to help us, and the Austrians then defeat us and we lose our freedom, our state, and the whole of Macedonia?"

The windows rattled; once more a caravan of carts passed by carrying wounded. They could hear their groans, and the curses of the drivers. Mišić struck a match—a bit too loudly—and lit a cigarette. Still gloomy, he betrayed himself by a quick look. *Does he too think I'm a traitor*? thought Vukašin.

"Shame on you!" shouted the officers and ministers. "What will your son say—a volunteer? And your daughter, who is working as a nurse? How will you face her tomorrow? And who will vote for you after the war, Mr. Katić?"

"You can't offend me or frighten me, since you have no power to judge me here tonight," he said quietly and thoughtfully. "Time will give its verdict—and that, far beyond this Valjevo conference chamber—on your patriotism and my treason. I can say with a clear conscience, if we do not obey the Allies and win over the Bulgarians to our side, we will make a disastrous mistake. Serbia will lose the war, however it may end."

He would have liked to add one more sentence, but was unable to do so because of the sudden hush that enveloped the conference table. Would Ivan and Milena really feel ashamed of their father? Pašić was speaking; he must listen to him.

"If nobody has anything more important to say, I wish to make the following announcement: I cannot act as the leader of a government that would agree to the Bulgarian annexation of Macedonia. I don't think our people would agree to such a sacrifice and disgrace under any circumstances."

He raised his eyes from the map toward Vukašin. The officers and Opposition leaders nodded their approval. Pašić continued.

"But we must be clear about one thing, gentlemen. We can resist the Allies' ultimatum only if we wage the war with our maximum effort. Whatever the cost. Do you agree that the government should inform the Allies that Serbia is ready to fight side by side with them to victory, provided they withdraw their demand that we surrender Macedonia to Bulgaria?"

The ministers agreed; so did the Opposition leaders. The officers were even more decided. Prince Alexander smiled ironically at Vukašin.

"That means you are in favor of fighting to the bitter end, to victory, Putnik?"

"Yes, I am. But how, and with what resources, Prime Minister?"

"With what we have. And in the way that only we can fight."

A sound on the cobblestones broke the silence; the street was shaking from the oxcarts full of wounded. That shaking, thought Vukašin gloomily, was both a warning and a threat to the members of the conference, who decide the fate of those who would die. Their fate was sealed. So was the fate of those who were deciding their fate. And the black night, pressing on the windows of the conference chamber like a wall, confirmed this.

"In the name of the King, my father, and in my own name, I wish to announce, gentlemen, that the Crown will not agree to any demands that would humiliate Serbia or infringe her sovereignty." Prince Alexander spoke in a sharp, curt, serious tone, sitting between the two old men, Pašić and Putnik.

Vojvoda Putnik cut through this solemn hush, crying, "What about ammunition? How are we going to get ammunition for the guns and artillery?" Restraining his cough, he looked at the men around the table: it was a look of despair.

"Today I have again sent urgent messages to France and Russia," replied Pašić. "I have sent them telegrams saying that if we do not receive munitions within a week, the Serbian army will have to stop fighting. But the Greeks are giving us trouble in Salonika, and Bulgarian guerrillas are crossing the frontier and destroying the railroad." Pašić spoke slowly, hardly raising his voice.

The secretary handed him a telegram. As he opened it, he mumbled: "We'll have to deal with them too. Well, let's hope God will pitch in."

"Yes, indeed, only God can help us," Vukašin said to himself. "Everything conspired that it should be so, and we are doing everything to make it so." And what was he going to do now? He felt miserable—so miserable that there was no room for any other feeling. The men around the table were suddenly shrouded in darkness; the lines and arrows on the map were no longer visible; the shape of Serbia was blurred; even the angry murmuring against her Balkan neighbors had died down. Everything around him was growing smaller and moving into the distance. From the street he heard the cries and curses of the men in the supply unit.

He could barely understand what Pašić was saying.

"And I must tell you, gentlemen, about this other telegram. The American embassy in Vienna is very concerned about the Austro-Hungarian prisoners of war. The Americans are not satisfied with the amount we pay captured officers and soldiers. That's what they say. They also assert that prisoners of war do not have proper conditions for the practice of their religion. They ask us to build them chapels and give them Catholic priests." He raised his eyes from the telegram. "Well, we can build them chapels, but how can we give them priests? Unless we take them prisoner too!"

Mišić suddenly interrupted the Prime Minister. "Everyone who can carry a gun must be sent to the battlefield immediately—policemen, clerks, draft dodgers, everyone. And all students—at once!"

Vukašin started. Did he really mean that? Mišić was looking at Pašić and the ministers; above his clenched fist he twirled his thumb as he pronounced his sentence.

"All our intellectuals must be spread throughout the army. The students must bring to our exhausted and decimated troops the first prerequisite of survival: spirit and will. There should be two students in each platoon. No student is to remain on the staff."

Mišić's thumb grew larger as it twirled, and became strangely intimidating: the heads of the officers and ministers were shrouded in a mist.

"Must we give our children—all our children?" Pašić whispered.

"Yes, we must. The Student Battalion must leave Skoplje for the front immediately," said Vojvoda Putnik.

"To the trenches—of course!" added the officers.

"Let's think it over a little. Can't we postpone the decision for a few days?"

"That will be too late, Prime Minister—there is no time for delay," said Mišić implacably.

Mišić too was a father, with two sons at the front and daughters working as nurses; and this Mišić was passing judgment on him, Vukašin Katić. He couldn't say a word; he couldn't even breathe. He stood condemned; that he understood clearly.

Why hadn't he opposed sacrificing the students? Was it simply because he was afraid of those men who had called him a traitor? Was it his ambition, his concern for his political reputation?

Vukašin heard someone coughing behind him. The persistent cough had been following him through the town, a steady accompaniment to the rumbling of wheels on the cobblestones, the creaking of carts, the heavy thud of oxen, and the shouts of drivers. He turned around and saw a peasant walking behind him: a poor wretch weighed down by his fur hat and bent almost double under a big bag. He too was going to the hospital.

"So Ivan must go to the front!" he whispered. He pictured Ivan in the trenches—replacing a sergeant who had been killed, leading his soldiers in a charge, with stones and earth spurting up in front of him. Seething darkness, pouring rain, the smell of gunpowder. No escape from the stench of exploding shells.

Vukašin walked alongside a cart, walking through the puddles: the broken light from an occasional street lamp stabbed at the night; groans and piteous cries for help rose from the carts; drivers beat their wet and exhausted oxen with sticks. Whenever the peasant caught up with him, Vukašin heard his footsteps and heavy breathing. He felt a sudden urge to turn around and look at the little black heap of a man. Perhaps his son was already dead. He wanted to see the man's face. He stopped; the man's back seemed even more bowed, his head lower. What could he say to comfort him? Vukašin continued on his way toward the hospital, walking alongside the cart, immersed in thought. War is a great leveler. Our powers, our actions, our hopes are the same; time allots the same span to us all. The more you try to be different from the rest, the heavier the punishment and the deeper th misery. He hurried to get away from the peasant's heavy breathing. The generals and ministers, Prince Alexander and Pašić, all those dignitaries in the Valjevo courtroom had convinced themselves and others that they were speaking on behalf of this peasant, this poor wretch bowed down under his hat and his bundle, on behalf of those men groaning and bleeding in the carts, cursing their mothers for having borne them, and on behalf of those wet and hungry drivers beating their wet and hungry oxen. What were so many people dying for? Why the boundless suffering? What kind of freedom could compensate those poor wretches whose blood, mingled with rain, was dripping onto the road for even this one night of suffering? Union with those who were fighting to prevent such a union? Unification with those who were killing them and being killed by them—was this the national aim for which absolutely everything should be sacrificed today? Vukašin stopped and leaned against a tree; he saw the peasant standing against the next tree. Where had he come from and how many days had he been hauling that bag with food and a change of clothes for his son? The son might already be dead. He must see Ivan. He would ask General Mišić where he should wait for him. In a passing cart a man was weeping aloud and groaning feebly. Vukašin raised the collar of his coat and hurried on to escape the weeping, but he was overtaken by the heavy labored breathing of exhausted oxen, stinking of excrement and urine, the smell of Prerovo and his childhood.

The hospital grounds were jammed with oxcarts; lamps illuminated the steps leading to the entrance. Vukašin slowly pushed his way through the lightly wounded men being lifted down from the carts. Reaching the steps, he was suddenly overwhelmed by the groans and the clatter of stretchers. He asked an orderly to call Milena.

"Who are you?"

"I'm her father."

"I'm afraid that relationship won't admit you to the surgical unit, sir."

Offended, he pressed himself against the wall. A nurse hurried by. "Can you, please, take me to Milena Katić?"

"She's in the operating room. No one is allowed in there, you know."

"Then would you mind telling her that her father would like to see her for a moment?" The nurse went away without a word. He trembled; the steps loomed over him.

Milena came out of a lighted room; she ran toward him, as she always did, her eyes shining. As though escaping from hot pursuit, she tore open his coat and tried to unbutton his frock coat, to thrust her face right into her father's heart: she nestled under his arm, shaking violently, as if she would stay forever in that protective warmth!

Too agitated to speak, he dropped his cane and clasped her firmly. What would life be without her and Ivan? Nothing was more important than her breathing, her warmth. How could he have let her go off and work as a nurse in wartime?

"Let me have a look at you," he finally whispered.

She pressed her face against his chest with even greater yearning. She would love only her father during the war, no one else. Frightened by the vehemence of her feeling, she suddenly moved away and looked at him tearfully.

It was not enough to stroke her cheeks, as he always did, to kiss her forehead, as he did whenever they met. "Tell your boss you'll be dining and staying with me tonight."

For a long moment she did not speak. *What if they bring Vladimir in and I'm not here*? she thought.

"Hurry and get yourself ready," he urged, hurt by her silence.

"Impossible, Father."

"It's my last night in Valjevo, Milena. And the hospital is sure to be evacuated in two days' time."

"Is Mother very unhappy?"

"You should write to her more often. And longer letters. She's sent you a parcel. You can come and get it."

"I can't come with you, Father," she said, straightening her nurse's veil.

Her eyes were dry now and her apron was flecked with blood. Was she really going away?

"The doctor will be operating all night, and there are only two of us to help. How can I leave him?"

"Are you actually helping in surgery? Looking at operations?"

"Oh, please, Father!"

For a long time he did not speak. She knew he would be hurt if she told him that it was because of Vladimir that she did not want to leave the hospital that night.

"But you couldn't even catch a butterfly," he said, looking at the bloodstains on her apron.

"That was before the war."

"And now, Milena?"

"Now, we're at war, Father."

"You need experience for operations. You have to be tough."

"No. All you need is love. I must go. Come again tomorrow morning about eight."

She started to go and then turned around, trembling: if only she could nestle under her father's arm for one more moment! But she dare not; she would burst out crying.

"Get some rest, Father. I'll be waiting for you at eight o'clock tomorrow morning," she whispered, and quickly ran down the dim corridor.

Vukašin stared at the door of the operating room through which she had vanished. Numb with pain, he picked up his cane and stumbled toward the gate.

On the road he stopped and leaned against a tree. Behind him he heard the familiar cough. He turned around with a shudder: it was the same peasant with the fur hat and the bundle.

"Who are you?" he asked.

"Give me a cigarette," muttered the peasant in a strangely familiar voice. His face was indistinguishable in the darkness.

"Where do you come from?" he asked. The peasant sighed. "Where do you come from?" he repeated. The peasant took a step back. "Is your son in the hospital?"

"I don't know," the peasant whispered.

"What do you mean?" he asked, handing him a cigarette.

"I didn't find him. Light it for me."

Vukašin had heard that voice before somewhere—a long time ago. It had asked him for something, threatened him, quarreled with him; it had groaned and cursed, insulted him and begged him. He had suffered much because of that voice, felt remorse and shame, despised himself, tried hard to forget it; how many lifetimes ago he had heard it, and yet he hadn't forgotten it. He struck a match. The flame lit up the black beard; the small eyes under their heavy brows flashed briefly in its damp, expiring light. He had not changed.

"Djordje!" exclaimed Vukašin, and stepped back. Djordje stood motionless, just as he used to stand in the stables, in the apple orchard, at the door of the winery, and in front of Aćim, who never bothered to conceal his hatred of Djordje when he was angry. Aćim loved Vukašin unjustly, but more because Djordje was silent and motionless, an old man before his time. Even before he married Simka he was an old man with a bristly black beard, an old man in a fur hat. Vukašin had heard that he had a son named Adam in the army. If Adam took after his mother, he must be very handsome. He had been born late in the marriage, and Djordje certainly wasn't his father. Never mind, Djordje had accepted him as his son. If this young man was killed, there would be no more Katići in Prerovo.

"Where's your son?" he whispered.

"I'm looking for him, Vukašin."

Vukašin groped for his brother's hand but could not find it in the darkness. "Is he in Valjevo? He hasn't been wounded, has he?"

"Yesterday I heard he was wounded. Worse yet, today two people told me he wasn't wounded. He's been with the Fourth Regiment since his squadron was wiped out. And now the Fourth Regiment will be wiped out. It's raining, raining bullets," he whispered.

Life hasn't changed us, thought Vukašin. *I too am the same as I was in Prerovo. What can I say to Djordje now?*

"Who told you I was here?"

"Your daughter. And my troubles have driven me to you."

"D'you think it's any easier for me?"

"Everyone thinks he's got it worst," said Djordje, stepping toward him. "I've never asked you for anything for myself," he muttered.

Vukašin drew back, appalled by the barely audible words.

"Save him for me. You can do it. He'd make a good telephone operator. He can read and write, and he's got a clear, strong voice, just right for the telephone. Can you hear me, Vukašin?"

"But why a telephone operator?"

"He won't be an orderly, the obstinate young devil. Doesn't want to be anybody's servant. Last summer I arranged for him to be an orderly to a regimental commander. Out of spite he did some damage and was sent back to the ranks. Then I gave thirty ducats to have him made a hospital orderly. But he wouldn't hear of it, the silly fool. He wrote me: 'I'll be an orderly if you'll let me cut my hands off after the war.' That's what he's like, the silly young devil."

We're brothers, thought Vukašin, stifling an urge to put his hand on Djordje's shoulder. Djordje was coming closer; he could feel his breath.

"For pity's sake, Vukašin, save him for me!"

"How can I save him? I can't even save my own son. Or my daughter; you've seen where she is."

"Yes, you can. You must save Adam for me! He'll die for nothing. Nobody can stop the Fritzies; Serbia is done for. Let somebody survive the disaster."

"We must go on fighting. We must, Djordje," he whispered defensively.

"We must live, not die to suit those generals and ministers, the swine! We lived under the Turks, under the pashas and janissaries, and we'll live under Franz Josef. What do I care about the state? It's my son I need."

"I can't do it. My son is going off to the trenches. I can't save him."

"You can, but you won't. The party, the state, the homeland are more important to you than life itself. You're just like our father; you love power more than anything."

"Don't ask me to do what I can't do even for my own son," cried Vukašin in despair.

"You love nobody but yourself—you and Aćim," groaned Djordje, moving away. The rain poured down on him; his bag sagged even lower. A cart with wounded clattered past. "Then tell me the name of a powerful man with a heart. I've got a bagful of ducats for him." Djordje beat his breast with his fist. "Whatever he wants, I've got it."

"Don't you understand, Djordje? To whom can I say: Here is a bagful of ducats; now please transfer Adam Katić to the telephone service? We can't save ourselves that way; we really can't, Djordje." His voice died away.

"I always knew you were a swine," muttered Djordje, walking off toward the town.

Vukašin leaned against the tree, shaking. In a passing cart a wounded man was singing a wedding song.

Djordje vanished into the darkness. Vukašin had not seen him for twenty-one years; and here tonight they had again bounced against each other like two pebbles; once more they had parted with Djordje hating him. This simply confirmed his fate: he could not even get along with his own brother on this accursed planet. But now the hurt was more poignant.

"Djordje!" he called, running down the muddy road. "Djordje!" No answer. It must have been raining since the beginning of time; a primeval wind was blowing through the bare trees. A cart with wounded rumbled past.

Vukašin hurried toward the town. He must find Djordje and explain what had happened to him since he had left Prerovo forever that Christmas morning. Tonight he would tell Djordje everything. They were both sons of their mother, Živana; Djordje would understand him better than Olga. Tonight they were in the same boat. His flight from Prerovo hadn't made any difference.

He scoured the streets and cafés for Djordje until he was exhausted. General Mišić was waiting for him at the High Command; now he was ready to tell Mišić what he thought about sending the students to the front. An orderly escorted him to Mišić's office with exaggerated formality. He found Mišić sitting at an empty table in his overcoat and hat, staring at the floor.

"I've been waiting for you, Vukašin," he said sternly, rising from his chair.

"I've been with Milena at the hospital. On the way over, some peasants from my village detained me." Vukašin shook the rain from his coat and hat and sat down on a chair placed against the wall. "How are Louisa and the children? Any news of your sons?"

"They're all as well as can be expected. Actually, my boys don't write me from the front. I suppose they think I can learn what interests me from their commanders." Mišić took off his sheepskin hat and put it on the edge of the table. "You were right this evening, Vukašin. You talked sensibly, like an honorable man. I was impressed by your political logic. I began to feel much more cheerful as I listened to you."

"Are you making fun of me, General?"

"Of course not, Vukašin. I'm speaking absolutely sincerely, as your friend."

"But you didn't agree with me."

"True. Not because you didn't talk sense, but because today we dare not act as you suggest."

"Why not, since that would be the surest way out of our present hopeless situation?"

"We cannot and we dare not."

Mišić's orderly brought in some plates and a pan of steaming hot food. "I told Louisa I wouldn't be home to supper. I wanted to have supper with you alone." He stood up to let his orderly set the table. "There are times in the life of a nation, Vukašin, when you can't take the wisest course of action, but must do what has to be done and what can be done."

"What you're saying is that the course of action must be determined by circumstances and by what is possible."

"That's right."

"But I did put forward a realistic proposal based on actual circumstances and alternatives. I was the only one who urged what can and must be done today to assure the safety and future of Serbia."

"The trouble is that both you and Putnik forgot about the people. The people are never all in the same predicament; nor do they necessarily see the best way out."

"But their leaders must find the best way. Otherwise they can't justify their right to rule, and they will lose their vital link with the people."

"I disagree. Those at the top need not always know the best course to follow. But they must always be aware of what the people definitely do *not* want. And that's what that wily old fox Pašić knows perfectly well. Just now our people will not do the most sensible thing from the point of view of their future."

"I'm not at all convinced of that." Vukašin rose and walked up and down the office, hardly able to hide his dissatisfaction with Mišić's attitude and his way of philosophizing about the people.

"Vukašin, I know military commanders of genius who in critical times have made decisions even their corporals would have had the sense to avoid. Sometimes these decisions resulted in victory, sometimes in defeat. These men were not fools; they must have known what was the wisest thing to do. And yet for some reason they didn't do it. They had to act as they did. Perhaps in our present trials we are behaving unwisely in precisely the same way. Come and have a bite to eat."

All through supper, General Mišić recounted military incidents and decisions to justify his position; he seemed to be testing himself, and he had no desire to hear Vukašin's opinion. Vukašin for some reason again found himself unable to say that it was a tragic mistake to send the students to the battlefield. He was still troubled by his parting with Djordje, by the old rancor. As soon as they finished eating, Vukašin excused himself on the pretext of going to see Milena at the hospital and went into the street.

It was after midnight when Vukašin, worn out by his fruitless search for Djordje, entered Valjevo's one hotel. Every bed was taken; he stretched himself out on a bench in the corridor and covered his face with his damp coat. He simply must save Ivan!

An explosion shattered Vukašin's sleepless night; he relived over and over the judgment passed on him by the High Command. Feeling stiff in every limb, he rolled off the bench and tottered to the main door of the hotel: under the low overcast sky refugees were streaming down the street. From the west came the rumble of artillery; each explosion sent a ripple through the river of refugees flowing down the street.

"Good morning, Vukašin." He stared at his friend and political ally Ljuba Davidović, amazed that anyone could still say those familiar words.

"The High Command is leaving Valjevo for Kragujevac. The government is going there too, and so are we."

"Why, for God's sake? Nothing was said about this last night."

"Our situation has suddenly deteriorated. The Fritzies really are in a hurry! How is your daughter?"

"But this is terrible! I've exchanged only a few words with Milena. Will the hospital be evacuated?"

"I know we have no way of taking the gravely wounded men from Valjevo. Our train leaves at nine. Pašić called me early this morning. He insists on forming a coalition government immediately. That clever old politician is now pushing his new policy of national unity. He's offered me the Ministry of Education, and he's going to offer you Economic Affairs."

"Me?"

"You. He's not at all bothered by the opinions you expressed last night. He doesn't care if you infuriate Prince Alexander and the generals. He's decided to silence you and tie you to his apron strings. You know yourself that he's always had a soft spot for people who make mistakes and people who won't kowtow to anyone."

"What do you mean?" asked Vukašin, deafened by the splashing of passing feet.

"Pašić always looks at things from more than one angle. Now that

Prince Alexander and the officers think you're a traitor, it's of course to his advantage that you are his old opponent. But he needs you more than anyone else. Hurry, we can talk on the train. Be at the station at nine sharp."

A series of explosions brought Vukašin to his senses. Davidović disappeared into the crowd of refugees. Vukašin stepped back into the corridor. Quickly collecting his coat, hat, and cane, he dashed out into the street and hurried toward the hospital through the tumultuous throng of refugees, sheep, and cattle. A peasant hurried along in front of him, carrying on his back a bag and some blue laths sticking straight into the air high above his head.

What if Milena stayed in Valjevo with the hospital? Could he leave her to be taken prisoner? How could he go away?

The blue laths on the back of the tall, stooping peasant dissected the low sky, the bare plum orchards, and the hills. The state was collapsing, and here was this peasant saving some blue laths. What pettiness! The laths on the peasant's back disappeared into the general hubbub of the hospital, into the groans of the wounded and the shouts of the orderlies who were loading them onto oxcarts.

Vukašin stopped, not knowing where to look for Milena. Lightly wounded men with bandaged heads and arms were streaming out of the hospital, wrapped in overcoats, blankets, and sheets. They stopped to look at the sky, strained to catch the sounds of artillery, and exchanged fearful glances. Vukašin pushed his way through the crowd, asking for Milena; the orderlies and doctors waved him away. Reeling from the stench, he made his way into the hospital corridor. Orderlies carrying wounded men on stretchers pushed him against the wall.

"Good morning, Father," said a voice behind him.

He stared at Milena: there was blood on her hands and a hopeless look in her eyes. "Didn't you sleep last night?"

"No. They never stopped bringing in wounded."

"I'm terribly worried about you, Milena." He looked silently at her bloody apron.

"We're still alive, Father. When are you leaving?"

He was silent for a moment, then whispered: "What about you, my darling?"

Milena gave a start and frowned. A dead soldier was carried past them on a stretcher; they saw the blue face and wide-open mouth.

"Do we have to stand here?" Vukašin whispered.

"Where else can we go?" She took his hand and pulled him toward the wall.

Her brisk, efficient movements intimidated him; he dropped her hand. What could he say to please her?

"How is Vladimir?" he asked cautiously.

She looked at him fearfully: had he heard something?

"Does he write to you?" asked Vukašin, even more softly.

"Yesterday morning he was rushing furiously toward a machine gun. I don't know what happened after that."

"Don't be afraid. Brave men know how to take care of themselves."

"I forgot to tell you that last night I saw your brother from Prerovo. He was looking for his son, Adam. Your brother—my uncle—seems terribly unhappy. Did he find you?"

"Yes."

"His anguish over Adam really distressed me. Now I'll worry about Adam too. Why are you frowning?"

"I'm not. Why should I be frowning? Adam is your cousin."

"But what happened between you? You've never told me why we don't go to Prerovo. That peasant with the blue laths who's going around with Uncle Djordje, looking for his own sons, told me about Grandfather. As soon as I get a leave I'm going to the village."

"By all means go as soon as you can. Do you know that the High Command is leaving Valjevo today?"

"Yes. They began evacuating the hospital at dawn. The lightly wounded are leaving for the station, as you can see."

"What about you?"

"I'm staying behind with the serious cases."

"Can't you leave with the wounded who are being evacuated?"

"No, Father. Two doctors are staying and three of us nurses. We have several hundred badly wounded; someone must sacrifice himself."

"And you have chosen to sacrifice yourself? Is that sensible, Milena? Or absolutely necessary?" He put his hand on her shoulder.

"Do I have any choice, Father?"

"You're right," he muttered, and fell silent. *That's just it,* he thought, *we have no choice, we can only do what we're doing. But why must she do so much so soon?* He gripped her shoulder convulsively and drew her face close. "What will happen to you when the Austrians get here, my child?" he whispered, looking intently into her eyes.

"Whatever happens to the wounded will happen to me." She lowered her eyes and her chin quivered. "I do understand you, Father," she whispered, "but I can't do anything else."

"How can I possibly leave you here?"

"How many times you've said to me: 'Our lives are not our own, Milena; we have obligations to others.' " Tears welled up in her eyes. "Suppose Vladimir is wounded. They bring him to the hospital, and I've run away. Just imagine how he would feel!" She leaned her head against his chest for a moment, then drew back quickly, as if frightened. "I must stay."

"I understand, my child. Your love is that self-centered feeling that makes the world go round."

"Are you trying to justify what I'm doing, Father?"

"Don't push all your feelings to the limit." He looked at her tears and could not speak for the lump in his own throat.

"My hands are dirty; we can't shake hands. Good-bye, Father. Kiss Mother for me and try to comfort her."

She wrenched herself away and walked slowly down the corridor, pushing her way past the wounded men and orderlies pouring out of every room.

Heartsick, he took a few steps after her, then stopped. The stream of wounded men carried him, stumbling blindly, out of the building.

Near the hospital gate Vukašin collided with the peasant carrying the blue laths on his back. The bent old man, who was gaping at him, reminded him of someone. He tried to walk past him, but the man cried: "Wait, Vukašin! Don't pretend you don't recognize me! I'm Tola Dačić. I know you're a big shot now, gone up in the world, but we can still shake hands like neighbors. Before you went off to that place Paris, we were good pals." Tola wiped his wet hand on the shirt under his sheepskin jacket. "God bless you, Vukašin!"

Vukašin held out his hand awkwardly, ashamed of his discomfort.

"Are you worried about your daughter? You needn't upset yourself over her. A nice-looking girl like that—only fire and water can harm her. She's safe from man and beast. When I tell Aćim what sort of granddaughter he has, he'll be tickled pink!"

"How is he?" Vukašin remembered that he hadn't asked Djordje about his father last night.

"Well, to tell you the truth, Vukašin, he's getting on. Mellowing, you might say. He looks about the same, but he's not the man he used to be."

"Tell him his granddaughter is working as a nurse, and his grandson has enlisted as a volunteer. He's going to the front any day now. Well, good-bye, Tola! I have to catch a train."

"You've time for a few more words. Since last summer my four boys have been doing their bit for Serbia, three of them with rifles and bayonets and Aleksa with his cannon. I lost Živko, the youngest, at Cer. Now I'm looking for the other three, to help them out. Tell me—you must know—can we do anything to stop the Fritzies?"

"I think we can. I hope so. We must."

"Don't give me 'I hope so.' That's not enough to help me stick it out. We Serbs have done a lot of hoping, Vukašin. We've put our hopes in God and in the devil. And nothing's come of it. Tell me what's going to happen, even if it's bad."

He had to say something reassuring to Tola, his old neighbor from Prerovo. "We won at Cer last summer. And we'll win again. The Allies won't let Serbia be defeated." Vukašin saw from Tola's glance that he wasn't comforted. What more could he say?

"I too have faith that Serbia will win. But tell me—since you're close to Pašić, although you're often snapping at each other—can Serbia hold out on her own, without being pushed along by the Allies? With all due respect, but suppose the Russians and those folk in England don't help us? They can't manage it for some reason. Got more important things to think about. I know what a master is, even when he's got a kind heart. He's good to you as long as he needs you."

Disbelief gleamed in Tola's watery blue eyes, not the eyes of an old man. What would convince him? Faith alone was not enough. And what would Tola say to Aćim? But Tola, smiling magnanimously under his huge, grizzled mustache, released him from his predicament.

"All right, Vukašin. You're in a hurry. So am I. Have a good journey. Come see us in Prerovo whatever happens. Plants and animals cheer you up no matter how black things are. And every evil is more bearable when you're on your own turf. Good-bye!"

Vukašin shook hands and rushed down the muddy road, hurrying past the wounded. In front of the railroad station he stopped, paralyzed by the thought that he had left Milena to be taken prisoner by the Austrians. What would he say to poor Olga? That a father was powerless to avert the fate of his children? That one should not be consumed by love and fear? Some consolation!

He heard voices calling him to the platform. In the milling crowd he caught sight of Pašić, who was being besieged by refugees and wounded.

"Pašić, you devil, what are you doing to Serbia?" "Where are we going now that you've got us into this mess?"

"We're going to freedom, friends! To freedom."

"Where? How? Bless you! Hurrah for Pašić!"

"Just have a little patience, folks. I promise you faithfully that we'll soon be back in Šabac."

"Šabac! You'd better defend Belgrade and Valjevo! Hurrah for Pašić! Where's your family? Fleeing to Salonika! Hurrah for Pašić!"

Women and old men swarmed toward Pašić, to see him and touch him, to trample him and throw him under the approaching train, which was scattering the crowds of wounded and women and children standing on the tracks. A cordon of policemen fended off the angry mob.

Pašić slowly raised his hat and called out in a firm, calm voice: "Bear up a little longer. Victory is ours, my friends. Good-bye!" Then he climbed slowly into the train to the roar of curses and cheers.

Vukašin followed Pašić, borne along by the fury of the crowd and a vague desire to show some sort of solidarity.

"What is your son's name?" whispered Pašić to him in the corridor, which reverberated with the yells of the desperate crowd.

"Ivan. Why do you ask?"

"Good, I've got it right. Give him this when he leaves for the front." He handed Vukašin a sealed blue envelope bearing the name of the High Command.

"Who is this from?" Vukašin asked as he took the envelope, instinctively divining its contents.

"Tell your son to give it personally to the divisional or regimental commander where he is posted."

"I'm sorry, but there can be no question of special favors for my son. He is a volunteer, Prime Minister."

"I know that. He's a good boy. They tell me he was the star pupil in the Belgrade High School. Let him just keep out of the way until the storm blows over. Afterward it will be easier. I tried to postpone the departure of the students to the front for a few days. But the High Command . . . you've seen what they're like. Come, let's sit down."

Pašić withdrew into his compartment. Vukašin could not bring himself to put the envelope in his pocket. Ministers and Opposition leaders saw the name printed on it. He had nothing to do with this envelope; he would make it clear that Pašić had given it to him. Yet there he was: bribed, blackmailed, caught with dirty hands around his throat. He alone would have to decide Ivan's fate. Whatever happened, he would be guilty. Pašić had nailed him to a cross. What fiendish game was he playing? Vukašin stared out the window.

On the empty platform some wounded men were fighting savagely over a tent flap. The engine gave a frenzied whistle, and the train pulled slowly away. The wounded man with the firmest grip on the tent flap was stabbed with a bayonet by a one-armed man, and sank down on the rails. But the victor did not take the tent flap; he threw away his bayonet and walked slowly toward the field beyond the station. Another wounded man caught up with him and walloped him over the head with his crutch; the murderer staggered, folded his one arm over his head to defend himself, and rolled down the embankment. The man with the crutch hobbled back to the murdered soldier, took the tent flap, and set off toward the station. Behind the train the mob overflowed onto the tracks.

"Aren't you feeling well, Vukašin? You look pale. Bring some water!" said Pašić to a sergeant.

"No, thank you. I'm all right. I spent the night in the hospital. The wounded men, the blood . . ." He put his hand in his pocket and took Pašić's letter between his trembling fingers.

The engine gave a long whistle, and the train stopped suddenly. Vukašin collided with somebody and almost lost his balance. He quickly put his hand over the pocket containing the letter. The ministers came out into the corridor and crowded around the windows. Children's cries and whimpers filled the air.

"Look at all those children! Where did they come from? A school is being evacuated. But where are their teachers? Where are your teachers, children? No adult in sight, not even a railwayman. How odd! What on earth is happening? Look, Vukašin!"

Vukašin went up to the window: children were standing on the tracks and crying; more children were pouring onto the platform of the small station. They rushed to board the train, attacking the policemen barring their way. The ministers silently fled to their compartments. The engine whistled and lurched forward.

To Milena the train's long anguished whistles were announcing its departure from Valjevo forever. Her hands trembled and the tweezers clinked in the instrument dish. Doctor Sergeev looked up from the piece of gauze he was putting over a large wound in the spine of a soldier. The tears that had welled up in Milena's eyes fell rapidly onto the soldier's torn, bloody jacket, thrown down beside the operating table. Doctor Sergeev gave her an imploring glance and whispered something in Russian. The tweezers jangled more loudly.

She might never see her father again. And she didn't even have supper with him, or spend an evening under the deep, tender protection of his presence, his quiet omnipotence. Ever since she could remember she had feared nothing when she was with her father. Not even death. Before she met Vladimir she had looked for her father's features, his strength, in the young men she met. The faults she discerned in her mother confirmed her belief in her father's superiority. Before she met Vladimir she had loved to sit on her father's knee and lean her head against his chest to listen to his heartbeats and the metallic voice of his pocket watch, to feel those strong, deep pulsations in his chest which made the whole house resound with their dark warmth, to ask him questions simply for the sake of hearing that reverberation in his chest. Had Vladimir prevented her from having supper with him, spending last night with him?

She was oblivious of the tears dripping onto the operating table. Doctor Sergeev said something softly to her in Russian, then in a loud voice ordered her to get some sleep; Nurse Dušanka would wake her in time for the night shift. The train whistles faded away.

She put down the dish with the surgical instruments and went out of the room; she pushed her way through the corridor crammed with wounded men on stretchers. Outside stood several newly arrived oxcarts full of wounded. As she walked over the cobblestones to the sleeping quarters the thought struck her that Vladimir might be lying in one of the carts. She wouldn't look, though. She would punish herself for hurting her father—because of a man who suspected her of flirting with doctors and wounded officers. She, Milena, a flirt! Just because she had kissed Vladimir in the hospital when he was wounded! It was her first kiss. She ran into the room in which her friends were sleeping fully dressed, lay down on the bed she shared with Dušanka, thrust her head under the pillow, and cried herself to sleep.

She was awakened by a soft whisper but could not open her eyes. She trembled on hearing "my dear girl" spoken in Russian, recognizing the familiar, slightly drunken whisper of Doctor Sergeev, the most extraordinary man she had ever met. His menacing tenderness sent a shudder through her. She opened her eyes: it was dark. The streetlight illuminated Doctor Sergeev's knees and bloodstained coat as he sat by the door, smoking. Her teeth began to chatter. She would wait for the Austrians with him, he had said. He was now her only protector. A protector and a potential danger: the nurses and doctors laughed at his romantic love for her.

"Has everyone gone, doctor?" she whispered.

"Yes, Milena, they've gone," he whispered, and walked out of the room.

Now she dared to turn around: she rolled on her back and stared at the ceiling. Maybe the Austrians would arrive tonight. They would rape her, kill her. Should anything in the world have stopped her from spending one last night with her father? She felt she was choking but couldn't cry. Outside the orderlies were quarreling and cursing, and the Valjevo dogs were barking.

Someone came into the room. She gave a start: it was Dušanka, with whom she shared the bed. Dušanka sat down beside her and, sighing deeply, took her hand.

"Vladimir has been wounded."

"Where is he?"

"Sit down, and calm down."

"What's happened?" said Milena, looking straight at Dušanka.

"He's badly wounded, but he'll survive. Doctor Sergeev has operated on him. He'll certainly live."

"So you've seen him? While I was asleep? My God, why didn't you wake me? Which ward is he in? Take me to him."

"Please calm down! He hasn't recovered consciousness yet. He's been wounded in the head. You can't see him now."

"I must! Take me to him!"

"Be sensible, Milena. You mustn't disturb him. It would be dangerous to excite him. You can't see him tonight."

Milena kneeled down and rested her head on Dušanka's knee. Vladimir must have been lying in one of the carts; she had walked past him and gone to bed. Her body began to shake; Dušanka bent over her and whispered something in her ear.

TO THE AMBASSADORS OF THE KINGDOM OF SERBIA IN ST. PETERSBURG, PARIS, AND LONDON:

THE CHIEFS OF STAFF SUGGEST SEEKING PEACE WITH AUSTRIA-HUNGARY OR ENDING RESISTANCE SINCE WE HAVE NO MUNITIONS. THE GOVERNMENT WILL SURRENDER BEFORE TAKING THIS STEP. ASSEMBLY MEETS IN THREE DAYS. WE WILL SEE WHETHER WE CAN COUNT ON HELP IN THE DIRECTION OF OUR POLICY. EXPLAIN OUR DESPERATE SITUATION. REMOVE FROM SERBIA ALL RESPONSIBILITY FOR FAILURE IN UNEQUAL CONTEST. AFTER TWO WARS AND AN ALBANIAN ATTACK IT WAS IMPOSSIBLE IN SEVEN OR EIGHT MONTHS TO PREPARE FOR WAR WITH AUSTRIA.

PAŠIĆ

TO SPALAJKOVIĆ, AMBASSADOR OF THE KINGDOM OF SERBIA, PETROGRAD:

IT IS OUR FIRM CONVICTION THAT NO CESSION OF SERBIAN TERRITORY TO BULGARIA WILL PERSUADE HER TO JOIN THE WAR ON THE SIDE OF THE ALLIES. BULGARIA AWAITS SERBIA'S COLLAPSE AND WILL THEN ANNEX ALL MACEDONIA AND THE MORAVA AREA OF SERBIA. THEY CAN CONTROL THE BULGARIANS ONLY BY PUSHING THEM AGAINST TURKEY. REPEAT TO OUR RUSSIAN BROTHERS. IF THEY DO NOT WANT TO SEE AUSTRIA IN SALONIKA AND ON THE BOSPORUS LET THEM GIVE SERBIA ALL POSSIBLE HELP. THAT IS ALL THEY CAN DO FOR THEIR GOOD AND OURS. WHAT IS THIS ABOUT ACCESS TO THE CZAR? KNOCK ON ALL DOORS DEMANDING ADMISSION.

PAŠIĆ

TO VESNIĆ, AMBASSADOR OF THE KINGDOM OF SERBIA, PARIS, FOR POINCARÉ:

AT THIS DESPERATE MOMENT WHEN WE ARE EXPIRING IN THE CAUSE OF HONOR AND DEFENSE OF ALLIED INTERESTS WE ARE REQUIRED TO GIVE BULGARIA THAT PART OF OUR TERRITORY DISPUTED BY AUSTRIA ON ACCOUNT OF WHICH SHE DECLARED WAR ON US SO THAT BULGARIA WILL CEASE HOSTILE ACTIVITY. INSTEAD OF COMING TO OUR AID ALL OUR ALLIES AND THE RUSSIANS FORCE AND COMPEL US TO STRENGTHEN BULGARIA WHICH HAS BEEN AND ALWAYS WILL BE ON THE SIDE OF THE ENEMIES OF THE TRIPLE ENTENTE AND PEACE IN THE BALKANS. IF A PRICE MUST BE PAID FOR BULGARIA'S PARTICIPATION IN THE WAR AGAINST TURKEY THEN IT SHOULD BE PAID BY TURKEY THE ENEMY OF THE TRIPLE ENTENTE POWERS AND NOT BY SERBIA YOUR MOST LOYAL ALLY. IT IS NOW HIGH TIME TO CEASE ALLIED PRESSURE ON SERBIA IN HER LAST HOUR. SERBIA WOULD BREATHE AGAIN IF SHE COULD BE SENT IN SEVEN OR AT MOST TEN DAYS AT LEAST TEN THOUSAND SHELLS FOR FIELD ARTILLERY AND FIVE THOUSAND GRENADES FOR HOWITZERS AND SUBSEQUENTLY THE MUNITIONS ALREADY PROMISED AND PAID FOR. WITHOUT THIS HELP SERBIA IS FINISHED.

PAŠIĆ

4

Therefore man is so fortunately constituted that there is no reliable measure of truth, but many excellent measures of falsehood.

Ivan Katić whispered Pascal's dictum for the third time. He was sitting on his pallet, in his shirt and undershorts, looking intently at his notebook of quotations culled from philosophical works he had read at the Sorbonne; he was reading by the light of a candle placed on a footlocker. He would spend another evening with Pascal; after the pulverizing exercises on Golgotha, only "The Misery of Man Without God" could restore some sense of belonging to his own body, humiliated and alienated by the bullying of the sergeants. He was too exhausted and the room was too noisy for sleep. Nor could he act like the others in the room. He couldn't sing—nor did he want to—like those in the middle of the room, under the two lamps. He hadn't any funny stories to tell, like the young men from the First Platoon. He couldn't laugh at the things the forty people in the room found amusing. He couldn't talk endlessly about weekly adventures with girls—grass widows and real ones—like those in the "Don Juan Corner," who needed someone to listen to them; he hadn't had any such adventures, nor would he be able to express such repulsive activities in words. He might have played cards with Bora Jackpot, his neighbor on the left, but he wasn't interested in playing cards. As for joining in discussions on the imperialism and militarism of the bourgeoisie with Bogdan Mustachios and Danilo History-Book, with whom he shared two pallets on the floor, he just couldn't see any point in it. So he was reading his notebook from the Sorbonne, whispering to himself as he read: . . . *Imagination, that is the most impor-*

tant ruling faculty in man, the creator of fallacies and false thinking, and the more deceptive in that it is not always so. . . .

He went on whispering, but couldn't help hearing the others.

"You must discover man, that is the point of war. Well, look for him in the barracks! Or, better still, look for him in his shorts. Now listen, fellows, it isn't the money that matters; it's the game. The battle is important, not the victory. Come on, let's play cards and wage war. Long live the generation of card players and fighters! Well done, Don Quixote!"

. . . *For imagination would be an infallible yardstick of the value of truth if it were an infallible yardstick of falsehood. . . .*"

Ivan whispered, but still he could hear the others.

"The only thing that matters is the law of the universe. Right now it's controlled by Minor Chaos. Yes, Minor Chaos in blood vessels. Now what would you rather have in your hands: a crown or a woman's breast? Don't hurry to answer. A woman's breast. A woman's breast. A woman's breast. Then you're pessimists. Science and the proletariat will save the world. When there are no exploiters and exploited, there won't be any more wars. But, Mustachios, what about those who are neither proletarians nor scientists? Who doesn't believe in progress? I tell you, after us there'll be a funny generation. Well, I despise future generations. Put the light out; they've sounded taps. Tomorrow Don Quixote will break our balls on Golgotha."

. . . *Imagination has her winners and losers, her healthy and her sick, her rich and poor; she causes reason to believe, to doubt, to deny; she has her wise men and her fools. . . .*

Ivan whispered, but still could not help hearing.

"Put the light out; the duty officer is coming around—honest! I know that you know all the parts of a gun, but what are men and women made of? And was the woman naked? I bet you five turns on duty that ninety-nine percent of the Student Battalion haven't seen a naked woman. They're lovers, do you hear? I know the parts where we're different. You don't even know that. Put the light out. The duty officer's already at the Fifth. The universe is a secret. The homeland's a secret too. So are women. That's enough of metaphysics—Valjevo is going to fall tonight. If Valjevo falls, so will Belgrade. The next thing, they'll be in Kragujevac. If they get to Kragujevac, Niš can't be defended. Oh, what pessimists we are! But Skoplje won't fall, because we're here! I'd give my right hand for something sweet. I'd attack Vienna for a bit of my mother's cake. What I'd like is a piece of cherry pie. That's a heart; don't move. Here's a diamond, old man. Capitalism brings mankind misery and wars, tyranny and ignorance. If only I had one of those women we met last week! England's to blame for the war."

The words were lost in laughter. Ivan stopped reading. Two people were running between the pallets, mimicking Don Quixote on horseback—that is, the commander of the Student Battalion, Lieutenant Colonel Dušan Glišić. They raced through the room; Glišić–Don Quixote waved his arms and shouted:

"Every one of you can die for his country! Every one!"

The students rolled over on their mattresses, howling and panting for breath; Lieutenant Colonel Glišić—nicknamed Don Quixote because he was thin and had a long mustache—sputtered: "Aren't you ashamed to be alive? How long do you think you're going to stay alive? Tell me, you softies!"

Ivan smiled, recalling his enlistment and Glišić's words. "You're right, young man. It doesn't matter that you're blind as a bat: you won't be able to see the Huns, so you'll be less frightened. Just fire quickly, and remember that every hundredth bullet is bound to find its mark."

The door opened with a clatter; it was Second Lieutenant Bloodsucker, the duty officer. Don Quixote and his horse collapsed amid smothered laughter.

"Do you bastards know when they sounded taps? Do you fucking idiots realize that you're making fun of a Serbian lieutenant colonel, a hero of Kumanovo, an officer who's already given two brothers for the homeland? You book-lickers, you ink-stained shits! Atten-shun!"

Many of them got up and stood at attention in their shirts and undershorts beside their pallets. Ivan remained seated; he could feel the veins swelling in his temples and his cheeks burning. The insulting words dimmed his vision, made the scene seem unreal. Bogdan Mustachios did not get up; he simply stretched himself out from a sitting position, leaned on his elbow, and began to comb his mustache. Bora Jackpot did not get up either; he was picking up the cards from the blanket. Danilo History-Book stood at attention, and kicked Ivan to make him get up. He kicked him harder, and Ivan moved to the edge of the pallet, so that the duty officer could see him better; Bloodsucker's foul language incensed him so much that he no longer saw him. He remembered the jar of blackberry jam in the parcel from his mother; he could easily find it in his footlocker. Kneeling, he found the jar and with all his strength hurled it at the mouth of the man who had called him such foul names. The jar broke against a beam where the guns were; Bloodsucker was covered with jam and bits of glass. The duty officer, Second Lieutenant Dragiša Ilić, nicknamed Bloodsucker, the worst villain in the Skoplje Blue Barracks, who hated students more than any other officer in the Student Battalion, wiped away the blackberry jam with his fist and stared in front of him, speechless.

There was a burst of laughter; then the students lined up, still in their shorts, and piled up the guns. Ivan remained kneeling on his half of the pallet. He was still kneeling when they all lay down, hurriedly burying themselves under the blankets. He looked at the open door in the distance, through which sneaked a dwarf of a man in officer's uniform.

"Lie down, Ivan!" said Bogdan Dragović—Mustachios—seizing him by the arm; then Ivan realized that his glasses had fallen off, or that someone had removed them. The room stretched out to infinity, and the pallets and the people on them grew smaller and smaller, as in a distant dream, or after a narrow escape from death.

"Your glasses are next to your footlocker!" said Danilo Protić, nicknamed History-Book.

He groped along the boards; he found his glasses and put them on. Bora Luković—Jackpot—lifted his blanket and shouted:

"Well done, Blindie! Your deed was classically irrational!"

Bogdan Mustachios pulled him down by the arm, and he lay under his blanket. Then Bogdan sat up.

"Comrades, no one from our squad hit Second Lieutenant Dragiša Ilić with a jam jar. Nobody. Isn't that right?"

"That's right. None of us did it. We know nothing about it. We won't admit anything."

The room echoed with shouts and threats; darkness enveloped guns and eyes. The sound of regular breathing began to interweave the horror of the unknown with the hope of companionship. Ivan wanted to cry. After fifty-six nights in this room, listening to the regular breathing in the darkness, now for the first time he felt that he was listening to the breathing of his comrades, his friends.

In the formation of all ten platoons of the Student Battalion, Bogdan Dragović, leader of the Sixth Platoon, stood at attention, looking at the back of Ivan Katić's head; he could see it trembling.

He had been trembling all night, unable to sleep, receiving in silence all Dragović's assurances that he had nothing to fear, that he could be sure no one in the room would give him away. And he must on no account confess.

"You mustn't admit under any circumstances that you threw something at Bloodsucker. Glišić and the other saber-rattlers must realize that we can do more than just read and write. We've got to din into those thick military heads what human dignity and solidarity mean. Do you understand, Ivan? It depends on you whether the Student Battalion—almost an entire generation of the Serbian intelligentsia, apart from the shirkers—wins at least a small victory for humanity in the barracks before it perishes. That's very important."

He had whispered this to Ivan several times during the night, both before and after the arrival in the barracks of a group of officers who demanded that "the man who hit Second Lieutenant Ilić with a lethal object while he was on duty" confess. Dragović, holding Ivan firmly by the arm, was aware of his hesitation and torment; sensing that Ivan would stand up and admit he was responsible, he squeezed Ivan's burning hand more tightly, and pressed him down onto the pallet. Ivan made no reply to all his efforts to convince him.

The first time that Ivan spoke after smashing the jam jar on the beam above Bloodsucker's head was in answer to Danilo History-Book's reproachful remark while they were washing.

"From an objective point of view, Blindie, there's no point in acting irresponsibly nowadays; it's dishonorable."

"Did I act irresponsibly?" asked Ivan.

"Yes, you did. We've lost Mačva. The capital will soon fall, and you split the head of a duty officer in the barracks. Yes, it's true that it was Bloodsucker, but still, he's a Serbian officer."

"And what if there's something in my country that matters more to me than its capital?" stammered Ivan with quivering lips.

Bogdan looked at him with delight. "He's got ideas of his own; a talented man, this Katić!"

Then he turned on History-Book and made him shut up, but didn't let Ivan out of his sight for a moment; in an affectionate, brotherly way, he encouraged him not to waver and praised his actions, convinced that Ivan had the makings of a rebel. A man who dared to throw a jar of jam at a second lieutenant in the barracks would be prepared to throw a bomb at the King tomorrow. Great rebellions are born in the mind, whereas those that proceed from the heart and the stomach are easily quelled; Ivan was mentally rebelling against the bourgeois barracks. Only it was to be hoped he wasn't a softy, a spoiled darling of the gentry, who couldn't take a box on the ears.

Danilo History-Book suddenly turned around and whispered: "The C.O. is coming! I told you, Mustachios—we've disgraced ourselves and made a stupid scandal!"

"Step to the front and tell them all, you self-seeking swine!"

Flushed and speechless at these insults, History-Book turned around and stood at attention.

"Boys," whispered Jackpot, "Don Quixote is really acting the part! Look, he's galloping. And it's a glorious morning!"

"Don't break ranks!" hissed History-Book, standing still.

Over the heads of the battalion Bogdan saw Glišić, the commanding officer, galloping across the barracks courtyard; he was accompanied by his orderly, also on horseback, but not at the prescribed distance. The platoon commander shouted: "Atten-shun! Eyes right!"

Bogdan thought that Ivan would fall over; he seemed to be almost fainting as he jerked his head in response to the command. No, he wouldn't stick it out. Yet his ideas were so bold and subtle. So far, no one in the Blue Barracks had dared to do what he had done last night. A pity. Of course he was of bad stock; yet there was revolutionary fervor in his blood.

"Stick it out, Ivan! Anyone who isn't brave in the barracks will be a coward at the front," whispered Bogdan. Ivan's hair bristled under his cap as the commanding officer whispered:

"The man who tried to kill Second Lieutenant Ilić last night will step to the front."

"Just imagine, he's whispering—fantastic! Look at his whiskers, an absolute right angle," murmured Jackpot.

Bogdan wanted to see the eyes of the man who was practically speechless, who described the hurling of the jar as an attempt to kill. Lieutenant Colonel Glišić's mustache moved as he whispered. He sat on his horse in front of the platoon.

"I'm warning you for the last time: let the man who tried to kill Second Lieutenant Ilić come forward!"

In the silence the dry sand crunched under their boots, and their cartridge belts pinched. The commanding officer's horse pawed the ground threateningly. Ivan's gun strap creaked; he was going to step forward. Bogdan whispered:

"You're not going to be a reformer and philosopher like your father, are you? Keep it up, Ivan! Be worthy of your deed. You'll be the most famous member of the Student Battalion!"

"Even numbers from the first detachment of the Sixth Platoon, three steps forward!"

The commanding officer's whispering finished Ivan; he stepped forward. Bogdan grabbed him by the belt.

"You're an odd number!"

"What are you gaping at, you intellectual riffraff?"

"*Even* numbers forward, I said, you lazy, good-for-nothing students! In two months you haven't even learned to count, but you know enough to try to assassinate a Serbian officer!" Glišić whispered, jerking the reins of his mare, which was pawing the ground and arching its neck, as if about to jump into the ranks. The platoon commander picked out the even numbers, who moved uneasily, turning around and staring in fear and agitation. Danilo History-Book was the first to step out in front of the ranks; his partner, Bora Jackpot, moved a step to the left of Bogdan, stood up straight, and stuck out his chest.

"Atten-shun! Detachment leaders, go to the stables and bring the rope. Now *run!*" ordered the commanding officer, speaking in a loud voice for the first time.

Ivan turned to Bogdan, his eyes staring as if they would burst from their sockets.

"Don't move! I know what to do. You just keep still!" whispered Bogdan.

He really didn't know what to do. They will tie up the even numbers, of course, then march them off to prison, or else beat them in front of the whole formation to make them reveal the name of the "assassin." If they put them in prison, everything will be all right; nobody will admit anything there. But if they beat them in front of all six platoons, then he would rush out at Glišić, throw him off his horse, and tear off his epaulets. You lazy, good-for-nothing bastard, you royalist beast, you saber-swinging bourgeois! Hit out at the Austrians, not at Serbian students and volunteers! He would summon the whole battalion to the barracks; they would put up barricades, and no talks with the military! Antimilitaristic and patriotic slogans!

"Tie up this revolutionary riffraff!" ordered Glišić hoarsely, while his mare threw back her mane and shook her head.

How can we let the civilian population know about our rebellion? We must tell the socialist deputies first, thought Bogdan, staring at Glišić with eyes full of hate. A nationalist, an idiot, a pigheaded bourgeois thug! I'd like to tear out his mustache!

"Officers and sergeants, forward! Take these traitors to the parapet and shoot them like rebels and criminals! What are you dithering for? It's an order!"

The bound men swayed as they turned toward the ranks; they looked at the commanding officer, unable to believe what was happening; no one spoke. Only Danilo History-Book turned to Ivan and Bogdan and shouted scornfully:

"You fools! I swam across the Sava under shellfire to fight for Serbia, you mother-fuckers!" He moved toward the parapet, tried to step forward, pulled at the line of those tied behind him; but they jerked him backward so hard that he could barely keep on his feet. Ivan turned to Bogdan.

"I'm sorry, I must confess."

"No, you mustn't! I'll deal with Glišić!" he whispered, holding him by the belt.

The nearest of the bound recruits turned around; they had heard what he said. Bogdan met their frightened glances, then grew bigger and bigger; the whole Student Battalion could see him, all Skoplje, and Natalia too, as he walked slowly toward Glišić with a smile on his face—Glišić, that cruel officer, a bourgeois thug, a nationalist puppet! Bogdan's hour had come: his strength choked him; there was nothing he dared not do. Glišić shouted:

"And who are you laughing at? Yes, you! What's your name?"

"Bogdan Dragović."

"The one they call 'Mustachios'?"

"That's me."

"Are you the Dragović-Mustachios who calls himself a socialist?"

"Sir, I wish to report to you . . ." He stopped, feeling that he had made a stupid beginning. Ashamed of the way he had addressed Glišić, he raised his voice:

"I was the one who threw the jar of jam at Second Lieutenant Bloodsucker—I threw it right at his head. Unfortunately, I missed. My comrades are innocent."

"You? What did you say?"

"I did it. And if I'd had a bomb, I'd have thrown it at that fool of a second lieutenant. Did you hear me?" He smiled again, but he felt that he hadn't done it properly, because suddenly his lips felt numb and rigid with foreboding: Don Quixote would shoot him.

"Are you deaf? I'm asking you what you studied—law, or philosophy?"

He could only smile. They wanted him to smile, he thought. Because he could not, dared not utter a word. His voice would have given him away, and the entire Student Battalion would have heard his heart pounding and his voice quavering.

"Disarm this ass of a socialist and put him under arrest! The rest of the battalion can get on with its work!"

Bogdan heard these words above his head and let the corporal remove his rifle and belt, while he watched Glišić dig his spurs into the horse and gallop away toward his office at the other end of the barracks yard. The corporal gave him a shove in the back.

"Off you go! Straight to the prison!"

He felt the excitement he craved: the power of self-sacrifice. He walked firmly toward the stables and the stone prison, the eyes of his comrades fixed upon him. He believed they were looking at him with envy.

Ivan would have cried out "I'm guilty!" but he dared not; Bogdan had forbidden it. He would have run after Bogdan and caught up with him before he reached the prison. Bogdan would have stopped him and burst out laughing. Ivan turned to his comrades: he met looks of scorn and anger. In despair, he removed his glasses: he didn't want to see anyone clearly. His commanding officer gave an order; he rubbed his eyes and temples. He had no idea what to do.

Danilo History-Book stepped beside him in Bogdan's place, grabbed him by the arm, and turned him around in response to the command.

"It's all over now," said Danilo. "Let's get on with the job."

He pulled Ivan forward, shouting the words of command: "Left, Ivan, left!"

Ivan marched as though in a dream, doing everything that Danilo History-Book told him, obeying only his orders. He charged across a meadow, fell into thorn bushes, and fired his rifle repeatedly. Then he lay on his back to rest and thought more lucidly about what had happened since last night.

His companions from the squad came up and stood around him. "There's nothing wrong with hitting Bloodsucker; too bad you missed his head. But it's not fair to your friends, Blindie, to stand in line while they tied us up and Don Quixote told the sergeants to take us off to be shot. It's not right that Mustachios should suffer because of you."

"You think I was afraid to confess?"

"Well, why didn't you?"

"We agreed that no one in our room had hit Bloodsucker. You agreed to that; I didn't ask you to protect me."

"But you have no right to ask your friends to make a sacrifice for your blunders. You know damn well that Don Quixote is a fanatic."

"Do you really think I'd have stayed in line if they'd taken you off to be shot?" Ivan could feel the veins in his temples throbbing.

They did not reply.

"So you really think that I was afraid to confess, that I still am?" he said, looking at each one in turn, now sitting around him on the dry grass, remote and alien once more.

"Then why did you let Mustachios take the rap?"

"All last night and this morning Bogdan was persuading me not to confess. This morning he even threatened me. Bora, didn't you hear what he said to me?"

"Yes, I did, old boy. It's not Ivan's fault, so stop fussing. Mustachios is a fellow who likes to suffer; he could hardly wait for the cards to fall his way. He's a man who likes a dangerous game. Leave Blindie alone. Wasn't it just great when that blackberry juice dripped down Bloodsucker's shining face and over his heroic breast?"

"It sure was, but he'll tear out Bogdan's mustache. He'll court-martial him. You heard how Don Quixote said 'assassin' and 'assassination.' Before long he'll be calling it a mutiny, a Putsch against the dynasty. Franz Josef's supporters trying to seize Skoplje. If they don't give Mustachios five years' hard labor, I'll eat my hat."

"We'll see what happens. The best thing now, fellows, is to have one more round before the next charge." Bora took his cards out of his pocket, shuffled them, and called for partners.

Ivan took off his glasses; his face was burning, his temples throbbed.

"Blindie, if you'd said to Don Quixote: 'He didn't hit Bloodsucker, I did,' you would have spoiled Bogdan's noble act. You would have deprived him of it, and that would have offended and humiliated him. Mustachios is happy that he has a chance to suffer. You, Blindie, have chivalrously made a present of this noble deed to Mustachios," said Vinaver.

The commanding officer gave the order to fall in.

Ivan charged, fell down, fired his rifle. The thorn bushes and meadows were full of enemies. In the boundless sky the sun had never shone with such a blinding light. He did whatever Danilo History-Book did, because Bora Jackpot shirked whenever he could, as usual. Between volleys he wanted to touch Danilo's hand. Of all the students, this volunteer from Novi Sad was the least congenial—until this morning's parade—because of his fanatical nationalism and his penchant for drawing lessons from history, which earned him the nickname History-Book. After his resolute step toward the parapet to be shot, he was for Ivan a different man. It had been unfair to regard this highly disciplined soldier as a toady. How could he thank him?

On their way back to the barracks, the commanding officer ordered them to sing; Danilo History-Book was the first to begin "Serbia, our dear mother . . ." Only a few joined in. Bora Jackpot and Staša Vinaver made fun of the singers.

As soon as he stepped into the commanding officer's office and saw him standing at the window, staring into the evening twilight, Bogdan Dragović, his hands now bound, said:

"Sir, I wish to register a protest." He stopped, waiting for Glišić to turn around and to stop tapping his back with his whip. Lieutenant Colonel Glišić stood lost in thought, as though alone. "Your prison isn't fit for pigs, let alone Serbian intellectuals who are giving their lives for their country. A country that doesn't even have a prison worthy of its citizens." Again he stopped: Lieutenant Colonel Glišić gave no sign that he noticed his presence. Bogdan leaned against the wall and shook his arms; that was all he could do now: refuse to stand at attention with bound hands. It was the second time in his life that his hands had been tied up; the first time, during an apprentices' strike, he had felt deeply humiliated when the police had tied his hands. "First of all, sir, please tell me what law gives you the right to tie up my hands?" He raised his voice in a threatening, provocative tone.

Lieutenant Colonel Glišić neither heard nor noticed him; he was looking toward Skoplje. Bogdan could not see his eyes, but he sensed that a film of some old pain and suffering had spread over his bony face. The very first time he saw Glišić he had noticed this expression of suffering. Whenever Glišić was furious at their lack of discipline and berated them, heaping scorn and insults and reviling them as Serbia's ultimate shame and disgrace, "unworthy of the sacred calling of a soldier," he had been unable to conceal his suffering, which was so stark that it aroused fear and astonishment rather than sympathy. Unlike many members of the Student Battalion, Bogdan did not believe that the only reason for his suffering was the death of two brothers at the front; he was now quite sure that this fanatical and nationalistic militarist bore the marks of some deeper and more lasting pain than grief for his brothers. He moved away from the wall and again stood at attention. He would keep quiet until Glišić turned around. At last Glišić broke the silence. "What family do you have, Dragović?" he asked quietly, without changing his position and still tapping his back with his whip, as though flicking a tail.

Bogdan was completely bewildered by the question. "I have a mother and a younger sister," he muttered. "My father died ten years ago."

"How did your father earn his living?"

"With wax. He made candles in Valjevo."

"Does your mother also earn her living that way?"

"No, my mother is a weaver." Bogdan took a step toward him; he wanted to look into his eyes. He spoke more loudly than Glišić's tone warranted. "My mother spins wool for the ladies of Valjevo. And she weaves mats for their houses. For the officers' kitchens. That's how she has kept us, and educated me."

With a barely perceptible movement of the head, Lieutenant Colonel Glišić relaxed the severity of his profile, thereby deepening the layer of suffering. Here was a truly unhappy man. That was why he was so obsessed with the idea of sacrificing one's life for the homeland. He's full of despair, concluded Bogdan compassionately.

"Go back to where you came from," whispered Lieutenant Colonel Glišić, tapping his back with his whip a little harder.

Bogdan was baffled. He did not want to leave with his hands tied—at least Glišić could relieve him of that misery—but he did not venture to say a word.

He was still bewildered when the garrulous sentry lowered the grill behind him, and he found himself back in his dim stone cell with its small barred window near the ceiling. Was Glišić a victim of the errors of the bourgeoisie and the military, or a thug wearing the mask of an unhappy man? Was he a mean, loathsome creature or a man overwhelmed by despair? How could you fight an unhappy man? How could you hate an enemy who was visibly suffering? Glišić was a victim of the class whose clenched fist and heavy boot he was. If only he could write to Natalia. Presumably this unhappy creature would remember to untie his hands before tomorrow. He would demand it; he would go on a hunger strike; Glišić must let him write to Natalia.

The sentry opened the door. "Here's your supper, Mustachios."

"Go and tell the duty officer that I demand that my hands be untied immediately. Maybe I did hit Bloodsucker with a jar of blackberry jam, but I didn't kill the King. I'm as hungry as a wolf. I'll chew you up, I'll bite anyone I see wearing a uniform. Is that clear? First put a piece of bread in my mouth."

The sentry broke off a piece of hardtack and silently pushed it between his lips. Bogdan swallowed it voraciously and thought of how he would tell Natalia that it was impossible to hate a suffering enemy.

Before he had eaten half his ration Glišić's orderly came to take him to the commander's office. Bogdan believed that he was about to be released; Glišić would berate him in the name of the homeland as usual, then let him go; he was glad, and pleased with himself, that he had not been wrong about Glišić. An unhappy enemy is not capable of great wickedness; it is happy and satisfied people who have the strength for violent and inhumane actions. So he reasoned as he stepped into the commander's office, not a little surprised to find him in the same position. Only Glišić no longer held his whip, an important change, and a pleasant one. A lamp burning low on the table shed a warm light. Bogdan stood beside the door, watching Glišić and waiting. He could hear people singing in the barracks and someone playing a guitar. He would write Natalia tonight; it was three days since he had written her. He would tell her that if a revolutionary who hated tyrants and exploiters did not possess in equal measure the power of forgiveness, then he might become even more cruel than those he was trying to destroy. How did he come to have so much Christian compassion? Justice must not be the same as vengeance. Where had he read this? A great evil must be pulled up by the roots.

"What are you intending to be, Dragović? That is, if the enemy doesn't kill you for your homeland." Glišić spoke in a stern, quiet voice, still standing in the same position.

Bogdan hesitated, not sure whether to answer frankly, and looked hard at Glišić. The marks of suffering on Glišić's face seemed deeper. This decided him, and he said firmly:

"I intend to fight against our misfortunes, sir." He could hear the floor creaking under him, or was it that Glišić gave a start? "Because," he added even more confidently, "our nation will be the most unfortunate of all nations, even more unfortunate than Russia, if it isn't already."

"I didn't quite catch what you said."

Oblivious to the irony in Glišić's voice, Bogdan said more loudly: "Don't you think that we are a most unfortunate nation?"

"Why so?"

"Well, among other things, because the first machine was brought into Serbia to make instruments of destruction. As you know, our first factory was an armaments factory. The first molten iron in Serbia was not used to make tools and plowshares, but to make cannons. And we go on buying cannons and rifles, not iron plows and machinery."

"Go on."

"We are plowing the land with wooden plows, but we have the most up-to-date howitzers."

"So that's why we're an unhappy nation?" Still Glišić did not move, though there was perhaps a slight tremor in his voice.

"Yes, sir. The men who run the country have pushed us down the wrong road. We've become a poor nation, deeply in debt, a government of thieves, with the loftiest national aims. We want to unite all the Serbs, we want to make a great state—all on the backs of peasants and workers."

Bogdan stepped toward Glišić and raised his voice. "What have our people gained from the wars with the Turks, the Bulgarians, and the Albanians?"

"You're asking me that?" said Glišić, still standing motionless, still staring out the window into the darkness.

"Not you personally. You are a man of honor, but mistaken in your ideas. You are . . ." Bogdan fell silent as the commander of the Student Battalion suddenly turned around and glared at him in his customary threatening way.

"Stand at attention!" he hissed.

Disappointed, Bogdan obeyed the command, looking at the strange expression on Glišić's face, which his exceedingly long, pointed mustache somehow distorted and made really terrifying.

"I asked you what you wanted to be in this wretched land of ours, whose soil you also tread."

"In this wretched land of ours I mean to teach people the truth about their misery. And to prepare the working class for revolution."

"For destruction?" said Glišić, stepping toward him.

"Only a revolution can save Serbia."

"Serbia?" Glišić whispered, dumbfounded.

"Yes. I'm firmly convinced of that."

Lieutenant Colonel Glišić turned around and walked to the window; Bogdan could no longer see his profile, but he could hear him whispering:

"Poor Serbia! My poor, wretched country, what lies in store for you? What sort of fate are your educated sons preparing for you? What will become of you when these men rule our poor and illiterate people?" He turned toward Bogdan and asked quietly: "What mischief are you plotting for the homeland?"

"I thought we were having a serious conversation, sir."

"Now, when our front has cracked, when our army is reduced by half, and blood is flowing on all sides, you think of revolution," Glišić whispered, turning his back on Bogdan and taking his whip from the table.

The loud swishing of whip over boots drowned out Glišić's whispers and revived in Bogdan's mind the image of Glišić the militarist, reactionary thug. But if he took this unhappy fanatic prisoner in the revolution, could he bring himself to shoot him? What would he do if this man were brought to him one evening with his hands bound, as the commander of a counterrevolutionary regiment? He would first of all order his hands to be untied immediately, and apologize for holding to this tradition.

Lieutenant Colonel Glišić came up to him, eyes blazing, holding his whip behind his back.

"What mischief have you been thinking up? Out with it, you wretched socialist! I suppose you're studying law. Go on, I'm listening."

"Do you have the courage to hear the truth, sir?"

"The courage? Why do I need courage before you?"

"To hear my honest answer, in which you are so interested."

"Your honest answer? Go on, tell me what you've been scheming. Let's hear it."

Bogdan noticed the whip waving behind Glišić's back, and this provoked him. "I was wondering if I would shoot you if I took you prisoner."

"What do you mean, if you took me prisoner?"

"I mean, if I took you prisoner in the revolution." Their eyes locked. It seemed to Bogdan that his bound hands were bending forward toward Glišić. He heard Glišić's strained voice.

"And what did you decide?"

"I couldn't make up my mind," said Bogdan, speaking more loudly.

"You couldn't make up your mind? Why not?"

"Because of something I believe in."

"Then let this settle your doubts!" Lieutenant Colonel Glišić stepped back and quickly, with all his strength, whipped Bogdan several times across the face.

Bogdan stood stock-still from sheer astonishment. Glišić, the table, the light, splintered into a thousand fragments, transfixed in the quivering silence; his face and the pain from the blows swelled until they burst into the room, filling it completely, so that there was nothing but burning darkness.

"Why couldn't you make up your mind?" shouted Lieutenant Colonel Glišić somewhere in the darkness.

"Because you are unhappy! Because you are suffering."

"So you feel sorry for me? Is that it, you damned socialist!"

Bogdan heard the swish of the whip and felt his cap fall off.

"And this is to stop you feeling sorry for me!" Glišić hit him hard on the face.

"That doesn't help you at all. I'm still not sure what I'd do. I pity you, I sincerely pity you," Bogdan muttered, and closed his eyes; his head felt enormous and something warm trickled down his cheek. When he opened his eyes the lamp was no longer burning, and Glišić was staring out the window, silent and motionless. "I won't shoot you in the revolution!" cried Bogdan out of sheer perversity; he staggered in the darkness and leaned against the wall.

"Who told you that I was unhappy? What makes you think that I'm unhappy?" The words were spoken not by Lieutenant Colonel Glišić, commander of the Student Battalion, but by an imploring voice from the darkness.

"Because you act like an unhappy man. You're cruel because you're unhappy!" Bogdan cried, determined to punish him.

Glišić lunged at him; Bogdan jumped aside and raised his bound hands, not to defend himself, but to return the blow. However, Glišić brusquely opened the door and shouted to the sentry: "Take him back to the prison!"

Coming down the steps from the commander's office, Bogdan Dragović collided head on with the moon—a dark red, bloated pumpkin hurtling over the roof of the barracks. His sweating face was on fire, his head full of the swishing of the whip. He walked unsteadily behind his bound hands, stepping heavily through the moonlight, as though he were walking on sand.

As he lay in his cell, a rat sprang up from a shaft of light. It stopped, stared at him, and smiled. *A class isn't a man, the bourgeoisie isn't a man. Then what are evil and injustice?* The rat held out its hand to him, smiling sympathetically. A man had tied up his hands and struck him with a whip. A man who suffered and carried a whip; an unhappy man, quick to strike; a saber-rattler with grief in his heart. The rat straightened itself and gripped the bars of the window with its hand: its saber, epaulets, and medals glittered in the moonlight. *God help you, heroes!* Its fur cap fell down over its face. *Freedom has the right to redeem itself; can't you understand this, Natalia? The world is divided into those who beat and those who are beaten. The beaten have the right to avenge themselves; do you hear, Natalia? Yes they have, Ivan. That's how I want it, sir. Why shall we all be unhappy if we have to live in bondage? Whom shall we hate then, Natalia? We will shoot the blows, the whips, and the sabers.* The rat gave a frightened shudder, the fur cap fell off with a bang, like a barrel; he began to tremble violently: the cap was hurtling toward his feet, clattering like an empty barrel. He shook himself again, then curled up, thrust his head against the stone, and pressed his nose against a candle, against the warm, fragrant wax. His teeth chattered from the swishing of the whip, which contracted into the motion of his mother's loom, into the dull thud and creaking of the reeds.

Someone shook his shoulder and he heard a voice say: "The C.O. is waiting for you."

"I'm not budging," he told the sentry.

"But I have to take you to him."

"Just tell that thug that I won't come to his office. And don't give any explanation."

Trembling, Bogdan turned toward the wall, brought the candle close to his nose, and breathed in its fragrance. Blood was spurting from his face and the weals from the whip had swelled up; his head was a confused mass of dull, burning pain. Someone came into the room; he didn't care who it was. But he put the candle next to his feet.

"Why did you lie to me about hitting the duty officer with a jam jar?"

Was that Glišić? Or the man on guard?

"Give me an honest answer, like a soldier."

It was Glišić, all right. He turned around and looked at him, but remained lying down. He would not stand at attention.

"I asked you why you lied to me yesterday."

"I did hit the duty officer with a jam jar, and I'm sorry I missed his head. Another time I'll aim better. With a bomb. And not only at him."

Lieutenant Colonel Glišić strode toward the window. He was not carrying his whip.

"Untie my hands!" Bogdan said, waving his heavy swollen hands.

Glišić turned around and stared at him; for the first time, his face brightened with pleasure. "You're a splendid fellow, Bogdan Dragović! You're what a Serb should be. But you'll spend a month in prison for lying to your commanding officer. Unfortunately, the law does not allow me to give you a heavier punishment."

Bogdan could hardly believe his ears; he raised himself slightly and leaned against the wall. In this position he could more easily say what he felt.

"What a splendid officer you'd make if your head hadn't been stuffed with pernicious ideas and foreign books!" Glišić turned away from Bogdan. "Poor, wretched Serbia! Your best sons are preparing a shameful future for you." He whispered something else that Bogdan could not catch, then turned around suddenly, came up to Bogdan, bent over him, and breathed into the pains cutting into his face:

"You misguided anarchist! You're like a lost sheep. Just get hold of this, my boy: the First Army has been destroyed. Valjevo will soon fall. Then Belgrade is done for. Can you live in bondage, my boy?"

"No. I'll be no man's slave."

Glišić walked up and down the cell, his head bowed, talking as though to himself.

"Why do you believe that I'm unhappy? Do all the students think that?"

Bogdan opened his mouth to say "I believe it," but Glišić suddenly burst out: "Do you think I'm unhappy because my two brothers gave their lives for their country? Do you idiots think that I'm grieving for their heroic death? You don't even know that heroes aren't mourned. Their death doesn't cause pain. I envy them! I feel nothing but envy for them because they gave their lives for Serbia. I envy every Serb now on the battlefield. It is my punishment that I have to make soldiers out of you students, you spoiled, pampered brats, you mother's darlings from Belgrade. You don't even know how to number off and form double rows, and tomorrow you'll be the leaders, the intellectual spearhead of your country. It's pitiful!"

Glišić opened the door and shouted: "Untie his hands!" Then he rushed out of the prison.

In the ranks of the Student Battalion, Ivan Katić for the first time stood self-confident, smiling, and defiant; it was because of him, he believed, that Glišić had ordered the battalion to line up. No one in his platoon, indeed no one in the Student Battalion, knew that half an hour earlier he had been in the commanding officer's room and had told him the truth about the attempted "assassination" of Second Lieutenant Ilić.

"Sir, you must be told the truth about what happened in the dormitory of Squad One of the Sixth Platoon."

"Yes?" said Glišić quietly, staring at some lines on a half sheet of paper.

"It was I, not Bogdan Dragović, who hit Second Lieutenant Dragiša Ilić with a jar of preserves."

"So?" asked Glišić, still bending over his paper.

"I ought to be held responsible for this action, not Dragović. I should be punished, and he should be set free."

"And?" Glišić continued vaguely.

"It is only right that Bogdan Dragović should be released from prison immediately."

The Lieutenant Colonel leaned on his desk, rested his head on his hands, and bent over the few typewritten lines on his paper as if making a decision affecting the fate of his country. Then, in a startlingly quiet and ordinary voice, he said: "Go back to the barracks."

Unable to believe his ears, Ivan did not move. His head still resting on his hands, Glišić looked up at Ivan and repeated his order. Ivan left the office downcast, uncertain whether he had taken leave correctly, and walked around the barracks yard. He felt ashamed that he had allowed Bogdan Dragović to go to prison in his place. Then the officers started running around excitedly, and the bugle sounded assembly. He was glad: Glišić was ordering the battalion to assemble to announce his punishment. The tables would be turned on those who had insulted him and considered him a coward. Now he would be able to say in front of the whole battalion what he had had no opportunity to say in Glišić's office.

He looked impatiently in the direction of that office; without fear and full of self-confidence, he awaited his great moment. Behind him, Danilo History-Book warned him in a low voice not to spoil the line. Bora Jackpot hung his head and breathed an audible and mournful sigh. Shouldn't he tell at least these two what he had done and why they had now been lined up? No. Let them get a surprise, and reflect a bit—and all the others, too. But why was the battalion so quiet, so dejected? As though out of the whole thirteen hundred of them, only Bora Jackpot dared to release that prolonged sigh and express the general fear and anxiety, which during the day was dammed up with jokes, usually childish and often quite pointless; only in their sleep at night did they sigh, and groan at the terrors of their dreams. Behind the mountains to the west, there appeared a strange, enormous cloud. Ivan believed that they all had the same thoughts as they looked at that cloud, and heard the same sound as they listened to a starling whistling at the top of a tree with dangling black pods.

"Danilo, what's that tree called where the starling's whistling?" Ivan asked softly.

"It's some kind of acacia. Now shut up!"

"Blindie, how do you know about starlings?" whispered Bora Jackpot gloomily.

"Oh, I know. I like the starling and the titmouse best of all birds," he said, surprised at himself; he had never thought about which birds he liked best. The starling was whistling as though it were alone in a forest, as though there were no Sixth Platoon of the Student Battalion lined up in front of it, looking at a black bird on a bare acacia tree.

"Shhh! He's coming," whispered History-Book.

Ivan's heart began to pound, but not only from fear. He felt a joy he had never experienced before. Lieutenant Colonel Glišić galloped up on his horse, accompanied by his staff, and stood in front of the platoon.

"Heroes!"

What does that mean, Ivan wondered.

"The High Command summons you in the name of the homeland!"

"What's he saying, Bora?" whispered Ivan.

"Your country needs your lives. Pay your debts, my boys! I'm sending all thirteen hundred of you to the High Command as corporals! Tomorrow you will leave for the front."

"Hurrah! Hurrah!"

" 'Hail, bugler from the Drina front . . .' "

" 'Serbia, our dear mother . . .' "

The shouting and singing drowned the Lieutenant Colonel's voice.

Caps flew in the air as they kissed and embraced one another. Danilo History-Book ran off somewhere; Bora Jackpot disappeared too. The whole battalion scattered in high spirits. He didn't see the commanding officer depart with his staff. Ivan remained where he was, alone. He noticed that the starling was not silent on its branch. He felt confused, disappointed, frightened by the good cheer of his companions and by something other than the prospect of battle and death. He began to walk toward the barracks, but suddenly turned in the direction of the prison.

The prison reverberated with the songs and shouts of the prisoners: "We'll take our Bastille! We're corporals too! Down with discipline! Long live our struggle! On to Vienna!"

Bogdan Dragović listened but could not understand what was happening. He was lying on the bare boards with his jacket over his head, covering the pain of his stiff, swollen face; he pressed his melted candle over the marks left by the riding whip, and inhaled the smell of the wax, heavy with a keen sadness: why did they have to hit him on the face every time he was arrested? Why did they have to strike right at a man's vision, words, and smile? How long would man continue to strike the eyes and face of his fellow man?

Someone was calling him, pounding on the cell door with his fists. He got up and put on his jacket.

"What do you want?"

"It's I—Ivan. I've told the C.O. that I threw the jar at Bloodsucker. He'll let you out. We're leaving for the front tomorrow afternoon!"

"So that's what all the noise is about?"

"You just can't imagine what high spirits they're all in! The battalion is going to Kragujevac, to be placed at the disposal of the High Command."

"And when will you get to Kragujevac?"

"The day after tomorrow, I suppose."

"I'll run away tonight and come with you. Find out the exact time the train leaves. Then run into town and send a telegram. Write down the message."

"Don't worry, I'll remember it. Just tell me."

" 'Natalia Dumović, Prerovo, P.O. Palanka. Arriving Kragujevac in two days. Meet me at station. Bogdan.' Repeat it, please." Bogdan pressed his forehead against the door, but it made his bruises hurt and he winced as he moved back.

Ivan repeated the message and then continued excitedly: "My father was born in Prerovo. Have you been there?"

"No, I haven't. I met Natalia in Belgrade. She was studying philosophy. Her father is the schoolmaster in Prerovo."

"If we don't get killed—I mean when we get leave—how about us going to Prerovo together? My grandfather is there, and my uncle and my cousin. Maybe your Natalia is one of my relatives. That would be great!"

"Please hurry!"

"So Glišić struck you on the face."

"He did. Go to a pharmacy and buy something for my bruises. How can I meet her in this condition?"

Bogdan leaned forward with his hands against the door of the cell. He could hear cheerful shouting and singing in the barracks. Maybe he would see her for the last time like this, his face disfigured and one eye closed.

"You're still there, Ivan?"

"There's something I must tell you. Maybe this isn't the right time, and you can hardly see my face, so I'll say it. You know, everything gets dirty, just like our hands. Feelings can become warped, just like bodies. Especially in the barracks. During this awful time two people have really meant something to me, meant just as much as my country. And that's a big thing, Bogdan. I've written her about you, and what you mean to me here."

"Who did you write that to?"

"Sorry, I didn't tell you. I have a sister; her name's Milena. She's a nurse in Valjevo. She's my only sister, and she's perfect, if such a person can exist. I love her."

"But do you have a girl, Ivan?"

"No, I don't. Actually, I was in love with someone, but she ran off with a Bulgarian. I do have a sister though."

"So do I. But that's different."

They looked toward each other in silence through the thick old door of the prison.

"I know plenty of men and girls, Ivan, for whom I'd turn the world upside down."

"But I'm suspicious of people who love a lot of other people. We'll talk about that some other time."

Bogdan heard Ivan running up to the sentry and shouting. He thought of how he would escape if he wasn't released that night.

The door opened and the sentry appeared with a smile on his face. "My congratulations, Corporal. You don't believe me? Can't you hear the shouts of celebrating? Hurry up, the C.O. is waiting for you."

Bogdan buttoned his jacket and went out, sure that he was now free. If Glišić was waiting for him at the window with his back to the room, he would go out immediately, without even saluting him.

However, he found Glišić greeting him with a formal salute. "I shall make it possible for you to carry out your duty to the homeland," he said. "I will postpone your punishment. When you get to the front, tell your regimental commanding officer that you have to serve thirty days' imprisonment and that you are to serve this sentence as soon as conditions at the front are suitable. Now go to your platoon. You leave for Kragujevac at noon tomorrow."

"And if conditions aren't suitable for my prison sentence?"

"Your country will forgive you only if you die a hero's death."

Bogdan looked at him thoughtfully. Was he now suffering less? Was he less unhappy? He saluted Glišić and tried to smile, which made the bruises on his cheek and over his eye hurt all the more.

Not until today in the prison did the two of us really become friends, reflected Ivan as he walked back to the Blue Barracks from the town post office. In the stinking darkness of the prison, separated by the cell door, they had become friends for life. If he had been able to see Bogdan's face, maybe he would not have said those things about himself, the thought of which even now made him blush. Would his cheeks burn and redden after the war too, if he survived it, whenever he experienced or said something really significant? Had he not spoken those few sentences, he would not now love Bogdan as much as he did. He had heard the catch in Bogdan's breath, and had felt with all his senses how much Bogdan was suffering. It had impelled him to confide in Bogdan. This, he supposed, was the beginning of true friendship, this declaration of love through trust in which all fear was burned up, this liberation of one's whole being. All at once loneliness had been vanquished, the ugliness of the barracks obliterated, the fear of tomorrow forgotten. Even hell was not hell if a man had Milena and Bogdan. If friendship between people was born of Bogdan's revolution, he would become a socialist. The sacrifices demanded by the revolution would be justified; it had the right to destroy everything that stood in its way. He would tell Bogdan this tonight.

Ivan was halted by the autumnal splendor of a service tree and a wild pear in the hedge. It was Danilo History-Book who had first pointed out the service tree to him during a "detour around the enemy" through a wood; the wild pear was familiar to him from the family vineyard. Never had he seen such profusion of color, such intense light, or trees glowing with such autumnal beauty! He took off his glasses so that the light might settle in his eyes forever. He must remember that light was the source of everything; light even created man. Beyond light there was no truth. Had he read this somewhere? But why search for the meaning of anything now? He must look and breathe deeply, he must experience the joy of autumn. If besides books a man had Milena and Bogdan, and a service tree and a wild pear, what else did he need? A group of students came up from the barracks, hurrying noisily toward town. As he walked up to them they shouted:

"Mustachios has been released! Now we're all together."

"Where is he?" asked Ivan joyfully.

"Back in the room. He's doctoring his friendship."

"He's doctoring what?" Ivan felt the color rise to his cheeks. *They don't know that I've been to see Glišić,* he thought.

"His memento from Glišić."

"This morning I told the C.O. that I was the one who hit Bloodsucker."

"That's now irrelevant. Vojvoda Putnik fixed all that. Come along into town; why stick around the barracks? Soldiers always spend the last night of peace storming the mount of Venus, charging its foothills, right at the source, Blindie."

Walking past them with the sound of their jokes in his ears, he saw the corporal's stars on their shoulder straps. Were these future schoolmasters, doctors, and engineers really pleased with their stars? It didn't make sense. He hurried away to find Bogdan as quickly as possible. He could not think of going to town and enjoying himself without Bogdan. He met other groups hurrying into Skoplje.

"Why are you heading for the barracks now, Blindie? We're going to have a night on the town! We'll make Skoplje remember us!" Danilo History-Book called to him.

"I'm going to pick up Bogdan; we'll come together," Ivan replied. Then he went up to Danilo and said: "You know I went to see the C.O. this morning."

"I know."

"Does everyone know?"

"No, but it doesn't matter any more."

"It matters a lot to me. Please spread the word to the whole Student Battalion."

"Don't worry; just you two come to town. I'll make a conquest of that singer with the tambourine; you'll see!"

Danilo History-Book ran off with his group, and Ivan hurried up the hill toward the Blue Barracks. He had never gone carousing; this form of pleasure seemed to him stupid and incomprehensible. He had never gone on a spree with friends. At home Milena had entertained him with her funny impersonations, dressing up in her mother's clothes and her father's suits. And a few evening parties were held in their vineyard. That was the sum total of his amusement. He had never embraced a woman, and no girl had ever kissed him, except Milena; Ivanka had only touched his arm by chance from time to time. It was books he had embraced, and books he had slept with. During the past year he had been carried away by the notion of light, inspired by his reading of Indian philosophy. But what if this was his last peacetime twilight, his last day untouched by war, his last night as a civilian? What if, from the moment he had seen the starling on the acacia tree, he was doing everything for the last time?

Ivan smiled sadly at the rowdy corporals, elated by the prospect of a night of debauchery, rushing off to their last evening of fun: he was the only one coming back from town to the barracks.

As he entered the dormitory through the wide-open door, he was astounded by the disorder: the room looked as though a marauding army had just left.

"Did you send the telegram?" asked Bogdan, lying on his bed with a wet towel over his face.

"Don't worry, everything is all right," said Ivan joyfully, jumping over open footlockers, pillows, dirty underwear, and empty boxes. He was glad they were alone. He sat down on a pallet.

"I'm here too, Blindie," announced Bora Jackpot, who was lying in his boots, half buried under pillows, and smoking. "Doesn't our dormitory look terrific, Blindie? At last it looks like it really should. We've had our revenge for two months of tidiness and discipline. I wouldn't have gone off to the front before trampling on our pallets, which Bloodsucker himself said were like packets of tobacco. Just look what Don Quixote did to Mustachios!"

Ivan leaned over Bogdan, who moved the towel, revealing his closed eye and the bruises on his cheek surrounded by congealed blood.

"Oh, no!" whispered Ivan, trembling. *It was because of me that he was struck,* he thought.

"It's nothing; it will pass. The main thing is that my right eye is still good—for aiming and other things." Bogdan would have liked to ask them whether his bruise would disappear during the next two days, before they reached Kragujevac. How could he kiss Natalia with such a disfigured face?

Bora Jackpot raised himself on his elbows.

"Listen, Ivan, last night there was unimaginable chaos in the universe. My cards were personally carried off by Her Majesty Fate. The universe was dominated by numbers and colors that came nowhere near my circle. I lost with the ten of diamonds, and then with the queen of spades; I fell asleep convinced that I would wake up to find some great event had taken place. Honestly, I was expecting that either a separate peace had been signed with Austria-Hungary, or that Bulgaria and Rumania had entered the war on our side. But all that's happened is that I've lost the buttons on my overcoat and been proclaimed a corporal."

"How much do you need?"

"Whatever you can give me. I've been waiting for you. Nobody wanted to lend me a single dinar. The corporals, like all devotees of death, want only wine and women tonight. Give me thirty dinars to spend on my last night in Skoplje."

Ivan handed him the money gladly, without hesitation.

"Be a good sport and give me another ten dinars."

Ivan gave him some more money without counting.

"Good luck, boys!" Bora Jackpot strode across the pallet in his unbuttoned overcoat and hurried out of the dormitory.

"I'm sure he's the most sentimental fellow in the Student Battalion. Yet he hasn't any friends. All people are the same to him," said Ivan, and felt himself blushing. "Who knows why he's unhappy," he added, just for something to say. He wanted to get out of the barracks with Bogdan as soon as possible.

"When will the telegram arrive?"

"The girl in the post office promised that it would reach Palanka this evening, and arrive in Prerovo by noon tomorrow at the latest. What did Glišić say to you?"

"He has magnanimously given me the opportunity to die for the homeland. But if I don't die immediately, as soon as we've driven the Fritzies across the Drina, I must serve thirty days' imprisonment. He's an unhappy man, a sick man. Ivan, take my cigarettes out of my pocket and light one for me; my hands are wet," Bogdan said, but he was thinking that if the telegram arrived by noon the next day, or even by nightfall, she could reach Kragujevac before they did.

Ivan carefully placed a lighted cigarette between Bogdan's lips. "The war will never be over for us, Bogdan. Even if Belgrade and Kragujevac fall, if all of Serbia is occupied, the war will still go on as long as Glišić and a single student corporal exist. Our Danilo History-Book, for instance. War is half illness, half idea. Or an illness from a great idea. Don't laugh," Ivan said, but he was asking himself why all the socialists and revolutionaries he knew despised those who did not share their opinions. And yet he was not opposing Bogdan.

"That's a naïve notion, Ivan. War is plunder, justified by a lofty idea. The greater the aims of the conquerors, the loftier the ideas that are used to justify the crimes committed by states and nations."

"Please don't talk politics! Who cares what war is." Ivan leaned over Bogdan and grabbed his arm; he shivered from the intimacy. "It's getting dark; we should get out of this damned barracks."

"Fine, Ivan. I want to look something like myself when Natalia sees me the day after tomorrow; that's why I'm holding this compress over Glišić's signature. But there's plenty of time; I'll do it on the train."

Bogdan got up and dressed quickly. Ivan felt that he was sacrificing himself on his account, and this both pleased and discomfited him, since Bogdan's face really was disfigured. He followed Bogdan out of the room, striding over the pallets.

"But why must we have a revolution and turn the world upside down to live and be happy? Isn't a girl's love and the devotion of two friends enough?" Ivan asked as they left the barracks.

"That's too little for life and happiness, Ivan. We need more."

Ivan smiled faintly, more from pity than disbelief. For the first time since they had become acquainted on the train to Skoplje two months ago, he felt superior to Bogdan. He was sorry to contradict him. He could hear the quiet chirping of a cricket. He had never actually seen one.

"What does a cricket look like, Bogdan?"

"It's black and very beautiful. When I was small I used to hunt them with my friends. We had competitions to see whose cricket chirped best," Bogdan said, gazing at the setting sun.

"Let's catch one and take it to the front! Just imagine a cricket in the trenches!"

Bogdan stopped and picked up a few leaves from a service tree; he put them in the envelope containing Natalia's letter.

"I have renounced love until I've discovered certain truths," said Ivan caustically.

"Whom did love ever prevent from discovering truths?"

"You can't love a woman and strive after wisdom at the same time. Politics and power are also enemies of truth."

"Those are outworn prejudices. Any truth that love interferes with is no truth for humans. And any human aim that love interferes with is not a valid human aim, Ivan. I'm ashamed of philosophizing; it's not in my line. But I can tell you this, simply as a friend: if I weren't in love, I would have deserted tonight."

Ivan stopped suddenly. *Why couldn't I have deserted tonight?* he asked himself. *Was it out of pride, or vanity, or some idea about man and the world?* He gazed at the moon; the moon and the sun were both in the sky. A lump of ice and a huge ball of fire, both giving out light. There was no boundary between day and night: night was mingling with day as day grew longer and stretched far into the heights.

Bogdan stopped too, but he was thinking about Natalia.

I'll be killed for certain, Ivan repeated to himself as he paused outside the door of the Sloboda Café, where singing and loud music could be heard. How could he prolong this day, abandoned by the sun and overtaken by the moon? Could he prolong this night beyond Skoplje? It was as if he had cleaned his shoes for the last time until the end of the war, taken pleasure in the wild pear for all his twenty years, and gazed at the light of the autumn dusk for at least one impoverished lifetime.

From behind the open door, Bogdan called to him to come in; Danilo History-Book was shouting to Bogdan to come to his table.

"Do you know what time the train from Niš will arrive?" asked a man in a straw hat.

"I've no idea."

"It's terrible. It's seven hours late."

Ivan marched into the bright lights and smoke, into mounting waves of music, singing, and noise. Bogdan was pushing his way toward the corner where Danilo History-Book was sitting at a table. He couldn't join them at that moment. First he had to savor the joy that so intoxicated his companions. All the tables were occupied by singing and shouting student corporals. The space between the tables and the platform on which musicians were accompanying a singer with a tambourine—right up to the bar and the entrance to the kitchen, from which came the sizzling sound of broiled meat—was filled with civilians, local people, and refugees. They were talking in a subdued manner amid the smell of food, sweat, and tobacco smoke; the bleary light cast a gray shadow over their faces, making them look old and frightened. Ivan made his way toward the bar.

"Why do you think the train from Niš is so late, young man?"

"It has nothing to do with me, sir."

Ivan stood at the bar: what should he drink? They all begin with brandy. He had tried it a few times and found it repulsive. Beer? It would take a bucketful to get drunk. He was too hungry to start with wine. No, he would try them all in turn. Strong brandy, beer, then wine.

Bogdan called to him to sit at their table. But he wouldn't join them while he was sober and they still looked strange and foolish to him. He drained his glass of brandy to the last drop. He ate a piece of cheese. He drank a mug of beer. It tasted stale and bitter. He ate more cheese, with green pepper. Then a glass of red wine. He shook himself and refilled his glass. He would sit down with them when he was no longer conscious of any difference between them and himself, when he wanted to shout whatever they were shouting. He was beginning to enjoy the music and singing. He drank another glass of wine. He would move when he wanted to sit beside one of those women whom several corporals at once were trying to pick up. Yes, when he had decided just which one he would sit next to; then, after midnight, regardless of fights and blows, he would step over the flushed faces of the men—warrior preparing to storm the mount of Venus—and lead her into the street, into the darkness and moonlight—it was all the same. Then he would take her to the park, or the bank of the Vardar. Yes, that's what he would do.

"Another half liter, please!"

Danilo History-Book would be killed. And Bogdan. It was sure to happen; he smiled so darkly. That woman with the hat, she was beautiful, though old; he would take her under the service tree, onto the leaves—red, brown, purple, and yellow leaves, which smelled of earth and sunshine—and for the first time he would become a man. Tonight, this last night, he would lie with a woman; how would he put it to her? Yes, on the leaves, like a shepherd—like his father, when he was young.

"Has the train from Niš come in yet, gentlemen? Nobody knows when it'll be here. The whole front has collapsed. Valjevo has fallen!"

He would like to smash that man's nose. Milena was in Valjevo. He grabbed the man by his shirt.

"How do you know Valjevo has fallen, you rat?"

"Don't you know the High Command has fled to Kragujevac, you silly schoolboy?"

He let go of the man, and drank up his wine. His cheeks were burning, but not from shame; he didn't feel ashamed any more. Wine was a cure for shame, wasn't it? How come he hadn't known that? Of course, it wasn't just chance that so many people drank, including the whole of his platoon. He had never heard such a mournful song. And what a row they were making!

"What's happened to the train from Niš, gentlemen? Belgrade will go in two days. In Sofia they're delighted with our defeat. The Bulgarians will attack us in three days. If as many refugees come tomorrow as today and yesterday, we'll have to push them into the attic. They've eaten us out of house and home. The Allied forces are moving up from Salonika. That's not true! Why go to Greece? Who's going to feed us? And *why* hasn't the train from Niš arrived?"

"What use is our state and our freedom if you're going to die?" someone whispered, placing his hand on Ivan's shoulder.

"You're a coward, sir!"

He thrust the hand away from his shoulder; he wanted something to drink. He felt he must drink because of that sharp sweetness, that slash of redness cutting through the unbearably mournful Macedonian songs, and the sound of the violins, which seemed to stretch right back to those evenings in Skadarlija during his last year at school, when he had first learned the meaning of jealousy. Since then he had never spoken a word to her, he had entirely forgotten the girl—Ružica, she was called. Through the dark-brown shadows something yellow was moving; a woman was pressing her leg and buttocks against him. He leaned against the bar and looked at her. She was ugly, repulsive even. He began to move away, but the new arrivals pressed her toward him.

"What do you want, madam?"

"You needn't call me 'madam,' mister—I'm not married, and by the way, about when do you think the train from Niš will arrive?" Even her voice repelled him.

"Madam, I'm not interested in the train from Niš. Or in you!"

He turned away from her. She was a specter—a witch! He hadn't seen such an ugly woman for ages. No, he wasn't drunk.

"That's where you're wrong, sir. Your fate depends on the train from Niš."

She screamed in his ear, like that deformed milk vendor at the corner of Vaugirard Street and Monsieur le Prince, who had always smiled at him lovingly, and followed him with her eyes until he disappeared around the corner. She was even worse than the Belgian girl who used to wait for him after the lectures, and more repulsive than the washerwoman Cula, who had jerked him by his pocket and spoken some foul words to him when he was in the sixth grade. It was his fate—the law of his existence—to attract ugly women. They were the only ones who looked at him and desired him. His sister, Milena, had tried—with sisterly sympathy, because she loved him—to convince him that he was an unusual boy, out of the ordinary.

It was Ivanka who had first told him this, once when he had tried to walk home with her. "You're not like other people, Ivan," she had said, "but I don't like anybody to see me home." Ivanka Ilić. They had sat in the same classroom for four years; she was the worst student in the class in mathematics. "Excuse me, I haven't done my homework," she would say. A very serious girl, round-shouldered and rather plain, but very sweet and charming. For three years she had sat in the third row on the girls' side. Then one Speech Day, when he was reading his prize essay, he felt himself being watched by bright, slightly squinting eyes from somewhere at the back of the hall and he began to stammer—until he recognized Ivanka's eyes. His mother had noticed his momentary confusion. After leaving the school hall he had waited for Ivanka to have a closer look at her. But she had stolen away, alone as usual; she always came to school and went home alone. So it was until that last day, three days before their graduation examination. Why did drunkards always insist that wine tasted best at the bottom of the glass?

"Another half liter of red wine, please! And what about that shashlik?" he cried.

No, it wasn't mutual attraction; why nurse his wounded vanity tonight? When Ivanka had waited for him at the corner, it had been a question of mathematics. She had never smiled so before. And she was beautiful, really beautiful. How he had trembled when they stood face to face, so close that they might have kissed. It was the first time he had really looked at her, and he saw how beautiful her dusky face was, with its sharply chiseled features and large mouth with perfectly formed lips. No, it was her expressive eyes that captivated him, even if they did squint a bit. "I'll come home with you; I know where you live." He had been afraid, poor wretch, that he might meet his father and had at once turned into the next side street. That was a despicable trick. It wasn't that he was afraid. And she hadn't said a word about his going off in a different direction, but had looked at him sweetly with her shining eyes. He had talked to her about all kinds of things, culled from books he had read. If she hadn't found it interesting, she wouldn't have kept stopping and looking at him with such excitement. That was why he dared not stop talking, but babbled on and on. No, she surely couldn't have found him boring, when she had smiled so sweetly and gently as she took her math exercise book out of her schoolbag and asked: "Will you do my homework for me?" What else could he have said when he stood there, speechless with joy, leaning against the fence with a flowering creeper catching at his coat? "I'll come for the exercise book at half past six and wait in front of your house." "No, I'll bring it here." He must surely have said this, because she had said: "No, I'll come and wait in front of your house." It was a dirty, messy exercise book, and there were seven sums to do. How many times had he turned the pages of that exercise book! It was dirty and messy, just like her. No, that wasn't true. It was only after he had turned the pages of that exercise book three hundred times that he had begun to feel troubled and had tried to figure out why Ivanka Ilić had not come for her exercise book. And she hadn't come to school the next day either, nor had she appeared at the graduation examination. He never saw her again. He had prowled around that small padlocked white house with blue gates until an old crone told him reluctantly, as if concealing some crime, that Ivanka had vanished without a trace. All right, so she had run off with a Bulgarian; that was quite possible. She had fallen in love with a revolutionary, a nihilist. Didn't that prove that she was romantic, a girl of deep feelings, capable of noble deeds and sacrifice? But why had she given him her exercise book to work out sums for a math lesson she had no intention of coming to? Why had she made an appointment with him, knowing that she would not keep it? Why had she listened to him, and looked at him and smiled at him the way she did? Why had she kept silent while he talked to her of things he had never talked of before or since?

Danilo History-Book had climbed up on the table—or was it his chair? *Who am I?* thought Ivan. *If you take away my Christian name and surname, my origin and occupation, what is Ivan Katić?* He looked hard at the yellow witch: *Do you find me unusual?* He didn't say it, he was just thinking it. Ugly women are intelligent—that's the law of nature.

He pushed away this eyesore with the yellow scarf, enveloped in a yellow flame. Some gentlemen urged him to behave decently, even if he was leaving for the front the next day. The tambourine and the furious din deafened his ears. The words spoken near him sounded round, swollen, greasy. They smelled of barbecue meat and tobacco.

But why had Ivanka Ilić given him that messy exercise book, with only two sums right, when she knew she was going to run off with a Bulgarian that very night? He had taken the exercise book to Paris and thumbed through it every night, memorizing all her sums full of mistakes.

From a distance, Bogdan smiled at him. But he would not join them yet. It was interesting here at the bar. He would go over to them when he felt like singing. A boy in a white apron was standing in front of him; his eyes sparkled good-naturedly. Ivan whispered in his ear: "Do you know what a cricket looks like?"

Ivan leaned forward so that the boy could whisper back: "Don't you know yourself?"

"No, I don't, but I'd like to have one. I'll give you ten dinars if you can catch me two crickets."

"You're drunk! You'd better take some sesame seeds and walnuts. And later tonight, and again tomorrow morning, eat something sweet."

"And you can get ten dinars for two crickets, but only if you catch them tonight. They must be alive. Put them in an empty matchbox."

"Is your mother alive?"

"She sure is."

"Give me something on account."

"Here's a dinar. I'll wait for you here."

He pressed two dinars into the boy's hand, feeling light-hearted. He would take the crickets to the front, to the trenches, one for Bogdan. But what did they eat?

"Sir, do you know what crickets eat? I really want to know."

"Don't act so silly. In a couple of days the Germans will smash that clownish head of yours!"

"Do you know, sir, what crickets eat?"

They laughed at him but the sound was drowned out by the music. Yet there was no real gaiety. He looked around the tables, but couldn't recognize a single face. He called out:

"Boys, anybody here know anything about zoology?"

The woman with the yellow scarf leaned against him. People were dancing the kolo. One of the dancers pushed him from behind; his nose touched her yellow scarf, which smelled of something unfamiliar.

"Well, you tell me what crickets eat, and I'll tell you what time the train from Niš will arrive," he said, smiling into her large, shining eyes.

"You really are strange. It's a pity you can't just slip off to Salonika, instead of going off to that lion's den."

"Strange!" he shouted. Then he drank a few drops of wine, ate some meat, and said: "What did you say?" He put his hands on her shoulders.

"You heard me."

"How do you know I'm strange? Tell me why I'm not like other people."

The corporals who were dancing the kolo grabbed the girl with the yellow scarf and dragged her away toward the dancers. They were swallowed up in the sound of strained violin strings and tambourines.

"What do I care how far the Austrians have advanced? Look at the students! We're going to win! Yes, boys, I bet you my boots we're going to win. 'Serbia, our dear mother, you will be my land forever.' "

"Belgrade can't hold out, my boy. In five days they'll be in Kragujevac."

Again the same man pressed his elbow. He should hit the ape.

"That's deserter's talk, you dirty little civvy! D'you hear me?"

"And what about you, you poor things! A handful of salt thrown into the Danube and the Sava. You'll all be dead in a week, poor wretches. Dead on the altar of war."

"We're the Serbian intelligentsia! Corporals today, heroes tomorrow—immortal heroes, you coward!"

"Good for you, Blindie! Bring a liter of wine for Ivan Katić!"

He moved toward the bar. It wasn't Ivan who had shouted at that ape of a civilian. How had History-Book heard him? The music had stopped; that was it. The air in the café was thick with breathing, words, and the smell of food.

"Let's have another song! Get on with the music! We're leaving tomorrow and you can rest till Franz Josef dies!"

"Good for you, History-Book!" he whispered into the murk. The music and singing blurred the lamps and darkened the yellow scarf of the girl, now far away among the corporals.

"You shouldn't drink on an empty stomach, Ivan. Let's go have supper together."

Ivan turned around. It was Bogdan. They embraced.

"I want you to answer a question—straight from the shoulder. Do you trust me completely? No reservations?" He was sorry about the dark bruises on Bogdan's face; he wanted to kiss him exactly where Glišić had struck him.

"Of course I do, Ivan. Why should you doubt me?"

"I want you to drink a liter of wine first."

"I don't drink."

"I don't either. At least, I didn't until tonight."

"All right, I'll have a beer."

"Two mugs, bottoms up!"

"All right."

He ordered the beer and took off his glasses, to look at Bogdan without them. How awful! What would he do at the front with only one pair of glasses? Would his mother be waiting for him at Niš? His father must know when the students were leaving. Never mind; he would get off the train, pick up his glasses, and join his companions by a later train. Bogdan's smile stretched right across the room, over a pile of heads; it cut through the singing, dug deep into the sweat and the murmuring voices. He spoke straight into Bogdan's ear.

"I've wanted to exist in this world, not just to be alive. Do you understand the difference between existing and living, and the dilemma that it poses? To know what you are—or simply to live out your life. Well, that's clear enough. But from today on . . . The moment I heard the starling in that tree in front of the barracks, where our battalion was lined up, when Glišić told us that the time had come to die for our country—then, Bogdan old man, I saw how our hearts sank, in the whole Student Battalion. And that starling just went on singing. Yes, I wanted to *live*, just to live, nothing more. I wanted it desperately. I could feel my blood seething—and not from fright, honestly. Do you believe me?" He placed both his hands on Bogdan's shoulders.

"Yes, I believe you."

"Speak louder!"

"Yes, I believe you—honest!" He drained his mug of beer.

"I wanted to live life to the full. Life itself, not ideas—not the life of the soul, or some eternal verities. Real life, Bogdan. Life in this hellish din, with the foul smell of meat and wine—and that strange girl with the yellow scarf, who doesn't know mathematics. I bet she can't even add two columns of figures. And what do you want from this world, Bogdan? Forgive me for asking such a frank question."

"Since you ask a frank question, I'll give you a frank answer. I want something that can't be found in this world."

"But ideals are the most cruel deceivers. I hate them."

"Are you thinking of our country?"

"Not only that. I'm thinking of all visions of paradise and future bliss. I can't help it, I hate them! Please listen to me for a few minutes! Suddenly everything has become clear somehow, as though I were reading a book. As though these bottles and glasses themselves were the truth. Actually, in the Blue Barracks I doubted everything. I just couldn't believe in any of those ideals for which we are asked to give up our lives. I wrote about it to Milena, but she didn't answer."

"So you think that my ideal is some sort of asceticism?"

"I hate every kind of denial."

"So do I, Ivan. I don't want to deny or cut short anything. With my whole being, I want to change this world. I'm no monk."

"I'm not quite drunk yet, so please don't tell me what you think I want to hear. I only want to hear the truth. All of you who want a revolution preach about justice and equality; you want to make a paradise on earth, and you all want people to sacrifice their lives. I'm sorry, but I find that horrible."

"But the fact is, Ivan, old man, I don't regard the struggle for justice and equality as a sacrifice. I feel an intense joy, unlike any other sensation—and a terrible power. My whole being is filled with a feeling stronger than any other pleasure or satisfaction. Only someone who believes deeply can understand it. Am I making myself clear?"

"Yes, I follow you, but I'm not convinced. Nothing is worth sacrificing one's life for—absolutely nothing. Just look at our buddies. Which of them isn't sitting with a girl having a good time, for the last time?" He fell silent; the girl with the yellow scarf was smiling at him.

"Does your friend know when the train from Niš will arrive?"

Everything around him had become a yellow blur. He removed his hands from Bogdan's shoulders and drank up the rest of his wine. Bogdan took him by the arm and led him through the hubbub of the café, which was raucous with shouting and singing.

"Do you have a sister, Bogdan?" he whispered to his friend. He was grateful for Bogdan's support under his arm.

"Yes, I do. She's four years younger than me."

"Then you know what eternal love means. Loving a sister is the most innocent of all sins, isn't it? A secret sin, a sin of the imagination—the sweetest and the most painful. The one thing that's certain in a world full of uncertainties is love; I remember my father saying it once. If I didn't have a sister, I couldn't love you so much; honest I couldn't!"

He wasn't sure whether Bogdan could hear. It didn't matter; he was really just thinking aloud. As Bogdan's face came nearer, he could see the large bruises, a reproach to his laughter and whispers.

"And I love you more now because I love Natalia. But now let's go join those fellows with the girls and have a look at them, and enjoy ourselves."

"Just a minute, there's something else I want to tell you—something I thought of when I was in the sixth grade. Neither love nor any other feeling will stand the test of time. Don't you agree?"

"No, I don't."

"Truth is independent of time. It lasts longer, I tell you! One must be a devotee of truth and reason."

"Look here, that's enough metaphysics for tonight. Come on!"

"Just one thing more. I want you to tell me sincerely if you can be my friend, whatever ideas I hold. Be my friend forever, that is. You know what I mean."

"Of course I do. And I am your friend. How much longer are you going to doubt that?"

"I don't doubt it. You're a year older than me, and I feel—well, twenty. I don't really know what I mean. Maybe I really am drunk."

They sat down at a table beside two girls and a crowd of corporals.

Ivan knew for sure that the Sloboda Café was rocking and swaying, creaking and moaning on its way somewhere; so he sat with his legs apart, planted his elbows on the table, and held his head in his hands, carefully protecting the top of his head so that, when the inevitable crash came, he would not bang against the ceiling or the bar. He was most afraid for his glasses: if they fell off amid this black turmoil, not even Bogdan Dragović would be able to find them. And how could he die for his homeland blind as a bat?

Try as he would, he simply could not remember why he had kicked those civilians in the ass, three civilians altogether, including one in a straw hat and one in a fez. A fourth, wearing a frock coat, he had missed, hitting his foot against the wall. Maybe he had broken his toes; his foot sure hurt. Maybe he would die for the homeland without any toes. That stuffy old idiot with the straw hat, a member of the State Council, had berated Pašić and the Serbian intelligentsia right in the middle of the café; for those gentlemen the Serbian commanders hadn't as much sense as a German sergeant. Then he had kicked him hard in the ass, but first he had climbed onto a chair, or maybe it was a table, and shouted: *Dulce pro patria mori.* Straw Hat had shouted, "*Est, est*"; who does he think he is to correct me for leaving out *est*, and why did I leave it out anyway? There he is, that Straw Hat, at the bar. It was all his fault; he really had spoiled the mood of the students in the Sloboda, and if Bogdan hadn't caught hold of him (and Bogdan thought he was a coward) he would have thrown all those refugees, those draft-dodging rats and apes into the Vardar. He should not have done that; why did he have to hit people, practice for the war, have a drill exercise in the Sloboda; it was the first time he had hit anybody in all his twenty years. Bravo, Ivan! Only one blow struck in the Sloboda on the eve of their great and holy sacrifice for the homeland, and it was struck by the son of Vukašin Katić, the moral and intellectual sword of Serbia. *But really, Father, what* is *Serbia? For a great revolutionary like Bogdan, I'm just a petit bourgeois way off in the distance, down among the bugs and cockroaches; that's all.* The singer was crooning something to Bogdan Dragović; a great mass of whips encircled Bogdan, and the tip of Glišić's boot was on his face. Bogdan was singing too; he would surely fall down on his back and the singer on top of him—that cocotte who had humiliated him beyond anything; but still, that whore had brilliant insight into people: "You're the one decent sport here," she had said. "It's a pity you aren't a lieutenant; Skoplje would have been talking about our love until the Germans got here." He'd heard that quite clearly; he could still hear clearly then. After that he had drunk a liter of wine; the singer was standing right beside the pitcher with her hand on Bogdan's shoulder, even though he was the one who had called her over and given her the dinars he had got from his mother. "I adore men who hit each other. They're real men, the ones with scars and bruises. My, but how I love to kiss a man on the scar from a knife!" And Straw Hat had called Vojvoda Putnik an old fool, no better than a corporal, and said that Pašić was digging Serbia's grave. Then Bogdan had whispered—some whisper, when the whole squad could hear—"Madam, I'm head over heels in love. My girl, Natalia, will be waiting for me tomorrow in Kragujevac." *But you have me to thank for that, Bogdan; you didn't say it. Did I kiss Bogdan then because of his strong character and loyalty? That's the sort of young man Milena ought to love, and not some fool of a guerrilla. Or did I immediately jump on that member of the State Council wearing the straw hat? My father, Vukašin Katić, used to wear exactly the same straw hat, and he was a member of the State Council too.* "You ought to love my pal Ivan. He's the gentlest fellow in the Student Battalion, in all Serbia, in fact. Honestly, Draginja, I'm not lying to you." "Bogdan, old man, do you really know yourself? Have you any idea who you are?" "Yes, Ivan, buddy, I know. I know very well when I hate anybody, and even better when I love someone." "So, Bogdan, we must hate in the service of that truth of yours?" "Of course." Of course: there were the Serbian heroes, kneeling before the girls; as soon as they got outside into the darkness they would swear to love them forever; they would babble the most disgusting obscenities, from which not even death could cleanse them. *A socialist playing the part of a good friend, trying to persuade that cocotte to love me tonight because I wear glasses.* "God, I'd never kiss a man with specs, not even if he was a doctor, not even if he bought me a fur coat. He's drunk a liter of wine, so he sees all the way to Salonika. Order him a glass of milk and take him off to bed!"

Danilo History-Book was kneeling among the chairs, imploring a woman:

"Darling, I adore you! I've never felt like this before. You're my first love. I'll be faithful to you till I die. Shall we get married tomorrow? I'll give you a wedding ring. I won't deceive you—ask anyone in the Student Battalion. I'm a volunteer. I swam across the Sava under gunfire to give my life for Greater Serbia. And for you too. Come on outside, so I can embrace you. Please—just for a minute. We won't go far. I'll drink that too—yes, pour it into my mouth. Just a minute—where are you going? Give it to me. This sure is no big city; by God it isn't! It isn't Šumadija either, or Gračanica monastery, you whore-spittle! What horrible stinking females live in this world—and Serbian females at that. Pfui! Ivan, get out of the way. I want to smash my head against the wall."

There's no sense in degrading yourself like this when you're going to die for your country. Where's your masculine pride, Danilo? Now what on earth is Bogdan singing? The singers and the gypsies make a beeline for him, and he has very kindly left me a stinking, bloated Skoplje whore who doesn't want me; nor will I find out what she's got under her belly, or what her mount of Venus is like—all the animals know what that is. And I don't want to go to the front; I don't want to die for my country until I've had at least one woman. A woman, that's the first death; then you rush to fight for your country straight from your schoolbooks, straight from the Student Battalion. Tell me, Mirko, how much does one of these whores charge? I don't care if she's got V.D. It's not going to matter a damn in the history of Serbia whether those who have to die have V.D. or not. That's a fact, Mirko, old man. This night stinks, and freedom stinks, and life stinks most of all. There's no help for it. Skoplje's going to spew up everything around: my twenty years, my sweetheart Ivanka Ilić, the doctoral thesis I planned on "Light and Illumination," and the homeland too. There it is, moaning in torment; there's no help for it! The Sloboda is toppling, with its pile of dead and live bodies, into the black pit of bugs, glasses, and straw hats. Everything was yellow. He smiled, and a yellow death smiled back at him; the girl with the yellow scarf was sitting next to him and looking at him with her gentle blue eyes, her wonderful eyes.

"The train from Niš still hasn't come, Ivan. And it won't get here before morning."

"How do you know my name? You're the one young lady here who does. How strange, very strange!"

"I think it's awfully nice that you love your sister so much. A man who loves his sister will respect another woman. You won't deceive me. I only like men who respect women."

"Oh, Yellow Scarf, sweet little Yellow Scarf, you really are a very sensible girl, a yellow light. Did Bogdan tell you that I adored my sister?"

"Well, you've been talking about your sister, Milena, all night."

"Have I really? What have I been saying, Mademoiselle Yellow Scarf? And what have I said about Ivanka Ilić? Please, Bogdan, what have I been saying?"

"Nothing special. But you'd better not have any more to drink."

"Ah, no, sir, you're wrong. He did say something quite definite. I've never in my life heard a man talk about his sister like that. It even made that fair-haired, chubby Danilo cry—the one who was shouting so much about conquering Vienna and Budapest. Ivan is a real man. Give me your hand, Ivan. My name's Kosara."

"Yellow Kosara. Mademoiselle Kosara. You've got beautiful hands—and an old-fashioned name. Where do you come from, Kosara? Though it really doesn't matter; it's your eyes that matter. Eyes are the only thing that matter in this world. Shining blue eyes, really gentle eyes. Let's drink something."

"Ivan, old man, we really aren't a very lucky generation, are we? We've come into the world only to fight. We beget children so that they can fight. We live only for war, don't we, philosopher?"

"Leave me alone, Casanova!"

"No, I won't! Who says we Serbs are unlucky? On the contrary. The English are fighting for markets, the Germans for colonies and the Far East, the Russians for the Dardanelles and their historic role, and the French for Paris and their colonial empire. Only we Serbs are fighting for freedom! We're the last aristocrats on earth. Isn't that so, Bogdan? Lucky fellows we are—and what a great and powerful people!"

The tables were moving toward him; he turned around and was seized by an uncontrollable nausea. He shouted:

"Death is frightful, Bogdan! Run, Bogdan, run!"

He grabbed a soft, warm hand and tottered away, not knowing where he was going.

"You've nothing to be afraid of, my dear, I'm taking you to my house. I do like it that you're so tall—and that you wear glasses too. No, it isn't far. What a refined person you are; you adore your sister, you're not a swine who doesn't respect women. Oh, they've given me money, offered to marry me, three of those students pushed a gold wedding ring onto my finger, but I showed them my claws! You needn't be frightened, I'm holding on to you. And if you fall, I'll carry you in my arms. I'm not what they say I am, cross my heart I'm not. And let me tell you something: tonight the son of a minister knelt down in front of me and cried. It was the one you call Casanova—a fine, slim young man. And if I hadn't picked you out the very moment you came into the Sloboda, you bet I'd have taken that minister's son, even though he's only a corporal. You'll all be dead soon, but I only want to remember you. I won't take even a button from you. That minister's son, the one who knelt down and cried, he's a fine young man, and, my goodness, he's got strong arms, that Casanova. You have too—and nice, firm thighs. Now just you lean against the wall and have a rest. Don't worry. I won't let you fall. How does it matter what I did in Belgrade? How old am I? Who cares how old anybody is, when this is the last year for you and all the other corporals anyway? Well, I couldn't be your mother, but I could be your sister, indeed I could. I'd be your sister if I had to go through hellfire. But the Huns are right on top of your gun barrel. That's right—have a good vomit. Now you'll begin to see straight. Push your finger into your mouth; that's right; no, push it farther. How your forehead's burning, and you're sweating too! The world must be coming to an end when people like you have to be sent out to die. Go on, throw up again; you're all right. As soon as you came into the Sloboda tonight, I could see that you didn't belong there. You're not one for drinking wine, sweetie-pie. Since they've decided you're to die, they might at least have made you officers, Pašić and all those graybeards. Do you feel better now? Wipe your face with my scarf. It's a yellow scarf; you haven't forgotten that, have you? And take a deep breath. Now another one. Come on, we must hurry; it'll soon be daylight. No, it isn't far; just by that street light. Come on now, don't talk, just hurry. Don't worry, there's nobody else in the room. I picked you, though I don't really like being with a man only once. If you're a gentleman and not a swine, you'll respect me because I took you in late at night. You find me old and ugly, do you? You should be ashamed of yourself, a student and fine gentleman like you. I suppose the girls have spoiled you; that's it. Oh, no, I don't do anything in the dark. I was looking at you in the Sloboda all evening, and now I want to enjoy myself. What's your father, by the way? All right, I don't care. Now sit by the bed and take your shoes off. Believe me, I haven't had a man here today, honest I haven't; I just couldn't be bothered to make the bed this morning. When I heard that you students were being sent out to die, I looked to see what time it was, and I just hadn't the heart to make the bed. And that damned train still hasn't come! You'd rather I wore my nightgown? All right, I'll keep it on; you needn't be scared. How are you going to shoot at the Huns, I ask you? I was looking at you students tonight and thinking, in a week more than half of you'll be dead, and I just felt like howling! All those women with no love juice inside them, all those children that will never be born, and all you young men—such firm, fine, clean men! I couldn't do anything with a dirty man, not even if he was the czar of Russia! What are you waiting for, sitting there like a schoolgirl? Go on, take it; all men like that—you learn that while you're still in diapers! Come on, now. How nice that you're so fine and white and tall! There's nothing wrong with me; you needn't worry. If you want to be sick, you've got a bowl there, so just get on with it. Lean over, you spoiled brat; you're making a mess all over my bedcovers. Come on, throw up again. Press your head against the wall. That's what happens when you drink red wine on an empty stomach, especially when you know you're going to die. My, but your heart's beating like a pigeon's! I love to listen to a man's heart going pitapat like that. Don't worry, you've got rid of it all now. Wash your facc and rinse your mouth out. Why are you putting the lamp out? No, you're not going outside! I've got the key and there's an iron grating over the window. So you can't get out. Better get on with the job; you'll never have another chance. You're having the last one now with a Serbian girl who wants to give it to you. No, I won't move against the wall, I can't bear a man coming from the side. What are you doing with your hands, you idiot? You don't know anything, and I do so love boys like you. That's why I grabbed you! Now, Ivan, don't think any more about the Huns and going to the front to die. Just lie on your back and think about the girl who comes to mind when you first wake up in the morning. All fine, white, slender boys begin that way. And when you get bolder, you're on fire! I don't believe it—you haven't done anything, and you're going away to your death this afternoon. A fine sort of stud horse you are! But don't think you'll get away with anything. I'll track you down to the ends of the earth. Oh, honey, why did I pick you to have a good look at before a bullet gets you? Look what a mess you've made! And I hoped and hoped, when that damned train didn't come! Didn't I tell you to be careful? I don't care if it is the first time; you should be ashamed of yourself. And you such a fine gentleman. Now you'll go off to die, leaving me to worry. What's your surname? And don't you lie to me; I'll go to Glišić tomorrow and ask your name. Ivan Stepanović. You're sure it's Stepanović, and you really do live in Belgrade? Where are you off to? Now I must have a bit of shut-eye and forget there's a war on. What d'you mean, it's daylight? No sign of it yet. All right, then, shake out your pocket and run off to the barracks. I'm really disappointed in you, leaving me with my worries. If you lied to me about your surname, I'll tell all the people on the platform waiting to see you off. When did you start smoking—I didn't see you smoking in the Sloboda. Take a cigarette, I keep them for visitors. At least you might as well learn to smoke. Yes, my fine gentleman, my handsome corporal, Ivan Stepanović! Oh my God, when will that damned train come from Niš?"

"She's scratched me," said Bogdan, rubbing the mark made by her nail on the upper part of his arm. It was the singer who had wanted to sing for him "until she died"; she had shouted these words so that they would be heard by the rest of the corporals, all desperate over this one last woman as their night out at the Sloboda drew to a close. They had gone through their last pennies, and the best and most rousing words they knew; they told her how marvelous she was, and begged her to come for a short walk in the moonlight, or at least to stick her head out the door and look at the "incomparable moon," speaking first in whispers and then aloud, shouting each other down. She replied that the night was cold, and that moonlight gave her "the shivers, like stepping on a snake"; but she gazed at Bogdan, stroked his neck, and murmured: "I love it that you're so sad. I feel sad too. My father and my brothers are at the front; they'll all die. What beautiful eyes you have! And you're so handsome, the handsomest of all the students!" He resisted her advances, told her that he had a sweetheart, and kept an eye on Ivan, especially after the fight from which he had just barely managed to extricate him. But she continued to have eyes only for him, pushing away and kicking the drunk and indignant corporals. "Those other students are all fools. Any man I've loved has always turned out to be no good. They all want a woman for only one night, but for me it has to be for a lifetime. Oh, why didn't I meet you last week? Come on, Bogdan, let's make love! You can love me just a little, and I'll give you all I've got. If I kiss you, then I'll be faithful to you till the end of the war, if only my father and brothers don't come back." He moved away from her and told her how much he loved a girl who was far away.

He felt sick from the beer, ashamed of himself, and also angry that he had allowed himself even the slight temptation of finding the singer attractive; the next night he would be with Natalia—she was waiting for him. Danilo History-Book had insulted him by being indignant at his "indifference toward a fine lady who could have her pick from the entire Student Battalion," and swearing the most solemn oaths that he himself was not jealous. There were two kinds of lies he disliked: those inspired by masculine pride, and another kind that he didn't name, because just at that moment he was making a play for the singer: "Darling, let me put my hand on your breasts. The Germans will occupy those too. When they capture Šumadija, they'll take possession of your breasts. And you're a Serbian girl, by God! Your breasts aren't the domes of the Peć Patriaršija, my God they aren't!" Then Ivan had left the Sloboda with the woman wearing the yellow scarf, and Bogdan immediately rushed after them; the singer had overtaken him at the door, and something happened that he would prefer to forget. He saw Ivan disappear down the street with that decidedly plain woman.

Feeling glad and at the same time wretched because he had overcome the temptation to go off with the singer, he stood leaning against the wall of a small, protruding house, looking at the gate through which Ivan had passed with his "lady" after having vomited for the second time. He would not go back to the barracks without Ivan; he could not let him out of his sight. The moon shone gray in the chill before dawn. Bogdan shivered and tried to press closer to the protruding wall, through which he heard heavy breathing and subdued agitation. The house against his shoulders felt like a huge animal that had fallen asleep after overeating. If the house had started to walk through the moonlight toward the donkey braying nearby, he would not have been startled. And if the mulberry leaves that had patterned the moonlight up to the deep shadow of the minaret had started to crow, he would not have been surprised. He pulled his neck in, placed his cap over the marks on his face, and blew on it to warm the big bruise. Would it fade before tomorrow evening, and would he be able to look at Natalia with his left eye as well?

Someone was approaching, walking fast; it was a corporal, returning from the house of his "lady" or hostess. Bogdan pressed against the wall, placing his cap over his whole face.

"What are you doing here, Mustachios? Good thing I found you," said Bora Jackpot.

Bogdan removed his cap from his right eye.

"What do you want? Why are you panting like that?"

"Our battalion has been driven from its position and defeated. Wine, women, in some cases plain despair. Not a soul anywhere. And I can't go to the barracks yet."

"Wait for me at Dušan's Bridge, and we'll go together."

"Fine. Maybe the Great Wheel has changed its speed and direction. Anyway, let's try."

He placed his hand on Bogdan's shoulder; he was excited.

"Leave me alone. I'm defeated too."

"Now listen, Mustachios; if your girl hasn't shown up by now, she never will. It's getting light. So let's go straight to the bridge and have a hand of cards. Right on the bridge. Just one hand—come on, be a pal! Tonight's the night for spades and high numbers. The uncertainty is terrible—fatal. I've won every single game; my pockets are full of other people's cash. Whatever I play, I win. My hand's full of spades and queens; it's terrible. The Great Wheel has suddenly started racing! We're heading straight for disaster, Bogdan, toward events that will settle our fate—by God, we are!"

"Please, Bora, go wait for me at the bridge. I've never played cards in my life."

"That's fine, Mustachios. You're a beginner, so for you the Little Wheel will revolve at its normal speed."

"No wheel is going to turn for me at all. I'm waiting for someone. Please leave me alone."

"You've always been a good friend, so be a pal now."

Bogdan bristled at Bora's tone, but he could not abandon Ivan.

"All right, deal the cards here on the cobblestones," he said, kneeling down.

"That's the spirit, old man," said Bora, also kneeling, and shuffling the cards. But he stopped when he heard a dog barking and a woman's voice shouting: "Write to me, Žarko darling! Write every day." Two corporals came out into the street, accompanied by women. The corporals kissed and embraced the women for the last time in the moonlight, in the shadow of the minaret. A train whistled in the distance.

"Good luck, Mustachios. Wait for your woman till noon."

Bora stuffed the cards into his pocket and ran after the corporals, who were walking slowly away, dragging their shadows wearily behind them and waving to the two women standing by the gate with their shadows in the shadow of the minaret. The stars were moving away to the top of the sky.

Bogdan sighed. Again he covered his whole face with his cap, breathed hard, and warmed his bruises. But now he could hear voices.

"Well, at least be a gentleman and go to the station, to see if the train has come from Niš."

He moved his cap away from his right eye; Ivan was walking quickly toward him. He decided not to show himself, so as not to embarrass Ivan, and again covered his face with his cap, and pressed closer to the subdued murmurs in the house.

"Is that you, Bogdan?"

Ivan ran toward Bogdan and embraced him. Bogdan submitted passively, his arms dangling.

"Are you feeling better now?" asked Bogdan, moving away from the wall and from Ivan.

Ivan sensed pity in his voice, but that did not offend him. He leaned against the wall.

"Let's go back. No need to hurry. By the time we reach the service tree, the sun will be out."

A fiacre full of corporals thundered past; they were singing, each to himself. One shouted: "Get a move on! Drive us to the end of the world!"

While the moonlight drained off through the street behind them in the silence of the dawn, Ivan and Bogdan walked, frequently brushing shoulders.

"Do you know what I'd like, Bogdan? To be hit by a bullet that has lost its death-dealing powers. A slow, weary bullet from a long way off. A bullet at its last gasp. Are you listening?"

"Yes, I am. Very carefully."

"A limp bullet, that's what I mean. So that I can experience clearly the sensation of it penetrating my muscle tissue or bone—it doesn't matter which. I want to feel it coursing slowly, like blood, through all my muscles and bones except my skull, before it moves to my heart. I want the process of dying to last at least a few minutes."

"What makes you talk like this, Ivan?"

"Because I want to know something for certain. Who I am, and what it is that . . . I also want to know if you are right. And what my Light is. Watch out, Little Light," he whispered.

Bogdan stood still and looked at him; could he be in love? Since midnight he'd done nothing but ramble on about love. It didn't matter that the woman was ugly. *Tonight there was only one girl in the whole world for all of us—the girl who was with you.*

"So anyone who wants to find out the truth shouldn't go into a library, but into the trenches? Is that what you mean?" He tried to smile, but stopped short. Ivan's eyes were full of tears.

"I'm absolutely convinced that the key to it all is the manner of dying. Who cares about death? The only thing that matters is how we die. If we want to know the real truth, we must die slowly—really slowly, old man. I've no doubts at all about that. And if I still believed in God, I would kneel down here and now, on the cobbled street, and pray: God, grant me a slow and lingering death, as slow and lingering as possible!"

He steadied himself by leaning against the wall, then spoke slowly and deliberately, with bowed head.

"Let my bullet be slow, O Lord. A weary bullet. A bullet coming from far away that scarcely has the strength to pierce my thin skin, my flaccid muscles. Then right into the center of my heart. And there let it remain. In the warmth of my heart. And let it get warm for a moment. But let it not touch my forehead—on no account let it come near my head!"

Ivan was weeping. Bogdan felt that it would embarrass Ivan if he embraced him or tried to comfort him. He took off his cap and placed it over the bruises and his left eye, then set off, shivering, in the direction of the Vardar. Ivan tottered along behind him, but with no desire to catch up.

They walked without stopping past a group of their companions who were singing loudly. Bogdan was the first to stop, when they reached the courtyard of the barracks. The light was still on in the commanding officer's room, and he saw the stooping, motionless figure of Lieutenant Colonel Dušan Glišić.

"So he's been up all night too," whispered Bogdan, more to himself than to Ivan. "Or maybe he just wants to see us coming back to the barracks for the last time."

On Golgotha, above the barracks, the company commanders were snapping out orders for inspection, which Ivan Katić heard as in a dream; he had no strength to stand up straight, bring his knees together, and look directly at some nonexistent point on the horizon, along which the dark shape of Šar Mountain seemed to be moving in headlong flight through space. His head and his full cartridge belt anchored him to the ground; but his heavy Russian rifle pulled him to the right, and he was at the head of the platoon. So he fixed his eyes on the cloud moving across the autumn sky above the mountains, toward the sun, now at its zenith. He would have collapsed but for that life-saving cloud. If only that cloud would blot out the sun and replace it by darkness—eternal darkness. Why could this miracle not happen? He must wish for it with all his strength; then it would happen. Behind his neck, Bogdan Dragović whispered:

"Do you think Natalia got my telegram? Will she be waiting for me in Kragujevac?"

"I'm sure she did. Imagine what it would be like if the earth was suddenly engulfed in eternal darkness!"

"That's impossible!" said Bora Jackpot aloud.

The company commanders shot out the last orders, for Glišić was galloping up on his mare. Ivan stared at the cloud, entirely consumed by the wish that the miracle would indeed happen before Don Quixote arrived shouting:

"God bless you, heroes!"

The sun tore at the edge of the cloud. Don Quixote prayed:

"My children!"

It was no use. The cloud was attacking the weary, light-bearing malefactor. The battalion yelled: "Hurrah!"

A fateful battle was beginning high up in the sky. The battalion pierced the cloud. A priest began to recite the Lord's Prayer.

"Is he praying for the sun or the cloud? What do you think, Bora?"

"For death, Ivan," replied Bora, and spat a long way through his teeth.

The priest was for the sun, not the cloud. But the cloud was winning. So why didn't the darkness come? He turned around to look at his companions, who were praying.

"Take the oath, Ivan!" warned Danilo History-Book. His face, like the rest of the faces, was composed of earth and cloud. They would be devoured by the fire. He turned to Bogdan.

"Are you praying?"

"No."

"Nothing can help us. I'll have to run away."

"You can't do that, Katić!" warned Danilo.

The minute they got out of the barracks yard, he would leave the ranks and make his way to the station alone by a side street. Then that specter in the yellow scarf wouldn't see him. The sun burned up the cloud; the battalion shouted "Amen." None of them would survive. The company commanders shot out a new order.

"Move left, Katić, left! What are you staring at?"

"We're going, Ivan." Bogdan grabbed him by the shoulders and turned him around.

He started off down the hill like a whipped cur.

"One, two! One, two! Turn left—*left,* Blindie. Come on, step out!"

Don Quixote rode into the cloud, pulling a song behind him.

As soon as they left the barracks yard and set off toward the town, Ivan Katić understood the situation: Ivan Stepanović was not at the head of the company. In front of him was the Obilić choir, and in front of the choir a military band, with its commander and other officers. Kosara wouldn't so much as get a glimpse of him! If he could just get out of Skoplje!

"Into battle, into battle,
Into battle for our people."

"Knees up! Step high, Corporal!"

"Long live the students! Happy journey, heroes!"

What did that mob want from them? They would kill them with apples and cakes, poke out their eyes with flowers. He set his glasses more firmly on his nose. Would his mother be waiting for him in Niš with a spare pair? It was now late autumn; why were those girls and women wearing yellow now? Wherever possible, he would trample on their weeping, their flowers and smiles, their fat tears which were flowing even from the walls of the railroad station, in front of which Don Quixote was sitting on his mare, his mustache like a lance, spreading all over the station, the warehouse, and the surrounding houses. He was growing thinner and thinner, until he was only a skeleton among the flowers and oranges which the girls kept throwing at the ranks of corporals. From a great height, Don Quixote shouted:

"Atten-shun! That's no good—again! Atten-shun! No good—again!"

"Stand at attention! That's the sixth order!" shouted Danilo History-Book.

"Attention, Ivan!" said Bora Jackpot. "That's the seventh order. Belgrade will fall before Glišić is satisfied with our lines." Bora spat through his teeth all the way to the other end of the platform.

But before Ivan could stand at attention, the corporals were rushing into the cattle cars. He frantically pushed ahead, jumped in, and toppled into a corner. He was safe! Kosara hadn't seen him, hadn't found out that he'd given a false name. Two long whistles from the engine announced his final deliverance. His eyes began to close as the car shook and rattled amid heart-rending farewells from the people on the platform and along the tracks. Then he was deafened by the raucous singing in the overcrowded train moving northward, toward the battlefield.

5

General Mišić left Prince Alexander and Vojvoda Putnik at the High Command just before midnight, without a word of apology; he was deeply upset by the devastating reports from the entire front and by the terse communication from General Bojovič about the relentless Austro-Hungarian advance toward Valjevo and the collapse of the First Army. Although the doubts he had felt during the last two days were now essentially resolved, he intended to postpone announcing his proposal for another night. It was not only an understandable hesitancy before risking all he had achieved as a man and a soldier that prompted him to wait until morning to disclose his plan for reestablishing the shattered front. He was also revenging himself for the humiliation he had suffered when he had twice been forcibly retired, especially on the last occasion, the previous year, when Putnik had dismissed him from the General Staff like a village policeman, without any explanation; Putnik had done it at the request of Pašić and Apis, and certainly with the endorsement of Prince Alexander. Although Mišić had been his assistant, Putnik, the senior officer who had presided over all his examinations for promotion, had refused even to talk to him. So let him and Alexander spend one more night feeling powerless to do anything; yet all that day their looks and their words had indicated plainly enough what they wanted. Well, they could at least admit to themselves that they had wronged him. As soon as he left the High Command for home, accompanied by his adjutant, he felt ashamed of his vengeful feelings at a time when the homeland was perhaps on the verge of extinction. During the remainder of the sleepless night this shame gradually trickled into the reasons for his final decision to sacrifice himself.

At daybreak he returned to the High Command and sat down at his empty table for a few more moments of reflection. Someone placed before him the latest reports from the army commanders; he pushed them away without looking either at them or at the messengers. All the facts and extrafactual considerations for his decision were inside his head. Unless the First Army could immediately regroup and halt the enemy advance into the heart of Serbia, this hopeless resistance could hardly last more than ten days. Then they would face capitulation and bondage, humiliation, and death. If his plan did not succeed—and the prospects of success were minuscule even with God's help and no interference from the devil—if the First Army received its *coup de grace* under his command, he would bear the entire responsibility for the defeat; although it would not be his fault, for centuries it would be stamped with the name of Živojin Mišić. And he was doing this without any external compulsion, but at his own request, simply by throwing himself in front of the wheels of another man's cart which was hurtling into an abyss. But when the nation was in mortal danger, dare any man be guided by considerations of success? Had any general the right to draw back from the possibility of failure if there was the slightest chance of preventing a calamity for his people? Even if this chance was no more than the human will to exist, and to endure and suffer for the sake of survival, whatever the outcome; even if all his efforts did no more than confirm the will to live in honorable freedom, then he, Živojin Mišić, must act according to his conscience. He must do his duty because of his knowledge and his power over people.

When he opened the door of Vojvoda Putnik's office and saw both him and Prince Alexander in the same positions as he had left them in the previous night, he was startled out of his self-absorption and alarmed by their appearance; he saluted briskly and stood at attention.

"Forgive me, Your Highness; I was not told that you were waiting for me. I have been in my office since daybreak."

For a moment he was embarrassed by their silence and their stern expressions, but that slight feeling of guilt immediately helped him to pull himself together; he strode toward the window and addressed them from there, at some distance.

"I am taking the liberty, Your Highness, of asking you to entrust me with the command of the First Army. Bojović has been wounded and is in no condition to control the demoralized troops."

Prince Alexander jumped up joyfully, took a few steps toward him and cried:

"All night long I have been thinking about how I could induce you to undertake this task, which only you can perform. If it's not too late."

Vojvoda Putnik gazed pensively out the window at the bare crown of a pear tree, and did not betray his thoughts by so much as the flicker of an eyelash. Mišić was deeply affected by his indifference.

He doesn't believe I can accomplish anything, Mišić thought. He's quite sure I can't. Putnik's impassivity impelled him to speak more forcefully than his own belief warranted, as he looked at Putnik, trying to catch his eye.

"It's not too late, Your Highness. As long as the people are struggling for their survival, they can be saved."

Pacing up and down Putnik's large office, the Regent expounded his views on the measures that should be taken to bring the demoralized troops of the First Army under control. Mišić did not listen to him: he was looking at the aging, bloated face of Vojvoda Putnik, still gazing impassively out the window; he waited apprehensively for Putnik to say something. It was only when Prince Alexander turned to Putnik with the words "I am waiting to hear what you have to say, Vojvoda," that he said quietly:

"I gave you my opinion two days ago, Your Highness: if anything can still be done on the front of the First Army, only General Mišić can do it."

Mišić decided to break the long silence that followed.

"I may be able to. In any case, Vojvoda, I will do everything in my power."

Vojvoda Putnik turned toward him and looked at him severely. "I don't doubt that, Mišić. You must leave today."

"You must leave at once, General. My car will take you to Mionica," added Prince Alexander.

"Try to reach headquarters by nightfall. And when you get there, Mišić, don't waste a moment! If you can't take time by the forelock, then at least don't let go of its tail. Because if time slips out of our grasp, we're finished."

"You must indeed perform the impossible, General. Or the First Army is finished," said Alexander.

General Mišić was silent for a moment before answering.

"Forgive me, Your Highness, but I do not agree with Njegoš. Only poets and fools do the impossible. An army commander, in my opinion, must do only what is possible."

The Regent frowned and then shook hands cordially with General Mišić for the first time, wished him success in his difficult task, and left him with Vojvoda Putnik for one more look at the plight of the First Army.

General Mišić stepped onto the porch and shook the rain from his cap and coat.

"What on earth's happened?" asked his wife, Louisa, as she came out to meet him.

Only when he had shut the door behind him and they were alone did he answer his wife, who was trembling with excitement, her dark eyes wide with curiosity. He spoke in a subdued voice.

"I've been appointed commander of the First Army."

"Now that the Germans have taken Valjevo, and all is lost?"

"Perhaps not all is lost, Louisa. Perhaps I can save the First Army," he said caustically, looking her straight in the eye.

"Why doesn't Putnik command the army that's fallen apart?" asked Louisa, bursting into tears.

"That's not the job for Putnik," he replied. He sat down on the little stool by the kitchen stove and lit a cigarette from the embers that glowed through the open doors.

A little girl with pigtails came in carrying a kitten; her smile dispelled his gloom. She wanted to climb onto his knee.

"Calm down, Louisa! We can't be other than what we are. Pack some underwear for me, and the other things I need. You heard me say that the car will be here in half an hour. Prince Alexander's car, of course."

He took the little girl onto his lap and stroked her hair, but did not hear what she was whispering to him; he was visualizing the positions of the First Army, and the area in which they were operating—in rain and mud, under gloomy skies, in trackless country.

"But why on earth did you agree, Živojin? They've seized an opportunity to disgrace you in front of the army! They've decided to stamp the defeat of the First Army with your name," said Louisa, standing in the doorway.

"I'd rather not discuss it, even with you. But since you ask me, well, I accepted the command of the First Army because it's my duty to perform every task I'm ordered to undertake. If that means taking command of an army on the verge of collapse, if it means going down with it, if there's no other way, if . . ."

"If the homeland really does require this from you, if it's not just somebody's whim! If it's right, Živojin," she whispered in strangled tones. "Oh, God, what wrong have we done you?"

"In order to become a general, a Serbian officer must deserve it; what's more, he has to prove it and justify the decision of those who chose him. Well, that's enough of parting words. Pack me as many handkerchiefs as possible. And hurry!"

"Daddy, how many times will it get dark before you come home again?"

"As many times as you have fingers on your hands. And on your mother's hands too."

"And what if Mummy cries tomorrow?"

"If your mother cries tomorrow, you take her on your knee and tell her the bogeyman will come. Put the kitten down and sit next to your father just a little longer!" He hugged her, held his hand against her heart, and felt its beating with his closed fist and his fingers. His sons Alexander and Radovan were in the trenches, and up to three days ago were still alive. But what about Voja? Olga, being a nurse, would at least keep her head. But what would happen to them all if Serbia were crushed? Resting his chin on the little girl's head, he stared through the window at the damp wall, on which there was a creeping vine shot with red and purple leaves.

"Do you want to see what I'm packing for you, Živojin?"

"No. I'll leave it to you. In any case, I'll have more than the soldiers. And as soon as Daddy gets to Struganik, he'll send you some of Grandma's walnuts, nice big white ones, the best walnuts in the world. You've come in the nick of time, Vukašin!" he said, letting the little girl off his knee and rising to greet Vukašin Katić, who said as he removed his coat and hat:

"They told me you were leaving for the front, so I've dropped in to say good-bye."

"Louisa, make some coffee. I'm glad to see you. I intended to find you."

"An unexpected decision. Was it Putnik's or Prince Alexander's?"

"A joint decision, theirs and mine."

"Good afternoon, Mrs. Mišić. Forgive me. I didn't see you."

"Sit nearer the stove; you're wet. Perhaps it's my fate to end my career in disgrace and cursed by my people. Not for nothing was my poor deceased mother alarmed when I told her that I'd been promoted to colonel."

"In Kragujevac they already know that you're going out to join the First Army. The people have faith in you. In the cafés they're drinking the toast: 'May God help Živojin Mišić!' Do you realize how much people believe in you? It's a lucky man whom people believe in today. I hope you don't mind my telling you this to your face."

"Perhaps it's too late, Vukašin. But what else can I do? If it's within my right to order that a position be held to the last man, then it's my duty to take command when it seems that all is lost. Two shirts will be enough, Louisa. I'll wash and wear them in turn."

"I feel that I'm living in a dream, Mr. Katić."

"You just make the coffee, and don't tell us what you think. The less said the better, today."

"But there are some things that do need to be said right now, General," added Vukašin quietly. "I hear that an order has been sent to the Student Battalion."

"It had to be, Vukašin. There'll be two of them in each platoon. We've given them the rank of corporal, and told them they must get to the front with all speed. We're scraping the barrel for an all-out defense, and calling up the police too. Everyone who can hold a rifle is to go to the trenches. It's going to be a fight to the end."

For a moment, neither of them spoke.

"The man at the head of the government and you army commanders think you have the right to demand everything in the name of the homeland. But history has proved you wrong, my dear General. Even freedom does not have a mandate for everything. You have no right to sacrifice everything, even today."

"If we except ourselves, then certainly we haven't."

"Nor in any other way, General. While an individual can sacrifice everything, the people—the state—may never do so. History shows that only tyranny defends itself by all possible means. Freedom has never done so. It is not right, Živojin Mišić, to sacrifice the future of a nation."

"But aren't you forgetting that our guns are now silenced, that our regiments have shrunk to battalions, and our battalions to companies? Teachers are now commanding battalions, and peasants are leading squads and platoons. The students are now all the country can give for its defense. When you're fighting for your existence, then you have the right to ask everything. That's what I firmly believe."

"Oh, I know all that. It's that . . . The time has now come when everything is stretched to the limit. But enough of this—I've come to say good-bye."

"Which platoon is your Ivan in?"

"The sixth, I suppose."

"He'll be in my army," whispered Mišić. "In time of war one must believe in God, my friend," he added, then leaned over toward Vukašin and put his hand on his shoulder.

"I don't want any comfort in misfortune. I don't want to deny pain or run away from it—even to God."

"I don't know how to comfort people, and don't want to. I think there are always solid reasons for being a believer. But you are not really a believer, are you, Vukašin? You doubt everything. How can you be a politician—and in the Opposition, at that?"

"That's why I'm *in* the Opposition!"

"That means you have been—and must be—a man of faith."

They fell silent once more.

"So you don't think I'm much of a believer?" said Vukašin.

"You haven't much faith in yourself. That's why you worry so much."

"You don't think, General, that it's my personal faith I'm worried about? Thank you, Mrs. Mišić, I'll just let my coffee cool a little."

"No, I don't think that, Vukašin. Quite frankly, I don't like such an excessive anxiety for the nation as you feel. Concern for one's children, family, and friends, yes. But for the rest, one does one's duty. One does what has to be done."

He fell silent. A car stood in front of the house with the engine throbbing. Louisa took a roasted chicken out of the oven and wrapped it in wax paper. The adjutant entered the room and announced that Prince Alexander's car had arrived and was ready to start immediately.

"Have the orderly put my things in. Andja, come to Daddy. I want you on my knee."

The little girl threw down the kitten and hugged her father. They whispered to each other that when he came back they would spend time together, without Mummy. Louisa pointed out his foot locker to the orderly and furtively wiped her tears. Vukašin rested his elbows on his knees and stared at the floor.

"If you don't save the First Army and halt the German advance, Serbia is done for."

"Please don't expect me to work miracles!" said Mišić, raising his voice. "All I can do is to direct the will of the people toward survival and living, and organize their defense of their lives and possessions. I shall be working for life to the utmost of my ability."

"You really are overmodest today, General," said Vukašin. He put out his cigarette and drank up his coffee.

"Well, what of it? I regard it as my job, or, rather, as my duty. I hate war, Vukašin—more than the most ardent pacifist. I would not fight for victory, and still less for glory. I work simply for life, for survival."

The little girl extricated herself from his embrace and went to her mother in the next room. He frowned, and continued somewhat irritably.

"Other people, more powerful than I, have decided that my work for life should be the strenuous and bloody business that it is. If the cause of life and survival could be served by picking acorns, I would lead the army to pick them. And I would feel much more honored and important if I commanded an army of acorn-pickers. But Franz Josef and my opposite number, Field Marshal Oscar Potiorek, are not pelting Serbia with acorns, but with shells and bullets—and lethal grenades, much heavier than our pigs."

The little daughter came back into the room with some apples, stuffed them into his pockets, then sat on his knee and began to play with his epaulets.

"Yes, indeed. When a man thinks as you do, General, then he certainly has the right to give any order he thinks fit. Your conscience is clear. But history shows that peoples and nations have suffered most under such leaders." As though alarmed by his own words, Vukašin suddenly straightened up. "Forgive me for this dubious notion."

"I respect it in you because your inspiration is pure. But you know, Vukašin, in war one must have a firm faith—in both God and oneself. In oneself, in order to endure to the end, and in God, in order to avoid actions that an honorable man would later regret. For war dishonors more people than it kills." He spoke these words in a reproachful voice, slowly and deliberately, as if dictating to his adjutant.

Vukašin rose, and took his coat and hat from the hook.

"Well, I must say good-bye, General. You must spend a few moments with your wife."

Vukašin's voice trembled; Louisa entered the room. Tenderly General Mišić lowered the little girl from his knee, went over to Vukašin, and spoke to him in a low voice.

"If Louisa and the children should need a friend while I'm away, I would like you to know that I rely on you. And on no one else.

Perhaps you could somehow manage to pay my damned bills of exchange. Sell some things, but at any rate pay them."

"What do your debts matter now? Forget your bills of exchange! If the First Army collapses, the Serbian banks will collapse too!"

"Well, let's hope that neither of them will. But my good name could suffer. You know that nothing in my life has caused me more trouble than debts. Nothing else has irritated and humiliated me as much as bills of exchange."

"You can leave with an easy mind. Good-bye, General. Louisa can count on me like a brother. And you too, Živojin, always!"

They took leave with a long handshake. Then Vukašin went out and walked slowly down the cobbled street. His footsteps became slower and heavier: In his pocket was the letter Ivan was supposed to hand to a regimental commander in Mišić's army. A pungent smell of chrysanthemums and burials rose from the courtyards of Kragujevac. In front of Mišić's house the car throbbed, waiting for the commander of the First Army.

Natalia Dumović was returning home under a dark, cloudy sky lit by fitful gleams of moonlight, stepping lightly over patches of mud. Whenever she heard wailing she would make a quick detour through meadows and plum orchards to avoid discovering that night which of her neighbors would not return to Prerovo. At dusk the village mayors had read new lists of killed and wounded in all the villages. She was carrying a heavy stick to use against the dogs, and under her left arm was a bag containing a clean exercise book, envelopes, stamps, and a pencil. She was coming back from Šljivovo, where since noon she had been writing letters to soldiers at the front and reading the letters they had written to their wives and mothers. She felt brimful of the words spoken to her pencil, spoken in moaning voices, or sometimes only with sighs uttered in dejected silence above the paper. These words buzzed in her head like bees, milling around in confusion, sinking down, then rising up again. All had faces and all were clearly audible.

The soldiers' letters, written from the battlefield, were wet and spattered with mud; between the words stretched an endless void of misery; the words themselves seemed on the point of exploding from anxiety and despair. The first words were usually written in large characters, but the signatures often showed signs of haste, as if they had been written just before flight, or the soldier's sufferings made his name seem worthless to both himself and those to whom he was writing. And it was just the name that their illiterate mothers stared at in the hope of finding out exactly how their sons felt as they penned their names; then they would move away, tight-lipped and obviously unhappy because those marks on the paper bore no resemblance to their sons. Words that had been blotted out by rain or tears particularly held their attention; they gazed at them as if trying to guess when the war would end. Fathers and grandfathers stared longest at the envelopes and addresses, as if amazed that these pieces of paper could reach them at all from such distances, through the bad weather. Women writing to their husbands spoke openly of their grief and enumerated all their troubles; mothers writing to their sons groped for words of comfort; fathers expounded maxims and particularly exhorted their sons to obey their officers; grandfathers talked about the general situation at home, about the stables and sheepfolds, sometimes injecting a joke or two. As Natalia went from house to house the people would be waiting for her: they would seat her beside the hearth, bring her grapes, apples, and sweet wine, and touch her tenderly and timidly with their rough, work-hardened fingers. Walking home alone through the dark meadows and plum orchards between Šljivovo and Prerovo, surrounded by wailing and barking, Natalia gave full rein to her feelings: it was as though she had husbands, brothers, and sons by the battalion! Even the thought of Bogdan couldn't drive out of her mind those swarms of words she had read and written that day.

The darkness of stables and barns, the bare crowns of plum and apple trees, the hearth flames visible through open doorways were pierced by loud lamentation and quiet weeping. About to jump over a fence, she was arrested by the sound of a man groaning: "Ah, my son, my son!" The voice came from Aćim's apple orchard. Had Adam been killed? "Why didn't I answer his letter?" she asked herself, shuddering. "Even if it was a silly love letter." Adam was the first man who had disturbed her girlhood, the first to cause her sleepless nights in which sadness was mingled with other feelings, the first object of a desire she had mastered. She listened intently, but could not recognize the man's voice. Jumping down from the fence, she hurried toward the plum orchards and the haylofts, defending herself against the listless dogs with her club or with coaxing words.

In front of the school and their house she stopped: through the window of the schoolroom she could see her father lighting candles for his dead pupils on the benches where they used to sit. She hated this custom of her father's; his behavior since the outbreak of the war was altogether intolerable. One day he had announced in a terrifying voice: "I'll have no more singing and laughing in my house while Serbia is at war." Ever since mobilization, he would wake her and her sisters unnecessarily early, banging on their doors and shouting: "Aren't you up yet? You ought to be ashamed of yourselves! Here you are sleeping yourselves silly while the boys in the trenches never slept a wink last night." Then he would heap scorn on himself and scold his wife because they had "bred only females," and so must feel ashamed before their countrymen who had sons at the front. He would cut short meals, reproaching her and her sisters for not being young men "fulfilling their duty to the homeland": he was always thinking up jobs for them to do.

Natalia struck the trunk of the acacia tree provocatively with her stick, but her father did not stir from the blackboard, where he stood motionless, staring at the fluttering flames on the benches. She could remember how he used to cane these same boys mercilessly, and make them kneel on corn seeds with their bare knees for hours on end, and yet there he was grieving for them in his own way.

She walked past the school and opened the house gate. Her mother appeared in the lighted doorway of the kitchen, holding a piece of paper. A letter from Bogdan! She hurried up the cobbled path, throwing her stick into the hedge. Her mother handed her a telegram from Bogdan. Natalia read it several times, then irresolutely put it down on the kitchen table. What reason could she give her father for going to Kragujevac? She would go, even if she never came back to Prerovo again! She sat with bowed head and her hands pressed between her knees, trembling.

"Your father says you're to go to Kragujevac," said her mother in a worried voice, standing at the stove.

"Father?" she muttered. He, the schoolmaster, was ordering his daughter to go to a farewell lovers' meeting with a young man he didn't know, about whom she had never even spoken to him?

"I was more scared than you are when he shouted at me: 'Of course she must see this soldier off to the front! No two ways about it!' He says there's a train that gets into Panjak at eight in the morning, and you're to leave at daybreak. I'm supposed to roast a turkey and make some pastries."

"What's this you're telling me, Mother?" Natalia jumped up and embraced her mother, who began to cry.

"The hot water's ready for you, Natty," said her sister, coming in from the next room.

"What hot water, Milica?" she asked, letting go of her mother.

"Hot water for your bath. For your trip," said Milica, a tall girl with pigtails, smiling mournfully.

Natalia went into the room she shared with her sisters, feeling depressed and ashamed; she caught sight of a large tub and a copper pan of steaming water. Her mother called her to supper, but she flung herself down onto the bed.

"Not now. Shut the door. I'll call when I'm ready," she said. *You'd think I was getting married,* she thought. *Could this be happening to me?* Her lips felt numb and dry. Her sister brought in a wreath of dried flowers, hovered over the tub and rubbed the dried flowers between her palms. Natalia could hear women wailing in the village. Her sister came up to her and whispered something. Natalia sobbed against her swaying, girlish breasts. Then alone in the dark she plunged her white, trembling nakedness into the hot water and the fragrant steam. *Tell me, Natalia, what will it be like when we are free again? What will it be like on our first day of freedom? Please write and tell me, Natalia.*

First I'll look at you: I'll look at you until my eyes hurt, as long as I can see, as long as I have sight.

The first time she saw him he was standing on the steps of the university building, leaning against the wall, waiting for somebody; at the sight of the huge mustache on his childish face she had laughed aloud. He saw her laughing, and smoothed and pulled his mustache tight, just as if he was alone in front of a mirror. She again burst out laughing as she walked past him; he had slowly and solemnly closed his large, dark eyes, but without showing any ill humor. She laughed whenever she saw him; she told her friends he looked "ridiculously terrible"; she laughed aloud at the very thought of him. As she met him more and more frequently at lectures and student meetings, she noticed that he did not feel at all awkward about being probably the most poorly dressed of all the students who lodged in an attic room above a café and often went hungry. She was curious about this young man who was so self-confident that even his poverty was a source of pride. Because of his seriousness and his habit of attaching the same importance to every word he pronounced, he did not sound particularly clever, and she felt rather sorry for him. For a long time she found him unattractive because of his severity toward other people and his penchant for telling his friends their faults and other unpleasant things. But she thought about him more and more often. Try as she might, she couldn't construct a clear and complete image of this student from what he showed to the outside world; she knew he was already a well-known revolutionary, with whom Dimitrije Tucović would stroll around Belgrade whenever he was out of prison. Even though she admired him for his daring, she thought him alien and remote because she had never heard him laugh or whisper.

So it was until that May Day excursion to Topčider, until she heard that exhilarating masculine laughter from a stream. She left her companions and walked toward the stream from which the laughter came. She wanted to turn back when she caught sight of Bogdan in the midst of a group of workmen who were sitting on the bank of the stream; he was sitting on a rotting tree trunk washing his feet, his trousers rolled up to his knees. But a young man with a tambourine had caught sight of her and called to her to join them; it would have been awkward to turn back. Bogdan was absorbed in what he was saying to the workmen and took no notice of her arrival. She sat down just above him. "Am I disturbing you?" she asked. "We know who disturbs us in the world," he said without turning around, and went on denouncing craftsmen who were socialists only until they acquired their own shops and apprentices. He was splashing his feet in the clear, chilly water, and she was afraid he might catch cold. "Dry your feet; you'll catch cold," she said, speaking into the nape of his neck and touching his dark, curly hair with her forehead. He turned around quickly, as if stung. A tremor ran through her body; she could not run away. She looked at the water flowing rapidly between the clumps of grass, shining in the sunlight. And when something made Bogdan laugh, she turned her eyes to the fresh young leaves in the wood. She didn't move away until he took her by the arm, without any embarrassment, familiarly; evidently he did not think, or perhaps care, that this was the first time in her life that her arm had rested in a man's hand in this way. He led her up a small slope where the trees were already turning bright green under the song of the cuckoo. And as soon as it grew dark she became convinced that he could indeed whisper—and in a very exciting and persuasive way.

After that she often heard his laughter and his whispers as they strolled through Kalemegdan or the Deer Park. When the lime trees were in flower, she had said: "Bogdan, never tell me that you love me. Love is trust. So always say to me: 'I trust you.' Because I trust you. We trust each other, Bogdan."

Why, then, had she jumped out of the train in Lapovo when she was on her way to see him in Ralja? So that she did not arrive in

Ralja in the evening, where he was waiting to see her for the last time before going off to war. But why after the parting in Ralja, when they wept beside the train, after so many letters from Skoplje—and what letters—why was she afraid now? *I'll look at you, first I'll take a long, long look at you, until my eyes hurt; as long as I can see, as long as there's sight left in my eyes. And then, if you really are so crazy, let your freedom come. . . .*

Natalia felt easier when her sleepless night was rudely cut short by her father at daybreak.

"The train won't wait for you, and the Command won't wait for him!" he said, going out without shutting the door.

She jumped out of bed: he had seen the herbs in the bath water! As she met her sister's laughing eyes, she felt ashamed right down to the soles of her bare feet. She began to dress quickly, unable to overcome the feeling of shame and the oppressive anxiety born of uncertainty.

In the kitchen her father was angrily reproaching her mother because the turkey was overcooked, and because she had made an apple pie instead of walnut pastries, which would keep for up to ten days in cold weather and might save the life of a soldier in the trenches. Natalia could hardly believe her ears. She combed her hair slowly, hoping he might leave the kitchen before she was ready. She selected a kerchief, a white one. *Why white?* she thought. *I'll take a blue one.* The wailing in the village mingled with the sound of pails clanking in wells and axes striking woodpiles. Her father was waiting for her in the kitchen with some money in his hand.

"This is for the train and whatever else you need. And this is for him."

She looked at the bag of food and murmured:

"Father, I must tell you who it is that I'm going to see off to the war."

"I know he's a Serbian soldier going to the front. That's good enough for me. Now have a bite to eat and hurry to catch the train."

She drank a cup of milk without sitting down, hoisted the bag onto her back, silently kissed her mother, then turned toward her father, but he was already hurrying toward the gate, frowning gloomily as usual. As she hurried after him she remembered that she had not kissed her sisters good-bye. A bareheaded, bearded old man was standing at the open gate; his son had been the first casualty from Prerovo in the war against the Austrians.

"My daughter-in-law is in labor, Mr. Dumović!" he cried. "Milutin's wife. All the women who know about these things are with her, but she's been in a bad way since dusk yesterday, poor thing. I've come for Natalia."

"But I'm not a doctor. I can't do anything to help her."

"Go and see what's happening, Natalia," ordered her father.

"But I've never seen a woman in labor, Father. I daren't even look."

"I said leave your bag and go with this man!"

The quince trees bent over her, the hedge pressed against her thighs: she could not put her bag down. The old man in his white underpants and sleeveless jacket stood weeping in front of her.

"But I haven't learned anything about it. I don't know what to do."

Her father removed the bag from her shoulders. She pushed the old man aside, then hurried out into the lane and began to run toward the old man's house.

In the corner beside the fireplace, in which the flames were leaping around a copper pan of boiling water, a woman lay on a coarse blanket, a man's shirt covering her head; the Prerovo midwives were bending over her long-drawn-out groans, whispering something. The girl's mother-in-law stood above her head, holding a lighted candle. Fortunetellers were making their predictions: one was "extinguishing the embers" in a dish on the doorstep and asserting that all the embers were turning to the sun; another was breaking apples into pieces to see the seeds and smashing pumpkins in the chimney corner; a third was tearing off pieces of red yarn above the head of the woman in labor. Natalia pushed her way through the midwives and knelt down in front of a pool of blood on the blanket.

Time stood still. Natalia forgot herself. When she heard the midwives whisper, "It's dead," she realized that day had long since dawned; she caught sight of the old man kneeling on the doorstep, crossing himself.

"It's a girl," she said as she walked past him, surprised that she had remembered that he might derive some comfort from the lie that the stillborn child was a girl. She could scarcely manage to totter to the gate, against which her father was leaning. He handed her the bag. "Run straight to the ferry!"

She ran toward the Morava River through the dewy unharvested fields of corn. She reached the river, choking with fear and panting for breath, and saw the ferry on the opposite bank, without the ferryman. She called out. The Morava roared over the sluices. Low, thick clouds hid the sun. She turned around and stared at the fields and banks of the river: nothing but willows and fallen tree trunks, not a man to be seen anywhere. In the distance, along the bank toward the village she could see the black and white kerchiefs of women working in the cornfields. She called frantically for the ferryman. The river roared past, and time with it. She put down her bag and ran along the bank toward the water mill, still calling out desperately for the ferryman, deafened by the roar of the Morava. The water mill was shut; she pounded on the door. Then she rushed back along the bank toward the ferry. Her throat ached from shouting. She remembered that it was wartime and yelled to the women in the fields: "Please help me!" The next train was tomorrow. But for her there was no next train. She would wade across the river. She stepped in and stood still: the autumn floodwater covered the fords. Well, she could swim. She undressed quickly, down to her chemise: how could she board the train wet through? She began to take off her chemise as well, then, suddenly frightened, let it slip over the lower part of her body; she tied her blouse, skirt, underskirt, and shawl into her kerchief.

She ran down the bank and waded into the turbid waters. The dark chill of the river cut into her knees and crept up her thighs, up to her hips, then up to her breasts: she felt the current tugging at her feet. I must swim, she thought; but she was startled and deafened by the long-drawn-out whistle of the train as it drew into the station. She stood stock-still: the river rushed at her, biting at the pebbles under her feet, clutching her by the chemise around her hips, drawing her into itself. Her heart floundered on the surface of the river. Then the Morava turned with its banks, willows, and poplars, and began to flow upward, eroding the long, gray skyline, falling on the poplar trees. Natalia dragged herself out and sat down on the bank. The train whistled again; the sound was lost in the clamor of the Morava as it broke over the floodgates of the water mill. She pressed herself against the bank like a wet leaf.

"It's fate," she said aloud, a little later. That was why she had left the train in Lapovo; that was why a stillborn child had been born that morning, to delay her. When the crows fleeing from the echoes of the Prerovo church bells flew over her head, she took off her wet chemise and slowly began to put on her blouse and skirt.

Through his deep sleep Ivan heard shouts and cries and realized that they had reached Niš: that meant his parents and yet another patriotic scene. He did not want to see anybody and remained huddled under his overcoat while the others jumped from the train, greeting their relatives and friends. The muffled sounds of commotion and shouting rose from the platform. Was he the only person still lying down in the carriage? He could hear Bogdan's breathing behind his back, and felt grateful to him for this protection. What would he do without him? If they were separated at the front, he would flee to Bogdan's platoon. He felt suffocated by something more than shame and remorse for yesterday's conduct. He heard someone call his name; it was his mother. Her clipped, strained voice sent a stab of pain through him; his father, of course, would be his usual stern, dignified self. For a few moments the noise of people laughing and talking prevented him from distinguishing anything clearly. Could anybody really be laughing now? He heard his name again. Bora Jackpot was calling to him; he would not answer. If he uttered a single word, he would burst into tears. Then someone ran through the carriage and shook him crossly by the shoulder.

"Your mother's waiting for you, Blindie. There's no sense in staying there like this! You're in Niš."

"We've already said good-bye, and in Niš too," he muttered; but he got up and jumped over Bogdan, the only person left in the car.

"Forgive me for waking you up, dear."

She spoke in a quiet, tremulous voice and stood pressed against the side of the car.

He seemed to tower above her; she could not see his eyes.

"I've brought you some warm underwear, and socks," she called up to him. "All the things you need now."

"I don't want to take any cakes to the front!"

He jumped down onto the platform and embraced his mother, somewhat reluctantly.

She had no strength to move. She could hardly keep on her feet under the overwhelming weight of her child—now a grown man going off to the battlefield.

He sensed that his mother was on the verge of collapse and moved away suddenly. He looked at her in confusion, then his face brightened. *How beautiful my mother is,* he thought.

She leaned against the car and looked at his chest, at the large wine stain on his jacket. *He seems much older,* she thought. *How much he has aged during these last two weeks, since I last visited him.*

"We're having a lot of rain now; soon it will snow," she whispered.

"Have you brought my glasses?" He turned around, but could not see his father. "Where's Father?"

"He's waiting for you in Kragujevac with your glasses. I had a telegram from him last night. Did you know that Valjevo has been taken? And that Milena has stayed there with the hospital?" She looked straight into his eyes. "And now you're going away too. . . ."

"What else could she do?" he said, and fell silent because her tears would begin to flow if he said more. And if she started to cry now, he would run back into the car. He turned his eyes to the dense, milling crowd in the background. Until this moment he had never once thought Milena might be suffering, and in danger. Why hadn't it entered his mind?

Olga saw that his lips and chin were quivering. *I shouldn't have said anything to him about Milena,* she thought. If only the train did not leave soon!

"Yes, dear, she couldn't do anything else."

"It's true they're barbarians and scoundrels, but I don't think they'd do anything to the wounded and the hospital. Anyway, there are international agreements about hospitals in wartime. And there's the International Red Cross, Mother." He put his hand on her shoulder. He must somehow convince her that Milena was not in serious danger.

"What shall I do with the parcel, Ivan?"

"Oh, I'm sorry," he said, and took from her a large box, beautifully wrapped, his mother's handiwork. He carried it into the train.

She saw him throw it down. *It doesn't mean a thing to him,* she thought.

"Someone will take it," she said, with a note of reproach in her voice.

"Oh, for God's sake, Mother! We're the Student Battalion! We're a family of specially chosen brothers." He stopped, surprised at his words and the confidence in his voice. "We're creating a legend." He stopped again; he was echoing Vinaver. "I'm serious."

"Are you now spouting ideas and principles? Just like your father." She said no more of what she was thinking.

He turned his eyes away from her astonished, no longer beautiful face. He looked at the crowd on the platform and recognized some people from Belgrade, civilians, draft dodgers, people behind the lines who were fleeing southward, to Greece. A feeling of scorn welled up inside him, and then defiance: he and his friends were going to the battlefield, to the north; they were the only people traveling northward today. He turned to his mother, embraced her tenderly with his right arm, and led her toward the engine.

"Listen, Mother. A country that has fifteen hundred people like us can't be defeated. I suppose you're thinking: What are fifteen hundred against so many Austrian divisions? It's happened more than once, though, that a few people, or even a single man, changed the course of history and transformed the worst defeat into victory. When it's a question of spirit, numbers are not the decisive factor. And we are spirit. This is our great moment, Mother."

"But I—and all wives and mothers—would be happy if you were not that spirit, Ivan. If you were simply children, children in our arms."

She tore herself away from his arm and hugged him tightly. He bent down slightly and let her cover him with kisses, now at last. He abandoned himself to her despair too. He sensed that, kissing him, she was also kissing Milena, and stroked her back. The engine coughed and hissed out its black anger and its dull, muffled strength. A cloud of steam enveloped them; the hubbub on the platform receded. She could no longer restrain herself.

"Why did you come back from Paris?" she whispered.

"If I hadn't come back to fight, I would never have come back to Serbia at all," he said, speaking into her head, resting on his breast.

She breathed in the unpleasant smell of wine and dirt from his jacket. But she did not remove her face; she wanted to breathe in his skin, the smell of him as a child, the smell of her milk, the smell of him as a baby after his bath, before he fell asleep.

He felt impelled to say something more. "I don't like all this talk about why we Serbs are fighting, about why I'm a volunteer. Really, Mother, is there any sense in us two talking about that now?"

He released her from his embrace and moved away. She held onto his jacket, staring at some nasty stains. When he was little he had been very squeamish; he would eat only what she gave him with her own hands.

"Please, Mother!"

"But I'm *not* crying, Ivan." She removed her hand from his jacket. No, she wasn't crying.

"Everything that we're losing today we *had* to lose."

"Don't repeat your father's principles at this time, please!"

"You're right, forgive me. Just now one should . . ." He didn't know what to do now. There was no sense in parting like this, in leaving her in despair. He could hear his companions singing behind him.

She paused from time to time to have a look at him. He didn't used to walk with a stoop. The singing was getting on her nerves;

what they needed now was quiet. Eyes have the longest memory. If only the train did not leave soon; if only it would never leave!

"Let's walk a little farther along the tracks."

"Yes, that's a stupid song. But the spirit is there. What's the latest news from the front, Mother?"

"We're finished, Ivan. They say our army is no longer putting up any resistance. There was a story going around this morning that the High Command is asking the government to begin peace talks with Austria immediately. And last night they were saying in the town that Pašić had been murdered in Lapovo, and that the King and Prince Alexander have fled to Montenegro."

"These people behind the lines are absolutely disgusting! What else is happening?"

"It's terrible, dear. Everybody is getting ready to flee."

"And what about you?"

"Do you really think that I could flee from Serbia, Ivan? Drag around suitcases and bundles to save my own life?"

"All isn't lost, Mother, not by a long shot. The people behind the lines have lost faith. They're a vile, filthy lot, the scum of our nation. If the homeland consisted only of people of that ilk, we ought to betray it immediately." He spat.

She had never seen him spit like that. Why does he have to console me like this? She caught up with him and walked alongside him, touching him; she had always felt so proud and happy walking beside her tall son. Her tall, slender son. But they would stick a bayonet in his chest.

"What were you saying, Ivan?"

"I'm happy that I'm going to the battlefield. I really am, Mother, I swear it. I'm not playing the hero." He turned around and looked into her eyes: he saw only tears. *What wonderful eyes my mother has,* he thought.

"I believe you, dear." She felt for his hand and gripped it. She could feel him in all her veins, feel his hand embedded in her heart. But she did not understand what he was saying. She could hear the singing on the platform, behind her. "It's cruel to sing now, Ivan. It's like mixing a wedding and a funeral." His fingers were calloused from handling a rifle, but they were long, like Vukašin's. He got his hands from his father. If only the train would not leave!

"If those of us who can think, if all thirteen hundred and twenty-one of us students on this train, do not admit defeat, then Serbia is not defeated."

"Ah, my boy, you're very innocent," she whispered, throwing caution to the winds. Then she was sorry and kept silent for some time. She could not hear him breathe; all she was aware of was his hand. "I know it is very difficult now to draw the line between wise men and fools, between patriots and cowards. Let's not talk about it."

"It's the shirkers who know that best just now. But I repeat that I really do believe that neither the government nor the High Command, nor even the war, has anything to do with our fate. Our fate is determined by some higher law. The fact that the Austrians have crossed the Kolubara means nothing. Nothing at all."

She leaned against the switchman's hut and sighed deeply. "That's not you talking."

"I'm speaking absolutely sincerely, Mother. Look at me."

She raised her eyes to his face; then her whole body drooped.

"I'm terribly unhappy, Ivan. In the eight days since Vukašin went off to Valjevo with Pašić, I haven't slept more than eight hours. I no longer know what I've been living for; it's as though our life before the war was but a dream, and real life is the war." She covered her face with her hands.

Her whispers shook him. He looked straight at her, breathed into the fingers covering her face.

She removed her hands and looked at him with deep longing, drinking in his very being: *He is my son,* she thought, *he belongs to me!*

He saw how suffering had ravaged her delicate face. These lines had not been etched simply by her anxiety about Milena and himself.

She looked toward the station: the train was not leaving, not yet. The noise and singing from the platform rolled down the valley.

He put his hands on her shoulders: she had an inkling of why he was prepared to die, and she was the only person who would not deceive him.

"So you really don't know what you've been living for?"

She chose her words carefully, trying not to distress him.

"Suddenly we've lost everything. And we're totally alone, Ivan. Being alone is the one misfortune that doesn't pass through the soul; it stays there."

"Is this an idea you've borrowed from somebody, Mother?"

"Is it really an idea?"

They looked at each other with a flash of recognition.

"There were always a lot of people around you. All sorts of people, some of them very amusing. Forgive me for talking about this. I didn't like the company you kept."

"I don't reproach you for it, dear. And now I don't reproach your father, either. You men don't know who gives you life and who loves you. All you know well is whom you hate, and, better still, who hates you. When you come back from the war . . ." She fell silent, dropped her hands, moved away from the wall, and stared at the low, overcast sky, closed and shut up forever.

"What will it be like when I come back from the war?"

"You tell me, dear. I want to hear what you have to say about it."

"What will it be like when I come back from the war?" he exclaimed. He took off his glasses and wiped his forehead. "Well, I don't know. I can't see. In fact, what I do see after the war is really so little, so unimportant. I wouldn't have gone to war for the sake of the future. I would have been a deserter."

She remained silent. *Perhaps he's fallen in love?* she thought. She turned toward him; he was suddenly looking at her with an inexplicable smile. If only the train would not leave! Someone shouted that the train wouldn't leave for two hours. Only two more hours! She was ashamed to ask him whether he had a girl, and yet she badly wanted to know; this had been bothering her ever since he had enlisted as a volunteer. She felt sorry that no girl loved him, that he did not love anybody.

He took her arm and led her toward the train again, onto the platform. Now he must talk to his mother about something vitally important; it was pitiful and stupid to die surrounded by lies and illusions. He wanted to know the truth when he went into the trenches, the truth about his parents and the truth about his own life.

"You haven't told me what it will be like when you come back from the war, Ivan."

She watched carefully every flicker of expression on his face. He was always ashamed when anyone praised him, always frowned as he was frowning now. When he was little he always played alone; he would hide under the bed, in a closet, or in bushes in the garden. Suddenly he let go of her hand.

"I don't want to think about the future. I'm interested in other things. I'd like to know what you and Father looked like when you were young."

"What we looked like? I really can't remember. After all that's happened, I don't know what we looked like, Ivan." She fell silent.

"You won't disappoint me, Mother. You can speak freely."

"I would have to go back to our house, back to my own room, among my own things, to remember how it all used to be."

"I don't quite understand."

"You and your father, all you men, can live on ideas, on the future. But we women live on our feelings, so we are condemned to live on the past. And when we lose the past, when war breaks out . . . You were asking me what your father looked like?"

"Yes. What did he look like to you when he came back from Paris? Why does it make you uncomfortable to talk about this?"

"But it doesn't, dear. On the contrary. Vukašin was an exceptional young man, refined and dignified, nothing of the peasant about him. Very serious. And concerned and anxious, but in a charming way. It was marvelous to listen to him talking. All the young people in Belgrade adored him, I can tell you."

"And in what way has he changed most?"

"Well, he's become very silent over the years. Because of all his worries, I suppose. Those damned politics crush a man's soul to dust."

"In what ways am I like him, Mother?"

She stopped and gazed at him with tears in her eyes; her look seemed to express something more than maternal love.

"But do you want to be like him?"

"I don't want to be like anybody," he said firmly.

He drew her aside in order to retrace their steps. Some corporals had formed a circle to start the kolo; he would rather fight than dance the kolo in front of his mother.

"Mother, I want you to give me an answer to an important question. And please don't be noble, or I'll feel depressed. Did my father ever harm anyone?"

They were walking into the steam from the engine and could hardly see each other. He stared hard at his mother. Were her lips trembling? Her expression had changed. Had she perhaps been disappointed? And yet she had behaved as if she was the happiest woman in the world.

She looked at him standing there, covered with steam up to his waist, his legs invisible. How well could he see in the autumn mists? She answered his question quietly, almost fearfully.

"Your father is an exceptionally honorable man."

"I know that. But how much good has he done?"

"Vukašin never told anyone that he had nothing to give him, Ivan. If anyone asked him for money or any kind of help, he never refused. He'd signed ever so many bills of exchange for people he hardly knew. I can't tell you how many poor students he's helped. And he did it secretly, like a gentleman. He never once boasted about his acts of kindness. The only thing he couldn't bear to do was to ask for special favors. He would never do anything against the law. Because of his principles," she whispered, then fell silent.

"You don't think Father was kind and charitable because of his political ambitions?"

"Nonsense, Ivan! How could you think such a thing about your father?"

"There are people who do good out of ambition."

"I haven't met them, Ivan." She fell silent. He would knock against a branch at night and his glasses would fall off. He would be in a forest, in a thick mist. She felt an overmastering desire to kiss his forehead, to press his head against her bosom.

"Why did he break with his father and brother?"

She took his hand and stroked his fingers as they walked along the embankment.

"I know them only by hearsay. I've never seen them, but I know very well that your father's father and his brother are not good people. His brother is a tight-fisted peasant moneylender, and his father is a Radical scoundrel. All their elections end in bloodshed. But Vukašin is an intellectual, a man educated in Europe; you've read his books and articles."

A train was arriving from the north, crowded with refugees; its thundering progress drowned their words. Soon his train would leave. She gripped his arm convulsively. What should she do? What should she say to him? O God, do such words exist? "My child, my child," she kept repeating to herself.

"What is Father doing in Kragujevac, Mother?"

"I don't know. I suppose Pašić is trying to persuade him to join the government."

"Tell him he'll lose my respect if he does. Tell him that I'll lead an attack out of shame. . . . Forgive me, Mother, I'm talking nonsense. I'm not interested in politics, and it's all the same to me who rules Serbia." He heard people calling him from the platform. The train was leaving; and a good thing too. If only he could get away as quickly as possible, away from everything. "Come and let me introduce you to my friend. My only friend. I think the world of him; he's a real man."

They turned back. Olga was exhausted and could hardly walk. He bent down toward her. A bayonet would get him, a bayonet would get her child. She wanted something to remember of his feelings, his soul.

"Are you in love with anyone, Ivan? Do tell me, dear."

He stopped dead, removed his arm from her shoulders, and hung his head. The train full of refugees was backing out of the station; the clank of the couplings and the whistle of the engine filled him with shame and disgust: he had given that horrible whore a false surname; the steam and soot stank of his vomit in her room, and in the singing and shouting on the platform he heard the words spoken by her between the Sloboda Café and her bed in that pigsty, words that had pierced the very marrow of his bones. But how could he tell his mother that he was in love with Ivanka, who had run away with a Bulgarian?

"There's nothing to be ashamed of. A lot of your companions have sweethearts. Look at them, beside the train."

"Oh, no, it's not that. Why should I be ashamed? I just don't like to talk about it," he snapped, staring at the slag beside the tracks.

"Do I know her? I suppose she isn't a girl from Belgrade? I don't mind if she's French; I'd be delighted. Even if she's a German, or a gypsy. It's all the same to me, if you love her. How pale you are, Ivan! You must be feeling sick."

"Yes, I do feel sick. It's unbearable. I don't know what's come over me," he whispered, moving away from her as she clutched at him, seeing him turn so pale. "A man has something inside him that he can't fathom. Which works against him. Don't be afraid, Mother. I'm sure nothing will happen to me out there." He ran off to the lavatory.

She started to walk after him but stopped, frightened by the shouting and singing on the platform.

"Get into the train, Corporals! We're leaving!"

Ivan was coming back to her, smiling; he was much smaller now, a little boy just beginning to walk, staggering uncertainly toward her; but he was wearing an enormous soldier's overcoat, belonging to someone else, somebody's cap, and boots he could hardly drag along. He smiled at her. She took his hand and led him toward the car labeled *42 soldiers or 8 horses,* smiling and talking gently to him.

"I'm also quite sure that nothing will happen to you there, Ivan. Don't be afraid, Ivan. Mothers can feel danger and evil. And I don't feel them for you, so don't be afraid, dear. I can see you coming back to me from the war. On the station platform in Belgrade. We'll be waiting for you."

"Mother, I have a girl."

"Splendid! I'm so happy, dear."

"Get in, Katić! Good-bye, everybody. See you again in Zagreb. See you in Ljubljana! In Vienna! In Budapest! Hurrah! Hurrah!"

"My girl's name is Kosara, Mother. She lives in Skoplje, 36 Prince George Street. That's my sweetheart, Mother, my last love. You don't seem to like her name?"

"Oh, no, dear. Why shouldn't I like it? Kosara is an old Serbian name. Mind you write to her often. Don't be like other men."

"I will; don't worry. She's a charming girl, Mother. She's beautiful, intelligent, and has a wonderful soul. She's well educated and refined. You'd love her queenly manner. That's why I'm so excited. I'm immensely happy. I'm going to the battlefield, and I'm in love—can you understand, Mother?" he cried as he wrenched himself from her embrace.

The train started its journey toward the north.

Returning from the Morava in the pouring rain, numb with despair, hardly able to carry her bag of food, Natalia stopped short as though confronted with an unforeseen danger: Aćim Katić was calling to her from his porch. He was the one person in Prerovo to whom she could pour out her woes. She stood before him, head hanging, grasping a porch post with one hand. She had to confess that she had missed the train.

"Throw down your bag and sit down. Where were you going?"

She sat down at his table, clasped her hands together, and remained silent. She should have told him where she was going; during the last few days he had kept asking her if she had received a letter from Skoplje. He was waiting for some news of the grandson he had never met.

"Were you going to Skoplje to see that young rebel of yours?"

"I was going to Kragujevac. They'll be arriving there this evening. Then they'll go on to the front, I guess," she whispered, her tears blurring the newspaper on the table.

"How did you miss the train, for heaven's sake?" he shouted suddenly, banging the table with his fist.

His anger pleased her; let him hurt and offend her, let him beat her numb body, which had not felt cold even in the Morava that morning. She waited in silence.

"Why didn't you ask me for the dogcart? When must you be in Kragujevac?"

She raised her eyes to his white forked beard. She could hear the newspaper rustling from her trembling.

"I should have got there this afternoon and waited for the evening train from Skoplje."

"Then you've time to get there!" He banged his fist on the table again. "You'll still get there, my girl. If you leave immediately in the dogcart and go through Levčo, you'll be in Kragujevac before ten o'clock tonight."

She gazed at him in disbelief. She could not even move her lips. Once again she heard the whistle of the train as she stood in the river with the water up to her breasts.

"I'll have the mare harnessed to the dogcart at once. And one of Tola's young devils can go with you. Zdravko's just a child but he can drive the dogcart. If it weren't for the deluge, maybe I'd come too—to see my grandson."

"Do come, Grandfather," she stammered, and began to cry.

He grasped the railing with both hands and stared at the ash trees and the sky; his misery turned into fury.

"I can't, Natalia! I won't leave Prerovo while Serbia is being ruled by Pašić and his toadies! I haven't set foot out of Prerovo for twelve years. No, I can't come, Natalia. You must go by yourself, my girl." He got up and ordered the mare harnessed to the dogcart.

Natalia still did not believe her good fortune. She looked in amazement at this powerful and extraordinary old man, who had changed her life by helping her to go to Belgrade to study. She silently placed her hand over his large fist resting on the table.

"I'll drop in and tell your father you've gone. I'll be going for my newspaper. Those damned Serbian newspapers. Just look at this, Natalia, for God's sake. . . . Our front has cracked like an old fence before a herd of bulls. Franz Josef has grabbed a third of Serbia. All Mačva, Podrinje, and Posavina are on the run. And the government, if you please, devotes half a page in all the newspapers to the promotion of officials. Serbia is on the verge of collapse, and the government is pushing forward those pen-pushers, those bloodsuckers, pushing them up the promotion ladder. What are our wretched peasants dying for? We again had long lists of men killed read out last night; whose state were they defending?"

She did not hear what he was saying. She was seeing the indifferent sky above the Morava when the whistle of the train drove deep into her brain and coursed through her veins.

"I could have died today, Grandfather," she whispered absently.

"There is no end to the evil in the world, Natalia. The women mourning their sons are worse off than you. It's harder for a mother who has lost two sons than for a woman who's only lost one. Even those who have lost all the sons they bore haven't seen the end of their troubles. Perhaps the time will soon come when people will not even dare to lament their dead. That's the way of the world, my child. You live to endure." He caressed her arm with his thumb.

"Are you sure I'll reach Kragujevac by this evening, Grandfather?"

"Of course I am! Didn't I once drive pigs to Zemun and Budapest by that route?" He began to enumerate all the villages, bridges, and crossroads, not failing to mention his political friends and enemies in every village. It was only when the servant led out the white mare already harnessed, and told Tola's grandson Zdravko to put a knife in his belt and an ax under his feet, that Natalia really believed that she was going to Kragujevac to see Bogdan. She picked up her bag and hurried into the dogcart; as she took the reins from Zdravko, Aćim handed her three ducats: "One for you, and two for Ivan." She clenched her fists and blushed. Each time she left Prerovo for school, he slipped some money into her hand. She took the money and drove off.

As soon as they left Niš and were hurtling along the southern Morava, Bogdan Dragović left Ivan Katić in the corner of the railroad car scribbling in his notebook and settled himself beside the door, opening it slightly: as he looked at the Morava he thought of Natalia. Danilo History-Book was passionately trying to convince everybody of the necessity of unifying the South Slavs from Varna to Trieste. As if they needed convincing! Bogdan flattened his father's candle, placed it over the big bruise, and pulled his cap over the wax to warm it. His eye had opened up almost completely, but a dull pain lingered in his eyebrows and the bruise discolored his temples. The ugly marks left by Glišić's whip would not disappear in the few hours before he saw Natalia. He felt melancholy; the sporadic outbursts of singing jarred his thoughts. Bogdan looked intently at the rain-swollen river, flowing between groves of bare poplars, unharvested cornfields, and blackened meadows and plum orchards. He was seeing it through Natalia's eyes: a clear river meandering through green willows and silvery aspens, through fields of young corn in the moonlight, past meadows not yet mown. He saw himself with Natalia on the bank of the river.

The engine braked sharply, and the train came to a standstill. The rattling and creaking, the reverberation of wood and iron, died away.

Bogdan open the door a little farther: it was a small empty station on the bank of the southern Morava. Some letters had peeled off the name, leaving only the stump of a word. The mutilated word made a strong impression on him. The stationmaster came running along the train.

"Boys, where's the officer in charge of the train?"

"In front, near the engine. What station is this?" cried Bogdan, alarmed by the sudden stop. Had they been rerouted to by-pass Kragujevac? The rain drummed on the roof of the car. Someone began to sing in a deep, weary voice and abruptly fell silent; the wind whistled through the wet elm just outside their car.

"Why are we standing here? Where are we? Not a soul around! So where are the Serbian people? Bogdan, bring the stationmaster over to sing the national anthem with us. Come on, boys, let's sing."

Bogdan stuck his head out into the rain, without removing his cap from the left side of his face; he felt suddenly chilled as he looked toward the engine. Danilo History-Book and a few others broke off singing after the first verse; Danilo shouted:

"Listen, boys, did we unload our cargo of military enthusiasm in Niš, to comfort our despairing parents and unhappy sweethearts? I don't believe it!"

"Nor do I. We are traveling along the highroad of history. Armies have marched up and down the Morava ever since wars were fought. I assure you, my friends, that the earth remembers every foot that trod this way, and the heavens have not forgotten a single voice. So let us not keep silent! We are now living for eternity!"

"Wrap Vinaver's overcoat around his head!"

"What's happening out there, Mustachios?"

"Something that doesn't look good for us," answered Bogdan as he watched the train's commanding officer and another commander following the stationmaster into his office.

"Maybe a revolution broke out in Germany. Why not? Maybe our brothers and fellow students—two Croats, two Czechs, and one Slovenian—have blown Franz Josef to smithereens with bombs. Why shouldn't they? Nothing is impossible, gentlemen. And the war might have stopped suddenly, just like our train. The war also has its engineer and motorman."

"And maybe Belgrade has fallen, Staša. Maybe Pašić has gone to Belgrade with a white flag. Why not, boys?"

"Enough of this draft-dodger's nonsense, Bora!"

Ivan Katić pushed Danilo History-Book aside and leaned against Bogdan. "Do you still believe in the future?" he whispered gravely.

"If they've changed our route, and Natalia arrives in Kragujevac this evening, damn them to hell!"

"So if a man is to believe in the future, a girl must be waiting for him, preferably this evening. Is that it?"

Bogdan turned to Ivan and frowned with the right side of his face.

"Yes, that's how it is, Bogdan: for you to have a future, someone must be waiting for you somewhere."

"That's how it is, sometimes."

"Still you must admit that man's future is a paltry thing. What do we know about it? What can we know? I've been thinking about this ever since we left Niš, and I've come to the conclusion that the concept of the future is the most pitiable of all ideas. Truly, Bogdan. The future is something narrow and confined, a brook that drains the Pacific Ocean of the present reality. It's just a drop, a wisp of the present. The power of imagination is poor indeed compared with the power of recollection."

"Is that what you've been writing in your notebook? Who is it for?" Ivan blushed slightly. "What I mean is, this shows how much you believe in the future, and how important it is for you."

"Man has no future. Not only today, because there's a war on, but because what we can visualize as happening in the time to come is so very meager. In fact, man has only a past; his present is also unknown and indefinite. Why are we standing in this empty station? Are we waiting for somebody? Or have we met a trainload of refugees? Our train full of corporals, with a future in which they will die heroically for the homeland."

"What if they've diverted us from Kragujevac!"

"Do you believe Tolstoy, Bogdan?"

"I don't believe many writers. Especially counts."

"Do you remember how Bolkonsky grasped in a flash the entire purpose and futility of his life as he lay dying? I believe that's true, and that's why I want a slow, weary bullet."

In front of the cars carrying their respective platoons, the commanding officers were shouting: "Get out of the train. With weapons and equipment! Line up!"

Bogdan stared apprehensively at his commander: they were taking another route; he would not see Natalia tonight. "Where are we going?" he yelled at the officer.

"What business is that of yours, Dragović? You heard the order!"

Bogdan pushed his way through the melee of arms, knapsacks, rifles, and shouts. "The line's been cut. We're going to the front on foot. Where is the front? You'll see, that old coward Pašić has signed an order for capitulation. Can Putnik and Stepa really do that? Something really big must have happened. God, what a downpour! There's nothing worse than fighting in the rain, boys. Hurry up! Hurry up!"

Bogdan picked up his rifle and Ivan handed him his knapsack; he was among the last to jump down from the car; he stood in line uncertain what to do and looked around the station for a way of escape.

The commanding officers shouted; the sergeants cursed and threatened: the line of soldiers curved four deep a long way in front of the engine. Bogdan's head was enveloped in steam.

"I'll run away. I'll be in Kragujevac this evening even if they shoot me tomorrow," he whispered into the back of Ivan's neck, and out of sheer fury refused to button his overcoat. The officer in command of the train came out of the stationmaster's office, walked to the middle of the ranks, and ordered the corporals to stand at attention. Bogdan did not obey. Danilo History-Book muttered a warning, and Bora Jackpot aimed a mouthful of spittle right at the commanding officer's boots. Bogdan resolved to hide under a railway car and then dash off into the unharvested corn.

"We found waiting for us here an order from the High Command," shouted the officer in charge of the train, "an order bearing today's date. The High Command has promoted all the corporals in the Student Battalion to the rank of junior sergeant. I congratulate you on your promotion, Sergeants!"

In the sudden hush the rain drummed on the railroad cars. The students looked at one another in disbelief.

Bora Jackpot spat loudly.

"Long live the Serbian army!" cried the officer in charge of the train.

Silence.

"What kind of joke is this, promoting us to sergeants?" said Bogdan aloud.

"Long live the High Command!" cried Danilo History-Book.

"Why are you silent?" shouted the platoon commanders, running alongside the ranks.

"What are we supposed to do?" yelled Bogdan. He was ready to grab the C.O. by the throat, something he had often wanted to do while drilling on Golgotha.

"Hurrah! Hurrah!" The cheer spread through the ranks like a mounting wave. Mutely Bogdan watched a lime tree shake off its raindrops and a window of the station fill with children's faces. He was thinking of how to get to Kragujevac that evening if the battalion took a different route. He did not even hear the command to get back into the train, but stood leaning against the car facing the stationmaster, who was looking at him with an insufferably stupid expression. He heard Bora Jackpot talking behind him.

"They've promoted us just in time to die. I bet you fellows didn't know how sensitive the homeland is to human vanity, what a subtle sense of hierarchy it has. Our homeland is as vain as an old maid. If our country were as big as Russia, we would have come to the front as majors."

"Bullshit, Jackpot! History has chosen us to create a legend for our nation, to provide a myth. The phoenix is no longer a bird; the Serbian phoenix takes the form of a student."

"Bravo, Vinaver! Just the same, I'd rather be a Serbian rooster than a Serbian student, Staša."

"We're sitting on a powder keg, you idiot! Now different laws apply—the laws of tragedy. Njegoš was right: the impossible is becoming possible."

"Still, the fact of the matter is that we're the last reserves of an army that's abandoning its positions without a struggle."

"But, Jackpot, that's just why I'm so happy, you fool. I'm happy to be a soldier fighting for the honor of Serbia. My patriotism has nothing to do with politics; it's a religious faith. We believe in the homeland the way the hermits on Mount Athos believe in God."

"That's right, big shot! The homeland isn't the government, political parties, or bureaucrats. What connection has Serbia with Pašić and Apis? We mustn't mix up our concepts. It's politicians and demagogues who confuse the homeland with the state and politics," said Ivan Katić crossly.

"Take it easy, Blindie. Someone must be to blame for the fact that the army has no ammunition for its artillery, and is going into the winter naked and barefoot."

"Come and sing, Raka! What do you care about army contractors!"

The engine whistled. Bogdan was racked by uncertainty. "Jump in, Bogdan!" Ivan called as the train gave a sudden strong jolt.

Bogdan leaped into the car; the train creaked from the weight of the singing. The air in the car was oppressively heavy. He stayed beside the door, gazing at the wet, empty fields. Once again he put the wax on the bruise over his left eye and placed his cap over it.

"The homeland is eternal! Serbia is eternal! But kings and governments, parties and politics pass away like dust, like the foam on the river!" Danilo History-Book's words were mouthed by Ivan Katić.

"What about our economic system, under which some people go naked and hungry, while others are well fed and have everything? Right, Mustachios?"

Bogdan did not feel like talking. The train seemed to be moving more slowly since leaving the station.

"Shoemakers' apprentices might still believe your socialist claptrap about fighting for profits and markets, because the craftsmen have been drafted. But let the facts speak for themselves. Where is the European working class now? What is the proletariat of Austria and Germany doing? Show me workers who don't have a homeland today. What do socialist comrades say to that?"

Bogdan could not ignore Danilo's challenge. "The homeland is a stepmother to all workers everywhere! The Serbia of shirkers and profiteers is not my Serbia. Nor is the Serbia of Pašić and Apis."

"Then why are you socialists fighting today, Comrade Dragović? Why is your leader, Dimitrije Tucović, commanding a platoon in the Serbian army?"

"We're fighting because those who want to enslave us are even worse bloodsuckers than ours. We're fighting so that after the war things will be different. We're fighting . . ."

"So that's how it is, comrades! You're fighting for revolution!"

"Of course we are, you stupid Radical! We're fighting so that we'll never have to fight again. The workers of Europe will go from the trenches to the barricades of Paris, Berlin, and London! And the Croats, Slovenians, and Czechs will rise up and destroy the Hapsburg Empire."

"That's the one thing you've said that I believe. The Croats and Bosnians and the people from the Vojvodina won't give their lives for Vienna and Budapest for very long; they won't kill their brothers for the sake of Franz Josef. I grant you that!"

The whole squad joined in the conversation, bickering about the boundaries of the future united South Slav state. The majority were in favor of Trieste as the boundary; the minority were satisfied with Istria as far as Pula. Nobody doubted that the unified state would include the whole of Koruška, as well as Temišvar and Baja, naturally. If the Greeks did not join the Allies, so much the better; it would not be difficult to take Salonika, a Slav city. The Italians might sail up and down the Adriatic, but in South Slav ships.

The sound of singing could be heard from the other cars. The engine gave a shrill whistle as it hurried northward.

After they left Bagrdan, word passed through the train that at Lapovo the battalion would be divided: two platoons would go to Arandjelovac to join the Second Army, and would be deployed by tomorrow; three platoons would go to Kragujevac to be placed at the disposal of the High Command.

"Which three platoons are going to Kragujevac?" cried Bogdan Dragović, poking his head out. No one in the adjoining cars knew. He turned to his companions, their hearts racing under their tunics, their unshaven faces pale from lack of sleep. He could read their unspoken thoughts: too bad they couldn't all go to the same place together, begin as a single unit. If his platoon went to Arandjelovac, he would run away and keep his rendezvous with Natalia; they would be together for one night, then he would go straight to the nearest battlefield. If he was shot as a deserter for it, so be it; what kind of a life could a man have in such a country?

"Lapovo's the next station," said Dušan Casanova, breaking the silence.

"Surely not?" groaned someone.

"Yes, it is; geography is a most exact science."

Ivan Katić moved closer to Bogdan Dragović and whispered excitedly: "If they separate us, I'm coming with you."

"If they send us to Arandjelovac, I'm going to Kragujevac first!"

"I'll come with you!" Ivan said, delighted with Bogdan's decision.

Bogdan removed his cap and the wax from his face, put the wax in his pocket, and placed his cap firmly on his head. "Fine. We should at least live this wretched life of ours like sergeants."

Ivan wanted to embrace him; he would go anywhere with Bogdan, right to the end.

The train whistled.

"Lapovo," said Bora Jackpot; he threw back his head and spat on the ceiling.

At the front of the train the Obilić student choir was singing the requiem: they looked at each other silently.

"Have they really gone through all our songs?" asked Danilo History-Book aloud.

"Yes. All that's left now is the requiem," said Bora Jackpot.

Ivan clutched Bogdan's arm, frightened by the pale, quivering lips of his companions. Bogdan was thinking of how he would escape if his platoon was sent to Arandjelovac. In the next car they were singing the requiem as if their hearts would burst out of their tunics. Ivan thought he would never survive Bogdan's death. Danilo History-

Book sighed and sang the first words of the requiem in a hoarse, quavering voice. They all joined in. Ivan saw tears on the faces of his friends, traces of tears in Bogdan's eyes too. The whole Student Battalion was singing the requiem. Ivan found himself joining in for the first time in his life. Bogdan turned his back on them to hide his unwillingness to sing the requiem, even now. He stuck his head outside and stared straight ahead, toward the station.

The engine was slowing down, without whistling, although the platforms and even the tracks were crowded with refugees and their bundles. It pushed forward as if on tiptoe, restraining its fiery breath, gently puffing its way into the mute crowd too frightened by the requiem to move back from the tracks; the refugees gaped at the freight train, which seemed about to split in two from the singing. When they realized that it was young men and boys singing their own requiem in angry voices, the mass of women and old men began to moan. The train crawled through the weeping throng; the clanking of iron died away. At the sight of the weeping crowd, the singers let go even more powerfully.

"So this is the homeland!" murmured Ivan.

"Now do you believe in the brotherhood of man?" asked Bogdan, gazing at the weeping multitude.

"You're right. Nothing unites us like pain."

Suddenly the song stopped.

Their car came to a halt in front of a sea of women's faces. *Perhaps Natalia is among them,* thought Bogdan.

"If you see a beautiful blonde girl looking for somebody, point her out to me," he said to Ivan.

"I'll stay with you; I said I would," said Ivan, squeezing his arm tightly.

The commanders shouted to their platoons to line up beside the train. Slowly and silently they picked up their knapsacks, fastened their overcoats, and climbed down from the train. Ivan, unable to look at the weeping women, kept his eyes lowered; Bodgan surveyed the crowd agitatedly.

The battalion stood at attention while the officer in charge of the train quietly gave his orders, barely audible through the weeping and snuffling of the women and children.

"The First and Second Platoons will return to their cars and go on to Arandjelovac. The other three platoons will board the train on Platform Two immediately. They are going to Kragujevac."

Bogdan embraced Ivan. Ivan felt ashamed of his exuberance, the only sign of joy among the thousands of people at Lapovo station.

The battalion of junior sergeants turned into a milling crowd as the platoons rushed to embrace each other. Bogdan felt Bora Jackpot shaking him.

"Be a pal, Mustachios, and give this money to Žika and Mića in the Second Platoon. They'll take it from you; you're all socialists. All the way from Stalač to Jagodina only diamonds were any good. I won all the time. I can't part from them and take their money."

"Then shove it into their pockets!"

"They won't take it. They're furious. Some sort of petty superstition. They're glad they've lost."

"What does your money matter now!"

Bogdan ran off to hug somebody. Bora Jackpot turned to Ivan, but Ivan was too excited to listen.

"All platoons into the trains! We're leaving immediately!" shouted the commanders.

The engines whistled. The women wept quietly; the old men snuffled. Bewildered children pushed in front of their mothers to look at this extraordinary army. Peasant women came up to the nearest sergeants and stuffed apples into their pockets. The battalion broke up, ripped apart by fragments of military songs and barracks jokes, and spattered with despairing cries of masculine affection as the sergeants milled around on the tracks, squeezed between the two trains. Everything quivered in a tearful blur; names and nicknames rose to a shriek; vows to die a heroic death for the homeland threatened the murky, rain-soaked sky, and perhaps brought some comfort to the tear-stained and dejected refugees who had been waiting for days for a train to the south. Ivan did everything the others did, shouting jokes and nicknames to the members of the First and Second Platoons, whom the persistent whistling of the engine was summoning to the cars.

The train containing the First and Second Platoons was the first to leave. "See you in Sarajevo! See you in Novi Sad! See you in Zagreb! See you in Ljubljana!"

The clang and bang of the departing train drowned out the words and songs; the engine cut short the embraces and broke up the handshakes; the wheels ground up the last conversations and pulverized the final messages. In every man, something died: they would never all see each other again. The members of the Third, Fourth, and Fifth Platoons ran after the train, clutching the hands of their friends in the First and Second, touching their fingers, no longer distinguishing faces. Then they stood still.

Only Bora Jackpot ran behind the last car, shouting something unintelligible at the top of his voice. The rails grew larger as he rushed behind the train; the space between them broadened and grew longer. The train was slipping away, a moving ribbon of faces still faintly pink as it receded into the distance; then the rumble of iron drowned the last voices; the waving hands grew blurred. Bora Jackpot threw after them the money he had won at cards; the coins lay twinkling on the gravel. The thin, stooping figure of Bora Jackpot swayed between the gleaming rails. Behind him stretched emptiness—between the bare trees, above the embankment, beneath the low Morava sky.

Ivan Katić saw inexorable fate exacting retribution for every hope, revenging itself on anyone who for a single moment forgot that he was mortal.

Turning a deaf ear to commands, the remaining platoons hid themselves in the train bound for Kragujevac. Bogdan led Ivan in; the last to climb aboard was Bora Jackpot, nonplused by their tight-lipped silence.

Ivan surveyed his companions: which of them would be killed? He had heard, or read somewhere, that death lurks in the eyes of those who are about to die. He looked at them closely: whose head would be shattered by shrapnel? Whose forehead would be pierced by a bullet? Whose face would lie rotting in the mud? Whose jacket would be reddened by blood below the upper pocket? A red stain was spreading over all their jackets, his own too. As for himself, he would surely be killed. The car was full of dead men. He'd better stop this. Who was *not* traveling by train for the last time? Who would return to Kragujevac, or Lapovo? Most of them were sitting with their hands bowed. So they would all be killed. The train grew dark. What if death was peering out of his eyes? Perhaps that was why he could see it in the eyes of the others. And Bogdan? He went into the corridor and found Bogdan gazing intently out the window. Surely he wasn't smiling? His jacket was clean and there were no mud stains on his face. Bogdan turned around: there was no sign of death in his eyes. He was the only happy person in the train. He put his hand on Bogdan's shoulder.

"You're happy, Bogdan," he said, with no trace of reproach or envy.

"Maybe I am. I admit it."

"And are you self-absorbed like this when you're suffering?"

"Probably. I'm beginning to see that there's something inside us that belongs only to ourselves." Ivan moved closer. "I used to be sure there was a fixed order of feelings and ideas inside me. But since we left Skoplje they've been jumbled up. Tonight I've caught hold of ten deserters inside me."

"But are you those deserters?"

"They look like me, but they're blind and deaf to facts as I see them. I don't acknowledge them as myself."

"What will you do to them?"

"I'll knock them down and look them straight in the eye. They're strong, but I'll master them. Are you surprised?"

"Not enough to make me disappointed. Maybe the whole world will be changed by this war."

Silently they watched the bare trees rush at them.

"Do you notice anything in my eyes?" asked Ivan. "Can you see any special change in me?"

"Now what should I see in your eyes?" asked Bogdan gently, smiling as he put his hand on Ivan's shoulder.

"I believe that death has a seed of its own. It germinates, grows, flowers, and bears fruit. In Skoplje, death germinated in all of us. Now it's growing. Look at those who are trying to sing. You'll see something in the eyes of every one of them."

"I don't see anything and I don't want to predict the future. You'll only see these things until the first time you're hungry, until the first night in the snow. Until the first charge and the first big battle. After that things will be different."

"What will it be like then?"

"You'll be a tough fighting man who'll drill his soldiers, like all the other sergeants in the world."

Ivan felt the color rising in his cheeks, so he moved away and opened his mind to the rumble of the train, the bare trees, and the dark muddy fields. What did it mean to be a tough, hardened fighting man? To be like all the sergeants in the world? Presumably girls like Kosara did not drag such men off to their lairs, to copulate with them and empty their pockets. Such men did not bungle their leave-takings with their mothers, as he had done in Niš. These sergeants did not suffer, did not feel ashamed, did not see the shattered heads of their companions, or their flesh rotting in the mud. How would the war change him?

Bogdan was distressed by Ivan's sudden dejection. How could he cheer him up? To overcome one's fears of the battlefield and the horror of this early dusk, a man had to have a Natalia. It wasn't enough to love one's mother and sister. Nevertheless, he asked:

"Don't you think your sister might be waiting for you in Kragujevac, Ivan?"

"My father's waiting for me."

They fell silent, leaning against the window, against the gathering darkness seeping out of the woods. Ivan was worrying about Milena; Bogdan's thoughts had returned to Natalia: the moment he saw her he would jump out of the train and hug her in front of everybody. Then he would take her by the arm and lead her away; he would hurry off to Paja the shoemaker, who was his old friend and would surely take them in for the night.

The engine whistled. From the car came unenthusiastic cries of "Kragujevac!" With a loud sigh Ivan returned to the compartment for his knapsack and rifle.

Bogdan leaned out the window: he wanted to jump out and beat the train to the station. The train slowed down to a crawl; he saw a yellow gleam of trumpets and clarinets and heard march music. The train stopped: a military band was playing on the empty platform. The station seemed to shrink in the emptiness and silence; the band played on. Dusk lay over everything.

Ivan stood behind Bogdan with his rifle over his shoulder; there was nothing he could say to him. He saw the band, and some women and children huddling under the eaves of the station. But there was no sign of a beautiful blonde girl. To avoid meeting Bogdan's eyes, he stepped down from the train quickly and silently and stood in line beside Danilo History-Book.

Bogdan was still standing at the window, staring at the platform, and at the women standing against the wall of the station. No sign of her! Maybe she was behind the car? He took his rifle and knapsack and jumped onto the empty tracks: she wasn't there! The platoon commanders gave the order to stand at attention. To avoid going around the train he crawled under the car. He ran into the station past the bewildered sergeants and officers: no sign of her. He crossed the waiting room and went into the street: no sign of her. He stood looking around. It just couldn't be.

"What's the matter with you, Dragović?" cried his commanding officer from the station entrance.

Bogdan looked at him mutely. The officer shouted and motioned to him to join them. Bogdan stared at the empty street decorated with small black flags. The military band marched past him, rending the silence, the low sky, the stillness. Ivan and the rest of his platoon came into view. He went up to them.

"Where are we going?"
"To the barracks," replied Ivan.
"She's sure to be waiting for me there."
Ivan made no reply and looked at the black flags. He couldn't sing along with the platoon, and not just because of Bogdan. He looked at the black flags, then at the muddy cobblestones. It was starting to rain.
"Left, right! Left, right!" shouted the commanding officers. "Make the cobblestones crack!"
"Ivan, look at those sweet little children peeping at us from the flowers. Poor kids, they don't know there's a last march through some Kragujevac in store for them. And that gentleman in the black coat carrying a cane, there's a snooty fellow for you, even though he's probably a patriotic Serb," said Bora Jackpot.
Ivan stared at the gentleman, who was walking along the pavement in front of them, but slowing down so they could overtake him.
"Why, that's my father!" he cried joyfully.
"Where's your father?" asked Danilo.
Ivan was afraid of meeting his father in front of the others, while marching, and in the presence of Bogdan, who silently stared into the face of every woman he saw. "Keep in step, Katić!" the platoon commander warned him. He hurried, caught up with his father, marched past him, and managed not to catch his eye. They would meet later, in the darkness, alone. He was grateful to his father for not stopping him, for letting him walk past him without a word. When the platoon turned into the main street he looked back quickly and noticed his father walking behind them with his head bowed. That night they would talk their fill. He wasn't going off to the battlefield tomorrow like some spoiled brat, grateful to his parents for a happy childhood. To face the ordeal that lay before him, he had to arm himself with the truth.
The sidewalks of the main street were crowded with townspeople, refugees, wounded soldiers, and women with children and bundles. The student platoons sang as they marched, but they were plainly angry and bitter. Here and there someone on the pavement shouted: "Long live our Serbian heroes!"
At the gates of the barracks, Bogdan handed Ivan his rifle and knapsack and slipped away into the refugees crowding the banks of the Lepenica. Ivan couldn't bring himself to ask Bogdan where he was going. He too felt somehow hurt and betrayed. He was relieved when the band music and singing stopped. In the stillness of the

barracks courtyard the ranks broke up; Ivan looked back toward the gates and saw the black figure of his father.

Vukašin Katić was amazed at how cheerfully the students jumped out of the train, at how boisterously they set out from the station, full of enthusiasm and self-confidence. Their unexpected, defiant, almost wanton strength wrenched him out of his despair, fascinated him, pushed to the depths of his consciousness the thought of Pašić's letter in his pocket. He was thrilled by Ivan's manly step, the stern, slightly scornful expression on his face as he walked past the dejected crowds; it seemed to him that Ivan was ten years older, and that he was coming back from the war. This completely new feeling dissipated as soon as the student platoons passed through the gates of the barracks: the march degenerated into a walk, the column became a crowd, the song subsided into the murmuring of a mob of soldiers pouring into the barracks.

Vukašin stood on the bank of the Lepenica, staring through the open gates at the empty barracks courtyard. No, he would *not* change his son's fate by a shameful act! He would not part from him feeling humiliated. Each must go his own way, right to the end. He walked up to the river, took out of his pocket his own letter addressed to Ivan "to be read some evening in Paris," and put it back; then he took out Pašić's letter, crumpled from prolonged and anguished handling by fingers that were sometimes nerveless, sometimes furiously angry; trembling, he tore it up and threw it into the turbid, muddy waters. How many days and nights he had carried around Pašić's blue envelope, the most tormenting burden of his life!

He still had not responded to Pašić's invitation to discuss the formation of a coalition government. As long as he had Pašić's letter in his pocket, a letter that would certainly remove Ivan from the front, he would not discuss his entry into the new wartime government of national unity. He avoided his friends, all except General Mišić. Before Mišić left for the front he had listened attentively to him as he affirmed his faith in victory, a faith founded on his confidence in the peasants' power of endurance and their steadfastness in adversity. Vukašin's suffering was making nonsense of his convictions, and his fear for Ivan blinded him to all general aims. Nothing meant anything to him, nothing mattered except whether Ivan lived or died. In his distress he even forgot about Milena, although Valjevo had fallen.

When the last scrap of paper had disappeared into the foam of the swollen Lepenica, he returned to the open gates of the barracks courtyard and stared at the main door, feeling cleansed and purified, as though a burden of pain and shame had fallen away from him. An electric lamp lighted the doorway. Small groups of students poured out of the barracks, talking noisily and cheerfully as they hurried over the bridge into the town: the sight of them revived his earlier elation, and he felt happy in the conviction that he had acted rightly.

Ah, there he was, alone. A huge, tall, clumsy fellow, easy to spot a long way off. A good target. Every piece of shrapnel would find him. Ivan was again chasing his shadow; he caught up with it, trod on it, and left it behind. Ivan was smiling at him; Vukašin had never seen him look so cheerful.

"Good evening, Father. Please forgive me for keeping you waiting."

Vukašin could hear the excitement and sincerity in his voice. He didn't dare hug him; he simply took both his hands.

"I haven't been waiting long, my boy."

Ivan trembled on hearing the deep, broken tones and left his hands in his father's. He felt both happy and confused as he looked at his father's exhausted and agitated face under the feeble electric light.

"You're a lot thinner, Father. You're not ill, are you?"

"No, everything's all right, Ivan. I'm fine."

"Did you bring my glasses?"

Vukašin did not reply immediately. "I did."

Now it was Ivan's turn to fall silent. "You'd better give them to me now." He smiled. "We might get drunk and forget about my eyes. We're marching to Gornji Milanovac at six in the morning."

Vukašin held Ivan's hands even more tightly, but his eyes turned to the noisy, turbid river. They'd have thirteen hours together. What would give Ivan pleasure? Could he make it up to his son and himself for past mistakes?

"When must you be in the barracks?"

"At midnight. But no one will follow orders tonight."

"The two of us will certainly get drunk tonight! We'll have supper and make a night of it at the Talpara Café." Was that all he could do to make Ivan happy tonight?

Vukašin let go of Ivan's hands and quickly handed him two pairs of glasses. They headed for the town. The rain was coming down in torrents; Vukašin didn't dare wrap his coat around Ivan: after all, Ivan was a soldier.

Does my father want to go on a spree tonight? Ivan stopped and stared into his father's face, but could not see his expression. In the evening shadows his face was dark, like his hat, coat, and cane. Was this his way of hiding himself from people, even from his children? Perhaps Mother didn't really know him. There was something different about him; and he was not going to the front without knowing the whole truth about his father. He would get to know the Ivan of the future, himself in his forties, the Ivan who would survive the war.

"I'd like you to take me to the liveliest café in town. If there's still such a thing. The people look as though they're at a funeral."

"To the masses, Ivan, funerals and weddings lie side by side. They go easily from one to the other. Let's have supper with your best friends. Afterward the two of us can go for a walk."

"Fine. We can go for a stroll before supper too. We've never walked together in the rain."

"I never had time, and you always wanted to read. Let's go down another street. This one is full of refugees." On a darker street he could put his coat around Ivan to shield him from the rain.

"What do you hear about Milena, Father?"

Vukašin hesitated before replying. "Don't worry about her. The hospital was evacuated from Valjevo in good time."

"You're sure she didn't stay in Valjevo?"

"I was in Valjevo when the hospital was evacuated. As soon as I can find a car to take me, I'll go to Milena."

"Do go tomorrow. And tell her that every day I write her a letter in my notebook. I'll send it when we drive the Fritzies back over the Drina." They turned into a dark, narrow street. The lighted windows promised warmth and excitement, rooms full of mothers and children. He eagerly breathed in the primeval smell of the chrysanthemums in the gardens. "Why are chrysanthemums regarded as cemetery flowers, Father?"

"I suppose because they're the last flowers of the year. Actually, they remind me of summer—summer that refuses to yield to winter." Vukašin fell silent, dissatisfied with his observation, since Ivan made no comment. He continued, speaking quickly and a bit too loudly. "And they have a clean, pungent scent; there's something green about it. I love its pungency."

Vukašin felt ashamed of these trite words; he swerved to avoid getting caught on a black flag nailed to a gate. With some trepidation he threw part of his coat over Ivan. He did not resist, but moved closer. They were touching each other as they walked along. He must not abandon Ivan to the fear and anxiety that would face him after tomorrow.

"Who are your close friends, Ivan? I mean, what sort of people are they?"

"Perhaps it will be awkward for you to have supper with a socialist. My best friend is a fanatical socialist! He's a bitter opponent of yours."

His father's nearness was awkward yet dear to him. His footsteps were shorter. But if he moved away from that hand lying heavily on his shoulder, he wouldn't be able to utter a single word; if his father removed his coat from his shoulders, he would be left naked in the November rain.

"I'm very glad you have such a friend. Socialists are the best friends in the world when you're young, and in wartime."

"Why in wartime?"

"Because by conviction they have no patience with officers, so they don't try to flatter them. Then, comradeship is part of their ideology, so they're always loyal and ready to sacrifice themselves."

"You were once a socialist, Father."

"Yes. And I believed it would be possible to establish a Balkan Socialist Republic with tailors and shoemakers. All great beliefs are a matter of experience and maturity, Ivan. In other words, an illusion. Anyone who hasn't been a socialist in his youth has never been young."

"Well said, Father," said Ivan with a smile. "Tell me what you think about courage."

Vukašin promptly answered. "I think that courage is the commonest of human virtues, definitely. I don't particularly admire a man whose greatest virtue is courage."

"So you still believe that knowledge is worth more than courage?" He took his father's hand so that they could stop for a moment. He gave it a squeeze before letting it go. "So you don't think that courage is the most valuable of all virtues?"

"For me, as I've told you many times, love of truth and of dignity are the highest virtues." Vukašin fell silent; Ivan could not see his face.

"Even if courage is the commonest human quality, as you say, cowardice is the most disgusting. Not just because of homeland and freedom. Cowardice prevents us from knowing anything."

"Very few people in this world are unhappy, Ivan, because they don't know your eternal verities."

"Ever since I began to read and think, I've believed that life is valuable insofar as we know the truth about it."

"You're exaggerating. Men live by very few truths."

"But knowing the truth is the only thing that makes me happy, Father."

"Since we're on the subject of life's troubles and the eternal verities, I would say that the hardest thing of all, my boy, is to recognize evil. It has as many faces as there are people in the world."

"Go on!"

"In the first place, I don't even know what evil is. It's not for lack of imagination that people are unhappy, and it's not cold and hunger that cause the greatest suffering. Even certain death does not drive them to despair."

"How do you know that?"

"In my experience—if this means anything to you—it's only other people who make us unhappy. Even when they love us, and we love them."

"I'm not convinced of that, Father."

"Knowing how to get along with people is the only knowledge that can make us happy, for a short time at least. In any case, the source of both happiness and unhappiness is other people."

"Yes, if we're ambitious and conceited. And very selfish."

"I don't mean just ambitious or conceited people, Ivan. We're born into a hostile world in which we're dependent and vulnerable from the moment of birth. In such a world it's a miracle how much goodness there is in man."

"Are you disillusioned, Father?" Ivan whispered suddenly.

"Disillusionment is not the worst consequence of experience, Ivan. You can escape from it. And you can find someone to blame for it."

"Does that make things any easier?"

"While you're young it does."

"There must be something important in a man's life that he must know from the outset, that is decisive for his future."

Vukašin remained silent for a moment. *That's the bane of my existence,* he thought. *Is it already his too?* "Perhaps the worst thing is that a young man can't understand his father's experience. He can't understand the experience of either those who have been successful or those who have been defeated by life."

"I don't believe it."

"You ought to. We can do little, my boy, to defend ourselves from the evil around us. And which we ourselves do." He wanted to hug Ivan.

"What should I be doing now, in your opinion? What would you do in my position?"

"The same as you, probably," said Vukašin, giving Ivan a gentle hug. "Yes, you must follow your own lights to the end. Don't try to imitate anybody else." He reached into his pocket for the letter "to be read some evening in Paris." Then he remembered that he hadn't given Ivan any advice useful in time of war.

Hearing music blaring from the Talpara Café, Ivan slipped from under his father's coat and his father's hand on his shoulder. "What do you think is going to happen to us? Don't answer as if I were a political supporter or voter. Or a son whom you want to comfort."

For a long time Vukašin said nothing. What would cause Ivan the least pain? He remembered how Ivan had marched through the streets of Kragujevac, singing victory songs with the others. He was cheerful and self-confident, all the happier for their long talk. He must not do anything to destroy Ivan's faith. Yet how could he deceive him in the name of patriotism? And on what was perhaps their last night together.

"You don't believe we'll win?"

"It's not a question of belief, Ivan. Belief is a feeling that is quite often independent of facts and objective truths. I'm sure you know this yourself. As for the situation at the front, it would take a miracle to turn the tide."

"You mean they're slaughtering us. The best and the bravest."

"It's not quite like that, my boy. Serbia will win the war; I'm sure of it. But the war won't be decided on the Sava and Kolubara rivers." What should he say to Ivan? Especially when he hadn't said the things he should have said at the High Command. "Oh, yes, I forgot to tell you. Two days ago Mišić was appointed commander of the First Army. You'll be in his army." He fell silent, suddenly struck by a horrible foreboding.

"On what do you base your belief in our victory?" asked Ivan, gazing at his father's face, now illuminated by the lights of the café. The din of singing and playing pounded at their ears.

"On you and your friends, and people like you." Ivan's face was in the shadow. "You people who were singing as you marched through Kragujevac this evening cannot be defeated. There's another thing: our victory will be decided by the Allies, and they will win this European war."

"You're right," said Ivan, magnanimously putting his father out of his misery.

Danilo History-Book and Bora Jackpot arrived. Ivan introduced them to his father, cheerfully and rather volubly. Vukašin led the way into the crowded café and ordered supper for them.

"Have you seen Bogdan anywhere?" asked Ivan at the door, uncertain whether to go in; he had been pulled up short by the café smell, the same as the Sloboda in Skoplje. It brought back Kosara and vomiting, the fight with the man in the straw hat, and himself masquerading as Ivan Stepanović! Once again he felt disgusted with himself. In the morning he would write to that wretched Kosara and give her his real surname.

"Have any of you got a piece of paper and an envelope?"

"Yes, I have. I've been meaning to write to my mother for a month. But I can't do it this evening," said Bora Jackpot, taking a crumpled envelope out of his pocket.

Ivan took the envelope and went into the café. The hot steam clouded his glasses; he could not see his father, and stayed beside the door. The café was full of fellow student-sergeants. He must put things right with Kosara immediately; he would write and tell her the truth. His father was introducing him to the proprietor of the café, who was smiling and spouting the usual pompous words about heroism and the fatherland. He excused himself and went off to write to Kosara, giving his real surname. He pushed his way through the patriotic rhetoric and raucous demands for music and love songs, ignoring the jokes at his expense as he hurried out through the clouds of tobacco smoke and the smell of wine and shish kebab.

Vukašin sat down at a table and followed Ivan with his eyes. What had suddenly depressed Ivan? Where was he going?

Bogdan was sure that Natalia must have arrived in Kragujevac; it could not be otherwise. She was there somewhere in the streets, looking for him, just as he was looking for her. The rain poured down over his bare, exposed heart, and dripped into his brain. It was impossible to see far in the feeble light of the street lamps. Silent ghostly figures stood under the eaves as if waiting for something, or walked slowly and aimlessly. He had to say something, anything. So he asked the refugees where they had come from and where they were going, so that Natalia could hear his voice, and also to release something inside himself. Whenever he saw anybody in front of him, he would catch up to see whether it was Natalia—only to have his hopes dashed once more. Every woman standing beside a fence or leaning against a tree looked like Natalia; he would go up and peer into her face: another refugee. He started every time he heard a woman's voice, stopped and listened for a long time; but all he heard, apart from the thumping in his own chest, was some dull, ominous echo reverberating through the town. The gathering darkness alarmed him, and he began to run; he crept up to one group of refugees after another, coughed to announce his presence to the people taking shelter under oxcarts, sitting in silence around small fires, and asked them where they came from. Many did not reply. He took to peering into the tents pitched beside trees, where women and children sat huddled together on sacks. Perhaps she was waiting for him at the station; that was logical.

He rushed toward the station. It was crammed with refugees. He stepped between the bundles and recumbent bodies, stopping frequently so that they could all see him; the light was so dim that his face would not be recognized a few paces away. What would she be doing in this mass of refugees? He went out onto the platform: more people were crowded together under the eaves, silently staring at the tracks and his now empty train. He walked up and down the platform so they could all see him, then once more crossed the waiting room. Maybe the train from Palanka had not yet arrived? He ran into the stationmaster's office. "Has the train from Palanka come in yet?"

The uniformed men did not reply; they were looking at various papers, at their cigarettes, or at the silent telephone. These damned idlers, safe behind the lines! He repeated his question in imploring tones.

"The last train from Palanka arrived this morning."

"When's the next one?"

"We haven't been told anything."

"Look here, how dare you not know what time your trains arrive!"

"You'd better ask Pašić and Putnik about the timetable. They're the only ones who know."

"What if the High Command has sent me to ask you?" He wanted to slap the man's bloated, bewhiskered face.

"If it's the High Command that's sent you, tell them we have seven cars and one broken-down engine. We'll be lucky if it's repaired by noon tomorrow."

Bogdan hurried outside. Maybe she was waiting for him in front of the barracks; that was the logical place to wait for him. He ran through the streets at top speed. Some friends called to him from the pavement; they were laughing. Well, let them. He reached the barracks, panting, hardly able to question the sentries.

"Has a girl been here asking for Bogdan Dragović?"

"No."

"You didn't notice a girl standing around or walking up and down the riverbank?"

"No."

"How long have you been on duty?"

"I came on when you students arrived."

Bogdan walked slowly back the way he had come. On the bridge he stopped: had she taken fright as she had done last summer on the way to Ralja, and got out of the train at Lapovo? She had wept and been full of remorse; in her last letter she had again reproached herself for "that lost night at the beginning of the war." No, that was illogical, impossible. Surely the telegram must have arrived. It must have arrived in two days; Palanka and Prerovo were still a long way from the front. Maybe she had arrived by the morning train and was waiting for him at the house of Paja the shoemaker, the friend with whom they had stayed last May Day. He ran toward Paja's house. He would not go to the front without seeing her. Only refugees and soldiers were still walking the streets, so it would be easier to spot her. On the steps of Paja's workroom he stopped, arrested by the sound of women's and children's voices. He listened, but did not hear her voice. Then he opened the door: the small room, with its empty shelves and shoemaker's bench, was full of women and children lying on the floor with bundles under their heads; the kitchen, separated from the workroom by an open door, was crowded with people sitting around the stove. *She must be there*, he thought dully. He loitered on the doorstep, waiting for them to call him by name.

"What are you doing here, Comrade Dragović?" Paja the shoemaker came out of the kitchen, jumped over people lying on the floor, and invited him in.

"I'm looking for Natalia. She isn't here? You know who I mean? The friend with whom I stayed here on May Day."

"Sure I know her! Come right in. No, she hasn't come. But I'd be darned pleased to have her here, even though my house is full. These are the wives and children of our comrades in Šabac and Valjevo."

Bogdan pushed his hand away. He went down the steps onto the sidewalk, Paja following him. Paja shut the door and pulled Bogdan under the eaves. They were in darkness.

"For God's sake, comrade, what's happened to the European proletariat? What's our International doing now?"

"Excuse me, Paja, I'm in a hurry. I'll drop in later." He had to get away from Paja's senseless questions.

"All right, but at least tell me why our Slav brothers are giving their lives for Franz Josef. Where are those fine South Slavs from Zagreb and Ljubljana? Surely Gavrilo Princip wasn't the only one?"

Bogdan hurried into the darkness; behind him Paja was asking about the Bulgarian comrades. To hell with them! She must surely be in a café. What would she be doing in the street in this rain? Why hadn't he thought of looking for her in the cafés? He turned into one; it was packed. He managed to push his way through the gloomy throng to the center. No sign of her; what would she be doing in a vulgar place like this? He went out into the street and learned that the best café in Kragujevac was the Talpara. Arriving there, he stood in front of the door, rooted to the spot by the music and singing, the only music in Kragujevac that evening. Could she really be waiting for him here, in a place where draft dodgers and officers with safe posts behind the lines were living it up and getting drunk? He leaned against the wall, shaking from fear and grief: suppose she wasn't here? He heard the voices of Casanova and Danilo. Of course she must be here, and Ivan and Mr. Katić too. He was ashamed to have Ivan see him in such a state. What state? Whose business was it how he now felt, or that he had been deceived? Impossible, absolutely impossible. He went into the café and heard Ivan calling to him. In all the racket no one would hear his heart thumping. He stood still in the middle of the café so that everybody could see him. The only people who called out to him were his companions from the squad. No, she wasn't there. He tottered over to Ivan, who stood up to introduce him to his father; Ivan was in good spirits. He shook hands and sat down; his face was distorted by the spasms and rigidity he felt inside.

"Didn't you find her?" whispered Ivan.

He looked at Ivan for a few moments before replying. "Are you quite sure that telegram went off?"

"Of course I am!"

"Then she's sure to come on the midnight train."

"You haven't had supper. Father, please order something for Bogdan."

"Thanks, I've had supper. I must be off to the station," he said, getting up from the table.

"Stay a while; we'll have something to drink," said Vukašin Katić. Bogdan felt an irresistible urge to punch his face.

"Aren't you feeling well?" asked Danilo History-Book, grabbing his arm.

Ivan was saying something to him in an anxious voice. Everything turned black. He pushed Danilo away and went out into the rain, bathed in sweat. He sped into the darkness and stopped only when he felt that no one followed him. What had come over him in the café? Vukašin Katić had not offended him; he had been kind and pleasant. Why had he wanted to punch his face? The rain sent a shudder through him.

He walked on, seemingly toward the station. Probably she would come on the freight train from Palanka, which arrived at midnight. Once more he walked through the waiting room, then along the platform, beside his empty train, where he had been so happy and full of hope. He would wait for her in the train. He went into a cold, dark car, felt for an empty seat, and sat down; burying his face in his hands, he shook with weeping. Could it possibly hurt so much?

"This evening I feel like the father of all three of you. And I would be very happy if you felt as if you were my sons," said Vukašin emotionally.

"Fine, Mr. Katić! Tonight you are my father, and the three of us are brothers!" said Bora Jackpot, clapping Vukašin jovially on the shoulder, while Danilo History-Book said in a quiet, serious voice: "From tomorrow on we will be everything to each other."

Their glances met; the songs, the violin, and the guitar swallowed up their silence. Ivan was comparing their present mood with that in the Sloboda at Skoplje. There they were cramming a lifetime's enjoyment into one evening and chasing women to save themselves in some way. Here in the Talpara the merriment was more an expression of sadness, a desire to escape from themselves, a gesture of defiance toward the darkness and rain, and the despair of the refugees he had just passed under his father's coat; they had never before been so physically close and so intimate. He was not mouthing empty words when he told his father that the value of life depended on knowing the truth about it. He should have added "love." Truth and love. This night was not a span of time; it was his father—and his father was truth and love. His father warned him kindly not to drink on an empty stomach.

"Don't worry, Father. I'm used to drinking wine on an empty stomach." He blushed; they all knew he was lying. "I've learned it from the French."

"I hadn't noticed. We haven't been together much since you came back from Paris."

"This Talpara is the finest place in our country. We are now in its warm, rosy, fleshy heart. We're in the cheerul heart of the homeland. Just think, Mr. Katić, how would we have felt tonight if our way to the battlefield had not passed through a café?" began Bora Jackpot, but Danilo kicked him under the table and frowned. "On my word of honor, the café is our national holy of holies," continued Bora, even more cheerily. "The café symbolizes the Serbian victory over the Turks. It belongs to our time of freedom."

"Since when are you so enthusiastic about cafés? Those hot, stinking dens where people's fates are decided," said Ivan, now serious again. He suspected that Bora might be alluding to the events in the Sloboda.

"Why, everything in our fate as citizens begins and ends in a café, old boy. People do business in a café, talk politics, found new parties, change governments and dynasties. This is where we get married and commit murders, live it up till we drop, write patriotic and love songs, and finally come to grief. Wouldn't you agree, Mr. Katić?"

"Yes, you've put it very well indeed. Of course, the same is true of an older society than ours. The café came in with the French Revolution. It is in some ways a consequence of the Declaration of the Rights of Man. Clearly it's a democratic institution."

"I also like cafés because nobody respects anyone else there. Such equality is wonderful. And then every denizen of the cafés is christened again, but with his true name."

Vukašin poured out more wine for Bora and Danilo, toasted them, and drained his own glass, smiling at Ivan, glad that he was feeling more cheerful, albeit with the help of wine. He thought that Bora, with his eccentric appearance and his precocious exaggerated cynicism, would end up as a celebrated wit in some small town; Danilo, with his round head and chubby, rosy face, a typical specimen of "healthy Serbian manhood," was destined to become a district chief, a pillar of the state, perhaps even a minister. If they survived the war.

Ivan did not listen to their bickering, familiar from the barracks. He looked stealthily at his father, hanging onto his every word; everything he heard his father say tonight seemed somehow new and significant. He was also beginning to enjoy the music and singing. Why had he despised the guitar music and the sentimental love songs? They were noble and stirring. Why hadn't he reveled in cafés or serenaded young girls? The sadness and yearning of the café might be superficial, but still, it broadened a man's experience, moved apart the enclosing walls of his temporal existence. It softened the blows and clenched fists of which his father was speaking and cast a glow over everything, at least for the moment. Even fear was more intimate now. He leaned toward his father, who was talking animatedly, to hear him better; his father's hands were restless and unsteady as they cut up the meat, and there was something voracious in the way he was eating.

Vukašin was cudgeling his brains for ways to push from their minds the fear and anxiety of war. He was not one to tell jokes or funny stories; if he had led an adventurous and amusing life, he would have regaled them with anecdotes. He groped for the right words to cheer them up and make them laugh before battle. All he could do was to prevent them from lapsing into silence by sharing with them some of his peacetime worries as an Opposition leader. He raised his voice above the din.

"You know we are a people who have made freedom our destiny. But unfortunately for us, the most important thing in our freedom has been political power. No sooner did we drive out the Turks than we founded political parties to fight for power—since we had correctly grasped during our centuries of bondage that to exercise the greatest power you must have political control."

"You're right here too," interrupted Bora Jackpot. "That's why our so-called modern history is riddled with paradoxes and all kinds of nonsense, as we read last summer in the *Echo*. 'Vasa Pelagić, our first doctrinaire atheist, was the abbot of a monastery. Pašić as a student was an anarchist and a follower of Bakunin; then he became a stronger pillar of the state than Ilija Garašanin. Not to mention that selfish, corrupt, bloodthirsty, and ambitious ruler Prince Miloš, whom we call the "father of our country"!' Have I quoted you correctly, Mr. Katić?"

Vukašin was amazed that Bora Jackpot had remembered his article "Paradoxes of Our Time"; he was all the more pleased because Bora had actually quoted it here, in front of Ivan.

"In fact, neither good nor evil, neither wealth nor poverty asks as much of a people as freedom. But we've been too obsessed with freedom, both as individuals and as a nation. Because we lived so long in bondage we attach too great a significance to freedom. Such nations can only have a tragic history."

"But a history worth remembering!" exclaimed Danilo. "And to be proud of too! What other Balkan or European nation had so many revolts against bad government and injustice in the nineteenth century, deposed or killed so many rulers in the name of freedom and democracy?"

Vukašin listened to him solemnly, unwilling to contradict him or attack his fervor and convictions. He should not have begun such a serious discussion; he must not shatter their illusions tonight.

They turned to eating. Vukašin observed Bora closely: What had happened to embitter this bright, lanky young man so early in his life? Was he perhaps afraid of the front, consumed by fear?

"Are you a volunteer, Bora?" he asked quietly, so that the others would not hear.

"Yes, I am. What else could I be? I was studying philosophy."

"Where is your father?"

"I don't remember him. For me, my father is a national concept, like tradition."

"I don't understand."

"My father was a district chief, and some peasants killed him while he was asleep, after an election, because he was going to build a road through their meadow; at least that's what my uncle told me. First they entertained him well, and when he had eaten his fill and was feeling content with life, he fell asleep. They cut him to pieces with an ax—him and a constable and his horse. They chopped off the horse's head and took it away. That's the one thing I can't understand in the whole affair." Bora Jackpot bent even lower over his plate and glass.

Vukašin was tempted to caress the boy's hairy neck; he remained silent for a moment, then moved closer to Bora and began to whisper, as though confiding in him.

"With us, Bora, life is an endless round of conflicts and clashes; we feel threatened by something all the time. We kill each other for a foot of land because we dare not lose any of it—because we have so little. There are more mouths to feed, but the meadows don't grow bigger. Our people don't kill each other for a foot of land because they're cruel and heartless; you must realize this." Ivan moved closer so that he could hear his father, but without taking his eyes off the singer and musicians. Vukašin raised his voice. "Because those same people are the most hospitable in Europe. Those peasants who chopped off the horse's head in a fit of frenzied anger probably perished heroically at Cer; or they will die in the defense of Belgrade and freedom. Those same people who will strike a neighbor on the head with an ax because his cow trampled their flax will not abandon a wounded man and will share their last crust with you tomorrow. You'll see when you get to the front what their hearts are really like. When we are wicked and cruel, it's because we are poor and unenlightened. It's trouble and suffering that make us wicked, believe me."

"Is that any comfort to you?"

"Yes, it is. If I didn't believe that, I wouldn't have gone into politics, joined the Opposition, experienced as much as I have."

Ivan gave a start and stared at his father. The singer had finished her song, the guitar was silent. Ivan felt the café sinking deep down somewhere. The officers from the High Command and the student-sergeants, as if frightened by the sudden silence, clapped timidly and called for another song and more wine. Vukašin went on eating and drinking so that Ivan would not ask him any questions or notice that he could barely swallow his food. But Ivan did notice the effort he was making; he was grateful for the consideration his father had shown Bora, and was reflecting on his father's last sentence. Ivan was sorry that Bogdan wasn't around to change his mind about his father, whom he had judged unjustly and too harshly; this was because he had only read his political articles, and had never dined or drunk a glass of wine with him while the old gypsies played their violins. *I don't really know my father either,* thought Ivan; *I've also judged him harshly and wrongly.* What was the most important thing he should find out about his father tonight?

Bora Jackpot was toasting Vukašin and saying: "Please tell me what I should be thinking while my platoon is being pounded by Austrian artillery. Because we have no more shells, or so we hear. That's true, Danilo, so stop muttering. Since our government has not supplied us with ammunition for our artillery, let the Opposition supply us with some ideas that will make us feel sorry for ourselves. That's what I said, Danilo: sorry for ourselves!"

Bora's words and tone made the food stick in Vukašin's throat. What should he say to him? His head felt fuzzy from wine and apprehension.

"Life always ends just opposite to how we expect it, Bora. People are rarely buried where they were born. We all end up betraying something or somebody. But this does not always deserve pity." He spoke quietly, more to himself than to Bora, and fell silent at the sight of Ivan's astonished glance.

Bora put his hand on Vukašin's shoulder. "Go on, please. We're leaving at six in the morning. If any of us come back, no one will remember who said what in the Talpara tonight. But I wish to announce that I'm joining your party. I'm not joking. After tomorrow we must die with honor, like legendary knights."

"You will be dying not only for your honor, Bora, but for a different fate for your country. This war will change the entire course of Serbian history. We will become a different nation. We will become a European state. The consequences are incalculable. Just think of that!"

"If that's our most important war aim, there's no sense in fighting."

"But why, Danilo? Surely that's no petty aim?"

"I hate Europe, Mr. Katić! Throughout history, Europe has been not only unjust and cruel toward us, but also stupid as well. But by our victory at Cer we made Europe find Serbia on the map! We compelled her to realize that Serbia is not ruled by Carmen Silva, and that Belgrade is not in Bulgaria."

The students at nearby tables, carried away by drink and enthusiasm, called out angrily:

"That's right, Danilo! We'll teach Europe a lesson—a history lesson! We poured our Slav strength into the exhausted Byzantine culture! We became her nobles and landowners. After this war, our peasants will no longer remind European diplomats of Zouaves! We've had enough of them admiring our folk dances and our hospitality!"

"Father, that man who's talking now is Staša Vinaver from Šabac. We studied together at the Sorbonne."

"Serbia will never again be a Slav Theocritean idyll, the incarnation of a myth about a happy nation, or a nostalgic picture of the simple life!"

"*Novitas florida mundi,*" added Vukašin quietly, with a faint smile.

"At last you have a chance to use your Latin!" whispered Ivan, without a trace of malice. "Go on."

Staša Vinaver heard him, and got up and shouted joyfully:

"Yes, Mr. Katić! *Novitas florida mundi.* Yes, indeed, gentlemen!"

It was now dark. Natalia Dumović reckoned she must have reached a crossroads, since they had been going downhill for quite a long time; she did not know where to go next. The weary mare shook the rain off herself and gave a helpless snort. Young Zdravko had fallen asleep long ago, curled up on the seat of the dogcart. They seemed to have come to some sort of straggling village. Here and there a dog growled; women were wailing higher up the slope. No gleam of light anywhere, not for a long time. No sound but the trickling of water.

"Oh, please help me! What's the name of this village? And which is the way to Kragujevac?" cried Natalia from the dogcart.

A dog barked in the distance and then fell silent. She turned toward the barking and called out again. Behind her a stream gurgled noisily under the small wooden bridge they had just crossed—she realized it must be a bridge because of the rumbling of the planks. She climbed down from the dogcart; wading through the mud she concluded that this could not be the way to Kragujevac. Then it must lie straight ahead. But where was straight ahead? Was it past midnight? She had not heard the midnight cockcrow. She jumped back into the dogcart, whipped the mare, and set out in the direction from which they had just come. The soggy clay squelched under the wheels and clung to the mare's hoofs so that she could not trot. If she could just see Bogdan; if only he could see her now and know that she had not betrayed him! Nothing more; then she wouldn't care what happened. In the darkness the sluggish steps of the mare and the slow turning of the wheels echoed dully through the mud. A dog growled. She jumped into the mud and groped for a gate.

"Is there anyone there?"

She went up to the door of the house and begged the owner to come out.

"Who are you? And what do you want at this time of night?" asked a woman's voice in the darkness.

"For God's sake tell me the name of this village!"

"Belušic."

"And is this the way to Kragujevac?"

"Yes."

The mud became thicker; the wheels turned more and more slowly. She could hear the splash of puddles under the mare's hoofs. If she could just see him, if he could only see that she hadn't betrayed him! Just that. But they were going at a snail's pace; and there was no sign of dawn. Suddenly the mare stopped. Natalia jerked the reins and struck her with her whip. She cried out, beat her, begged her to move on. The mare wouldn't budge. She climbed down into the mud and took a cautious step forward; hearing the stream in front of her, she trod even more cautiously. Then she saw that the water had carried away the bridge: it was impossible to go on. She went back to the mare and clutched a wheel.

"So this is the way to Kragujevac?" she cried with a groan. "Why did you deceive me, you filthy bitch? Why? *Why?* Who were you revenging yourself on tonight?"

She sobbed bitterly. Zdravko slept on. The mare was silent. The stream roared through the darkness.

"Well, boys, it's after midnight; time we got some sleep. We'll be marching from the café to the battlefield!" cried Danilo.

"You haven't finished, Mr. Katić," said Bora Jackpot.

"Sing us the happiest Serbian song you know!" Ivan called to the singer; she seemed to be bobbing up and down on the platform, which itself sank every now and then.

"Which song would you like, sir?"

The singer looked at him with a sweet, charming smile, but he couldn't think of any happy songs. Feeling somewhat abashed in front of so many eyes, he turned to his father.

"What's the happiest Serbian song, Father?"

"I don't know, Ivan."

"But which song would you choose?" he asked, leaning toward his father and putting his hand on his father's gray head. That thick gray hair had once made his father seem stern and remote; now it made him strong and reliable.

"The one you like," muttered Vukašin. Seeing Bora's sudden dejection, he whispered: "Let me tell you this, Bora: those peasants did not kill your father because he was no good, but because he represented authority. He wore a red cap and a uniform, he had his constables. He could put the peasants in prison, or give them a thrashing. He could do this because he had authority, and the peasants hate authority."

"You're quite sure about this?"

"I'm positive, Bora."

Ivan came back from the singer laughing. He put his hand affectionately on his father's shoulder.

"All through supper I've had this sentence running around in my head; I don't know where I got it from: 'Our parents teach us how to live when life is over.' "

"Ivan!" Vukašin started and clutched Ivan's hand.

"Oh, it's nothing. Just a sentence spinning around in my head. It doesn't matter. I'd like us to have a little time to ourselves. As soon as the singer finishes her song, pay her and let's go."

Ivan sat down beside his father. The tables and the people bobbed up and down under the low, blackened ceiling; heads were jumbled up, words seethed and bubbled, the song was weaving through a gray haze of tobacco smoke and steaming food. The walls could hardly stand up straight. And beyond them was the darkness, the rain, and the war.

The evening he had told his father he was enlisting as a volunteer, his father had behaved as if he had said he wouldn't be home for lunch the next day. He had been flabbergasted. My father can't possibly be indifferent about my going off to war; after all, I was rejected for military service because of my poor eyesight. His father had sat there in gloomy silence, showing no surprise. He was quite sure his father didn't feel any pain. His face had hardened—maybe he was piqued because he felt deceived. Suddenly Ivan had desperately wanted his father to oppose him, to condemn his decision, to say it was unreasonable. Not because he wanted to play the hero. He would not have dared to indulge in heroics in front of his mother, who had turned deathly pale; for ten minutes she had not raised her eyes from the floor, and her hands were shaking as she whispered: "Is this really true?" No; he needed his father's resistance, his protests as proof of his love, and his fear for him, his son. If his father had said firmly: "You can't enlist as a volunteer" instead of saying "Go, my boy" and "Talk to your mother about the things you'll need to take along," would he have spent the whole night thinking about it and feeling hurt and angry? And the next day, would he have set out so casually for the station, as if he were going on a trip? He'd drunk too much tonight, so his present conclusions really weren't worth anything. He must not think now about his mother and all the other things that had happened before the fiacre came to take the three of them, as silent as if they had been quarreling, to the Niš station. He must forget everything to do with his father, until their meeting in front of the barracks gates this evening. Except for one detail from the ride in the fiacre: his father's hands had been resting on his cane, and his own on his knees; for the first time he noticed that their hands were absolutely the same, except for the tobacco stains on his father's fingers. The thought struck him: *If my hands are like his, then I must be like him in other ways, perhaps in everything.*

As he gazed at his father now, he tried to remember what his father had said tonight in the café. To be like him. That was no mean thing in life.

They stepped outside into the rain and darkness. Vukašin shuddered at the thought of the tremendous uncertainty ahead. He would have liked to wrap his coat around Ivan again, but waited for the student-sergeants to pass; they were going off to the barracks with cries of "Good-bye, Talpara!" How dared he not oppose that crazy decision of the generals to sacrifice these young men? Bora Jackpot called to him from the darkness:

"Don't forget me, Mr. Katić. I'm your supporter! Even though you haven't convinced me why my father's murderers cut off his horse's head!"

"Good night, Bora, and good luck! When you get leave, come and see us in Niš with Ivan. You too, Danilo."

"I'm Pašić's man, but I'll come! Good-bye!"

Bora Jackpot came up to Vukašin and whispered: "Swear to me by everything you hold sacred . . . that my father was not a scoundrel."

"I swear it. He was a victim." Bora Jackpot hurried off into the darkness.

We met yesterday, went for a walk in the rain, had supper in the Talpara tonight, and now it's today, said Ivan to himself. His first day as a soldier was beginning. He moved into the shadow of a streetlight and called to his father. Now they would walk alone in the deserted streets and talk some more. He was glad it was still dark. He must not let the conversation flag or he would hear the time passing and his father's stifled sighs. He must draw his father out, find out more about him.

"We're not parting yet, Father. Let's get that straight first. And then let's talk as if . . . as if day will never dawn, as if I weren't going off to the barracks. Can you do that?"

"Of course I can, my boy."

They walked slowly through the mud, but not in the direction of the barracks. Vukašin threw his coat around him; this gesture of affection pleased Ivan. They turned into a street and saw rows of fires: the refugees had lit fires under their covered oxcarts and were warming themselves, wrapped up; the women were holding children in their laps. Ivan did not want to look at them; he pulled his father into a dark street.

"Father, I want to know why you've never taken us to your village? Why don't Milena and I know our grandfather and our uncle? We must have some cousins in Prerovo."

"I'll tell you why I parted company with my father and brother when you come back from the war."

"But I want to know now. Why should I fight just for King and Country? Why not for my grandfather and Prerovo too? There are some truths worth going to war for."

"There's only one truth worth considering when a father is seeing his son off to war."

"Don't get upset, Father. And don't make this night any shorter. It will be daybreak soon enough. To fight this war I need my grandfather and his village, I need woods and vampires. Let's turn left here. The carts and fires of those refugees make me think our nation is migrating. I'm listening, Father."

"How can I explain it to you? For my father, I was everything he could not be but wanted to be in our country. And yet he wanted too much for one son. Not just ordinary happiness, peace, and joy. Not even wealth and a successful career. What he wanted for me was power, power over people. And for my father, Aćim, power meant being in a position of authority."

"All the same, he did love you. In his own way, obviously."

"People like my father, Aćim, even when they're doing good to others, go to extremes and have no regard for justice. And when they love, their love becomes tyranny. They demand total submission. And naturally they justify their own inviolable position by their good intentions. Such people are indeed tyrants, Ivan, but tyrants with convictions. And they deserve to suffer."

"I don't know any people like that."

"They are fathers, my boy. Old, powerful fathers!"

"Fathers? But are you that kind of father?"

"I've tried to be different."

"Well, perhaps I understand. Or at least I have an inkling. All right then, Father, how did it happen? How did you break with your father?"

"Break with him? That's not the right way to put it. I tore myself away from him. From his desires and hopes, from that love of his . . . I tore myself out by the roots. From my homeland, my childhood, from practically everything in my youth . . . But I did it by my own will, my own decision. There were no external circumstances that forced me to do it. And I didn't do it for any particular reason, such as following a career or pursuing worldly success. On the contrary, I threw away all the opportunities that would have easily brought me success of this kind. I would like you to believe this, if you can."

"But it bothers you. This evening you said: 'We all end up betraying something or somebody,' so it must be bothering you."

"It doesn't trouble me from a moral point of view, Ivan, but as part of our fate. I left everything that was safe and dependable and leaped into the unknown. I rejected my father's love and power, the support of his friends, the many joys a man has when he lives in harmony with his surroundings and his family and his birthplace, not to speak of his own generation. I sacrificed myself, in fact. Can you grasp this, Ivan?"

"And now you're finding it difficult, you're sorry for what you did. You have sinned in your own eyes."

"No, I have no regrets. I had to do what I did."

"Still, you're unhappy."

"Not at all. I'm not hiding anything from you. I had to do what I did, and I was able to do it. I don't know how much you know about what Serbia was like at the time when I was your age."

"I know that people yearned to avenge the defeat of Kossovo, and dreamed of liberating and uniting all the Serbs and making a great state. It's the same today, of course."

"Yes, we were all preoccupied with great national aims. Student idealism, the fervor of youth . . . But Serbia was ruled by old men. Men like Aćim and Todor and Pašić. And by the greed of petty shopkeepers. Everybody was ambitious for something. The ruling dynasty blocked the way to freedom. And knowledge was valuable only insofar as it served the needs of those in authority. As soon as you wanted to use your head and your knowledge for something else, you were in danger and you were ridiculed."

"Is that the sort of people we are, Father?"

"Let's move on; you've stepped into a puddle. No, my boy, that's not just a national trait of ours. It's always been the same everywhere: all a servant wants is to acquire a servant of his own. When the peasant who has been oppressed by the Turks for centuries becomes a constable, when a farmer who has toiled for years becomes an official, he has attained all that God can give to man. What is the point of knowledge, ideas, ethical values? Whereas the human experience of fighting, deceiving, and subjugating one's fellow man, and of cheating and lying, is proverbial."

"How horribly that dog is barking! Can you hear it? Well, go on with your story. And please don't leave out anything."

"I remember standing in the Belgrade station with my father beside the train for Paris; I had on a new outfit, the kind we wore in Šumadija, and there was a wooden box at my feet. My father put his hand on my shoulder. An unforgettably heavy hand. I bent under its weight, Ivan. Then he said to me: 'Vukašin, learn as much as you possibly can. Show those folks in Europe what a Serb is like. Show those damned fine folk that we're not just handy with rifles and daggers; let them see that we're just as clever with books. Show them you've got brains, and don't be stingy with money. Spend it like a lord. Let those Frenchmen see that we Serbs are not afraid to part with our money, that we're people who like to enjoy life and have a sense of honor. Write home for money before you spend it.' That's what my unhappy father said to me. 'Spend money freely, but don't stop wearing your fur hat and jacket. Don't feel ashamed of these things, because they haven't got them. Cock a snook at Europe. Show them what a Serbian head and a peasant's son can do.' "

"My grandfather is a strange man!"

"He is indeed. His sort have practically died out."

"What happened next?"

"When the train crossed the Sava, I began to cry. I was convinced that nothing in the world would make me disobey my father's instructions. But you know, Ivan, as Serbia receded farther into the distance, and as everything became so different the farther we moved westward—not only different, but better—my grief subsided. I protected myself first by being stubborn. But as soon as I set foot in Paris, I began to have doubts about everything in my life. I walked all over Paris, didn't even remember to eat. That first night the thought of my homeland was still very painful. You know Paris, so you can imagine how I felt: you only have to compare it with Belgrade, not to mention our village. All night long, Ivan, I saw Serbia, my homeland, as an old man . . . an old man in a fur hat and jacket holding a club between his knees, on a boundary between fields, always on some boundary. No end in sight of hardship and suffering. And then before my eyes rose this enchanting, ominous mystery of a great city, of Europe, civilization."

They were silent for a time as they walked through the dark lanes of Kragujevac, striding through puddles, listening to the rain and the early-morning cockcrows. They were very close together, under one coat, matching their unsteady footsteps.

"And when you came back from Paris, Father?"

"I came back from Paris firmly resolved not to join a political party and to have nothing to do with politics. My intention was to build a factory to make plows and other agricultural implements, so that Serbia would first of all exchange the old wooden plowshares for iron ones. That was to be the starting point. But people believed—not just my friends, but the whole nation—that the most important and urgent thing was to change the dynasty and institute democratic elections. Actually, I didn't share this opinion. That's a long story, and the details wouldn't make any sense tonight."

"Still, you did become a politician."

"Yes, I did. But only when I saw no other way of achieving my aims."

"Do you feel defeated, Father?"

"No, I don't, because I believe that I'm right. But I'm no longer sure that I'll win. This war will defeat us all."

"I still don't understand all the reasons for your breach with your father, but I think I'm lucky to have such a grandfather." Ivan leaned against his father. "The fact that the two of us may be talking to each other for the last time . . . that's more important; this night is more important than ten thousand ordinary nights! It's worth being born to have one conversation like this."

"A few days ago I attended a meeting of the High Command at which I could not bring myself to state my opinion. It was about sending you students to the front."

"You know what conclusion I've come to, Father? No doubt it seems very simple to you. I've come to the conclusion that life is very, very murky and complicated."

"I'll regret to the end of my days that I kept quiet."

"Sometimes for a moment," Ivan went on, "a light flickers inside us. Perhaps it's best to go off to fight as young as possible. Don't you think so, Father?"

They walked in silence toward the barracks. They crossed the bridge and came within sight of the barracks gates. Ivan stopped, not wanting to stand under the electric light.

"Here we are, Father. I must get a little shut-eye before we leave. But I want you to know this: a night like this is worth a bit of fighting."

"Would it be easier for you if we went together? If I came with you to the front?"

"Why should you do that? You've given me plenty of facts and arguments to help me to endure the rain and cold and the hunger."

"You still don't understand me very well, do you, Ivan?"

"Everything is just as it should be. I mean, as far as the two of us are concerned."

"Can I really believe that, Ivan?"

"Yes, of course. I understand you very well."

Ivan put his hands on his father's shoulders and felt him grow smaller under their pressure. He embraced him lightly and kissed his cheek.

Vukašin kissed Ivan's shoulder, then moved away and took the letter out of his pocket. "I ought to have given you this when you left for Paris."

Without a word Ivan took the envelope and pushed it into the pocket of his overcoat. Then he turned around and hurried toward the barracks.

At the same moment Vukašin also turned around, and hurried over the bridge on his way back to the town.

Vukašin Katić strode along the short streets and lanes with Ivan's kiss on his left cheek. There was no highway to take him from the dawn, the roosters, the daylight, which was already filtering through the rain along the edges of the hills. Ivan was probably asleep; he was tired, he had drunk quite a bit, he was feeling well. Children are not anxious or afraid for long, nor do they suffer for long. He was surely sleeping, the more sleep the better. When Ivan got up, at their final parting, he would ask him if he remembered the night they had gone sledding in Belgrade. Vukašin remembered it as soon as they had separated on the riverbank. The night they went sledding was the last time Ivan had kissed him, until tonight, in front of the barracks gates. When Ivan was leaving for Paris, and even this summer when he was going to Skoplje, they had not embraced. He would ask Ivan if he had forgotten that sleigh ride in the moonlight, after a historic meeting of the cabinet, when it had been decided to buy French instead of German cannon. The decision marked a major shift in foreign policy, culminating Vukašin's long struggle to turn Serbia toward France, away from Russia, and to effect a final break with Austria-Hungary. He had not wanted to celebrate his victory publicly, in a café, drowning it in wine; he went home alone, knowing that Olga was at the theater, and the children would be asleep. He found Ivan curled up on a couch, reading. How delighted he had been to see him! He had greeted him in a loud voice, but Ivan simply muttered something in reply and went on reading, with a frown on his face. He wanted to tell Ivan that something very important for his future and his generation had been accomplished that night, and that his father had had no small share in it. For a long time he stood leaning against the door, watching Ivan reading as if he were alone; his joy evaporated, his victory seemed less important. Suddenly he felt an urge to go out again into the moonlight and snow. "Let's go sledding, Ivan," he had said. And Ivan had replied joyfully: "Why not? It's moonlight, and the street's empty." Ivan rushed off to get dressed, and he had asked himself why he didn't play with him, go sledding with him, every day? Why did he deprive himself of such a harmless pleasure? Suddenly, remembering Prerovo, he felt depressed. His melancholy disappeared when he was coasting down Birvanin Street with his son on his lap, laughing with delight. He had never seen Ivan so enraptured. On the empty, slippery track he was struck by the thought that his political victory had not brought him so much pleasure as sledding with Ivan, seeing Ivan's intense enjoyment. It was long after midnight when they plunged into the snowdrift in Prince Miloš Street for the last time, and Ivan, laughing and powdered with snow, had hugged him and kissed his cheek.

Sitting there in the snow, he had pulled his son close to him and held him in his lap, their shivering bodies and chattering teeth uniting them. The icy, sparkling track was rising to the sky between the shadows of houses and trees. The next day neither of them mentioned the midnight sledding. And it would have remained their secret if someone hadn't written in the *Little Magazine:* "After the cabinet meeting at which it was decided that Serbia would purchase cannon from France, Dr. Vukašin Katić went sledding with his small son. That was their last ride on a sled. From now on Vukašin Katić will be driving around in a French car, and the rest of Serbia will be riding on sleds as before. But bare-assed." And although he'd grown inured to political mudslinging, this time he couldn't take it in stride; it hurt him for a long time, and he felt ashamed before Ivan too. He must ask his son whether he remembered that sled ride.

In spite of the mud, Vukašin walked with his usual long stride. He was soaking wet, and his head was growing larger and heavier. A bugle sounded: reveille! Yes, it was already daybreak. He leaned against a tree. The bugle sputtered and squeaked; it was wet. Should he have one more look at Ivan as he marched away? Just to wish him a good journey and wave to him from the ditch by the roadside? No, they had said good-bye. To escape from the sound of the bugle, he hurried away to the house of the friend with whom he was staying. No, he must not go back; they had said good-bye.

Vukašin shook off his shoes, went into his room, threw down his hat and coat, and lay down on the bed fully dressed. He shut his eyes: he could not hear the bugle for the sound of the rain rushing through the gutters. Were they getting a warm breakfast? Though

Ivan couldn't be hungry. He suddenly realized that he hadn't given Ivan any money! Probably Olga had, when she gave him his underwear. His knapsack was rather flat, so she can't have given him much. Ivan would be washing up now; he hadn't slept much, not nearly enough. The rain rushed through the gutters, in his veins; he shivered. Go, my boy. He opened his eyes and saw his friend's wife standing in the open doorway, weeping as she listened to the military band and the tramp of marching feet.

"The students are leaving."

He turned toward her, then lay rigid and motionless.

"They're leaving. Can't you hear?"

He shut his eyes, petrified. When he again heard the rain in the gutters and church bells ringing, he suddenly yearned to see Ivan once more, and rushed out into the street without his hat and coat.

Natalia could not believe her eyes, although it was already daylight: Kragujevac lay before her, shrouded in mist. Zdravko was leaning against her, asleep; the mare, soaking wet and covered with mud, was too exhausted to trot. Natalia had ridden through darkness, mud, and pouring rain, hearing the sharp barking of dogs and the muffled wailing of women as she passed through villages, climbed slopes, and crossed streams. It was not until just before dawn that she managed to pull the mired cart out of the stream and turn back. An old man had shown her the way; and after that she had relentlessly urged on the weary mare with entreaties and endearments, shouts and blows.

"Maybe they're not gone yet," she repeated aloud to herself. She jumped down from the dogcart to lighten the load for the mare, jerked the reins, struck the mare with her whip, and ran alongside her to get her to run too. The mare's only reaction to the blows was to prick up her ears as she stumbled along.

"Zdravko, we've reached Kragujevac. Get down; it'll be easier for the mare. You can sleep later." She poked the boy and pulled him down into the muddy highway. She whipped the mare, who broke into a trot on the downward stretch of the highway. Suddenly the mare stopped, trembling. Natalia struck her, pushed her, coaxed her; Zdravko pulled at her halter. The mare did not budge; she just stood there trembling, her head hanging.

"I think she's done for," said Zdravko.

The mare started to move of her own accord, and Natalia's eyes filled with tears. She stroked her flanks and walked along beside her.

And so they came into the town, through the milling crowd of refugees, soldiers, and townspeople.

"Sir, do you know where the Student Battalion is?"

"You'd better ask the High Command."

"Where is the High Command?"

"Can't you see I'm a civilian?"

"Do you happen to know where the Student Battalion is staying, madam?"

"I know they were marching through the town last night with a band. And a short time ago we heard the band playing at the barracks."

"Can you tell me where the Student Battalion is now, Captain?"

"At its position."

She asked a passing soldier: "Where are the soldiers who marched through the town with a band last night?"

"If you mean the students, the band played them out a short while back."

"In what direction did they go?"

"They took the Milanovac highway."

"What's the quickest way to the Milanovac highway?" she asked an old man.

"Go across the Lepenica, then straight ahead. Why take a road every living soul is running down?"

"Is this the Milanovac highway?" she asked a little later.

"Damn right."

"It's the students I'm asking about."

"Well, they've left. You can see the band coming back."

"Could I catch up with the students?"

"On a horse you could."

She hit the mare, who didn't even prick up her ears at the sound of the blows, just hung her head lower. Natalia decided to pull her into the roadside ditch. "Give her a push!" she said to Zdravko. But he was staring at the weeping men and women trudging back to the town. "Wait for me here until I come back," she cried to Zdravko, and ran down the muddy road: if she could at least see him and tell him she had lost her way in the dark, missed the train because of a woman in childbirth. He would see her wet through and spattered with mud: he would see that fate had been against her. If she could only just see him! A stream of people and animals poured toward her from around a bend in the road. The sky was no longer visible; it had toppled over the hills toward which the road was leading, where the students had gone. Water trickled, dripped, and flowed from earth and sky.

"Sir, are the students very far from here?"

"I'm afraid you won't be able to catch up with them," said Vukašin Katić, leaning against an old elm by the roadside, staring at the bend around which the four-deep column of junior sergeants had disappeared forever, with hardtack stuck on their fixed bayonets. When he caught sight of its rear guard, and the bread on the bayonets, when he heard them singing as they marched along, he could go no farther. Somehow he had jumped across the muddy ditch and leaned against the elm. The song died away; the soldiers disappeared behind the black underbrush. He stared at the empty road.

Natalia came up, flung herself down on the bare roots of the elm, and writhed at Vukašin's feet, moaning. He gave a start as he looked at this young girl, only a little older than Milena, moaning in a voice from which he could not escape.

"Who did you want to see off, my child?"

The turgid, muddy stream coursed through the ditch; the bare thorn bushes showed black against the sky. Natalia moaned even more despairingly.

"Where do you come from?" he asked, putting his hand on her shoulder to lift her up; she pressed her face against the damp tree trunk. "Please tell me where you come from."

"I'm from Prerovo."

He snatched his hand away from her shoulder. "It can't be!" he whispered. For some time he did not speak; then suddenly struck by a new fear, he murmured: "Who do you have in the Student Battalion?"

"A friend. My boy friend, Bogdan Dragović."

"He's all right. You needn't worry about him."

"Have you seen him? Do you know him?" She clutched his hand.

"Yes, I've seen him. We were together in a café last night. He's a friend of my son."

"Please tell me all about it!"

Vukašin did not know what to say. He looked down the road along which they had gone away forever, with bread on their bayonets, singing. Milena was also in love, just like this girl. He could not find any words to comfort her.

"Was Bogdan expecting me? Did he tell you about me? Was he very angry?"

"No, he wasn't angry. He assumed that something had happened to hold you up. There's a war on. Of course, he was extremely sorry."

"I lost my way. And before that I missed the train. Have they gone straight to the front?"

"I suppose so. Who is your father, my child?"

"Kosta Dumović, the schoolmaster."

"Kosta Dumović?"

Vukašin jumped over the ditch. Kosta Dumović, a famous old Radical, a fanatical and quarrelsome man. He had been forced to change jobs several times under the Obrenović dynasty. In the Assembly, Aćim had several times accused the government of illegally discharging village schoolmasters. Perhaps they had been great friends at one time?

"Do you know my father?" asked Natalia.

"Yes, I do. I'm Vukašin Katić."

"You are! Why are you here? So you must be Ivan's father."

"Yes, I am. How long have you known Ivan? What is your name?"

"Natalia."

The thick, muddy water flowed noisily through the ditch that separated them.

"I know him well. Not personally; only from letters. Bogdan thinks the world of him. In his last letter he wrote all about . . ." She fell silent, remembering how she had read the letter to Aćim, and how he had reacted.

"All about what?"

"About Ivan. Nothing but nice things. How long were you with them last night?"

"Almost till daybreak. Actually, Bogdan left us a bit earlier to get some sleep."

For a long time neither of them spoke as they watched the muddy water gurgling between them. The wind shook the rain from the elm tree; ravens flew overhead.

"And how is my father, Aćim?"

"He's well. I came here in his dogcart, your dogcart. I forgot to tell you; he gave me some ducats for Ivan." She got up, jumped over the ditch, took Aćim's ducats from her bosom, and handed two of them to Vukašin. "Please find some way of sending them to Ivan as soon as possible."

His hand trembled as he looked at the ducats. For twenty-two years he had not held anything of his father's in his hand.

Natalia sensed his hesitation. "I'll tell Grandfather Aćim that you'll send Ivan the ducats right away. And please, will you send Bogdan a letter from me?"

Vukašin pocketed the ducats. "Yes, do tell him that. Give him my regards, and tell him not to worry about his grandson. But I'll write to him myself. Come back with me to the town, Natalia. I'll find you a place to rest, then we'll have lunch together. You must tell me about Prerovo. I haven't been there for a long time, a very long time."

Natalia looked at him in confusion: where were they going?

"Come on, let's go. They've gone now." He put his hand on her shoulder. "We have to go our own way."

They set off slowly together along the road back to Kragujevac, he bareheaded and without his coat and cane, she covered with mud, her wet scarf clinging to her hair and face. Neither of them spoke. She was still in despair because Bogdan would perhaps never know that it was not her fault she hadn't shown up, at the thought they had perhaps parted forever on the platform beside the train in the Ralja station. His silent thoughts were on his father's ducats weighing down his pocket, and on the war, which was making all the disparate paths of his life converge into a single fateful road. The sky lay on the plum trees and the underbrush like a crushing weight, about to break in two even the road that lay before them.

Late that evening Pašić's secretary took him to the Prime Minister's temporary office through a dim corridor filled with people. Nikola Pašić was on the telephone, talking so quietly that Vukašin wondered if there was anybody at the other end. Vukašin stopped by the door, still wearing his coat and holding his cane; he removed his hat, moving his arm slowly and cautiously.

Pašić ended his conversation and invited Vukašin to sit down on the chair beside his table, the only other chair and the only table in the small, square, empty room. A lamp hissed and flickered beside the telephone, which stood between them; they did not greet each other, but remained silent, resting their hands on the empty table. Above Pašić's head, King Peter in full-dress uniform hung in the shadows. Their own contorted shadows sprang out of their doubles seated on the chairs: Pašić's creeping along the wall, Vukašin's lying on the floor, which smelled of linseed oil. "I must get out of here as quickly as possible," said Vukašin to himself.

"I would like to tell you, Prime Minister, that I have torn up the letter you gave me for my son. But thank you for giving it to me."

Pašić remained silent for a moment, looking somewhere to one side of Vukašin; then he said calmly, raising his voice a little above the sound of the lamp and the wind: "There are a thousand ways in which a man can do both good and evil without behaving either honorably or dishonorably."

"Unfortunately for me, I don't know them."

"People will do anything to have their children survive them. It's been like that from time immemorial."

"But a thousand things can prevent children from surviving their parents."

"That's a terrible misfortune, Vukašin."

"I suppose it is, Prime Minister."

They listened to time burning away in the flame of the lamp and heard the damp wind choking around the eaves and strangling itself in the chimney, its special torture chamber.

"I summoned you today, Vukašin, to see what we can do about making use of your talents now. In three days I must announce the composition of my new government."

"I must ask you once more, Prime Minister, not to reopen this subject tonight. It is now of no real significance for the fate of Serbia."

"But really, Vukašin, there is nothing I can offer our exhausted country except agreement between us, the assurance that we stand united in a time of misfortune for which we are not to blame."

"The fate of Serbia does not depend on our being in agreement at the time of her collapse."

"If peace and victory in the Balkan wars could not unite us, at least let war and suffering do so now."

"Excuse me, but I can't accept that. There are people I don't want to work with even at a time of suffering, when our state is on the brink of collapse. I don't want to be a member of a government that includes people who have joined it to save their bank accounts. Just think, Serbia is in her death agony, and these gentlemen are squabbling over ministerial portfolios."

"True, Vukašin. But what can I do when Serbia has no better Opposition? I've got to come to an agreement with the Opposition. I'd embrace the devil himself, my boy, I'd stand yoked to a leper if it would make things easier for Serbia."

"To my misfortune and shame, I'm not prepared even now to embrace the devil or stand yoked to a leper. I will continue to serve the people and the Serbian cause conscientiously in opposition to you. And just because I oppose you"—their eyes met, and he added more firmly—"because I oppose you, I must serve our common cause even more conscientiously and with greater dedication Yes that's what I must do, Prime Minister; I am firmly convinced of it. No government in this world should ever be without people who oppose it, without an Opposition. Never! Times can never be so bad for any government that it should be spared having opponents and those who do not share its opinions. Because there is no evil from which the government will not emerge unscathed."

"Not everything happens so wisely and consistently in this world, Vukašin."

"But some things have been consistent, Prime Minister, ever since human beings existed."

"The time has come when the homeland needs more than just wise and honorable men. Besides, there are too few such people to defend it today."

"Maybe."

"Is there anything wiser or more important than working for its salvation, Vukašin?"

"If the government is left without an Opposition, then nothing that saves the government will save the people. And no victory will be a just victory."

They looked hard at each other. "There's something I'd like to ask you, Vukašin. If we are victorious, as I trust we shall be, with God's help, what will the people think of you for having opposed the government which won the war?"

"The people will respect me insofar as I urged and compelled the government to work as hard and as conscientiously as possible for victory and the subsequent peace."

"It's a lot you're asking of the people, Vukašin. Sometimes they have eyes to see great truths. But they're lazy about small ones. Only lawyers bring them to light."

"Neither of us is really in the mood for this conversation tonight, Prime Minister. But since we've begun, we'd better finish. There are many reasons why I'm your opponent. If my aim was to get power, it would be logical for me to do as you suggest; and I would become one of your ministers today. But if my aim is to be in the right, and to perceive and defend the truth publicly and honorably, then your advice and your immense experience in dealing with the people are beside the point. But I'm truly grateful, believe me."

Pašić said nothing but nodded as though in agreement. Then he looked straight at Vukašin and said:

"Pulling a cart through mud and storms is not the same as brandishing a whip and beating those whose backs you are breaking under the strain."

"I grant you that, Prime Minister. But I cannot sacrifice my convictions for anyone, not even the homeland. If necessary, I'll sacrifice my life for it."

"That's a lot to promise, Vukašin."

"Perhaps. But it's certainly not the easiest promise to make."

Pašić rose. His shadow crawled up the wall, breaking in two at the ceiling. The head of Vukašin's shadow touched the edge of the dark, empty floor. The lamp no longer saw their faces. The table between them seemed to creak under the weight of the lamp and the telephone.

"Good night, Vukašin. Your father, Aćim, would not have hesitated tonight."

Vukašin trembled as he whispered: "You think my father would have acted contrary to his convictions tonight?"

Pašić leaned over the table. "No, he wouldn't have done that. But he would have joined my government."

"Good night, Prime Minister!" said Vukašin in a firm, loud voice. Quickly he took his shadow from Pašić's empty room out into the corridor full of whispering and shadows. How soft and warm were the hands with which that terrible political engineer had tried to strangle him!

Vukašin felt better when he plunged into the wet, windy darkness. He set out along an unlighted street so that he would not meet anybody as he walked through the mud and darkness. At daybreak he would go to the station and take the train to Niš. But he would write to his father tonight; he must, after twenty years. "Tonight, Father, I refused once and for all to join Pašić's wartime government. I'm staying in the Opposition. Have I acted rightly, Father? This morning I saw my son, Ivan, off to the front as a volunteer; I destroyed a letter Pašić gave me for Ivan's commanding officer, which would have kept him out of the trenches. You would have done the same, I know. That's what we fathers exist for, to confirm the faith of Abraham and to carry out his decision—to sacrifice our sons." He slowed down. The wind, the darkness, the earth, even the rain were saturated with the smell of chrysanthemums.